# BROKEN VERSES

# BROKEN VERSES

## KAMILA SHAMSIE

**BLOOMSBURY**
LONDON • NEW DELHI • NEW YORK • SYDNEY

First published in Great Britain in 2005

Copyright © 2005 Kamila Shamsie

The moral right of the author has been asserted

Bloomsbury Publishing, London, New Delhi, New York and Sydney

50 Bedford Square, London WC1B 3DP

A CIP catalogue record for this book is available from the British Library

ISBN 9780747577249

10 9 8 7 6 5 4 3

Printed and bound in Great Britain by CPI Group (UK) Ltd, Croydon CR0 4YY

MIX
Paper from
responsible sources
FSC® C013604

## ACKNOWLEDGEMENTS

I would like to thank the Arts Council for a fellowship
to the Santa Maddalena Foundation during the writing
of this book – and Beatrice Monti della Corte
for her extraordinary hospitality at Santa Maddalena.

For Herman Fong and Elizabeth Porto

. . .

The Minions came again today.

That sounds like a beginning.

What else to say?

Can it be you, out there, reading these words?

# I

The old dream, once more.

I stand in a beach hut, looking out. The window frame in front of me reduces the world to a square of sun and sea. Into that square a woman falls, her arm drawn up in front of her face. She splashes into the water. I run out. Her body is caught in the surf, a dark tumbling shape. Above, there is nothing but sky. The waves recede, leaving her on the sand. I rush down, see scales where I expect legs. I have seen a mermaid once before, spent hours splashing water on to it to save it from dehydration. I remember the ache of my arm from the effort, but not whether I saved the creature. It is evident nothing will save this one. I turn towards the hut to see why people are shouting, and when I look back she is gone, only her impression remaining. I know what is necessary. I must cut out the sand which is imprinted with her body, lift it up, and bury it. But the sea is coming in again and I know that, faster than I can respond, waves will wash away the contours of her body, the graceful curve of her tail.

When I awoke, this line came to mind: Dreams, sometimes, are rehearsals.

I sat up in bed, scratching the faded scar which criss-crossed my palm, and a shark lunged at my shoulder. I really had to do something about these walls. The bedroom had been a children's nursery when the previous tenants lived in this flat, and the walls were covered with water-colour paintings of

1

sea-creatures: jellyfish, turtle, barracuda, flying fish, octopus, swordfish, angel-fish, shark, sea-horse, and a mermaid sitting on the back of a manta ray. I couldn't look in the full-length mirror without some creature extending tentacles, fin, snout or tail towards my reflection. If it were a fixed image it would be easy enough to get accustomed to it, but the mirror was attached to the closet door which opened and closed with any gust of air, and the angles of the room shifted even as I stood still looking into the mirror. Even so, occupying this room was preferable to moving into the master bedroom – directly across from a mosque which, my sister had warned me, broadcast fiery sermons just before the dawn azaan. 'If you sleep there, you'll wake up angry every morning,' Rabia had said.

I stepped, naked, out of bed and belted on my dressing-gown. Then I remembered: I'm living alone. I shrugged off the dressing-gown and for a moment I was giddy with imagining all the flats around me that might be filled with single occupants wandering nudely around their homes. But you can really only imagine people in states of nudity for so long before your internal censors step in and relieve you of the images. For me, it was the image of the madman of 3B doing push-ups on the hideous beige carpet I'd seen through his window which made me cast about for other things to fill my brain.

But what other things?

I stepped into the kitchen, and ducked right out again. There were no blinds over the kitchen window. So much for my one-woman nudist colony.

Minutes later, I was back in my dressing-gown, sipping a cup of tea and wondering whether to go next door and steal Rabia and her husband Shakeel's copy of the morning paper. I had told them earlier that I didn't want a subscription – what was there in the news these days that I could possibly benefit from knowing? – but I hadn't contended with the sheer boredom of waking into an empty flat. If this persisted

I'd have to take up yoga, or morning television. Or both. At the same time. I'd have to start watching morning yoga programmes.

Clever Beema, I thought.

My father and stepmother weren't flying out to Islamabad until that evening, but my stepmother – Beema – had still insisted that I move into this flat a day before they 'migrated', rather than spending one final night in the bedroom I'd occupied my entire life. 'Because the house will be in turmoil with everything being packed up,' Beema had explained, but I knew now that she hoped this waking up into silence would convince me to have a last-minute change of heart about staying in Karachi instead of going with them.

Looking around into the emptiness, I had to admit her hope was not without foundation.

You're a grown woman, I told myself. Behave like one!

Assistance came in the form of a ringing telephone. I picked it up with gratitude and an unfamiliar voice on the other end said, 'Aasmaani Inqalab?'

Aasmaani Inqalab – my first and middle names, self-important trisyllables that long ago pushed my shorter surname off everything except the most official documents. My mother's choice, the name. My mother had made all the important choices regarding my early life; the only thing she left to Dad and Beema was the actual business of raising me. Aasmaani Inqalab: Celestial Revolution. Such a name never really admits the notion of childhood. But Beema used to whisper in my ear, 'Azure.' Aasmaani can also mean azure. An azure revolution. Like Picasso's Blue Period, she'd say, without the gloom.

Picasso never had a period, my mother replied once, when she was around to hear Beema. Men know nothing of inevitable pain.

I wish I could say she had been attempting humour.

The unfamiliar voice was calling from Save the Date studios – fondly known as STD – to tell me my afternoon interview with the CEO had been moved up to the morning, so could I come to the studio straightaway.

'With bells on,' I said.

'Belzon?' echoed the voice, with a hint of panic. 'I think you're expected alone.'

One of the only fortunate things I inherited from my mother was the ability to be entertained by a mediocre joke for a very long time. I was still chuckling over Belzon when I got into my car to make the short drive over to STD. And when I pulled up outside the startlingly yellow house which had been converted into the STD studio a few months earlier the thought of encountering the voice behind the joke brought on a fresh bout of laughter which I had to try to suppress as I slid out from the passenger-side door of my car to avoid the gaping manhole next to which I had parked, walked up the palm-lined driveway, gave my name to the armed guard sitting on a fold-up chair near the front door and was ushered into reception.

Reception was a desk and unoccupied chair at one end of a long, freshly painted white hallway which led to offices, smaller hallways and – at the far end – an imposing staircase with rosewood banister leading both up and down. Two twentysomethings in jeans and short kurtas were walking down the hall, one saying, 'What do you mean they don't want any two-shots?' and the other one shaking her head, 'Yaar, celebrities, yaar.'

Standing there – seen but unnoticed – in a shalwar-kameez with a dupata tossed over one shoulder, I felt instantly old. They had that light in their eyes, those girls did, of believing they were a part of something bigger than their own lives. They were going to beam youth culture, progressive thought, multiple perspectives, in-depth reporting to a nation which until so recently had only known news channels which spoke with the voice of the government. 2002 would be remembered as the year of the cable TV explosion in Pakistan, and these girls were right bang in the middle of it, making history

4

happen. For a moment I tried to step into their minds, to remember what it was to be that hopeful.

Poor, enviable fools.

I looked around for something that wasn't younger and more stylish than me, and found a painting of a line of Arabic on the wall behind me. فَبِأَيِّ آلَاءِ رَبِّكُمَا تُكَذِّبَانِ The repeating line from Surah al-Rahman, beloved of calligraphers for its variedness and its balance.

فَبِأَيِّ آلَاءِ رَبِّكُمَا تُكَذِّبَانِ

Which of your Lord's blessings would you deny?

When my mother – in one of her attempts to give me career advice – told me that I should learn Arabic in order to translate the Qur'ān into both English and Urdu, in versions free from patriarchal interpretations, the Poet said, 'And translate Surah al-Rahman especially for me.'

'Because you want to know all about the virginal houris who await the faithful in heaven?' my mother teased. 'You want to know what you'll be missing?'

The Poet shook his head. 'Not that part. "He created man and taught him articulate speech. The sun and the moon pursue their ordered course. The plants and the trees bow down in adoration." I want to see how Aasmaani tops that with her translation.'

'It is beautiful,' my mother acknowledged. 'But don't forget the warnings of the Day of Judgment that follow. It's not all order and adoration.'

The Poet held his hands in front of him as he always did when quoting words that moved him, as though weighing them in his palms. '"When the sky splits asunder, and reddens like a rose or stainèd leather – which of your Lord's blessings would you deny?"'

The sky as stained leather. It was almost enough to make you desire the end of the world.

A middle-aged woman with a nose which changed character halfway down its length walked out of one of the offices and smiled at me. 'Are you here for *Boond*?'

I shook my head, more than a little regretfully.

*Boond* was a much-hyped, multi-part television drama which had fallen into a deep crisis the previous week when one of the lead actresses was fired, six weeks before the show's premiere, because her newfound antipathy to bougainvillea made filming outdoor sequences impossible. There was talk that the whole show would need to be cancelled, and speculation about how much of a financial setback STD would suffer, and then, in a stunning coup, one of the STD newsreaders had announced, in the headlines of the 9 o'clock news, that Shehnaz Saeed was going to take on the role of the lead actress.

I was listening to the news when the announcement was made and, I swear, I gasped out loud when I heard it. Shehnaz Saeed! If I'd heard that the ghost of Marlene Dietrich was taking on the role I suppose I would have been a little more surprised, but only because Dietrich didn't speak Urdu.

Shehnaz Saeed had been the darling of the theatre and the small screen, an actress of amazing range who had retired at the peak of her career fifteen years earlier in order to devote time to 'preparing for and raising' the children she was planning to have with the man she had recently married. Her son from her first marriage was raising hell at university by then, telling anyone who would listen that all mothers should stay at home with their children, otherwise the children would grow up like him. I had never met the first-born son, but I disliked him intensely for being the person who convinced Shehnaz Saeed there was a choice to be made between acting and motherhood. I had seen her on-stage for the first time when I was about eleven, in an Urdu translation of *Macbeth* – it was the Poet's translation – and I swear there was not a man, woman or child in that audience who would not have plunged a dagger into a king's heart for her. She never actually had any children with the second husband – the gossip-mongers said he always timed his frequent business trips abroad so that he would be away while she was ovulating –

6

but though rumours surfaced intermittently that she was considering an end to retirement, she hadn't so much as made a cameo appearance since her swansong – a one-woman show in which she played six different roles; it had been a one-night-only performance, sold out before the box office even opened (the leading newspapers ran editorials of protest).

It was to confirm that the newsreader wasn't on drugs that Beema rang an old schoolfriend of hers, whose brother-in-law was the CEO of STD (that he was a noted philanderer made the title hilarious to both Rabia and me); at the end of the call she didn't just have confirmation of the news, she'd also set up a job interview for me at STD. I had just quit working at the oil company and was having trouble figuring out, what next? So I thought I might as well go along with Beema's plans.

The woman with the extraordinary nose turned away from me to flag down a man with gelled-back hair. 'It's all a disaster,' she said. 'We have to rewrite the entire role.'

'Everyone is doing too much drama,' he said. 'She's just a has-been actress.'

The woman jerked her head in disgust, and turned to me. 'You. Tell me something. You planning to watch *Boond*?'

'Isn't everyone?'

'OK, so here's the thing. This role – this role Shehnaz Saeed is doing – she plays the ex-wife of a wealthy industrialist. They've been divorced for years. Now he's getting remarried. The drama starts with the proposal scene. His new wife, much younger, is completely and without reason insecure about the ex-wife. OK? So, the thing is this. The ex-wife becomes important eventually but she's supposed to play a totally minor role in the first episode. How do you feel about Shehnaz Saeed returning to the screen in a minor role? Don't answer! Your face has answered.' She turned to the gelled man. 'Look at that! Look at her expression.' I ran my palms along my mouth and forehead to see if my facial muscles were doing something of which I was unaware, but they seemed to be utterly in repose. 'I don't know if I can do it. Every idea I have for that first moment she steps on to the screen is inadequate. A nation's expectations are sitting on my bony little shoulders.'

The woman stopped speaking and turned sharply towards me.

'I just realized who you are,' she said. 'Do you mind if . . . ?' Before I could say anything, she stepped forward and held up her hand to cover the lower half of my face, so all she could see were my eyes – grey with a starburst of green in the centre – and my high forehead and straight, black hair.

'Amazing,' she said. 'Isn't that amazing?'

What was amazing was the way women in Pakistan took one look at me and assumed they were entitled to instant familiarity – as though I were the one who had sat in jail cells with them or knelt beside them in cramped railway carriages writing slogans on banners.

An office door a few feet away opened and a man in his mid-thirties stepped out. He saw me, and his face became bloodless. I stepped away from the woman, revealing my long nose and sharply angled jaw, and the man blinked, put his hand up to his eyes and rocked back on his heels.

'I'm sorry,' the woman was saying. 'That was presumptuous.'

But I wasn't paying much attention to her any more. I knew the man, just as he knew me. Even if Beema hadn't said he was working here and was the reason Shehnaz Saeed had agreed to do the show, I think I would have recognized him immediately. Those curved eyes straight out of a Mughal miniature, that sensuous mouth. How strange that they should be so masculine on his face, even while marking him clearly as the son of the most beautiful woman in the country. In sober tie and an obviously expensive shirt he looked nothing like the imagined hooligan in my mind who had forced his mother into retirement fifteen years ago.

He saw that I realized who he was and a look came upon his face which I recognized – a mixture of panic and self-deprecation allied to an acknowledgement of failure.

8

He stepped forward and held out a hand. 'Mir Adnan Akbar Khan,' he said, in mock-grandiose tones. 'But my friends call me Ed.'

'Nicknames and friendship rarely go together,' I said, taking his hand, and trying not to show how startled I was to have found a stranger wearing an expression I thought of as mine alone. He seemed to have no desire to let go of my hand, and as I pulled my fingers out of his grasp I wasn't sure if that was flattering or sleazy. He was one of those men who straddled the line between dazzlingly sexy and somewhat repulsive. All due to the heavy hoods of those Mughal eyes. 'My name is Aasmaani Inqalab. My friends call me Arse-Many Inflagrante.'

He laughed – dazzlingly – and beckoned me towards the office out of which he'd just walked. 'You're expected.'

Inside the office, a portly man sat behind a large, cluttered desk. He nodded as I walked in, placed both hands on the arms of his chair and pressed down with them, leaning forward at the same time. It was clearly his way of expressing that while he would like to rise and greet me, the effort was over-whelming – so I did what was expected of me, and said, 'No, please,' while patting down the air with both my hands to indicate he should stay seated.

'So,' he said, after we'd finished the formalities of whether I wanted tea or coffee, and how exactly I knew his sister-in-law, and why it had been necessary to move the interview up by a few hours, 'so you're looking for employment.'

'Yes—' and then I realized how unprepared I was for this meeting. 'I'm sorry. I didn't bring a CV or references.'

He waved his hand in dismissal. 'If you want a job here, that's all the reference you need. We're in no position to be fussy. And as for a CV,' he smiled and picked at his teeth with the corner of an envelope, 'your background is CV enough.' He leaned forward again with that anticipation I knew so well, and said, 'We're starting up a political talk show. Hard-hitting stuff, one-on-one interviews with our newly elected ministers. You could be ideal to host. If you have even a fraction of your mother's fire, the camera will just lick you up.'

'I'm entirely anti-flammable, I'm afraid. And I'd like to stay unlicked while at work if that's OK.' The CEO of STD held up his hands as though warding off an accusation. 'Is there anything off-camera I could do? And nothing about politics, please. It's not really something I'm interested in.'

He looked offended, as though I had made my way into his office under false pretences. 'I suppose you're not interested in poetry either.' Then he turned red, as strangers often did when they alluded to the Poet's position in my life.

I shrugged. 'I occasionally write haiku. Munchkin verse is how I think of the form, ergo I'm working on a *Wizard of Oz* series.'

So this is who I was planning to be in my media incarnation. A woman who penned constipated verse and who could use the word 'ergo' before her morning cup of coffee. This could be the most insufferable version of me yet.

The CEO's face brightened – not from any poetic feelings, I was sure, but merely because he was grateful to be past the awkward moment. He made a clumsy gesture of appeal, and my mind worked furiously, counting syllables and reaching for the most obvious way out.

'Follow the yellow/Brick road, follow the yellow/Brick road. Follow it.'

From behind his desk, he looked uncertainly at me, obviously unable to decide whether this was humour or an appalling lack of talent.

Someone behind me cleared his throat. I turned, and it was Mir Adnan Akbar Khan, known to his friends as Ed, standing in the doorway.

'There is wit in straw/Courage in fear. Love echoes/In vast tin caverns.'

He had his eyes fixed on me as he spoke. I kept my hands hidden beneath the desk as I counted syllables on my fingertips, unaccountably hoping that he'd got it wrong.

The man behind the desk had lost all interest in poetry – and me – by now, and indicated this by hiring me on the spot. 'Ed will show you your office. Wait in there until someone comes to talk to you about a contract and then you can leave. Or stay. Whichever suits you.' He raised his bulk out of his chair.

'But what's my job description?' I asked.

'Bit of this and bit of that. Same as most people here. You do actually want to work, don't you?'

'Sorry?'

'You're not one of the eye-liner girls? The ones who come here to find husbands.'

'No, I'm not.'

'Because if you are, I've got this nephew . . .'

Mir Adnan Akbar Khan cleared his throat again. 'Do you have any particular talents or abilities we should be taking advantage of?' he asked.

'Not really. Except, facts. I have many of them in my head. About all sorts of things. I don't know if that's at all useful. I take some pride in it not being useful, actually.'

'That's perfect,' the CEO said, smiling a gold-capped smile. 'We need a research assistant for our new quiz show. You have to come up with questions in different categories, and list four possible answers. Quiz show researcher. That's your official designation, but you'll soon find everyone here does a little bit of everything.' He addressed himself to the man behind me. 'I'll be at the golf course, Ed. Deal with anything that needs dealing with. That includes finding someone to read the five o'clock news. Amina has to leave at four – there's a tea at her place and her mother needs her to hand out pakoras. You, haiku girl, how do you feel about cockroaches?'

'The sight of their antennae makes me sneeze.'

'Well, then you can't be our newsreader,' he said, and waved me away.

I followed Mir Adnan Akbar Khan out of the office and up the staircase at the end of the hall. The ground floor's buzz of activity fell away as we stepped on to the landing which led into a lemon-yellow hallway with a window at the far end, framing a bough clustered with pink blossoms set against the pale sky. 'The creatives are on the ground floor,' Mir Adnan Akbar Khan said. 'Along with the CEO, of course, but only because he's too lazy to walk up stairs. The studio is in the basement. There's a lone cockroach living there at the moment, resisting all attempts to take him dead or alive – we call him Osama Bin Roach. He makes some of our live shows far more interesting than they would otherwise be. And up on this floor you've got producers, researchers, analysts and other people who prefer quiet. My office is down the end. This is yours—' He pointed to a door half-way down the hallway.

I pushed open the door and entered. A glass-topped desk and computer took up the bulk of space in the tiny room. It was hard to imagine being able to move in there without bumping into something – the desk, a computer peripheral, your own ribs. There was no window, only four blue walls and a duct for central air-conditioning, which didn't seem to be turned on.

'A room with a vent. How charming.'

'If it's luxury you're looking for, you're in the wrong place.' Mir Adnan Akbar Khan squeezed in past me, and reached under the desk for a pedestal fan, which he deposited on the desk. He reached down again, and pulled out a pile of books. He stacked the books vertically against the wall, and put the fan on top. The blades were rimmed with blackness. He turned to face me, amused. 'Think you can handle it?'

I walked around the other side of the desk, and sat down in the worn, leather chair, elbows propped on the armrests. My mother would tell me to count myself fortunate. She'd work out how many political prisoners could be squeezed, like pomfret, into prison cells this size. She'd refuse to say, 'Like sardines,' because sardines are a colonial residue.

'So, Mir Adnan Akbar Khan—'

'It's Ed. Short for Eddy. As in, a whirling current. And there's no need to laugh – it's a childhood name which just stuck.'

'Don't get so defensive, Eddy.' He looked annoyed and I waved my hand in a gesture of peace. 'It's just that I woke up thinking of seas and currents, and now here you are.'

'Oh.' He blushed, and that made me suddenly self-conscious. The office was so small that for the two of us to be sharing its space seemed like an intimacy.

He rested his hand on the edge of my desk, and, looking down, smiled. There was a tiny stick-on heart near his thumb, the kind I had covered my pencil-box with when I was a girl.

'Tell the Tin Man to call off the search,' he said.

'Who first did that?' I asked, levering my nail between glass and sticker to prise it off. 'Who made love a heart without arteries and chambers – a castrated organ?'

'The same people who turned angels into harp-playing, effete creatures in nightgowns, floating on clouds. The ones who like to domesticate the dangerous.'

I busied myself removing bits of sticky paper from my nail. It was an answer too near my own way of thinking for me to know how to respond to it. I didn't know what to say to him – there was a subject between us, a history going back one generation, which I couldn't decide whether I wanted to allude to or avoid.

'Look, there are plenty of jobs available here,' he said. 'You don't have to get stuck with this quiz show nonsense. It's obviously not what you want to be doing.'

I looked up, flicking the last bit of sticky paper into the space between us. 'What makes you think you know what I want to be doing?'

'Oh, please!' He rolled his eyes. 'The enigmatic-woman act is so overdone.'

*Don't you dare*, I found myself thinking, and then almost – almost, mind – before I knew what I was doing, I angled my head just so as to draw out the cords of my neck, clenched my jaw, narrowed my eyes to obscure the grey and make the green flash through.

Ed stepped back, the expression on his face telling me to what extent I had just left my own skin, allowed someone else's personality to brush its hand across my features and leave its ghostly mark there.

I looked away, aware of feeling smaller, more useless, as soon as I had returned to myself.

'What's your story, Aasmaani Inqalab?' he said in a tone of voice I couldn't decipher. He moved the fan on to the floor, and sat down on the stacks of books. 'No, don't give me that look. I hate that look.'

'You've just met me. You can't hate my looks already.'

'Your looks are actually quite stunning.' I raised an eyebrow at him, and he laughed. 'Don't worry. I'm not making a move on you. I'm just stating a fact. You like facts. You said so. Although, here's a question. Why?'

'What?'

'Why do you like facts? Or maybe you don't like them. You just collect them. See, we've just met and here's what I know about you. You say you're not interested in politics, you claim to write haiku though clearly you don't, which casts some suspicion on the veracity of your claim about politics, you pride yourself on collecting useless facts, you woke up thinking about currents, your friends call you Arse-Many Inflagrante, and cockroach antennae make you sneeze. You'll have to agree, this is a strange collection of information to have about someone you've only just met. It's . . . well, isn't that interesting?' He leaned back against the wall. 'You've given me a lot of useless facts about yourself. Huh. Clever. I bet you do that a lot as an alternative to actually revealing information.'

'There's something really creepy about you, you do know that, don't you?'

'You're just upset that I'm on to you.' He stood up. 'Look upon it as a gift. I've seen past the façade instantly. Isn't that a relief?'

14

'There's a difference between seeing a façade as a façade and seeing past it, Eddy. So enjoy the arches and parapets, take your pictures, buy your postcards. The guard dogs at the gate have been alerted to your presence.'

'I hear the clatter of a gauntlet,' he said, stooping down as though to pick something off the floor before walking out.

'Irritating sod,' I muttered after him.

It was a long time I continued to sit there, waiting for someone to come and find me. I recited *Song of Myself* in my head, not knowing why it had occurred to me until I came to the line about 'eddies of the wind'.

At length, my mind wandering back to my first moments in the STD building, I found pen and paper in the desk drawers and began to write:

*To: the woman in the hallway who asked me if I was planning to watch* Boond.

*My turn to beg forgiveness for presumption. But I've been thinking about your concerns re Shehnaz Saeed's role in your drama. It seems to me your biggest problem is knowing how to both use and downplay her status as A GREAT. That first moment the camera alights on her – how can you make that moment work both at the level of the television drama and at the level of the larger 'real-life' drama of Shehnaz Saeed returning to a medium she once owned more fully than any other actress in Pakistan's history? I have a suggestion:*

*Let the show start with her return to Karachi, after years away. Let those years be years of mystery, and silence. That allows her to step on to the screen both as a character who has been away from her family for many years and as Shehnaz Saeed returning to all our lives. Those initial moments of recognition that her family has when she comes back, those gasps of shock, those searching inquisitions of every aspect of her appearance to see how she has changed, can both mirror the audience's responses to her and set up the character's position as 'the familiar/unfamiliar-mother/friend/enemy/ex-wife'. You said the show starts with her ex-husband's proposal to another woman. Think how the drama increases if his proposal coincides with Shehnaz Saeed's return to town. Yes, this is staple fare of low-brow soap operas – but no less effective for that.*

As I wrote, I saw it in my mind. A woman is disembarking a plane in Karachi. On the walk from tarmac to terminal she pauses to light a cigarette and look around her. This terminal was not built when she last left, and for a moment she is terrified by all that must have changed, and all that must have stayed the same, in this city she departed without explanation so long ago, leaving behind her only child.

I put down the pen and bent my head forward to rest in my cupped hands.

Oh, Mama.

# II

'Don't you want to know what's in the water?'

My father extended his hand into the space between us, tilting a glass jug; the liquid inside flowed towards the mouth of the vessel and then receded – a captive ocean with a memory of tides.

'It's only rust.' Rabia took the jug from our father's hand and slid open the bedroom window. At a twist of her wrist a thick rope of orange-brown water spilled out of the glass lip. I imagined a variant on the Rapunzel story in that instant before the water scattered into thousands of drops, racing in their descent to the garden, three storeys beneath us. 'That tap hasn't been used in months.' She leaned out of the window. 'Look, the madman of 3B is proposing to a flowerpot.'

Dad reached over and pulled Rabia in, and I slammed the window shut. The weather had been bearable this morning when I set off for my interview at STD but now, in mid-afternoon, it was a different matter. The October heat was a haze over Karachi, yet despite its diffused appearance it could pummel its way into any room through even the slightest crack in the window. Dad walked across to the air-conditioner and held his face up to the vents. Outside, crows circled slowly in a sky near white. When I was a child, the Poet told me that the sky-painters' union had negotiated reduced working hours on days of oppressive heat, so the painters only slapped

17

on a single coat of blue under cover of darkness before packing away their brushes for the day. When I repeated this to Dad he sat me down and explained wavelengths and particles, which sounded so entirely unreal I thought he was making up an extraordinary story which I was too young to understand, just as I was too young to understand why *Wuthering Heights* was a story my mother could love when it was so choked with misery.

Rabia rested her chin on my shoulder and wrapped her arms around my waist. 'I think the flowerpot is turning him down.'

'Just as well. He was only after her money-plant.' I leaned back into her, feeling rather than hearing laughter ripple out from her body.

Rabia was really my half-sister, four years younger than me, married to an artist, and employed by an NGO. Her features were all soft curves to my sharp angles, and her sense of humour stemmed from joy rather than irony. The only thing we had in common was our father's gene pool – clearly filled with recessive genes since there was nothing of him apparent in either of us – and our overly protective attitudes towards each other.

'Make sure you look after each other while we're away,' my father said, and I couldn't help smiling at the unexpected – and rare – confluence of our thinking. Dad walked over to the two of us. 'And come and visit, often.' The air ducts had given his hair a windswept look and, seeing it, Rabia laughed again and combed it back into place with her fingers before leaving the room to find Beema – last seen with the customs official downstairs, deep in conversation about Shehnaz Saeed's return to acting.

'You're sure you'll be OK, living alone?'

'Dad, I'm thirty-one.'

'Yes.' He shook his head. 'How did that happen?'

'Linearity?' I suggested. His face had that slightly bemused expression I had seen at various points in my life when I announced my age to him, as though he couldn't quite believe the gap between my conception and the present moment.

'It's not too late to decide you want to come with us, you know.'

I threw him an exasperated look. 'Welcome to the third millennium, Dad. Single women in Karachi do occasionally live alone without the world coming to an end. Besides,' I jerked my thumb towards the lounge, 'there's the connecting door to Rabia and Shakeel's flat. I'm not exactly camping out in the wilderness. Subject closed.'

He nodded and ran his fingers over the network of hairline cracks in the paint which gave the turtle on the wall a wrinkled brow.

'I could go out and get some paint, and help you slap on a coat before our flight out,' my father said. 'Unless the marine life is growing on you.'

'Now there's a pleasant image. Barnacles on my skin, seaweed draped around my neck. It's fine, Dad. I can take care of it. You know, you don't have to be so useful all the time.'

He smiled and scratched his chin, as he always did when he wasn't quite sure what to say. The chin was growing more prominent as the passage of time carved itself into his frame, gradually removing all excesses of flesh. Old age would happen to his face suddenly, and soon, I realized, but for the moment, with his trim physique and thick grey hair, he looked better than he had since the days of his boyhood, just past adolescence – a time in which, if photographs were to be believed, there was a promise of extraordinary beauty in each angle of his face.

'What should I be if not useful?' he said, spreading his arms as if indicating a willingness to take on any possibility.

'It's a moot point. All you can be is yourself. Consistency, thy name is Dad.'

'You have this way, darling, of paying compliments that sound so very much like insults.'

'I know. I'm sorry. I will miss you, you know.'

'You say it as though it just occurred to you for the first time. Please, don't respond to that.'

It was my turn then to smile and not know what to say. So finally I said, 'What are you going to do in Islamabad? Couldn't the bank just have transferred you to their branch there instead of giving you time off?'

'They could have. They offered to. I said no. I thought my wife might have need . . . well, that she wouldn't regard it as unwelcome if I were with her during the day instead of behind some desk. The financial world won't be too disturbed by my absence, I expect.'

'Because we're only irreplaceable to those who love us? That's the subtle point you're trying to make here, right? Let's concentrate on the domestic and leave the world to take care of itself. Thank God Louis Pasteur didn't take that view. We'd all be out milking cows every morning for our daily cups of tea.'

He raised his eyebrows at me. 'The subtle point I'm making is that I'm not a very good banker. And anyway, someone else would have figured out pasteurization eventually – there'd just be a different word for it.'

'And if Shakespeare had stayed in Stratford with Anne Hathaway and the kids, someone else would have written *Hamlet* eventually, too.'

He half-shrugged, summing up his view of both *Hamlet* and this oft-repeated dance around our differences, and there was something approaching relief on his face as we heard the sounds of Rabia and Beema's footsteps and rushed voices headed towards the bedroom.

'Such excitement,' Beema declared, walking into the room, Rabia behind her. When my stepmother and half-sister stood next to each other, it was remarkable to notice the resemblance between them which had nothing to do with features replicating themselves from one generation to the next, and everything to do with the way personality can be a physical presence, particularly around the eyes and mouth. 'About Shehnaz Saeed's return. I was talking to the customs guy about it and next thing I knew I was in the centre of a throng, buzzing away about the Great Comeback.'

'I told you it would happen eventually,' my father said drily. 'Some people just need their spotlight.'

'Be fair to her.' There was a hint of rebuke in Beema's voice. 'It's been fifteen years, and why shouldn't she have her spotlight?'

'I never said she shouldn't have it. I'm entirely unconcerned with whether she has it or not. I'm just saying what I've always said. People don't change.'

'People change entirely,' I said. 'Look at Narcissus. Became a flower. I call that a change.'

'A metamorphosis, even,' Rabia added. 'Ma, you knew Shehnaz Saeed, didn't you?'

'A little.' Beema put a hand on my wrist. 'She was a friend of your mother, remember?'

My father made a noise in his throat, muttered something about something that needed fixing, and left the room. It was his standard operating procedure where anything to do with my mother was concerned.

'Oh, everyone who was ever within ten paces of Mama claims to have been a friend of hers at some point,' I said as airily as I could manage, though I knew it had been a different story with Shehnaz Saeed. 'No wonder she had to leave all the time. So many friends, so many birthday presents to buy.' I thought of Ed's initial reaction to me, that moment when he stepped back as though seeing something impossible, and it struck me forcibly that he must have known my mother when she was in Karachi – not just through pictures in the paper or from the viewpoint of audience, but actually known her.

'I met the son at work,' I said, to change the subject. 'Shehnaz Saeed's son. He seems to be in charge of the place.'

'The delinquent?' Rabia said.

'Doesn't seem like a delinquent so much as a jackass. He wants to be called Ed. And, despite this, he thinks he's so slick.'

'Uh-huh.' Rabia was grinning at me. 'So you like him?'

'Oh, shut up.'

'Don't be so judgmental, Aasmaani.' Creases appeared between Beema's eyebrows. 'Just because the name's silly it doesn't mean the man is.'

'Hear that, Celestial Revolution?' Rabia laughed.

'Beema, why don't you take the brat to Islamabad with you and give me some peace?'

It was the subtlest glance that they exchanged then, my mother and sister (because that's what they were, after all – never mind the steps- and the halfs-), but in it I saw a baton being passed, some responsibility for me transferring from Beema to Rabia. Beema saw that I had seen it and moved quickly into briskness.

'Well, whatever he's called, I hope he's going to give you proper work that makes use of your abilities, not just this quiz show rubbish you're pretending to be happy about.'

'Beema, I don't have abilities. I have acts of desperation which land me in occupations I couldn't care less about.' And then, because I was angry about that glance, 'I told you I just want to take a few months off to do nothing. That's why I quit the oil company. I don't even know why I let you interfere.'

She sat down on my bed. 'You never do nothing. You brood. And I don't like the thought of you living alone and brooding with Rabia off at work all day and Shakeel locked up in his studio.'

'I think you overestimate the importance of your presence on my sanity,' I said, sitting down next to her.

She stroked my hair. 'I fuss. I know. I can't help it. It's what mothers do.'

'No, it's what you do.' I put my arms around her, resting my forehead on her shoulder. 'Don't stay away too long, OK?'

As soon as I said it, I realized the awfulness of the demand. Beema was going to Islamabad because her mother was dying. She was going to Islamabad to watch her mother die and know herself incapable of reversing or stalling the process. No amount of love or pleading, no promises or entreaties, could slow the decay of that body of which she had once been a part.

'Now, don't say anything silly,' Beema said, as I lifted up my head to apologize. 'I know what you mean. And don't you start worrying about me. I'm not ready for that role-reversal yet. Oh listen, jaan, don't look so sad. Watching someone die gives you a new way of learning to love them. Imagine, knowing someone for five and a half decades and at the end of that finding a new way to love them. It's an extraordinary thing.'

Sometimes the sadness of the world can appear beautiful. That was what Beema knew and Rabia, without experience of wrenching loss, believed. It gave them the strength to hold out their arms to grief, their own or anyone else's.

*Do you want me to come with you? Will it help if I'm there?* I almost asked Beema as I had almost asked so often these last few days that it almost seemed a matter of habit now to leave it unsaid.

A few hours later, they were gone. Dad and Beema on their way to the airport, Rabia having tea at her in-laws' house. This was worse than the blankness of the morning, the emptiness vaster because it had sprung up where three people I loved had stood just a few minutes ago.

Rabia lives just through that doorway, I had to remind myself.

I walked through the flat, counting my footsteps from one end of the lounge to a corner of my bedroom, then counting them again from the kitchen to the front door. Such silence. In Dad and Beema's house there was always some sound – Beema on the telephone, the cook yelling at the gardener, the neighbours' dog barking, men pushing wooden carts piled with old tins and bottles calling out to announce their presence, whether searching for buyers or sellers I never knew. But here, three storeys up from the world, the windows closed – nothing. All this space and just me to fill it.

I walked over to the boxes of books which surrounded the empty bookshelf in the living room, and opened the one marked 'REF'. On the top was the dictionary I'd had since I was a child. I closed my eyes, opened the book, and ran my fingers down the page. Opened my eyes. My finger was halfway down the definition of COMBUST. I flipped past CONTRA MUNDUM and CORUSCATE and CUMULAS until I reached CURRENT.

I pulled out all my reference books, moved over to the coffee table, sat on the ground, switched on my laptop and loaded my encyclopaedia software. Currents. I knew something of them already.

I knew the currents of the oceans include the Agulhas, the Hunboldt and the Benguela, I knew currents move in gyres, clockwise in the northern hemisphere and anticlockwise in the southern hemisphere. I knew the Poet had told me, years ago, that if we could only view the motion of currents as metaphors for the gyres of history – or the gyres of history as metaphors for the motion of currents – we'd know the absurdity of declaring the world is divided into East and West. I knew my mother's voice at the beach, cautioning me against undercurrents.

I looked up into the emptiness around me, and was suddenly very grateful that I had an office to go to every day.

# III

A week later, long past midnight, I sat cross-legged in my lounge, watching the shadow-dance of leaves and stems on the window panes. The Xylem and Phloem troupe.

This lounge was my favourite room in the flat. Not for the minimal furnishings (one two-seat sofa, one bean bag, one low coffee table, one bookshelf which tilted forward if you put too many books in it) or the large red and beige rug or the flower-patterned curtains. None of these features – inherited from the previous tenants – held any appeal for me. But I loved the broad windows along the width of one wall, looking out on to the balcony with its profusion of plants and, beyond that, past two rows of buildings too low to obstruct the view from my third-floor vantage point, the sea.

When the touch of a hibiscus tongue sent the money-plant reeling back in anguished pleasure, I understood the performance had reached its crescendo, and turned my attention back to the blank screen of the laptop on the low table in front of me, beside an encyclopaedia opened to 'I'. I wrote:

*Which is the oldest poetic form still in popular use?*
*a) haiku*
*b) ghazal*
*c) sonnet*
*d) tendi*

*Answer: b*

I had reached that question via the entry on IAMBIC PENTAMETER, which led into a memory of the Poet's irritation when he read an English scholar's claim that the sonnet was the oldest extant form.

I flipped the pages of the encyclopaedia and was trying to think of a question which would have as its optional answers my four favourite mediaeval Ibns – Ibn Khaldun (which mediaeval historian wrote *Muqadammah*, which expresses many of the thoughts of modern sociology?), Ibn Battutah (which mediaeval traveller covered 75,000 miles from Spain to China, Tambouctou to Russia, and left behind written accounts of his journeys?), Ibn Sina (which mediaeval philosopher and physician wrote *Kitab-ash-Shifa*, covering a range of subjects including metaphysics, Aristotelian logic, psychology and natural sciences?), Ibn-al Nafis (which mediaeval physician was the first to explain pulmonary circulation, in *Sharh Tashrih al-Qanun*?) – when there came a knock on the newly fitted door that connected Rabia and Shakeel's flat to my flat (I had already started thinking of it as mine, even though it really belonged to Rabia and Shakeel; they'd bought it some weeks ago in expectation of a future in which their family would double in size and make their one-bedroom flat seem cramped. My timing in needing a place to stay had merely been fortuitous.)

I tossed a tennis ball at the door, signalling my willingness to be sociable, and Rabia walked in, yawning.

'How's it going?' she said, sitting down next to me.

'I've discovered all sorts of fascinating things about *I Ching*, the Ibibio, and the many suffixes that can be added on to "icthy-". You want to hear? It's gripping stuff.'

'You and all your information,' she grumbled, leaning her slight frame away from me. 'You should have been a mathematician – one who works with pure mathematics, not the applied variety. Just live in an abstract, self-referential world.'

It was an appealing thought, despite my inability to grapple with numbers at any level beyond the most basic. If you asked me which historical figure had the grandest death, I'd skip over martyrs and lovers and warriors, and settle on Archimedes, who was so engrossed in making diagrams in the sand one day that he rebuked a Roman soldier who came up to him. Don't disturb my diagrams, were the last words he ever spoke, so legend has it. Not that Archimedes was a man of pure mathematics alone; among his many inventions was a weapon of great power – a magnifying glass which could be used to direct the sun's rays to set the enemy's boots on fire. If all wars were fought using giant magnifying glasses as the only weapons, perhaps we'd have seen long ago the absurdity of armed combat as a means of resolving disputes. Oh, the tragedy of boots lost to friendly fire!

'What are you so amused by?' Rabia said. 'The idea of you as a mathematician? Believe me, Smaani, when we were growing up that would have seemed a lot more plausible than the notion of you as some low-level researcher for a quiz show which blatantly steals its format from foreign TV.'

Clearly, my sister's delight at my departure from the corporate world had given way to her customary stance of disapproval, which had followed me through the years as I taught at a school for the educationally disinclined children of the elite, edited a monthly cricket magazine, translated the Urdu diaries of a nineteenth-century, narrow-minded, petty bureaucrat from an Indian princely state for an Anglophone historian, and finally landed up in human resources at the oil company. 'I'm not low-level,' I pointed out. 'I'm the only level.'

Rabia placed one finger against my shoulder-blade and pressed down – her childhood gesture of ensuring you were paying her attention. 'It's such a powerful medium, television. Think of all you could do.'

'What could I do?'

'Influence people's thinking.'

'Ah.' I lay back, fingers interlaced in a cradle for my head, which rested on the bean bag. 'How can you be so certain of your own certainties, Rabia, knowing that if you trace back belief far enough it always leads to mist?'

'What mist?'

'Mists, really. There are so many. The mist of received wisdom, the mist which confuses subjective experience with truth, the mist that is afraid of believing otherwise, the mist which acts as panacea.'

She nodded, her large eyes fixed on me. 'Tell me just one thing, Aasmaani. Is it that you don't want to be your mother, or that you're afraid you'll fail so dismally to live up to her that you won't even try?'

I sat back up and bowed my head before her, my hand twirling away from my body in a gesture of submission inspired by the shadow-leaves. 'Either way, you've proved my point. All that I am, all that I believe or try not to believe, it's got nothing to do with larger truths, and everything to do with being the daughter of Samina Akram.'

Rabia sighed, and shook her head.

I leaned forward conspiratorially. 'And besides, the quiz show isn't all I'm doing at STD.'

After I'd written my plot suggestions for *Boond*, that first day in my cubicle, I had folded up the paper and put it in my desk drawer. Writing it had helped fill up the time I waited for someone from personnel to appear and, as far as I was concerned, that was the extent of its usefulness. But a few days ago, in the STD kitchenette, I had run into the harried scriptwriter again – by now Ed had told me she was Kiran Hilal, one of the most respected figures in the industry – and as we waited together for the kettle to boil she said she was going insane. She'd been working with her story-development team round the clock, but all they'd concluded was that the entire script would have to be reworked to accommodate Shehnaz Saeed. They'd torn up almost everything they'd already written, and been compelled to tell the director that she'd have to scrap most of the footage she'd already shot of the opening episodes (filming had ceased when the

28

bougainvillea-phobic actress quit). And the show was to premiere in less than five weeks. It was all a disaster, a total disaster.

The real worry, she admitted, was that Shehnaz Saeed wouldn't approve of the role created for her, and back out at the last minute. Her contract had an escape clause which she could invoke if the show didn't meet 'certain creative standards'. Meanwhile, the hype about her return to the screen had got so out of hand that if she withdrew STD might never recover. When Kiran said that I thought it was wild exaggeration, but then she told me how much money advertisers had paid to secure spots for their products during *Boond*'s run – with the caveat that they would withdraw from their contracts if Shehnaz Saeed wasn't in the show – and I almost dropped my cup of tea. (Later that day, the hoopla around Shehnaz Saeed's unretirement reached another level: as talks between the various political groups entered one more round in their attempts to form a coalition government, nearly a month after the elections, a leading politician was quoted in the evening papers as saying, 'Of course a powerful central government is possible under the circumstances. Shehnaz Saeed is acting again – doesn't that tell you all hope is possible?')

'Got any ideas?' Kiran Hilal said to me, as the kettle whistled and two jets of steam came shooting out of the holes in the spout. She meant it rhetorically, but I found myself repeating back to her everything I had written down that first day in the office about Shehnaz Saeed's return to the screen. She thanked me, spooned a staggering quantity of sugar into her tea and went away, leaving me feeling foolish. But the next day – that is, two days ago – she'd asked me if I would sit in on the next meeting of her team and pitch my idea.

'Seriously?' Rabia said. 'You'll be working on the Shehnaz Saeed show? Why didn't you tell me?' High political ideals did nothing to stand in the way of my sister's love of celebrity.

'Let's not get carried away. I'm sitting in on one meeting with Kiran's team. That's what she calls it – her team. I'm like the outside coach who's called in to help correct a particular bowling action, and then sent away again.'

'Yeah, but maybe when they see your own bowling action, they'll want you to be a part of the team, too.'

There she was again, in front of my eyes, walking from tarmac to terminal. 'I don't want to be part of the team.'

'Why not?'

'It's complicated.'

My sister put her arm around my neck. 'Once in a while, you need to let things be complicated.'

I stood up, aware of Rabia watching me closely as I walked towards the screen door, pulled it open and stepped on to the balcony. There was a mingled scent of sewerage and sea in the air which I should have found a great deal more unpleasant than I did. It was only at these early-morning hours that it was quiet enough to hear the waves, and then I loved this place despite how quickly window grilles and outdoor antennae turned to rust and how rapidly the paint on the façade faded. This proximity to the sea, I knew, might have as much to do with the mermaid dream – which had come back again last night – as the wall paintings did, but it was easier to blame the paintings since they weren't anything I loved.

The Poet used to say we all have a particular topography in which we feel ourselves at home, though not all of us are fortunate enough to find the landscape which makes us so aware of that thing called 'the soul'. It is mountains for some, deserts for others, wide open plains for the most obvious in our midst. But you and I, Aasmaani, he'd tell me, we are creatures of water.

I heard Rabia get up and walk back to her flat.

In a few minutes she returned, carrying a file full of news cuttings that I hadn't seen in many years, though it didn't surprise me that she still had it.

'Sit,' she commanded, when I returned to the lounge. When I failed to comply, she clicked her tongue – there were moments when it was frighteningly easy to see what she'd be like as a grandmother – and flipped through the various cuttings until she came to the one she wanted. 'Read it,' she said, and retreated to her flat again.

I ignored it for almost an hour, and contented myself with surfing the internet for further information about Archimedes' magnifying glass and checking e-mail. Just three new messages. One from my father, commenting on the latest news from the world of cricket and suggesting we switch our sporting allegiances to the game of curling. One from an ex-colleague at the multinational corporation, giving me an update on office politics and saying we must get together one of these days. I wondered if she was at all surprised to find how easily I had slipped out of her life, just as I had slipped out of the lives of everyone with whom I had ever worked. The third e-mail was a petition to ban some sport of which I had never heard, because it was endangering a species of animal for which I had no regard in a country that couldn't care less what I thought of its laws. I forwarded it to Rabia with the message: 'The modern woman's preferred method of political engagement.'

Finally I logged out, and hefted the green ring-binder file on to my lap. Its contents had increased quite considerably since I last saw it, which came as something of a revelation.

The article Rabia had left the file open on was an interview with Shehnaz Saeed, conducted in 1982 when she was touring festivals around the world with *Macbeth*. It had been published in Italian, and someone in Milan had mailed the article to my mother's Karachi address. Mama was having one of her bouts of self-imposed exile at the time, so I was the one who found the letter when I went with Beema on our monthly inspection of my mother's house. Attracted by the foreign stamps, I had opened the envelope and, finding the contents indecipherable, I had made Beema drive me to the Italian consulate, where a young official with the bluest eyes had taken pity on me and translated the article. Those were the days when you could just walk into a European consulate without encountering road blocks and several layers of security guards and the need for appointments. Those were also the days when it was me, not my half-sister, who maintained this file about my mother with a near-religious zeal. I shook my head to clear away the memory, and read the translation, which I had glued next to the cutting:

Q: Watching your performance of Lady Macbeth at the festival, even though I couldn't understand the Urdu, there was an Italian word which came to mind: *sprezzatura*. The illusion of ease with which the most gifted artistes imbue their most complex performances. Are you familiar with this word?

A (laughing): Yes, I am. Thank you. I'm very . . . thank you.

Q: If you had to name a performer who embodies *sprezzatura*, who would it be?

A: I can think of a number of actors. But, correct me if I'm wrong, there's an Italian word which is applied to performances which are a level above mere *sprezzatura*.

Q: You mean *grazia*. I have to say, I'm impressed.

A: Yes, *grazia*. Divine grace. The feeling that something almost out of this world is happening through the performer. You can admire *sprezzatura*, but in the presence of *grazia* you feel actually honoured, you feel you've changed. You've glimpsed something of the immortal mysteries. I've only witnessed *grazia* once – and it wasn't while watching a play. The feminist icon Samina Akram, I heard her address a crowd in Karachi once. In the interaction between her and the audience and some ineffable presence, *grazia* happened. I was in that audience – and I know without doubt that my most important performance was that, just being one of the crowd of several hundred people who created that atmosphere which allowed her to be so fully herself. I don't think I'll ever feel anything like it again.

*

That was my mother's greatest cruelty. She allowed you enough time to luxuriate in her *grazia*, and then she went away, taking it with her, leaving you with the knowledge that you would never feel anything like it again and you would certainly never produce it yourself. Small wonder my father was never able to look squarely at her after their divorce – in all my memories of the two of them sharing the same space he is always distracted by something on her periphery: a sunset, a fleck of paint, an ant. I used to think it was because he hated her too much to look at her, but it was only after she left that final time that I thought to wonder if he was afraid of glimpsing *grazia* in her again. They were married for eleven months; she left him after four months, but agreed to delay the divorce until after I was born.

'Which did you resent more,' I had asked Dad in one of the rare moments in which either of us mentioned my mother to the other, 'that she left you or that she married you to begin with?'

He said, 'If she hadn't married me, I wouldn't have you. If she hadn't left me, I wouldn't have Rabia.'

He was right to evade the question, I suppose. Even before my mother left, she was an unspoken presence standing between Dad and me. His disapproval of her, and my disapproval of his disapproval, made silence the only possibility between us in regard to her.

I ran my fingers over the plastic sheet which covered the newspaper clipping and held it in place. What did Rabia think she'd achieve by reminding me of this article? More reason not to have even the slightest involvement with *Boond*, that's all it was. And yet. I knew Shehnaz Saeed had really been a friend of my mother – and not just in the way of all those people who claimed to have been her friends but had really only fallen under the spell she could cast so quickly, so pervasively, over almost anyone she met. In those last two years before she disappeared, I would sometimes pick up the phone to make a call, only to hear my mother on the extension speaking to a voice I knew so well from all those hours of listening to it on the stage and TV. Mama would always hear the click of the receiver when I picked up and say, 'Who is it?' so I'd have to hang up, but even though I never heard their conversations, the mere fact that Mama was talking to Shehnaz Saeed in those years when she barely talked at all said volumes about their closeness during that period.

I had never met Shehnaz Saeed – this struck me as odd for the first time – though I knew that Mama went to visit her during those two years – sometimes several times a week, sometimes not for weeks at a stretch. After Mama disappeared, I sometimes thought of calling Shehnaz, but I never knew what it was I wanted to say to her.

But now Shehnaz Saeed herself had handed me a reason to call her. I walked over to the oversized handbag I had carried to work that day, and took out the envelope addressed to me that had been lying there, unopened, since the morning. It was from Shehnaz Saeed: 'Thank you for helping with my character' was scribbled on the envelope. One of the twenty-somethings at STD who'd been in reception when the package arrived had almost fainted at this evidence of Shehnaz Saeed's unstarlike attitude to 'underlings'. I hadn't been so convinced. I knew a thing or two about women who were legends. I knew how desperately they wanted to be treated as though they weren't legends – but only by people whom they deemed worthy of such impertinence. I was worthy, in Shehnaz Saeed's eyes. It didn't matter that we'd never met.

Despite the twentysomething's entreaties, I hadn't opened the envelope; doing so seemed to constitute an agreement – to *something* – so I'd kept curiosity at bay all these hours.

But now I prised open the flap and pulled out the contents – a piece of paper, neatly folded up, with a yellow post-it note stuck on top. I peeled off the note and read: 'I would love to meet you. Please call me. In the meantime, does the enclosed bit of writing mean anything to you? – Shehnaz.'

I unfolded the paper, laid it on the table, and smoothed

the creases with the palm of my hand. An unintelligible series of letters, beautifully calligraphed, filled the top of the page.

Ijc Anonkoh efac fyfno ikrfb.

That was the first line. The rest of the writing didn't make any more sense.

Why would someone I had never met put this in a box and imagine it might mean something to me?

I looked at the page one more time, then pushed it aside. Some foreign language, no doubt. Live in a port city all your life and you get used to finding pieces of paper with indecipherable scripts formed into paper cones for roasted pine-nuts, or just drifting along on the breeze in empty lots used as garbage dumps. Did Shehnaz Saeed think I was a linguist?

I walked away from the page, and was all the way to my bedroom before dormant neurons in my brain fired themselves awake.

*My ex calls the ochre winter 'autumn' as we queue to hear dock boys play jazz fugues in velvet dark.*

I turned. My feet were heavy lifting themselves off the bare floor and my body sluggish in response.

I reached the paper, lifted it up.

Ijc Anonkoh efac fyfno ikrfb.

The letters stepped out of their disguises – haltingly at first, but then all in a rush and swirl of abandon – and transformed into words:

The Minions came again today.

# IV

The edge of the low table bit into my skin, just inches below my elbow. I raised my arm, and looked at the diagonal indentation. Close up and out of context, this groove running through a square of skin could as easily be a dried river-bed in a desert as a thread of sap on the vein of a leaf.

I ran my thumb along the furrow, and returned my attention to the four lines on the page. It was startlingly easy to read the code after all these years, read it as though it were a language of its own – but it might as well have been Albanian for all my success at comprehension. From a writing pad on the table, I tore out a page and pressed it against the encrypted lines. The black calligraphy showed through as if covered by nothing thicker than the membrane of an onion skin.

I picked up a felt-tip pen, and traced the twirling letters on to the overlying paper. It took much longer than I would have thought to follow every line and loop of that intricate hand. I began to feel as though I were replicating an abstract painting, each stroke of my nib inscribing my inability to understand how a mind could conceive of those shapes and combinations. What was I hoping for as my pen moved in and out of curlicues? That the act of tracing would bring me closer to whoever wrote those sentences, allow me to slip between the words and understand the mind that placed them on the page?

What was I hoping for? It was a question that had been following me for a long time.

I put down the pen.

Other than me, who knew the code? Only my mother and the Poet. And the Poet had been dead sixteen years. He had been killed, so the story went, by a government agency which feared the combination of his national popularity and international reputation – although the military government in power at the time countered those claims by declaring a national day of mourning for that 'flower of our soil'. All over the country anti-government groups of every hue boycotted the government's day of mourning and announced their own day of mourning (on the same day) for that 'voice of resistance'.

Of course, there were those who believed he wasn't really dead. The art of storytelling, so ingrained in this nation, had turned – in all the years of misrule and oppression – into the art of spinning conspiracy theories, each one more elaborate than the one before. So when the Poet died it took only hours for the weavers of tales to produce their versions of what really happened. There were variants from one teller to the next, but the bottom line remained the same: that poor tortured corpse, they said, was a look-alike, his features slashed and gouged where they didn't match the Poet's. Where the Poet really was, and why anyone should fake his death, was a rather more difficult issue to contend with, but – just weeks after the funeral – when the conspiracy theorists were beginning to acknowledge the illogic of staging a death when it would be so much easier actually to kill a man, the doctor who claimed to have verified the identity of the corpse died in a car crash. And then all the tales spun with whispers and perverted glee were brought out again.

But my mother never accepted that claim of a faked death, and so I had never believed it either. Why would she, of all people, ridicule such an idea if it seemed to contain even a fibre of truth?

If only she had believed it. Perhaps hope would have allowed her to cling on to her own character, instead of setting it adrift like a widow sending her possessions out to sea in the wake of a bier.

I lifted the page off the table again. From what distance was I regarding this object? How long ago had it been written?

Long ago. Had to be. When they first invented the code. Surely they must have practised? I couldn't have been the only one who did that, turning Peter Pan into Ucicl Ufo and Mama into Afaf? I picked up Rabia's file again and looked through the cuttings once more until I found the one for which I was looking. An interview with the Poet, first published in 1971, the year I was born, and later reprinted in 1996, on the tenth anniversary of his death:

Q: The acclaimed Colombian novelist Rafael Gonzalez has said of you: 'He is my twin, in political and aesthetic temperament. It's a good thing he writes poetry because if he ever turned his hand to the novel he would write my books faster than I myself write them.' Has fiction ever lured you?

A: I'm lured frequently and indiscriminately. But in my life allure is always fleeting. Well, always except twice. The first, the allure of poetry. The second I'm too gallant to mention. Or perhaps, also, too cowardly. Newly-wed husbands can be violent in their jealousies. But, to answer your question more directly, Rafael and I have often played games of diving into each other's skin. I send him a fragment of a story in English, our mutual language, and in response he sends me a dramatic monologue, also in English. I tell him, that's cheating. You've written me a short story with line breaks! Then he sends me a perfect couplet, and I'm filled with envy. Yes, yes, for Rafael I have written prose. And sometimes I just do it to restore suppleness to my wrist which is locked in place from agonizing for days over a single word of poetry. It's interesting . . . always English, my prose. I suppose it's just habit now.

In all the interviews published during his lifetime, this is his sole reference to my mother as something other than his first reader and only editor. What had Mama felt when she first read it, just weeks into her marriage? And my father, how must he have reacted? That was easier to answer: with silent anger, directed less at the Poet's continued feelings for my mother than at the publicizing of those feelings. Omi must have known that, of course. Must have known how much my father would have hated to have himself referred to in print, in a discussion of something so tawdry as jealousy.

That might have been the moment you lost her, Dad.

But I didn't really believe it. That they had ever been together was not a mystery, just an aberration.

Regardless. For today, the interview told me all I really needed to know. The Poet wrote prose. Sometimes for Rafael Gonzales and sometimes just as an exercise. So, those cryptic lines were nothing more than some old writing exercise of his, written in code.

All that was out of my life now, and that at least was something for which I should be grateful. The need for codes and secrets, the conspiracies and cover-ups, the weightiness of History pressing down on people who insisted that it was their burden to bear though it showed nothing but disdain for them. All that was over. All that madness. All that life.

I touched my fingers to the calligraphed words. 'Omi.'

I walked to the balcony, and leaned out into the smell of the waves.

*I am so young I count my age in quarter years. In my mother's house, I turn circles in the master bedroom with arms spread wide. I turn circles and make it look like joy so the whole room joins in and turns with me. We are spinning, the room and I, turning into blurs. If we keep it up we'll spin right out of this world into some Oz – we can spin ourselves into cyclonic speeds. But I hear voices coming up the stairs, and leaving isn't so tempting any more, so I stop spinning. But the room doesn't. I must grope my way to the bed to sit down, my hands clutching on to the frame to make it stop. What will my mother say if she enters to find her bed has gone to Oz? She walks in, the Poet behind her, and her face is instant concern.*

*'What's wrong?' she says. 'Are you sick?'*

*'I'm diggy,' I reply, trying to bring her face into focus. She looks as though she's partway to Oz herself.*

*'Giddy,' says the Poet. 'The word is "giddy".'*

*Everything has righted itself by now, the bed, my mother, the walls. It seems terrible to be wrong. So I say, 'No, it's diggy. That's when you're so giddy even the letters in giddy turn topsy-turvy.' I can't believe I've said something so stupid, but the Poet throws back his head and laughs. He lifts me up in his arms.*

*'She'll be a poet, Samina. She'll make language somersault through rings of fire. Just watch.' He brings his face closer to mine and whispers. 'They say I can do that. Maybe you're a young me.'*

*'Maybe you're an old me,' I shoot back. And that's it, an appellation coined. Old Me. Omi.*

I turned, saw the paper lying on the coffee table, blurred through the smudged windowpane, and the thought slipped out: could it have been written by my mother, and recently?

I could almost hear the plants around me exhaling carbon dioxide. I leaned over the balcony again and looked to the right. Here and there, lights shone out of windows and street lamps. There seemed no numerical order to the illumination, no multiples or prime numbers underlying the logic of lights. But perhaps the order was pictorial rather than numerical. Connect the dots, and what do you get?

When my mother had disappeared, fourteen years ago, I saw dots of brightness everywhere. The universe, back then, reconfigured itself into an accumulation of clues and conspiracies. The clues looked like this: any tapping sound or flashing lights; a ringing phone which stopped ringing the instant before I picked it up; a news reporter speaking on a foreign news channel about an unexpected uprising; strangers who whispered indecipherable words as they passed me on the street; a dream of my mother set in a place that I would have known in another instant if the wind (how could I be sure it was just the wind?) hadn't banged on my window and woken me up. And the conspiracies, they took these shapes: a conversation which stopped the moment I entered the room; a fire burning down a restaurant my mother had loved; a letter intercepted at my gate (I had no proof of such interceptions, but that only made the conspiracy more powerful); the death of anyone she had ever known; the death of anyone, anyone at all, because how could I know for certain all the people she had known? And yes, I had seen patterns start to emerge amidst all those clues and conspiracies. Until, one day, some principle of self-preservation (brought on by Beema's intervention) had forced me to see that the only clear pattern in any of this was my own rush towards insanity. I was seventeen then, and resilient. I had been able to pull away from that course, and face the harsher truth that everything that happened was Mama's doing, Mama's choice.

But what if I had been wrong? What if there had been some conspiracy all along? I shut my eyes against the dots of light and I saw a gathering of people: the customs official downstairs, Beema's old schoolfriend, the CEO of STD, Kiran Hilal and Shehnaz Saeed. As I watched they discussed their various roles, plotted how each one of them would guide me towards the next one in line, so discreetly, so seemingly unconnectedly, that the arrival of an encrypted page at my door, after I'd been led all the way down the line, would appear coincidence, a confluence of random events. And there was another figure in the gathering: Ed. The man who tried a little too hard to announce himself as my ally from near the beginning of the game. But to what end, all of it, any of it?

I opened my eyes. A street lamp flickered Morse code. I turned away with a gesture of dismissal.

I walked back indoors, and into my kitchen. It had seemed absurdly small when I first saw it, accustomed as I was to the expanse of Beema's kitchen, but already I had come to enjoy its cosiness, every spice and utensil within easy reach as you stood at the stove. And I had grown, also, to love the little window at the right-hand side of the stove which allowed you extra elbow room when you needed to stir the contents of a haandi with extra vigour. Rabia said it was one of the great sight gags of the block of flats, my elbow jiggling outside the window for everyone to see, as much a source of amusement as the woman in number 9C who would flip her long hair over the balcony after a shower and squeeze, directing the water into a flowerbed below, ensuring that the snapdragons she had planted there stayed alive even through water shortages.

I gathered together all the ingredients I needed for biryani. Gestalt philosophy must have been born in a kitchen of the sub-continent, the Poet once said. In any successful biryani, the whole is so much more than the sum of its parts. I switched on the portable radio that perched on the raised back strip of the stove and listened to FM 100 as I soaked the rice, measured out and ground the spices, chopped the potatoes, tomatoes and chicken, and wept over the onions. Beema and Dad's cook, Abdul, had offered to come and work for me while they were away, but I had told him not to be a fool and just take Dad's offer of paid leave instead. The truth was, there had been nothing more appealing to me about the idea of living alone than the thought of having my own kitchen, without Abdul finding ways to mark his territory every time I entered it.

There was a burst of static from the radio, telling me it was 4 a.m. It wouldn't do to fall asleep tomorrow in the middle of my afternoon meeting with Kiran Hilal's team, I decided, so I put clingfilm over the ingredients, left the ground spices on the kitchen counter and everything else in the fridge, and went to bed, falling easily into a sleep without remembered dreams.

But the following morning, as I stood in the STD kitchenette shaking the remnants of the instant coffee jar into my mug, Ed walked in, and I had to wonder whether he knew of his mother's gift to me, and what it meant, and how I was supposed to react.

'How go the haiku?' he said, reaching across me to pick up a mug. I hadn't seen very much of him since that first day at the studio, and when we did encounter each other in the hallway he was professional to the point of being brusque. He was officially a producer, but seemed to take on all the responsibilities that the CEO couldn't attend to because of the pressures of the golf course and his philandering. When Ramzan started Ed was going to accompany a camera crew for the entire month as they filmed the preparation and eating of iftar meals across the country for a documentary about the culinary and cultural variations within Pakistan. He was producing the show, but everyone at STD knew that the show's presenter was the CEO's mistress and Ed's real responsibility was to ensure she stuck to speaking in Urdu (in her previous foray into television work she felt compelled to throw in occasional words of English which would result in perfectly phrased Urdu sentences interspersed with such gems as 'the women here do very good hand jobs'. This in regard to the production of local crafts in a Sindhi village.)

'Dot, how did you know/Yellow, Emerald, Ruby when/All your world was grey?' I said, pulling a new jar of instant coffee off the shelf.

'Ah. *Wizard of Oz* as philosophical conundrum.' He laughed as he took the jar from my hands and punctured the foil with the tine of a fork, slashing from side to side to widen the rent, and then held the jar up to his nose. His eyebrows rose in mock-pain. 'Ed, will you recall/The scent of coffee beans when/All you have is instant?'

'One syllable too many,' I pointed out, though I couldn't help laughing back.

'I knew this girl in New York – an English girl, always in search of a new expression. When she wanted to say someone had a screw loose she'd say, "He's one syllable short of a haiku."'

I was suddenly ashamed of my prickliness at our first meeting. 'New York, huh? Is that where you picked up your coffee snobbery?'

'Uh-huh.' He poured water from the kettle into his mug and mine, with the wristiness of a spin-bowler. 'It was my home until a few months ago. Lived there for ten years. Loved the place. The day I arrived I thought, I can just be myself here. Not my mother's son, just me. You know what I mean?'

'I have some idea,' I found myself saying, though normally I would not have allowed myself to be pulled into this particular avenue of conversation. But there was a lightness about him today, which made him seem . . . I couldn't find the word for it. Not boyish; it was hard to think of Ed as boyish.

'Yes, of course,' he smiled. He reached out as if to touch my shoulder, but in the last moment changed course and took hold of the sugar-bowl behind my head instead. Then I knew. The word I was looking for: irresistible. Something about his lightness, his assurance, was calling to mind all those men in screwball comedies from the 1930s. Men who'd crack one joke and smile one smile, and that would be enough for you to know the heroines would live happily ever after with them, with great sex lives, lots of laughs, and endless parades of parties. Even if the idea of endless parades of parties normally seemed unbearable, those men with their smiles and charms would make you forget that. If you can be this, I wanted to say, why are you ever anything else?

'So how do you feel about being here rather than there?' I tried to keep all tones of coquetry from my voice.

'Have you seen this?' he said by way of answer, passing me a magazine he'd carried in with him. It was the new issue of *Asia Now*, with an old picture of Shehnaz Saeed on the cover, and the words SHE'S BACK! emblazoned across her shoulders.

'Yeah, the security guard outside was looking at it when I walked in. Amazing. She hasn't even stepped on to the set yet, has she?'

'Stepped on to the set? She hasn't even seen a script. And here she is, on the cover of the largest-circulating magazine in Asia. On the cover. My mother! Fifteen years she's been away from the public eye, and here she is on the cover. Can you beat that?'

'Congratulations,' I said, handing the magazine back to him. I knew his last question was merely rhetorical, but I couldn't help hearing it as one-upmanship, and I found I wanted to say something cutting.

He took the magazine back, and shrugged. 'It's nice for her. The warm embrace of the spotlight, and all that.'

I had made him self-conscious about his own joy, I could tell. And though I was slightly guilty about that, I was also inexplicably irritated about the cloud of filial smoke into which the promise of a parade of parties and laughter and great sex had vanished. What self-respecting thirty-one-year-old single woman would want the man across from her to transplant himself from a screwball comedy into an episode of Happy Families?

'So.' I smiled brightly at him. 'New York.'

'New York. Yeah.' He shook his head. 'God, I loved it. Really, truly. I had the best life there; I had my job, my friends, my rent-controlled apartment, my local gym, a place round the corner for Sunday brunch which made Eggs Scandinave you would not believe.'

'And then?'

'And then the Towers fell.'

'And you stopped being an individual and started being an entire religion.' I said it in a haven't-we-all-been-down-that-road tone but he didn't seem to notice.

He let go of the sugar-bowl without disturbing its contents, and made a vague gesture of acquiescence. 'The thing of it is, I was never more a New Yorker than on that September day. But even then, almost right away, I knew. There are these moments,' he held up his thumb and finger, lightly pressed together, as though a moment were held between them, 'when you think, now history will happen and I can do nothing but be caught up in it.'

Extraordinary, that someone who'd grown up in Pakistan could say a thing like that, utterly straight-faced, as though history hadn't been breathing down our necks all our lives. You weren't looking, that was all, I wanted to tell him. When history seemed to touch your life less obviously, when it happened somewhere out of sight, when seeds were being sown and there was time yet for things to work out differently, you weren't looking. When my mother warned you, you weren't listening.

He would hardly have been more than a boy when she left, I had to remind myself. He wasn't responsible for making her words worthless.

'It wasn't anything specific that made me decide to leave,' he continued, rinsing out his coffee-mug. He was too involved in his own story to see I wasn't keeping pace with him any more. 'It was just everything, everything over the last year.' He wiped his hands on his sleeves, dragging his fingers across the blue cotton and leaving wet imprints that looked like the shadows of elongated fingers clutching at his arms. And then he started off. The INS. Guantanamo Bay. The unrandom random security check in airports. The visit from the FBI.

'Look, you don't have to do this.' I cut him off just as he finished saying 'The Patriot Act'. 'It's OK to tell me you were laid off.' It was the 'it wasn't anything specific' line that gave him away. It was always something specific; there was always that precise moment when you felt everything inside you break.

The anger on his face then was of a particularly male variety, one passed through the generations, which must have had its origin the first time a cavewoman told a caveman she knew the reason he was vegetarian was his inability to use a spear.

'I was laid off because I'm Muslim.'

There was something in his tone that said, 'You can't possibly be expected to understand anything outside your little world,' and it was that, more than the unjustified nature of his anger, that made me react as I did. In my most condescending tone I said, 'Yes, it is comforting to blame our failures on the bigotry of others, isn't it?' *So you gave up your Eggs Scandinave, whatever they might be, and moved back into the cushy life of the Karachi elite. And you think this is being caught up in history?*

For a moment his entire face changed, something hard and cold settling on it, and then he was smiling and leaning back on one elbow, saying, 'Are you always this unpleasant in the morning or is it just the instant coffee? Will our relationship undergo a remarkable upswing if we meet around a percolator from now on? I'm prepared to carry one on my person at all times when you're in the vicinity.'

There was an instant in which I thought he knew in practice what I only understood in theory: the falseness of character, the malleability of it. With that knowledge he could step from light to dark, from joker to knave in a heartbeat. But then I understood he was only playing with masks. Screwball comic hero, devoted son, angry young man, condescending jerk. 'Will the real Eddy please stand up?'

He pulled himself upright, and stepped closer to me. 'He will, if you will.'

'We're back to that again, are we? Look, you're not entitled to get to know me. OK? That's not a right you have which I'm depriving you of. That's not how it works down here on Planet Earth.'

'You're the one who just said you want to know me.'

'No, I didn't. I said I want you to stop being Mr Creepy-Many-Personalities.'

'Look, I'm sorry.' He seemed anything but sorry. 'I know I'm not entitled to anything. But we have this connection, you know, and it's stupid to just ignore it.'

'What connection?'

He lifted up the magazine and waved the cover at me. 'Larger-than-life mothers.'

'Oh, come on. You really think we're going to bond over swapping notes about that? You can complain about your mother going on location for weeks on end, and I'll reciprocate with tales of my mother exiling herself for three bloody years.' I crossed my arms, pressing them against my chest. 'Is that what that whole line about getting to New York to escape being your mother's son was all about? You thought I would embrace you to my bosom as soon as I realized the strong parallels between us? Admit it, Ed – if you so wanted to escape being your mother's son you wouldn't have returned to work at a television studio.'

'Are you done?'

'Almost. I just need your mother's phone number.'

'For what?'

'She sent me some calligraphy. I want to call and thank her. She's not anything like you, is she?'

'What do you mean, she sent you some calligraphy?'

He looked so startled that for the first time I knew I had the upper hand. 'Well, I guess Mummy's keeping secrets from you,' I said, and turned to walk out.

I felt so triumphant about my exit that it wasn't until I was back in my office that I realized what he'd done. He'd got past the façade. And worse than that, much worse – I knew he realized it, too.

# V

The month my parents married, the Poet wrote his most famous narrative poem, *Laila*. Reconfiguring the Laila–Majnu story, the poem centres on Laila, bereft after Qais has been banished from her presence. Unable to endure the thought of a life without him, she seeks out his likeness everywhere – in other men (she is soon regarded as the town whore), in nature (sometimes the wind brushing her neck reminds her of his touch), in art (she risks her life to steal a painting, because a man at the edge of its crowd scene leans forward in a manner suggestive of the angle of Qais's back the first time he bent to embrace her). But all her attempts to find her Beloved's exact copy lead only to frustration, so she starts to adopt his manner of speech, his gait, his dress, his expressions in order to keep his characteristics alive. She becomes an outcast, shunned by all for her madness and, driven out of town, she makes her way into the forest where Qais has been living – and walks past without seeing him. He watches her go and senses something familiar in her, but is too distracted by composing love poems about Laila to give the matter much thought. Years go by and one day, wandering through the forest, she meets a young man who greets her by the name 'Qais'. She realizes she has finally succeeded in becoming her Beloved and need never be without him again. In that moment of triumph she looks into the forest pool and sees Qais's face where her reflection should have been, and remembers: the one thing Qais could not live without is Laila.

I couldn't help thinking of that poem as I drove over Lily Bridge and headed toward Shehnaz Saeed's house in the colonial part of town. Kiran Hilal had given me her number and when I had called she didn't wait beyond the moment when I identified myself to invite me over for lunch that afternoon. I said I wasn't sure I could get away from work for an extended period of time, and she laughed, and said, 'We'll call it a professional meeting, then.'

What kind of meeting it really would be, I couldn't say. Even though we'd never met, she had been part of my memory since I was three years old. It was 1974 then, and one of the Poet's acolytes had adapted *Laila* for the theatre, with the Poet himself in the role of Qais and Shehnaz Saeed as Laila. Though the poem was less than four years old at the time it had already attained the status of a national classic, and though no one objected to the Poet playing the part of the impassioned young Qais, even though his age (forty-two), physical appearance (underwhelming, at best) and previous theatrical experience (none) all marked him as being wholly unsuited to the role, there was more than a little grumbling about an unknown actress taking on the role of Laila. An estranged relative of the play's director had spread the rumour that my mother was to play Laila, and Shehnaz Saeed had to bear Karachi's collective disappointment when it transpired that there was no truth to that story. 'The unbarked sapling whose pretty foliage will scatter before the cold blast of expectation, leaving only denuded branches, scabbed with the blight of inexperience and folly' is how one theatre critic famously described Shehnaz Saeed on the morning of the press preview.

The following day he was singing a different tune, with the rest of Karachi's critics acting as chorus. In the wake of the announcement that Shehnaz Saeed was to return to acting, one of the newspapers had reprinted the volte-face review from all those years ago.

*The script is appalling, the costume and set design absurd,
and someone should tell the greatest of our poets that it is
an embarrassment to watch a man whom we hold in such
high esteem brought so low by his own insufficiencies. He
cannot act. But despite all this, Laila is without doubt the
greatest thing to have ever happened on the Pakistani stage.
Can I write the words without swooning? Let me try:
Shehnaz Saeed.*

*As the young, infatuated Laila of the opening scenes she
is sublime. But as the play progresses and she becomes the
mad Laila who metaphorically casts off her own living
tissue to knit Qais's flesh on to her bones, she exceeds all
adjectives. The play's greatest failure is to dim the stage
lights as Laila looks into the pool and to bring them up
again to reveal Qais standing where she had been a second
before. After the brilliance of Shehnaz Saeed's performance,
even the original Qais seems an inadequate impersonator
of himself.*

If I ever saw a performance – or even part of a rehearsal
– of *Laila* I had no memory of it. But I did recall sitting at
my mother's dining table, colouring in a poster advertising
the play. I was young enough to regard the alphabet in terms
of shape rather than sound, and I loved the way my hand
curved into the bends of 'S' that appeared not just once but
twice in Shehnaz Saeed's name. I made a mess of the poster,
of course, but the Poet merely said, 'This one's too special to
hang up for the crows to shit on. We'll frame it and put it
in my study.' I knew he was saying it wasn't good enough for
public display, but I loved him for the way he chose to say
it, and for his free use of 'shit' in my presence, and when he
actually did frame and hang it between the paintings of two
of Pakistan's finest artists, with the words, 'I think you're a
perfect bridge between their contrasting styles, Aasmaani,'
then I loved him most. The poster stayed there until I took
it down and tore it up, years later, in adolescent embarrassment

at proof of my childhood. It was one of the few times he was ever really angry with me.

I drew up to Shehnaz Saeed's house, and when the chowkidar opened the gate I drove up the long driveway and parked just near the front door of the double-storeyed, yellow-stone house.

There were three steps leading to the carved wood door and potted plants all around the alcove within which it was set – some hanging from the ceiling, some not. Lilies, orchids, spider-plants. I rang the door-bell. An old woman opened the door, looked startled to see me, and then laughed without evident humour and pointed at my eyes. 'Descended from one of Sikandar's soldiers, I always used to tell her,' she said, and turned and walked away, gesturing for me to follow her.

How often had my mother been here between the Poet's death and her own disappearance? Those were the two years when conversation between us slowed to a trickle. I spent so much – the idiocy! – of those years slamming doors and saying things like 'It's none of your business where I'm going.' That particular sentence came out when something of her old self was awake in her, and she replied, 'Fine, then I won't tell you where I go when I go out.' It was in my hands, she made it clear, to choose to end the foolishness of that reciprocal silence, but I was too proud to do so. And where had that pride got me? Right here, in the doorway of Shehnaz Saeed's house, knowing nothing.

I looked around. The house was airy in the way that no modern housing ever is, and the ceilings were high. Along the whitewashed walls were portraits of Shehnaz Saeed by both acclaimed and little-known artists. It should have seemed an act of monumental egoism to fill the entrance to your home in such fashion, but as I walked closer to the row of paintings it seemed clear that the display mocked the adulation of beauty. They were so varied, the paintings, in their portrayal of her that what came through ultimately was the absence of any singular truth about her visage and how it is perceived. Next to the painting nearest the door was a mounted card with a single word on it: APPEARANCE.

As I stood by the mounted word, recalibrating my expectation of Shehnaz Saeed to encompass a subtle intelligence, the woman who had opened the door continued to walk down the alternating black-and-white stone tiles of the hallway. With her black chapals and black shalwar-kameez she seemed to appear and disappear as she stepped from light tile to dark, her existence a strobe-light illusion.

She stepped on to a white tile and looked over her shoulder at me. 'What, do you want a palanquin to carry you?'

I followed her through the hallway, past an open door through which I could hear the 'hmm . . . hanh . . . hanh' of someone talking on the telephone. The door was artfully ajar to allow passers-by a glimpse of a Gandhara Buddha, a Bukhara rug, and a bare arm draped over a sofa back. 'It's my house. I'll invite who I want!' the voice said, and it was Shehnaz Saeed's voice. I wondered if she were talking about me and, if so, whether it was Ed on the other end of the line, but my guide was looking back impatiently as I slowed my steps so I had to speed up and follow her. Then I was climbing up stairs and more stairs, feet echoing on the uncarpeted ground. It was surprisingly cool indoors; the slatted window shutters facing the sun were all closed, casting half the house into shadow.

At the top of the stairs, the old woman pushed open a set of wooden doors and gestured for me to step outside. I did so, and found I was on the roof, diagonally across from a cupola of yellow stone which gave shade to a table, laid for two, beneath it. The old woman disappeared back indoors. For want of something better to do I walked round the roof, looking down on the beautifully tended garden below and enjoying the view this height afforded of grand neighbourhood houses, more than one of which served as diplomatic housing for consul generals from countries which, after the Soviet invasion of Afghanistan, had made it known to the Poet that he need not bother applying to them for asylum. Freedom of speech was all very well, but there was no need to exercise it against a government that was helping in the fight against Communism – that had been the implicit message back in those days when our schoolteachers told us that the Russians thought of Afghanistan as a mere stepping-stone to the warm-water port of Karachi, so it was our national duty to . . . oh, why think of any of that? Any of that or any of what followed or what was still to come.

'You've sowed, now reap,' I announced to any represent-ative of the nation who might be listening.

I gave myself over to the view again. Karachi looked like a green city from up here, the usual vistas of unrelenting cement and concrete replaced by lushness. I closed my eyes and enjoyed the breeze. November had brought a change in climate and already there was an intimation of winter in the air. Soon, the breeze promised, you will sit outdoors at night wrapped in shawls, breaking open shells of peanuts just off the flame.

I turned the corner, back to the cupola. There was someone sitting there, facing away from me, one arm over the chair back, in the same posture that I had seen through the open door. She was dressed in a sari with a sleeveless blouse, a red rose stuck behind her ear. The theatrics of it!

I walked closer. My chapals slapped against the brick as I approached her, but she showed no signs of being aware of the sound. I wondered if she were a little hard of hearing. And then, for the first time, I realized she must have aged. In 1987, when she retired, she had been thirty-eight. So, fifty-three now. Where stunning women are concerned that change from late thirties to early fifties can sometimes be a matter of exchanging obvious beauty for a more subtle loveliness – the lines of mortality and the pull of gravity can alter an aspect to make it more moving, more precious for its own admission that it will not last. But sometimes, also, those years wipe a face clean of the memory of its own younger self and mark it chiefly with a premonition of the ravages that will befall it.

I stayed back, unwilling to walk straight up to her and have to see, up close, every emerging wrinkle delineated by the afternoon sun.

'Hello,' I said.

In a single fluid gesture she uncrossed her legs, turned, and stood. She did it with the sort of easy grace that can only come with practice. She had not exchanged obvious beauty for subtle loveliness. No, hers was still a quite obvious loveliness. She saw me and laughed; crow's feet around her eyes and the angles of her face no longer seemed quite so sculpted, but for all that she was just as unapproachably lovely as when she had played Lady Macbeth.

'It's a stunning resemblance,' she said in that lilting voice of hers which could deepen into gravity so unexpectedly. 'All in the eyes, of course. Come here and give your old aunty a hug.'

I did, and was surprised by the fierceness of her embrace. 'Samina's daughter. My God, Samina's daughter all grown up.'

Ed had something of her tempo of speaking. I hadn't realized that until now.

She released me and pointed to the chair opposite her. While I had taken my twirl around the roof someone had placed na'ans and chicken tikkas and chutneys on the table. I sat down and almost immediately a moist tongue licked my foot. I jerked my feet up, and a chihuahua darted out from under the table.

'Director, come here!' The bonsai dog turned to Shehnaz Saeed. 'Basket!' she said, and Director skittered towards the door leading back into the house.

'Did you choose that name as a tribute or an insult?' I asked. The question launched her into a series of tales about her theatrical days and all the triumphs and tribulations she had faced. She had the extraordinary ability to speak only in short bursts, creating the impression that she was allowing

55

me ample opportunity to be part of the conversation, yet she ended every series of sentences with the artfulness of Scheherazade drawing the night's story-telling to a close – 'Of course that wasn't the worst disaster!' or 'If only people knew the truth about his eyebrows' or 'We called her Peking Duck, for reasons you might be able to guess' – so ultimately my side of the exchange consisted of little more than 'Why?' and 'How?' and 'What do you mean?' The most aggravating part of sitting through her self-obsessed performance of her own past was the adolescent voice inside me squealing, 'IT'S SHEHNAZ SAEED!'

When she finally slipped up and broke off speaking at 'And that was that' I knew I should take the opportunity to ask about the encrypted page she had sent me, but I didn't know quite how to broach the subject. So instead I asked, 'Why return to acting now? And why on television? It's obvious theatre's where your heart is.'

'My heart . . .' she said dramatically, placing her hand over the organ in question as though to reassure herself it hadn't been left behind in a theatre somewhere. 'My heart is a spoilt child, demanding all the attention, insisting it remain central to all decisions. Isn't it time to attend to other, more neglected organs?'

I was sufficiently overwhelmed by my proximity to great-ness to nod knowingly at that bit of absurdity.

She laughed – not the tinkling laughter that had punctu-ated her Tales of Before but a deep, rolling laughter. 'Oh, Aasmaani, your mother would have tossed that chicken carcass at me for such a statement. And look at you, so earnest, trying valiantly to take me seriously. You've been doing it all through lunch.'

For a moment all I could do was stare at her. Despite my earlier self-vaunting about knowing a thing or two about women who were legends, I had walked in here with exactly the kind of attitude I had seen so many women adopt when they first met my mother – a determination to see some mythic being, a determination so strong that my mother occasionally found herself behaving in ways entirely alien to her personality just because it seemed impolite to shatter the illusions others had about her. So, for their benefit she'd turn into a woman with no time for trivialities, no concern except Justice with a capital J. And I, who had rolled my eyes at all those people, had come in here wanting – so desperately wanting – to have lunch with a star that I even interpreted the way her door was left ajar as a sign of theatricality. And Shehnaz Saeed had seen it right away, the way my mother sometimes saw it instantly in certain people. They-who-would-feel-betrayed-if-they-knew-I-love-disco, is how my mother referred to the mythologizers.

I hadn't thought about that side of her in a long time – but all at once she was before my eyes, laughing, 'Oh for endless summer days! Donna Summer days!' as she danced around her living room in outrageous gold heels, taking my hand and pulling me into the dance with her.

I picked up a chicken bone, and pretended to aim it at Shehnaz Saeed's head. 'You've been playing me this whole time!'

'That's better,' she said, and patted my hand, suddenly maternal in a way that made my throat clench. 'Now I'll answer you truthfully about my return to acting. It's quite obvious by now that I'm past any possibility of child-bearing, so that puts aside my initial reason for giving up the acting life. And while we're on the subject, I'll confirm the rumours for you – my husband really is my husband in name only.'

I looked down at my plate, discomfited. 'You don't have to tell me that.'

'Oh, it's hardly a secret. I find it so irritating when I meet new people and they pretend not to know, and there's all this tiptoeing around things. And with you it would be particularly silly. I mean, it's not as though I'm unaware my personal life is a topic of gossip in the gonorrhoea office.' We laughed together at that and I thought, yes, I can believe you were my mother's friend before her gold heels gathered dust and cobwebs. But did she ever laugh with you in those final two years before she disappeared?

'To return once more to your question,' Shehnaz Saeed said, dabbing at her eyes with a napkin. I was irritated to find myself noticing that the laughter had produced a single tear-drop which shimmered in the corner of her eye. 'Quite simply, I want to act again. But I'm more than a little frightened. So I need the safety nets that an ensemble piece on television, with all its possibilities of retakes and editing, can provide. When that's done, you're right, I'll go back to the stage. Lady Macbeth again, I think. I don't really have the heart to play Laila once more, even if it were a plausible role at my age.' She rolled her eyes just slightly at the last three words, and then smiled self-deprecatingly when she saw I had noticed. 'Think of it as a retired Olympic-gold diver walking to the edge of a low diving-board and jumping feet first into the water. It's obvious to everyone you're just limbering up, remembering how to use those old muscles. Maybe some people will wonder why you need to do that, but no one's going to criticize you for being something less than extraordinary in the way you perform the leap. But it gets you back at the pool. And you carry on doing those little boring jumps for a while until people get used to seeing you there, by the water's edge. They stop looking at you in that greedy expectant way. Then, no fuss, you get out of the pool, walk up the stairs to the high board, and execute a perfect jack-knife, the barest ripple as your body breaks through the surface.'

'Ah,' I said. 'Now that makes sense. Though Kiran Hilal will not be pleased to have her baby compared to a foot-first leap from a low diving-board.'

She smiled. 'Dear Kiran. You know, I acted in the first play she ever wrote for television. If she could forgive my retirement – which she did, but it took a while – she can forgive my analogies.'

'And then there's that other reason you have for going back to work.' She tilted her head to one side. 'Your son.'

'Oh, yes. Ed.' She pulled the rose out from behind her ear and ran her fingers over the petals. 'How are the two of you getting on?'

'I have no idea.'

She seemed unsurprised. 'He's not always the easiest man in the world to be around, I know. But he does like you. A great deal.'

'Oh? What has he said about me?'

'Nothing. I didn't even know you were working together until Kiran told me. He's furious that I've invited you over for lunch.'

'And this means he likes me?'

'Yes.' She smiled in a way that told me she wasn't going to say anything further on the subject. 'You know, your mother and I were once talking about the two of you. She'd just had an argument with you, I'd just had a shouting match with Ed, and we both wondered – what would our children say about us if we put them in a room together?'

I nodded, wanting her to go on speaking of Mama, but not wanting to have to add anything to the conversation.

'God, but we need her these days,' Shehnaz Saeed said, and in the shift of her tone I could tell that the 'her' she was speaking of wasn't the private Samina any more, but the Samina Akram of blazing eyes and fiery rhetoric who had crowds chanting her name as though she were a religion. 'It's already started. The assemblies haven't even convened yet and already the mullahs in the Frontier are saying, "Of course women can work, but only according to the guidelines of Islam." What guidelines? There are no such guidelines! Maybe that's another reason for coming out of retirement. I don't want to be one of those women the beards approve of, the ones who sit at home and cook dinner.'

I dipped my fingers into a handbowl with a bougainvillea flower floating in it. 'I hardly think you'd be their poster girl under any circumstance.'

'Regardless. We desperately need your mother now.'

'Well, then, perhaps she'll reappear. The nation needs her to be a heroine – how could she resist?' Early in October, the night the election results came in, I couldn't stop myself from sitting with Rabia and Shakeel, watching the news reporters trying to look unsurprised as they announced the gains of the religious alliance whom most political pundits had written off when they failed to muster any compelling street-power for all their anti-government rallies a year earlier. When the votes were counted and the newly united religious bloc emerged as the third-largest party, with forty-five seats, Rabia raged up and down the room, cursing anyone she could blame for the debacle – the Americans, the President, Al-Qaeda, the other political parties, the Americans again, everyone but the 11 per cent of the electorate who voted for the beards. But through all my own disgust at the situation, there was an undercurrent of hope. Now she'd come back. Back to her old self, and then back to us. She couldn't fail to come back, not with all that was at stake.

Shehnaz Saeed looked at me, shock on her features, and I felt instantly ashamed. Whatever Mama's failings, her activism was never about personal glory. I owed her that acknowledgement, if nothing else. And then I saw Shehnaz Saeed's expression soften into pity.

'She'll come back? Aasmaani—'

'This is not a conversation I want to have.'

She looked hurt then, and I was sorry.

'How did you first get to know her?'

She pulled petals off the rose in her hand and scattered them on the white tablecloth between us. 'Well, that story takes us back a bit. I married at seventeen, did you know that?'

'Yes.'

'Yes?'

'I read any interview of yours I could get my hands on around the time you did Lady Macbeth.'

She seemed to find that genuinely surprising. 'Your mother never told me.'

'I don't think she knew. She wasn't around in those days. Political exile is more glamorous than a daughter entering adolescence.' Stop it, Aasmaani. Stop now.

'Oh, I see.' She laid her hand flat, palm down, and started putting petals over her unpainted nails. 'I don't think I ever revealed in those interviews the extent of my misery. It was an arranged marriage, but it's not as though I put up any kind of resistance. I couldn't think of anything I wanted to do after school that seemed at all plausible. I mean, I wanted to go to London and join RADA. That was it. The only dream I could think of. But everyone convinced me, places like that they don't even consider Pakistanis. You won't look right for any of the parts in their plays, they told me.' Her voice became shrill, as though she were moving her lips in time to the performance of a twisted ventriloquist. 'Look in the mirror. Are you Juliet, are you Blanche Dubois, are you anyone except the foreign one with the funny accent? And I believed them so completely that I even believed there would be no place for me on a Pakistani stage. And, anyway, I was scared to do anything to risk my parents' anger, and what respectable family in those days would want to admit their daughter was an actress? So I tried my first major performance: I convinced myself I wanted to be a wife and mother and daughter-in-law and high-society hostess. It was my worst performance ever.' She scored rose petals with her thumbnail. 'Every day, every single day, I wanted to be on a stage, speaking lines that could wrap themselves around your chest and squeeze until your rib-cage cracked open and your heart lay exposed.'

She spoke about language the way the Poet and his friends used to – as a living, dangerous entity – and listening to her I felt the blood move quick through my veins and knew she – and they – were right.

Her eyes were bright with memory. 'I wanted to be Sarah Bernhardt at the end of her days – a seventysomething, one-legged woman playing Portia in scenes from *The Merchant of Venice*, reclining on a couch the whole time to hide her disability and, in so doing, making the character so coiled with languid power that any standing-up version of her seems feeble by comparison. And then, taking seven curtain calls when it finished.'

'So when exactly did you see my mother speak in front of a crowd and fill the air with *grazia*? I've read the Italian interview. Don't tell me her performance before the adoring masses is what convinced you to leave your husband.'

'No, actually my husband left me. I bored him, he said. Seven years of marriage, one son, and he wakes up one morning, says to me, "You bore me," and leaves. I was terrified for weeks that he'd come back. And when it was obvious he wouldn't, I was so lost, Aasmaani. Twenty-four and clueless. Mother of a six-year-old son. Soon after that I went to hear Samina speak. She had a remarkable capacity to make people imagine change. That's something we certainly need now, when the zealots are the only ones who appear to have that gift.' She picked up a rose petal between thumb and forefinger and traced circles in its velvet smoothness. 'The next day I got back in touch with a schoolfriend whose brother was a director, and before I knew quite what was happening I was Laila. I met Samina just a few days into the rehearsals.' She spread her hands as if to say, 'the rest was inevitable' and I acknowledged the gesture with a nod. 'But I was just starting out, and she and the Poet were in trouble with the government and both of them told me I shouldn't risk being associated with them or I'd never get any roles on television. I needed to work, Aasmaani, I needed money. So I kept it discreet, my friendship with both of them.' She touched my shoulder. 'I miss her terribly.'

We walked down the stairs in silence. When we reached the ground floor, I turned to her again. 'The gift you sent me. Tell me about it.'

'It meant something to you.' She caught my shoulder. 'What?'

'First you tell me.'

'Well, I don't know really. It came a couple of months ago. There was a covering letter – wait.' She walked into the room which I had glimpsed on my way in and came out with a piece of paper, filled with childish block letters. A clue or a conspiracy? She handed it to me, and I read:

*Dear Madame. I have bin a fan for many yers. I am sending this too you, though it could be dangarous for me, because perhaps it is the only thangs I have to give you that you might want. I do not undastand them but maybe you will. I know you know the person who rote them. There are more. I will send you more if you act again. Please act again.*

I offered the letter back to Shehnaz Saeed, and she gestured to me to keep it. 'It seemed like lunatic ravings when I first read it. I was about to throw the whole thing away – I've received some peculiar fan mail over the years, believe me, though I'll admit it had been a while since the last one. But it was intriguing enough that I kept it. I don't know, maybe this letter is what planted in me the idea of acting again, and made me more receptive to the idea of *Boond*. I don't know. We never really know how our brains work, do we? Anyway, I knew your mother and the Poet had some code they wrote to each other in and when I heard you were involved with *Boond* I thought, maybe, just maybe. That's why I sent it to you. Can you read it?'

Some old instinct of secrecy in all matters related to my mother caught hold of me. I found myself saying, 'No. I don't know the code. But it does look like some sort of code, and so, like you, when I saw it I thought it might be their code. But I don't know. Do you have more? If you have more, maybe if I look at them long enough I'll be able to think of a way to crack the code.'

I sounded entirely unconvincing to my own ears, but she merely nodded. 'That's all I have. But who knows, now that

I really am acting again maybe whoever wrote the note will send more. If he does, I'll give them to you.'

She kissed me goodbye at the door, and just before I got into my car she called out into the driveway, 'I don't want to get your hopes up. It's probably just some deranged fan.'

'Yes, of course. I know that.'

I was turning the key in the ignition when she came running down the steps and touched my shoulder through the open car window. 'But you will tell me, won't you? If it means anything to you.'

'Of course I will,' I lied.

# VI

That suggestion of winter which had coursed past me on the roof of Shehnaz Saeed's house was nowhere in evidence when I drove out of her gate. Heat rose off the streets, creating mirages – thin, shimmering bands of water. The mind would have to be fevered to believe they were anything other than an illusion – in this heat any puddle would evaporate in seconds, or act as beacon for the thirsty pye-dogs who roamed the streets.

After my mother disappeared I used to see her everywhere – not just in the form of other women but in empty spaces, too. She seemed lodged, like a tear, in the corner of my eye, evaporating in the instant I turned to look at her. I knew what hallucinations were, I knew what mirages brought on by psychological aberrations were, but somehow that seemed too prosaic – too predictable – to explain away my imagined seeing, even when I realized it was entirely imagined. Easier to think in terms of Orpheus and Eurydice – every time I turned to check that it was really her, I lost her. But with that explanation I was attempting to step into a story that wasn't mine. It was a story that fascinated my mother, but even when she first told it to me, I heard her unasked question, 'Would my Poet journey to Hades in search of me?' and though I had wanted to reply, 'I would, Mama,' I knew that wasn't the answer she was looking for. So when she placed herself in that borderland between seeing and imagining, I knew I would have to find something other than a Greek myth in which I didn't belong to explain her away. Quite by chance, I found mention of 'the Fata Morgana' in some piece of writing by Conrad, and when I looked it up and discovered it was 'a mirage of the looming effect' I knew I had finally found a name by which I could refer to those images of my mother. I still saw her continuously, but I now knew it wasn't her, just a Fata Morgana, and I would no more think to turn and look closer than I would think to worry about splashing a passer-by when I drove through the mirage of water.

I stopped at a red light and looked out of the car window at a grey sparrow swooping down on to the footprinted dust between the car and a boundary wall sprayed with political graffiti. As a child I used to believe the sparrow itself was layered with dust, and that if I ever got close enough to one to stroke its feathers with my thumb I'd erase the dust to reveal the colours – emerald-green, electric-blue, pomegranate-red – that were the bird's natural inheritance. My thumb still twitched, now and then, at the sight of a sparrow.

Someone rapped on the passenger-side window. I looked up and there was a man on a motorbike gesturing towards the traffic light, which turned from green back to red almost as soon as I looked up at it. The man on the motorbike gave me a look which said 'Women drivers' as he sped through the intersection, swerving out of the way of oncoming traffic.

I was left waiting for the light to change again. I reached into my handbag for a mint, and my hand touched my mobile phone. I wished I could call Rabia, or Beema, just to talk about the strangeness of Ed, the charm of Shehnaz Saeed. But Rabia was at the inauguration of yet another women's shelter her NGO had set up, and Beema would be taking her afternoon nap before heading back to the hospital to relieve her sister at their mother's bedside. My father – I could call my father. Since he and Beema had left Karachi, she had been the conduit of information between him and me, telling me how much he was enjoying his leave from the bank, telling him about my bouts of cooking and my new-found fascination with plants. It wasn't that he and I avoided speaking to each other, just that it was easier for both of us to speak to Beema and Rabia. But it would be a comfort now to hear his soft voice, its thoughtful quality equally in evidence if we talked about the phenomenon of mirages, the current form of the Pakistan cricket team or the significance of isotope decay in the dating of fossils.

I pulled over to the side of the road and dialled his number. He sounded glad to hear my voice, but our conversation merely skated from small talk to small talk – hospital food, STD coffee, my forward-leaning bookshelf, the light fixtures in his bedroom. Almost from the very start of our conversation I knew I wouldn't talk to him of Ed and Shehnaz Saeed. Unconventional mothers and their children – that was a subject that made Dad choke on his attempt to be honest without sounding chauvinistic. Which I knew he wasn't – particularly. Certainly Rabia and I had no cause to complain about his attitudes towards women. He was more than proud of Rabia's NGO work, and had never done anything other than champion my right to be single, even at the grand old age of thirty-one. But if a woman was a mother, Dad was simply unable to view her life in any way except as it might relate to the well-being of her child.

'And what about fathers?' I had challenged him once. 'Why are they allowed to be irresponsible?'

'It's not that we're allowed. It's just that we're less significant, and so less capable of doing damage,' he had replied, turning away before the sentence was finished.

When he'd exhausted the subject of light fixtures I said I had to go, and hung up. But more than before, I felt the need to call someone and talk, just talk. I scrolled down the names in my mobile phone, considered calling my brother-in-law, but knew he would be entirely uncommunicative during the middle of his work day. I put down the phone, ran my fingers over the steering wheel and, for a moment, had a memory – no, not a memory, a reliving – of sitting behind the wheel and learning to drive at the age of fourteen. I needed to speak to a friend, simple as that – and not just one of my ex-colleagues from teaching or human resources or the cricket magazine, who served so well as dinner or beach companions. A friend who had known me long enough to know me, that was what I needed. A childhood friend. Someone who had changed gears while I held the wheel and pressed the clutch because doing all three things at the same time had seemed a task too complicated even to attempt.

I shifted gears from neutral to first. A few months after my mother's disappearance, soon after I had stopped my blinding search for clues and conspiracies and waited, instead, simply for her to call or return, my closest schoolfriends had come over to my house, sat me down and said it was time to accept facts. They weren't going to collude in my delusions any more, they said, it was too painful for them and too harmful for me. Better to face that she's not coming back, and look, here are our shoulders. Cry on them.

It was their mothers' voices speaking through them, I knew. All those mothers in whose houses I had done so much of my growing up; those mothers who, even more than their children, had wrapped such a tight, protective circle around me when my mother disappeared that I had hardly been able to breathe in their presences. I stood up in front of all my friends and, one by one, reeled off a litany of complaints about those mothers. The mother who tried too hard. The mother who stifled her children. The mother who was holier-than-thou. The mother with her absurdly bleached hair. And finally I turned to the closest of my friends, the one whose mother had been most like an aunt to me and, unable to come up with any complaint about or accusation against that sweetest of women, I said, 'And your mother with her arranged marriage. She'd hardly even met your father before the wedding. That means she did it with a stranger. Like a prostitute.'

I knew exactly what I was doing. Mothers were sacred in all our lives, and even while our faith in their worthiness as objects of veneration might falter, it was not something we would ever dream of saying in public. To complain about your own mother was taboo; to insult someone else's mother was unthinkable. And so, my friends turned and left my room. The following day, in school, my closest friend walked past me in the school-yard, alone, three times, giving me all the opportunity I needed to call out an apology. But I didn't, and we hadn't spoken since.

In the weeks after my betrayal of my friends, I kept waiting for the moment when one of them, or more, would reveal to the world the reasons for their refusal to associate with me, and then, I knew, I would be shunned by everyone in the tiny circles in which I conducted most of my life. But that moment never came, and I knew their silence was a final mark of friendship which all of them handed to me, across that line which now separated us, before retreating from my life.

I looked up to see the traffic light changing from green to red again and I slammed on the accelerator, almost colliding with a bus which had replica nuclear missiles attached to its roof at jaunty angles.

There was one moment when I could have changed course and found my way back to those friends – and their mothers. It was the end of my first year at university in London – my mother had been gone two years by then, and my newly found method of coping with her absence was excess, which meant drugs, drink, men, or any combination of the above. That lasted most of the university year until Beema and fifteen-year-old Rabia arrived in London at the beginning of Rabia's summer holidays and refused to say anything disapproving at all for two weeks; the weight of their forbearance finally became too much for me and I broke down in tears and promised a reformation of character. The first step was finding a way to pass my exams – which I did, after weeks of dedicated studying which surprised me with the exhilaration it brought to my life. One of my most vivid memories of that year is of walking through Bloomsbury in the rain, after my last exam, repeating one phrase over and over: for peace comes dropping slow. The rain seemed to change its tempo as I whispered those words, each drop hesitating in its arrow-straight descent from sky to my outstretched palm. I, too, am of the sky, I said aloud. My mother named me.

I looked across the street then, and saw my former best friend sitting at one end of a long table in a pub, with a group of students celebrating the end of the exams. I had been avoiding her through the year, but right then if she had turned around and there had been anything at all except indifference in her eyes I would have broken down in tears, and told her of every fear that had made me so cruel. But she didn't turn, and the rain became a torrent, so I returned to halls and ate baked beans out of a can. It was all so obviously pathetic that I told myself I'd laugh about it one day.

'Still waiting for the day,' I said, driving past a police checkpoint that was absurdly blocking an entire lane of a busy road, without bothering to see if a policeman was flagging me down.

Who would I be now if she had stayed? How did I become this person, this quiz show researcher without real friends? I was the girl who could be anything – that's what my teachers used to say, and I believed them. I just never realized that 'anything' could include this.

What have I done to my life, Mama, in your name?

There was a slight tremor running along the back of my hand. It would be so easy to drift into the utter self-absorption of misery.

Absorption. Something or the other absorbs neutrons and then fission occurs, after which . . .

Aasmaani! There was my mother's voice. Are you thinking of nuclear weapons as the more cheerful alternative to thinking about me?

No one could ever make me laugh in more unexpected moments. Things I – and everyone else I knew – might find funny, she'd often deem outrageous, such as when Ronald Reagan insisted on referring to Pakistan's military-picked Prime Minister, Junejo, as Huneho during the latter's state visit to the US. 'Cowboys running the world, and treating us

70

like vassals whose names aren't even worthy of learning to pronounce', she fumed, and refused to see the joke. But on another occasion, a typo in a warrant for her arrest reduced her to tears of laughter. 'Aasmaani, look,' she said, as I clung on to her arm, terrified by the policeman at her doorstep. She handed me the warrant. 'I stand accused of having "beached the law".' I laughed all the way to the police van with her, entirely caught up in picturing the law as a giant whale and my mother as Jonah, the magnetism of her personality throwing off the compass that allowed the whale to navigate away from shore.

I was still thinking about that when I parked the car in my designated spot outside the STD office and got out, ducking my head in greeting at a group of co-workers who were standing around their cars. The ducked head, if executed properly, serves as polite salutation carrying with it the barest suggestion that you're really just nodding to yourself over some remembered incident and are not making overtures of friendship. It keeps both offence and familiarity at bay.

As the police van had driven away with my mother inside, and it occurred to me to be frightened, the Poet appeared from next door; when I told him what had happened, he said, 'Run, look up "breach" in the dictionary.'

So I did, and beneath 'to fail to obey or preserve something, for example, the law or a trust' I found 'to leap above the surface of the water (refers to whales)'. That was all the proof I needed that there was order in the world, and that – this followed naturally – my mother would come back soon. She did, that evening. All they wanted was to keep her locked up during a protest rally.

You had your moments, Mama, I'll give you that. In those – what was it? – ten years out of the first seventeen of my life when you weren't absent in one way or the other, you had your moments.

I pushed open the front door to the studio and walked in. On the ground floor, life was as chaotic as usual, with people

71

calling out to one another through open office doors, and a steady stream of employees walking from kitchenette to photo-copier to downstairs studio to upstairs offices. I stopped next to a group of men and women of mixed ages standing under the television mounted above our heads, watching STD's repeat broadcast of its mid-morning music video programme.

'But why is she sitting under an umbrella at the beach like it's the French Riviera instead of Karachi?' one said. 'Put her on an old shawl surrounded by kinoo peels, that's more like it.'

'You just go watch your MTV if all you can do with the local stuff is complain.'

'Oh, baba, I'm saying the local stuff should try less harder to be like MTV.'

'O-ay, listen. You really planning to boycott American goods when they attack Iraq?'

'Hanh, well, we have to feel like we're doing something, right?'

'OK, but does that mean boycotting movies and music as well? I mean, what if they attack before the new *Lord of the Rings*?'

'No, no, no problem. We get that on pirated videos and DVDs. So when you buy those you're just helping local industry. Same with music. And computer software.'

'Great, great.'

'Yeah, great, but there's one problem remaining. Petrol pumps. Between work, home, supermarket, sabziwallah, and my parents' house, there's only Shell and Caltex pumps. What do I do about that?'

A moment of silence. 'Well . . . you have to be realistic, after all. You need the car. The car needs petrol. What to do?'

'I'll tell you what to do. You want to piss off the Americans, there's only one thing to do. Vote in the fundos. I swear next election, I'm doing that. Last time I was tempted, next time I will, for sure.'

'You just shut up and go sit in your corner. You vote in the fundos, they'll do nothing about the petrol pumps, and just ban all your precious music videos and put us women in burkhas.'

'And anyway, the Americans like it these days if you piss them off. You piss them off, they bomb you.'

'Seriously! But listen, yaar, you think the mullahs are going to join this government?'

'God forbid. If they do, who knows what killjoy laws they'll try and pass. Remember in the eighties how boring life got with all that pretend-Islamization?'

Boring? What I wouldn't have given for some boredom in the 1980s. It was all prison and protest and exile and upheaval around me. Strange, how I was almost nostalgic for that. The battle-lines were so clearly drawn then with the military and the religious groups firmly allied, neatly bundling together all that the progressive democratic forces fought against. Now it was all in disarray, the religious right talking democracy better than anyone else and insisting, unwaveringly (admirably, I would say, if I didn't recall their political track record), on the removal of the military from power while all the other political parties tiptoed around the matter or see-sawed back and forth; and, on the other side of the equation, the President-General who had been the first head of state in my lifetime to talk unequivocally against extremism was tripping over his own feet in an attempt to create a democratic façade for a government in which the military remained the final authority and the only veto power. All those sacrifices, all those battles – and this is what we had come to. It wasn't a tragic waste – those lives, that passion; it wasn't tragic, just farcical.

I made my way up the stairs – leaving the groups below to argue about whether Pakistan's nuclear capability made America more or less likely to attack – and almost collided with Ed, on his way down.

We both moved away from each other, further than was necessary – him up two steps, and me down two steps – so the distance between us didn't imply the civility of two people making room for the other to pass but instead implied a mutual feeling of contamination.

The only way past this moment was brazenness, so I took two steps in one stride – at the exact moment that he came to the same decision – and then we really did collide, his foot stepping on mine, my forehead bumping against his nose.

We both cried out, extricated ourselves from the tangle of our bodies, and sat down, side by side, to nurse our injuries. And then, looking sideways at each other – him with a hand over his nose, me with my palm pressing down on my foot – we laughed.

Ed leaned sideways on his elbow and looked at me appraisingly. 'You're impossible to figure out, aren't you?' That struck me as particularly funny, coming from him. 'I just spoke to my mother. She said the gift she sent you was that strange nonsensical bit of writing she'd received some weeks ago. Why did you tell me she sent you calligraphy? I thought you meant she'd lifted her Sadequain painting off the wall and had it delivered to you.'

When he put it that way, I couldn't imagine why I'd said such a thing. I fanned my fingers in front of me, hoping that would convey some sort of adequately inadequate response. 'You did seem rather upset about it.' I was embarrassed to remember that it had crossed my mind at some point during the morning that his response had been an admission of complicity – in what, I hadn't worked out. That search for conspiracies hadn't entirely died.

'I have to admit I was a little concerned,' he said. 'I mean, you're quite lovely despite all your considerable strangeness, but Sadequain is Sadequain. I've loved that bit of calligraphy hanging in my mother's bedroom since I was a child.'

Lovely. When was the last time it had occurred to anyone to think of me as lovely?

I looked at him, and that thing happened between us. That fizz. Something electric. Our bodies reduced to single nerve cells and the space between us a synapse, pulsing an impulse back and forth.

It doesn't mean anything, ultimately – I've had some of

the most unsatisfying encounters of my life with men in whom
I've mistaken the fizz for potential of one sort or the other.
And I've had entirely satiating flings with men who've made
me feel every pleasurable physical sensation – except the fizz.
Thus, I know, it doesn't mean anything. But in the moment
you feel it, you forget that.

So who knows what would have happened right then with
Ed and me, both our offices just steps away, if Kiran Hilal
hadn't rounded into view with her team behind her, and said,
'Aasmaani, there you are. The meeting's in the conference
room. What are you doing just sitting there?'

We stood up, and as Ed moved aside to let Kiran pass
through, it was gone. The fizz – it had just disappeared, leaving
me feeling as though I had indulged in someone else's fantasy,
entirely in opposition to my own tastes. I didn't even look at
him, or say anything in farewell, as I followed Kiran up the
stairs and along the corridor to the conference room.

'We've just got a couple of things to wrap up from our
previous meeting before we get to you,' she said, opening the
door to the conference room. The room had the twin comforts
of an air-conditioner and leather chairs but managed to retain
STD's general air of dishevelment thanks to the scratched
surface of the long table which dominated the room and the
faded posters on the walls of temples and beaches and city
skylines, all advertising an airline which had been out of
business for years.

The *Boond* team – two men and two women in addition
to Kiran – settled round the table and launched instantly into
a discussion about fine-tuning a particular storyline after
seeing the unexpected nuance brought to it by one of the
actors before filming had stopped.

As the chatter around me dissolved from words into
sound, I ran through the cast list in my head and kept myself
entertained inventing monikers for all the actors who were
involved in the drama.

In addition to Shehnaz Saeed (enough of a star that her

name was a moniker unto itself), there was The Mistress's Issue (daughter of the 'hand-job' lady), Once-Leading, Now-Trailing Man (who had catapulated to fame when he had played Macbeth to Shehnaz Saeed's Lady), Hero Number Zero (a former cricketer who played brilliantly in a single one-day tournament, was reported for suspect bowling action, and found himself in need of a new career at twenty-one), God of Small Things (a remarkable, beautiful actor endowed with all that is pleasing in a man except – if persistent rumour was to be believed – for one tiny, very, very, tragically, tiny detail), Battle-Axe and Couple Who'll Get Written Out Soon.

But when I was done with the naming, the chatter about reshaping Hero Number Zero's role still continued around me, and despite my best efforts, I couldn't help but think back to that cryptic note Shehnaz Saeed had received, and those even more cryptic encrypted lines. Even presuming the lines had been written years ago, by either my mother or the Poet attempting some elaborate script, why? And who had possession of it, and why had he – or she – sent it to Shehnaz Saeed? And now that she was acting again, would more encrypted pages follow?

None of it made any more sense than any of the senselessness I'd latched on to at various points over the years.

*My ex calls the ochre winter 'autumn' as we queue to hear dock boys play jazz fugues in velvet dark.*

Aasmaani, put it from your mind.

*The Minions came again today.*

Aasmaani, stop it!

Ffhaffon, hiku ni!

Stop!

Hiku!

I closed my eyes and started to run through the multiplication tables, starting with multiples of thirteen, just to keep things interesting. Somewhere in the multiples of sixteen I lost my way, but even though I realized that sixteen times seven could not be one hundred and twenty I kept going –

sixteen eights are one thirty-six, sixteen nines are one fifty-two – until Kiran turned to me and said, 'Why don't you tell everyone your idea for Shehnaz's entrance, Aasmaani?'

So I did. When I finished there was neither the approbation for which I had hoped, nor the derision which I had feared – who was I to walk in with no idea of plot and suggest an opening that would overturn so much the people in this room had worked to create? – but instead a slight pause and then a cascade of questions.

'But where has she been all these years?'

'And why is she coming back now?'

'And what's she like? I mean, the ex-wife as written for Bougainvillea was all about "must protect my daughter" and this one clearly is not.'

'Yeah, this is my big problem with it. We want her to be a sympathetic character, right, for later if that black magic internet story is going to stay the way it is, which I'll admit I'm willing to fight for, because that's my baby. But now suddenly we've got this woman who just left her young daughter and took off. How are we going to make her anything but a monster? Ow! What?'

The woman next to the man who'd been speaking tried to lean her head in my direction with some subtlety.

'OK, how's this,' said the second man in the room, raising his bony fingers for attention. 'The mother left because of her daughter. She left because something happens which makes it necessary for her to leave, and stay away, in order to protect her daughter. Except, of course, the daughter doesn't know this.'

The man willing to fight for the internet black magic story looked sceptical, but another woman – one of the twenty-somethings I'd seen on my first day – was nodding her head vigorously. 'So now that the daughter is a little bit grown up, she's decided to find out what happened to her mother. And somehow her mother comes to know of this, and that's why she returns. Because now the only way for her to protect the daughter is by returning and keeping her daughter from uncovering the secret.'

'Isn't this getting a little too cloak and dagger?'

'Oh, and black magic on the internet is so down-to-earth.'

Kiran Hilal raised her hands, and everyone fell silent. 'What's the secret?' she asked.

What's the secret? What could be the secret? What could keep her away for so long?

Bony Fingers shook his head. I looked down at the scratched wood of the table.

'OK,' Kiran said. 'Never mind. I like that idea. We can work it in with either the industrialist slash criminal world story, or the black magic story. And it might just save the daughter from the Hole of Abject Boredom we've been digging for her.' She smiled at me in a way that meant thank you, you can go now.

The room was silent as I stood up and made my way out, but just as I closed the door behind me – in the instant before the latch actually clicked – I heard someone in the room exaggeratedly release a breath.

There was something unbearable about appearing transparent to people who thought up story lines about black magic on the internet. Get yourself an on-line exorcism, go! I wanted to say to them through the closed door, but that just sounded silly, so I turned towards my office instead. My footsteps echoed in the quiet hallway. Ed stuck his head out of his own office and called out my name.

'Aasmaani, listen!' He started to make his way down the corridor towards me. He was walking like a man who would rather be running, but is trying to affect casualness. It made him seem insincere.

'Hi,' he said, coming to a stop as both of us reached my office door at the same time. He put his hand up to the door-handle and started fidgeting with it. It may have been a sign of nerves – what was he about to propose that was making him nervous? – but it also effectively barred me from entering my own office without physically pushing past him. 'I just wondered. After work. How about getting a real cup of coffee? With me. I mean, us. Both. Going for coffee. Wait. Let's start again. Aasmaani, would you care to accompany me to Café Aylanto for a coffee?'

I had thought he couldn't appear boyish. I was wrong. Here he was, an awkward teenager in a man's body, with nothing even remotely appealing about him.

'I think it would be best to just keep things professional, Ed.'

'What is it you're afraid of?' he said, moving a little bit closer.

'Lizards. Snakes. Many sentences which start with the word "actually".'

'Come on, Aasmaani. No games, no masks. Just you and me and two cups of coffee. Would that be so terrible?'

'Actually, yes. Now, could you move your hand? I have work to do.'

His hand lifted abruptly off the door-handle, and he turned on his heels and strode away. I pushed open the door, switched on the fan, and sat down at my computer to work on quiz show questions.

*What's the secret which made the mother leave?*
*a) a really bad nose job which can't be fixed*
*b) she exchanged her legs for a scaled tail and went to*
*   live with her merman beneath the sea*
*c) she died. Someone who looks like her took her place,*
*   and finally grew sick of the deception*
*d) she doesn't love her daughter any more*

*Answer:*

The cursor blinked at me with steady patience, but I just sat there, unutterably weary, with no strength in my fingers even to press down on any one of the keys they were resting on. I sat there, watching the vertical line appear and disappear on the screen until time swallowed itself up in that repetitive motion and there was nothing in my mind but darkness.

# VII

Far enough into the darkness, I ceased to exist. I was a body, yes, but a body freed of everything that is other than corporeal. Sometimes the only way to be is to remove yourself from yourself. It cannot be done, of course. But illusions – no, delusions – are so much more effective than people give them credit for. I could live for longer than anyone imagined in the delusion that I was just the body of Aasmaani, with nothing within it.

There was an art to this, of course, a patiently learnt art. Or perhaps a talent. It bore some relationship to sitting in a classroom, with a look that signified attentiveness while the mind skated through every topic except precisely that with which it was supposed to be concerned. In the beginning, I didn't know how to enter the darkness without my face transforming into blankness, alerting all those around me to what was going on. But now, now I could smile and nod my head, follow key phrases in conversations, occasionally add necessary interjections, while all along I wasn't really there.

I was, instead, in that blank space where nothing could touch me. For hours, sometimes, blessed hours of silence.

And here was the CEO stepping into my office, a female co-worker I recognized but didn't know behind him.

'Got any gum?' he said.

I automatically reached into my handbag and passed him a mint. 'That'll do,' he said. He sat down across from me and pulled the telephone closer to him.

'Phones downstairs aren't working,' the woman explained to me, as though it were necessary.

The CEO punched in some numbers and sat with the phone to his ear. The woman compressed her features – lips squished together, eyebrows drawing close, nostrils constricted – as though putting on a battle-mask. The CEO turned towards me and raised his eyebrows in mock-alarm. I managed an upward flicker of my lips in response.

'My only point,' the woman said, 'is that a medical show should cover important medical issues.' And now the tiny part of my brain which continued to concern itself with such things recognized her as the presenter of one of the more boring of STD's educational programmes.

'BHS is not a medical condition,' the CEO said, before barking into the phone: 'Get Tahir.'

'BHS? No, I'm talking about depression.'

'Bored Housewife Syndrome,' the CEO said. His lips were startlingly red.

The woman put her hands on her hips. 'Seven out of ten people in Pakistan suffer some form of depressive disorder in their lifetime. In six per cent it's serious enough to . . .'

'Well, all the more reason to shut up about it. If they don't know they're sick they won't expect to be treated like they're sick. Too much damn whining in this country as it is. Tahir, round of golf? . . . I'm leaving now.'

He hung up and pushed himself out of the chair with no inconsiderable effort.

Leave. Go.

But in the doorway he turned back to me. 'You, what's the story with you and the Poet?'

I blinked. Two times, three, and then I was in my skin again. 'I'm sorry? What do you mean?'

'It's his seventieth birthday next year. We're going to do some grand programme about it.'

Seventy!

'Tributes, readings, homages, bla bla. It's going up on our

website as a coming attraction for the new year. Someone somewhere in this building thinks it's a good idea to have a link on the website to a bio of him. And we've found one, a bio, on some other website which we're going to shamelessly steal, just tweak a sentence here and there. But maybe we should check the facts because who knows where that other website gets its information. Last time we stole information off a site without checking it we ended up informing people that the game of cricket got its name because the sound of ball on willow was like the death-cry of the insect of that name. And you know, you're the research girl so we might as well give you some work. But if you've got some trauma associated with him, I'll tell someone else. Otherwise I'll be accused of causing depression in my employees, and you'll take medical leave.'

'It's fine,' I said. 'I can check facts.'

'I knew your mother,' the woman said, stepping forward. 'We marched together against the Hudood Ordinances.'

Great.

'Twenty years ago. Can you believe it? Next year it'll be twenty years.'

I looked at the CEO. 'Can you send me the bio?'

He nodded and put his hand on the woman's shoulder. 'Come on. Out.'

'She was a great lady,' the woman said, her eyebrows emoting, before the CEO pulled her out and closed the door behind him.

Seventy. He would have been seventy.

He once joked that in his old age he'd become respectable – a revered, toothless icon, sufficiently domesticated for governments to trot him out on state occasions so that he could snore his way through ceremonies and receive standing ovations for mumbling, inaudible couplets.

'No, you won't. I'd kill you first,' my mother cheerfully promised.

'Now, there's devotion for you,' he laughed, taking her hand and kissing it.

Against my will I found myself trying to age both their features in my mind, picture her as she might look and him as he would have looked. It was a mental exercise I occasionally applied to Mama's features, so that I would not fail to recognize her if somehow our paths crossed again.

There was an officious rapping on the door. When I made a sound of enquiry one of the CEO's underlings shuffled in, so apologetic in his mien that I couldn't help looking over his shoulder to see if someone else had boldly applied knuckles to door. He handed me a page which consisted of a single paragraph, printed in large bold font.

I scanned the sentences as the man shuffled out again.

How could anyone reduce that man's life to this?

HE WAS BORN IN A FAR-FLUNG VILLAGE IN PUNJAB AND MOVED TO KARACHI AT THE AGE OF ELEVEN.

That was the opening. Inaccurate, already. He moved to Karachi at the age of thirteen, in 1945, the year my mother was born there. They liked to say, later, that there was an element of fate in that. (And I could hear his voice: Far-flung? Far-flung? Far from where and flung by whom?)

FROM THERE HE WENT TO PUNJAB UNIVERSITY TO GET AN MA IN ENGLISH LITERATURE AND BECAME WELL KNOWN IN LAHORE'S MUSHAIRAS (POETRY RECITALS).

'Well known' didn't begin to describe the reception his poetry received, right from the beginning. His ghazals, in particular, drove the crowd to raptures – not just through the power of his imagery and his ability to mine a word for all its layers of meaning, but also for his capacity to surprise; he would start reciting a couplet, and after a line and a half the crowd would think they knew exactly what rhyme he was leading up to, and they waited with a keen anticipation for him to say it out loud, but suddenly, with just a few syllables to spare before the rhyme and refrain he'd turn it around completely, take it in an entirely different, and quite brilliant,

83

direction. The crowd – often numbering in the thousands – would roar with delight and repeat the rhyme and refrain back to him, shaking the edifices of buildings around them with the sounds of poetry.

DURING THIS TIME HE TOOK THE PEN-NAME 'NAZIM' BECAUSE IT MEANT 'POET'.

He took the pen-name Nazim because he adored Nazim Hikmet's poetry.

HALFWAY THROUGH HIS UNIVERSITY STINT HE UNFORTUNATELY ABANDONED THE GHAZAL TO EXPERIMENT WITH WESTERN IDEAS OF POETRY.

He wrote sonnets, pantoums, villanelles, canzones. For those who had loved his ghazals this was a profound betrayal, particularly in light of the nationalistic, anti-colonial feeling that ran high among young Pakistanis in the early 1950s, and they mockingly took to calling him 'The Poet' rather than 'Nazim'.

AFTER UNIVERSITY HE WENT BACK TO KARACHI which was then still a young cosmopolitan capital that was so busy experimenting with its own form that it wasn't going to berate anyone else for doing the same

AND STILL UNDER WESTERN INFLUENCES HE FORGOT POLITICS AND SOCIAL CONCERNS IN FAVOUR OF OBSCENITY AND WAS HAULED UP IN COURT FOR THIS CRIME.

'I don't know what goes on in the minds of these disgusting people,' he said, speaking in his defence at his trial for indecency. 'I'm writing about eating fruit, and they say I'm being vulgar. What exactly do they think the mango's slippery seed and dripping juices refer to?' And with that, he put a mango on the table in front of him, cut it open along its equator and started sucking on its seed in a manner so suggestive that the newly married judge ran home to his wife.

THE CASE WAS DISMISSED BECAUSE THE JUDGE HAD OTHER THINGS TO DO AND HE CONTINUED TO WRITE, WINNING ACCLAIM FOR HIS CRAFT BUT NOT FOR HIS SUBJECT MATTERS.

By the time he was thirty he was already acknowledged as a craftsman in whose hands language was plastic; even his detractors acknowledged as much, while still complaining that, in contrast to his impassioned student days, he made language do everything except engender 'worthy' emotions in those who were listening. In one public gathering he ran into his old teacher who told him that, for all his formal brilliance, he was an inferior poet to his former classmate, Maqsood. 'When you read a Maqsood poem you feel he's plucking his heart out of his chest and placing it in your hand,' the teacher berated him. The Poet replied, 'Personally I don't want any of Maqsood's quivering organs sweating all over my palm.'

BUT THEN IN 1963 HE TRANSLATED THE POLITICAL POEMS OF AN OBSCURE TURKISH POET WHO SHARED HIS PEN-NAME.

He said afterwards that in some ways Nazim Hikmet's death in 1963 affected him even more than the death of his own mother. He barricaded himself in the tiny cubbyhole which was his flat and within a few weeks produced his adaptations – he never used the word 'translations' – of some of Hikmet's verse with all its fiery politics. With discontent rife in the country over Ayub Khan's constitution and its Basic Democracy scheme that made a joke of democracy it was either a brave or politically naïve man who could publish such inflammatory verse; the Poet himself never said to which of the two categories he belonged.

THE AYUB KHAN GOVERNMENT IMPRISONED HIM FOR TWO MONTHS ON SOME CHARGE.

The deep scars across his face date from that first incarceration. He used to say simply that he got the scars from running into barbed wire. But one day I asked him, 'How did you manage to run into barbed wire?'

'Simple. The prison guards led me to barbed wire, put a gun to my head and said, "Run."'

HE EMERGED FROM PRISON WITH HIS SOCIAL CONSCIENCE RESTORED.

He emerged from prison with a scarred face and a poetic voice that seared every government in Pakistan for the next two decades.

BUT HE STILL CONTINUED TO WRITE ROMANTIC VERSE AS WELL, THE MOST FAMOUS OF WHICH WAS *LAILA*, PUBLISHED IN 1970.

Oh no. No, no. No leaping from 1963 to 1970. No erasing 1968. That momentous year around the world – student revolutions, a new era dawning, my mother's first meeting with the Poet. She was twenty-three and he was thirty-six. He was already immortal by then. Immortal and ugly – a short, stout, broad-nosed man with scars across his face. And she – she had just stepped into incandescence.

She was recently out of university at the time, and had been helping her uncle in his understaffed law firm as research for the book she was planning to write on 'Women and Jurisprudence in Pakistan'. Her timing, in joining the firm, was either fortuitous or disastrous, depending on how you viewed the path her life took thereafter because, just weeks later, her uncle was engaged to represent a woman who accused her former employer of withholding her pay for six months and locking her in chains when he left the house. As the woman was an illiterate villager and her employer was a wealthy crony of many of the most powerful people in the country, it was a wonder either she or my great-uncle believed she'd ever get a fair trial. Forget fair. The matter didn't even get to court before the former employer produced before my great-uncle and the woman 'credible witnesses' who were willing to attest to the moral depravity and pathological insanity of the woman. The woman walked out of my great-uncle's office, swearing to him that she believed in justice, broke into the former employer's house and when he returned she was waiting for him with his gun in her hand. She killed first him, then herself.

Somehow a Canadian film team which was working on a documentary about Pakistan heard of the story and came to interview my great-uncle. Too sickened by the whole thing to talk about it without exploding in rage, my great-uncle sent my mother to meet the film team instead. On camera, she was ablaze with beauty – and with a sense of justice so newly minted it shone through her eyes. The student revolutions of 1968 had found her on their fringes in her final weeks in the UK, listening, sympathizing, occasionally even marching, but it took the village woman's bloodied end to draw all those political ideals away from the abstract margins of her life and place them front-and-centre.

The Canadian film team must have scarcely been able to believe their luck that day – everything about her cried out, 'I'm ready for my close up!' She was wearing a plain white kurta, a thick karra on her wrist – silver inlaid with lapis lazuli – and had her hair tied back with a scarf. And she could speak with passion and intelligence and flashing grey-green eyes. 'Pakistan's Gypsy Feminist' was born. One of the members of the film crew was also a freelance journalist and he wrote a besotted piece about my mother for a hugely popular magazine with a global circulation. Even so, her newly discovered fame would not have penetrated below the upper echelons of Pakistani society – those households that subscribed to foreign magazines – had the Poet not seen the article and expressed an interest in meeting her when one of her cousins was in earshot.

It was Something at First Sight. Something heady and consuming.

It can't be an easy thing for a fiercely independent woman to become a muse. But before she knew how to react against what was happening, my mother found herself being defined by what the Poet wrote about her. He even changed the year of her birth in his poems, made her two years younger than she was so that she was the same age as Pakistan – in many of the poems of this time when he writes about the Beloved his poems have both the intimate resonance of a man speaking to his lover and the grand sweep of a poet declaiming about the nation. What twenty-three-year old could retain her sense of self amidst all this?

Oh yes, at first she enjoyed it – when he made her a figure of rebellion, of salvation, she played into it. That's when her initial incarnation as Activist came to pass, though at this point the term was wholly inappropriate – she was still little more than the dogsbody at her uncle's office, but people all over the country read the Poet's verse, all dedicated to her, and soon she was being invited to speak at girls' colleges, to join panels on Women's Upliftment, to cut ribbons, to pose for pictures. It helped that the poems placed her on such a high pedestal that is was possible to ignore the sexualized imagery and believe that it was the impossibility of ever winning the love of this young, beautiful creature that fuelled the Poet to write about her so insistently.

But by the time 1970 was exiting the monsoon season, with civil war beginning to loom and the absurdity of panels and ribbons and pictures asserting itself in my mother's mind, she walked out of the Poet's life and went in search of an identity that wasn't caught up in his shadow. At the outset of her search she found my father, plucked him up by the collar and, weeks later, married him.

The Poet responded by writing *Laila*. My mother remained unmoved, and proved this by becoming pregnant just a couple of months after her marriage. When the Poet heard of her pregnancy, he came to see her. ('He was wearing that grey shawl I loved – it was a hot, hot day, he must have been incredibly uncomfortable. But that didn't stop him from wearing the grey shawl,' she told me once when I asked her for details of their reunion. That was as much as I ever got out of her about it.)

They didn't move in together, of course – not then, not ever, at least not in Karachi. But her father had already died and left her the two adjoining houses in Bath Island, so she and the Poet became neighbours. Everyone expected a wedding to take place after her divorce with my father came through, but the Poet didn't believe in marriage – the illegitimate child of a rich landowner and a woman who worked on the lands, he grew up with a fierce dislike for the very institution which would have saved his mother from her outcast status, with only a widowed aunt willing to take her in and help raise her son. And in any case, my mother said, she and the Poet weren't temperamentally suited to co-habitation and much preferred adjoining houses so there was no need for a formal contract which couched the terms of marriage in monetary terms and demanded a declaration of religious beliefs. She came to see the idiocy of this view when he died, but by then it was too late.

For a good part of the first twelve years of my life the Poet was either in prison or self-imposed exile; and wherever he was, she wasn't far behind. I think the government moved him to jails in remote parts of the country just to make life difficult for my mother who would shuttle back and forth from Karachi to visit him whenever prison rules or bribery allowed. On the occasions he was allowed daily visitors she would find somewhere to live near the jail – he had admirers in every part of the country who offered her places to stay – which sometimes meant being away from home, and me, for weeks at a stretch. The times when he was jailed in Karachi rather than anywhere else owed themselves entirely to Beema, who had relatives in the military and bureaucracy, and who was the only person who seemed to see how much I needed my mother around.

Most of Karachi society disapproved of her, of course. Running around the country after some man she wasn't even married to, leaving her daughter behind. But they also said that letting Beema raise me was the best thing she could do for me, not that that excused her behaviour in any way. From 1972 on, however, the whispers about the 'coffee-party feminist' began to subside. This was the second phase of 'Samina Akram, Activist', and she inaugurated it by speaking out vocally against the false imprisonment of the Poet, who was in jail again, allegedly for the indecency of poems he'd written five years earlier, though everyone knew that the real reason for his imprisonment was his poem 'Ufuq' which condemned the generals and politicians he held responsible for the tragedy of the 1971 civil war. My mother's attempts to have him freed brought her into contact with other women who were engaged in similar fights for husbands or brothers or sons. Even after the Poet was released she continued to seek out, and later to be sought out by, women in search of justice. She offered them whatever help she could by pointing them in the direction of sympathetic lawyers and journalists or explaining their legal rights to them – the research she had done for the unwritten book about women and jurisprudence in Pakistan served her well over the years. But the fame she acquired was greater than the sum of everything she did – it had something to do with that *grazia* that Shehnaz Saeed spoke of.

And what of me in all this? I was just a few months old when the Poet was imprisoned in 1972, and my mother knew the ability of a smiling infant to cut through bureaucracy. I could instantly reduce both uniformed and inky-fingered men into cooing creatures – and though they tried to snap back into positions of authority, the damage had been done as soon as they started addressing me in baby-talk. The landscape of my first few months in this world was one of courtrooms, prisons, lawyer's offices. 'I would not allow them to tell me there was a choice to be made between motherhood and standing up for justice,' my mother used to say, and I never asked, 'But what about the choice to be made between motherhood and romantic love?'

I looked down at the paper in my hand again.

HE WAS IMPRISONED SEVERAL TIMES DURING THE 70s BY THE BHUTTO GOVERNMENT FOR HIS POLITICAL VERSE INCLUDING 'UJALA' (DAWN) AND 'AIK AADH LAMHA' (A LITTLE DISTANCE).

He was one of Bhutto's strongest critics, but even so he

was filled with apprehension when the anti-Bhutto movement pulled religion out from behind its veil of privacy and into the realm of politics as both secular-minded and hard-line religious politicians banded together to campaign against the government. Bhutto tried appeasing the hardliners by introducing Islamic laws, but the General in the wings took over and decided to show everyone how Islamization was really done. My memories of those days are all about fear. The Poet and my mother were in Karachi at this point but I used to feel claustrophobic in their presence, all that pessimism sitting so heavily on them, evident even to a six-year-old, that part of me was actually relieved when

IN 1977, FOLLOWING THE MILITARY COUP WHICH BROUGHT GENERAL ZIA TO POWER, HE WENT INTO EXILE IN COLOMBIA

to stay with his great friend Rafael Gonzales – my mother went with him.

HE RETURNED TO PAKISTAN OVER A YEAR LATER.

He was unable to write a word in his time away, and my mother claimed that following Pakistan's news from a distance had almost given her a nervous breakdown. They saw in the New Year – 1979 – with a promise to their friends that they weren't going to leave again, and I moved half my toys and books back into the blue bedroom in my mother's house with every confidence that I would have no reason ever to move them out again.

IN 1979 GENERAL ZIA INTRODUCED THE HUDOOD ORDINANCE WHICH NAZIM, WHO KNEW SOME WOMEN ACTIVISTS, WAS VERY CRITICAL ABOUT.

'How can words be used for such indignity?' the Poet said, when he heard the details of the laws being passed in the name of Islam. (And my father's father, the most gentle and pious of men, wept himself to death over it.) The Poet wanted to get back on a plane and leave the country, leave for anywhere. But my mother told him he'd have to go without her. Something in her broke free the day she sat at her dining table in dressing-gown and slippers, smoking a cigarette, and reading out loud every detail of the Hudood Ordinance. When she got to the part about 'Zina', which said an accusation of rape could only be proved in a court of law if there were four pious, male Muslim adults willing to give eye-witness testimony, she looked up at me and said, 'For the first time, I wish I'd given birth to a son.'

LATER THAT YEAR, ZIA HANGED BHUTTO AND THE POET WROTE 'ZEHER' (POISON).

When he heard of Bhutto's death the Poet locked himself in his cramped, dark store-room, and when my mother finally found a spare key and opened the door she found him whimpering and shaking. Within days of the execution he produced 'Zeher' and no one dared publish it. Undeterred, he made twelve copies of the poem, called twelve of his friends over for dinner and handed a copy of the poem to each one. 'It was all very Last Supper,' my mother later said, recalling the dinner. It was hardly the most accomplished of his poems ('"Eyes expelling barbed wire in place of tears?" my mother said, holding the page away from her, between thumb and forefinger. 'That's what you get with instant poetry.') but within forty-eight hours there were thousands of copies circulating throughout the country, being set to music, and through song entering the nation's consciousness. That's when he and my mother devised the code – they knew imprisonment was inevitable, and given previous instances in which letters smuggled into the prison ground had been intercepted, they decided a secret code would be a sensible safety measure.

HE WAS IMPRISONED YET AGAIN AND PLACED IN SOLITARY CONFINEMENT.

My mother knew the climate wasn't right to agitate for his release; she had nightmares in which he was hanged and she was taken to cut down his body with nothing sharper than her own teeth to sever the rope. So she turned her attention elsewhere. That's when the third and final phase of her activism began, and it's the phase people today almost always refer to when they talk of her life in the public realm.

In the wake of the Hudood Ordinance the women's movement in Pakistan began to assert itself, though it wouldn't be until 1981 that it went into high gear with the formation of the Women's Action Forum. But as early as 1979 my mother was going from city to city, and often to smaller towns, sometimes covered up so no one would recognize her, and talking to different groups and individuals about the need to politicize women, to bring them together, to do something.

HE WAS RELEASED FROM PRISON SOME MONTHS LATER with the understanding that he had a week to leave the country if he didn't want to be re-arrested AND WENT INTO EXILE AGAIN.

This time my mother told him she was staying in Pakistan. But once he was in Colombia she began to pine – after all those months in which she'd borne his imprisonment with remarkable fortitude. 'You yearn for his release so you can be with him – you fear that might never happen – but then he's released and further away from you than ever,' I heard her explain to Beema one day. So it didn't surprise me too much when Rafael sent word the Poet was ill, that my mother packed a suitcase and left. She said she'd be back in a few weeks.

HE REMAINED IN EXILE FOR THREE YEARS.

And she remained there with him. She seemed to be on the move a lot during those years; often at conferences and the like, drumming up support for the women's movement in Pakistan.

THE FIRST YEAR IN COLOMBIA, THEN IN EGYPT.

My mother insisted on the move – she saw that her own belief in secular jurisprudence was not sufficient to take on a government intent on claiming its laws were God-ordained, so she went to Egypt to work with women's groups there and discover the feminist traditions within Islam which would allow her to battle the hard-liners on their own turf.

WHILE IN CAIRO HE WON THE PRESTIGIOUS RUMI AWARD, CHOSEN BY A PANEL OF POETS AND SCHOLARS FROM THE MUSLIM WORLD AND RETURNED TO PAKISTAN

having received government assurances that he wouldn't be arrested on his return.

It was 1983 by then, and the Women's Action Forum, spearheaded by some of my mother's closest friends, was taking on the military government with an astonishing show of bravery. Between the Ansari Commission's recommendations that women should be barred from holding high public office, and the proposed Islamic Law of Evidence which equated the evidence of two women to that of one man, and the Safia Bibi case in which a blind eighteen-year-old girl who was raped found herself sentenced to a fine, imprisonment and public lashing on the charge of adultery, there was plenty of work to be done, and my mother rolled up her sleeves and entered the mêlée.

I decided to enter it with her. I didn't tell anyone about it beforehand, but I managed to convince one of my cousins to drive to me to a rally to protest the Law of Evidence. There were so many people there that my mother didn't see me, but I saw her as she addressed the crowd. *Grazia, grazia, grazia.* When I came home that evening, Beema saw the bruise that had been left on my arm from falling in the street while running from policemen who broke up the rally. We had the worst fight of our lives. Rabia, eight years old, phoned my mother to tell her what was happening, and Mama walked into our house in time to hear me say to Beema, for the only time in my life: you're not my real mother, anyway.

'Say that ever again and I'll disown you,' my mother said.

She told Beema she'd have no objection to having me locked in chains next time there was a rally if I refused to swear on the Qu'ran that I wouldn't attend any organised

94

protest unless Beema told me I could or until I turned eighteen, whichever happened first. So I swore, but I wasn't happy about it.

Of course, there was never a rally that she didn't attend herself. I remember going to her house one day and finding her with vicious bruises on her back and arms and stomach; and sometimes she was taken into police custody for anywhere between a few hours and three weeks, during which time Beema was almost constantly on the phone to her influential relatives. But despite how harrowing those days were there was an exultation about my mother; she had finally found an incarnation that suited her entirely. And there were significant victories too – Safia Bibi was acquitted by the Federal Sharia Court and the Islamic Law of Evidence was amended so that it was only in cases pertaining to financial matters that the testimony of two women was equal to that of one man (not enough of a victory, my mother said, but still significant), and the Ansari Commission's recommendation never became law.

And the Poet, during this time

IT IS IMPOSSIBLE TO KNOW IF HE REALLY WAS WORKING ON A COLLECTION AFTER HIS RETURN TO PAKISTAN, AS HIS ADMIRERS SAY, OR IF FEAR OF FURTHER IMPRISONMENT MADE HIM STOP WRITING, AS SOME WONDER.

Oh, he was still writing. Writing feverishly, though not publishing anything – he said if he was going to prison again it would be for a complete collection, not just an individual poem.

I think both he and my mother were happier with their own reflections in the mirror at this time than at any earlier point of their lives. And I, too, remember the next three years as happy times, despite – and in some way, as a result of – all the mayhem wreaked upon the nation. There was such a headiness at the centre of all the anti-government activity.

But then

IN 1986, HE WAS FOUND MURDERED IN AN

EMPTY PLOT OF LAND. NO POSTHUMOUS WORK
APPEARED.

And Mama became so incapacitated with grief that Beema
moved her into the room next to mine, in my father's house,
and she was there but not there for two years before she'd
had enough, and left.

The paper in my hand started to blur. I dropped it in the
waste-paper basket and sent an e-mail to the CEO saying:
The bio's fine.

Then I returned to the darkness and stayed there for the
rest of the day.

# VIII

*Who was the most civilized Crusader?*
*a) Richard the Lionheart*
*b) Frederick Barbarossa*
*c) Bahemond of Taranto*
*d) Frederick II*

*Answer: d*

The quiz show host raised his dyed eyebrows across the desk at me. 'They're very good questions except, as you know, for that last one.' He put down the list of questions and slashed a cross over my Crusader question without any sign of irony. 'But, as a matter of interest, why Frederick II?'

'He was excommunicated three times by two different Popes. That seems eminently civilized to me. But he never got his due during his lifetime, poor man. Instead of waging war on the Muslims, as any good crusader should do, he decided to enter into diplomatic negotiations and won Jerusalem in that shameful manner, while also settling a ten-year peace treaty with the Sultan of Egypt. He was ridiculed throughout Europe for this unmanly conduct.'

The quiz show host stretched his mouth into the smile with which he once recommended a brand of tea in a popular ad from my childhood. 'Well, we can't possibly have that question, then. No Christian who wins Jerusalem from the

Muslims, in any manner, can be deemed civilized by us without causing all kinds of problems.' He licked his fingertip and used it to smooth down his eyebrows. 'You know, the opening still exists for the host of the political chat show. I know the Big Man offered it to you. You might want to give it some thought.'

By now I had been at STD long enough to recognize that the CEO's offer hadn't been a sign of any incipient potential he saw in me, but just an indicator of his desperation to find presenters for the STD shows. All that would change soon – already it seemed that everyone I met between the age of sixteen and twenty-two had the word 'media' on their lips when asked about their future – but for the moment those of us who were 'reasonable enough' (i.e. reasonably attractive, reasonably intelligent, reasonably articulate) had a world of on-air opportunities to pick from. 'If it's a ground-breaking chat show, involving a séance, which allows me to interview Frederick II, then sure. Otherwise, I'll stick to being the brains behind your beauty.'

The quiz show host smiled – he was well aware of both his intelligence and his good looks – and shrugged his shoulders. 'Suits me fine.'

When he left my office, I checked my watch. It was approximately twenty-two hours since I had left Shehnaz Saeed's house. Twenty-two hours since she had given me the letter which had accompanied the encrypted page. In those twenty-two hours I had managed to restrain myself from reading the covering letter even once. Now there was a clear sign I was so much better than before – it wasn't that many years ago that every time I answered the phone and there was silence on the other end it was enough to make me call the telephone exchange and demand they trace the call. It was tempting now to phone Beema and tell her, you see, you see, all those attempts on your part to get me to 'talk to someone' weren't necessary. I'm doing this on my own, I'm getting there.

Fourteen years later, and as far as I'd got was being able to avoid reading a letter for twenty-two hours.

I knew exactly what that 'someone' to whom Beema wanted me to talk would say. She'd say, it's been fourteen years, Aasmaani. That's twice the length of time a person has to be gone before they're legally declared dead. You need to let go.

Let go. As though I were holding on to something outside myself; as though conclusions were ropes that could hang you. And whatever I tried to say, however much I tried to explain that my mother really was capable of vanishing, that she'd been practising it for two years before she actually left, that she had been practising shedding the skin that was her character and assuming another identity, right there, under our noses without any of us understanding what was happening – however much I tried to explain all this, and tried to explain, also, that there had been simply no reason for her to stay within her old identity, they would tell me I had created a story to avoid facing the painful truth. That they, too, were creating a story would not occur to them – if enough people believe a thing, belief becomes indistinguishable from truth, and they cannot see how anyone with the same facts as they possess could ever reach a different conclusion except through stubbornness, denial or a wilful misreading of the situation.

I opened the desk drawer which contained the cover letter and encrypted page, and then closed it again. I would give myself another two hours before looking at it. Self-imposed restrictions are absurd but not without effect; if you can't rid yourself of obsessions you can at least wean yourself off the number of hours you waste on them to the exclusion of everything else.

I forced my hands off the drawer-handle and on to my keyboard. But there really wasn't any work demanding my immediate attention. It was a particularly slow day at STD – the only event of note had been the firing of a pregnant TV presenter, whose energetic and efficient hosting of a current affairs programme had been brought to an end at the insistence of the show's primary advertisers who claimed that their product could not be associated with a pregnant woman without 'adverse effects'. The primary advertiser was a bank – and already the STD kitchenette was rife with ribaldry about 'direct deposits' and 'early withdrawals'.

Somehow my hand was on the drawer-handle again. I moved it over to the telephone and phoned Shehnaz Saeed to thank her for lunch.

'Don't be silly,' she said. 'My pleasure entirely. I don't know why we haven't been in touch all these years. You know, I was just going to call you myself to ask if you'd made any sense of that page of garbled letters.'

'No, sorry. Haven't had time to really look at it. But as a matter of interest, do you remember the postmark on the envelope?'

'I did check,' she said. 'But some of the letters were smudged so I only know it started with "M" and ended with "AN". Either Multan or Mardan, I suppose. The stamp was local.'

That really didn't help, but it wasn't as though I could think of any postmark that would have furnished a helpful clue about the origin of the letter.

I was going to end the call, but she said, 'Aasmaani, can I ask you a personal question?' Of all the rhetorical questions in the world, that is the one which irritates me most with its simultaneous gesture towards and denial of the trespass that is about to follow. But I merely made a noise of acquiescence, and Shehnaz Saeed asked, 'Is there some kind of problem with you and Ed?'

I had heard his distinctive gait – one stride followed by three short steps – outside my office several times today. Each time he passed I thought of opening my door and calling out to him, but I remained unsettled about how my feelings towards him could swing so quickly and so arbitrarily from irritation to camaraderie to desire to disdain, and not knowing what I wanted from him made it impossible to know what to say to him.

'Why do you ask?'

'I mentioned your name during dinner last night and he reacted strangely. Surly, in a way that was almost adolescent. And I'm not sure if it's because of your name or because I'm mentioning it, if you see what I mean.'

'Not really.'

'No. No, I suppose you don't. It's just that – I'm going to be very frank now – I think he likes you. A lot. And he's not going to want me befriending you, because then, you see, you'll be my person and not his. That's how he'll think of it. It's not easy, I suppose, having a mother like me.'

For a woman who had managed to maintain an air of secrecy around her private life for so long, she was surprisingly voluble.

'You're wondering why I'm telling you this?' she said, and I couldn't help laughing in embarrassment at being caught out. 'It's just that, my dear, when we were growing up no one taught us how to be mothers and something else at the same time. Motherhood was an all-or-nothing business. You can tell me, if anyone can, how should I be his mother and be famous? He's thirty-five years old, Aasmaani, and I still don't know what he wants me to be. When I acted, he hated that it took me away from him. When I stopped acting, he hated that I'd given up that part of myself. He kept hounding me to act again, and now that I've said yes, he's even more moody than before.'

If she wasn't going to be subtle, neither was I. 'You're trying to talk to me about my relationship with my mother, aren't you?'

'No, darling, I'm being much more self-involved than that.'

She was probably lying, but I liked her all the same. 'I'm really not the person to talk to about Ed. I can't even begin to fathom him. I'll try not to be unpleasant to him, that's as much as I can promise. But I'm trying for your sake, not his.'

She sighed then. 'If he hears that he'll say, you see, Ma,

you've gone and done it again. And I suppose I have.' Her voice dropped. 'Oh, I hear him. He's here for lunch. I'll speak to you later.' And she hung up.

What an odd household.

The thought had barely crossed my mind when I smiled at the irony. Who was I to talk of odd households, when between the ages of fifteen and seventeen I had lived under the same roof as a divorced couple, his second wife and their daughter? And before that I'd spent all those years shuttling between the picture-perfect normality of life with Dad, Beema and Rabia and the utter unconventionality of my mother's house with its connecting door to her lover's garden. How unremarkable those arrangements had seemed to me.

I put down the receiver and sent around an e-mail to a choice group of colleagues, enquiring, 'Time for a breakout, Chinese style?' and within minutes I'd assembled a group of three women and two men who were more than happy to join me at the nearest Chinese restaurant for lunch. (That was one of my carefully nurtured talents – the ability to enter a new workplace and almost instantly find people who would provide companionship to speed up the day without demanding anything so emotionally exhausting as friendship.)

Over chow mein, lemon chicken, egg-fried rice and beef chilli dry I brought the conversation around to Ed and everyone rolled their eyes or held up their chopsticks in gestures of confusion.

'If he was a woman, the letters PMS would be attached to his name like it was a university degree,' the news anchor asserted, picking off the little pieces of carrot from the egg-fried rice on her plate, and leaving everything else untouched.

'Oh, he's sweet enough. Leave him alone,' said one of the women on the *Boond* team. 'You can't blame a guy for getting frustrated if he's been working abroad and then has to come back and deal with goats in the budget.'

'Sorry?' I said between mouthfuls.

'Don't you know this?' The news anchor leaned in.

'Whenever there's some major production in the works the budget includes the cost of several goats – the bigger the production, the more goats. That way, when something goes wrong, a goat gets sacrificed without disrupting the balance sheet. Two goats if the problem is major.'

'*Boond* is a seven-goat production,' the *Boond* woman said, not without pride. 'But what with Bougainvillea dropping out, and then waiting to see if Shehnaz Saeed would agree to do it, we're already four goats down and filming has hardly even begun.'

The conversation moved on from there and I could find no seamless way of bringing Ed back into it. That felt like failure. Later, in my office again, I found myself tracing widening circles on my desk and thinking of them as Eddies. Then, my mobile phone beeped to tell me it had been twenty-four hours since I left Shehnaz Saeed's house.

It was with a sense of occasion bordering on the ritualistic that I pulled open my desk drawer and lifted out the covering letter. I set it down in front of me, an empty coffee jar filled with pens holding down one corner and the edge of my mouse pad holding down the corner diagonally across from it. It struck me instantly that the handwriting was too deliberately childish, the misspellings too obvious. *I am sending this too you, though it could be dangarous for me, because perhaps it is the only thangs I have to give you that you might want.* Though. Perhaps. Might. Those were words you'd associate with someone who was more than just marginally literate. And a sentence structure that employed a sub-clause offset by commas – that required a certain level of sophistication.

I felt a moment of satisfaction mixed with contempt. Whoever had written this could have tried just a little harder to make the fiction convincing. And yet . . . I adjusted the neck of the desk lamp so the light shone on to the letter, and tried unsuccessfully to find a watermark or some other distinguishing feature. And yet, if the intention of the writer of this letter were merely to disguise his (or her) identity, then the plan had been successful. I continued to look at the letter for a few more minutes, but no amount of staring could force it to yield up any clues, so I turned my attention to the encrypted page.

*The Minions came again today. That sounds like a beginning.*

I held my hands in front of me, as though in prayer, as understanding dawned. Of course. It was written by someone who was trying to write something – the Poet trying to write a story for Rafael Gonzales, perhaps – except his mind was having trouble forming plot and sentences. So he wrote one line, and then he wrote, triumphantly, that it sounded like the start of something.

*What more can I say?*

But having got his opening line, he didn't know how to continue. Of course, of course.

*Can it be you, out there, reading these words?*

That could only have been addressed to my mother. Why? Just to be playful, perhaps. Just to say, I know you can't resist picking up things I've been working on, and reading them. Except, she never did as far as I knew – she always respected the privacy of his work, never read anything until he asked her to.

Something else was troubling me. I looked at the paper again. Why do it? Simply that. Why write in code for any reason except to write letters to my mother that he wanted no one else to read? Yes, I used to write in the code all the time – I wrote stories, wrote letters to my mother, wrote in the steam of the bathroom mirror. But that was only because it gave me the thrill that children get from partaking in adult behaviour that is forbidden to them. It was the most illicit of pleasures to write in code, and then tear it up or rub it out instantly before anyone – anyone – could see. I was a child then, and the flexibility of my child's mind was able to grasp and learn the code with an ease that defied grown-ups. But for my mother and the Poet writing in code was hard, laborious work; it carried with it the scent of jail cells and dread. My mother told me so after the Poet had died – and

I had surprised her then by saying, yes, I know it. I still know the code.

It was supposed to be their secret, just the two of them. But I was eight years old when they devised the code – curious and small; an excellent combination when your mother locks up her study which has grilles outside its window to prevent any grown person slipping through.

In a drawer, in her study, I found a paper on which she had written:

*My ex calls the ochre winter 'autumn' as we queue to hear dock boys play jazz fugues in velvet dark.*

And below that, two columns. One which listed all the letters of that odd sentence, and another beside it listing letters of the alphabet:

M=A
Y=B
E=C
X=D
C=E
A=F
L=G
L= (Repeated)
S=H
and so on.

It wasn't hard to figure out after that.

I copied the sentence and the two columns of letters into the mini-notepad with the spy-sized mini-pen which I carried around in the back-pocket of my jeans, and that afternoon I asked, 'What's fugue, Mama?'

'What? Why are you asking me that, Aasmaani?'

'I saw the word somewhere. In a book at the school library,' I lied.

'Oh. Well, to start with it's not fug-you. That could sound rude.' She pulled me down into her lap and put her arms around me, her chin resting on the top of my head. The more conventional meaning has to do with music. A sort of call and response. Two or more musicians responding to one another's music. The second meaning is much more interesting. It means deliberate amnesia. You know what amnesia is, sweetheart?'

'Mama! Of course. But that's so silly. Why would you deliberately forget something?'

The following day, I handed my mother a card which said:

AFAF, N GKZC BKP.

When I first handed it to her, she thought it was nonsense words. I dug my hands in my pocket and rocked on the balls of my feet as the Poet did when he was offended by someone's misreading of his work. 'It says "Mama, I love you".' That's when she shook me, made me promise to forget about it, made me swear never to mention it to anyone. Then she tore out the pages of my notebook which contained evidence of the code – and though I wept to save the jellyfish which I had laboured over drawing on the reverse side of the page which contained the jazz fugues sentence, she shook her head firmly, told me there were consequences for taking people's secrets, and burnt the pages.

But she couldn't burn my memory. When the Poet was released from prison, and she followed him to Colombia, I wrote the sentence down again. Each time I started to think about her I would turn my mind to translating sentences into code instead, until I was so adept at it I sometimes had to concentrate hard in school in order to avoid filling exam papers with clumps of words unintelligible to everyone except me. I never broke my promise to her. I never told anyone else about it.

No one except her, years later, after the Poet's death. She had only a dim memory of the card I had written for her, and thought I was joking when I told her that there was still a muscle in my brain which knew how to read and write in code.

*Can it be you, out there, reading these words?*

I pushed my chair back and stood up. Maybe, just maybe.

Why would anyone send that encrypted page to Shehnaz Saeed? Because my mother wrote it. Whoever wrote that covering letter knew of the strength of my mother's friendship with Shehnaz Saeed in those two years before she left. *It is the only thangs I have to give you that you might want . . . I know you know the person who rote them.*

Oh, surely it was the only explanation that made sense?

A hoax. It could – think, Aaasmaani! – be a hoax. Someone else could have written it, pretending to be my mother. But then why write it in code, when Shehnaz might not understand it or know where it came from? Why not sign it, at least? Why send someone a forgery while making it as difficult as possible for them to guess whose words were being forged?

My mother had written those pages to me. That was it.

After she disappeared. She had written those words since her disappearance, knowing I was the only person who would understand it. But somehow, it never reached me. It fell into the hands of someone else who sent it to Shehnaz Saeed and, by some miracle – no, by chance, nothing more – the page had come to me weeks, months, maybe years after it was first written.

But why write something so mystifying? Why? And why, again, in code?

Because she was in danger. That had to be it. They only used the code when there was danger of the words being intercepted. But what was there in those words that she didn't want intercepted?

*There are more. I will send you more if you act again.*

I sat down, trying to breathe slowly, trying to control the rush of blood to my head.

What situation could make it necessary for her to send

encrypted messages? *The Minions came again today.* If that wasn't a line of fiction, what could it mean?

'Mama!' I called out, without understanding why.

The door was pushed open. There was Ed, with the curious faces of three of our first-floor colleagues behind him. He took one look at me and stepped inside, shutting the door behind him.

'Get out,' I said.

He made no move either to come closer or leave. Instead, he looked around the room, searching out clues. His eyes came to rest on the letter and encrypted page on my desk.

'Get out,' I said again, more softly, through clenched teeth. And then I saw the envelope in his hand addressed in childish block letters.

Not daring to speak, I pointed to it.

Ed glanced down and looked surprised, as though he'd forgotten he was holding it.

I lifted myself out of the chair, walked over to him, and caught hold of the envelope. Though it was mid-afternoon, a hint of aftershave still clung to Ed. It had the scent of a citrus tree growing by the sea. I leaned forward, very slightly, and then pulled away, only to find Ed was still holding on to the envelope. For an instant I thought he was gripping it so tightly in order to keep me near him, and then I realized that he had no intention of relinquishing the envelope to me.

He said, 'What's going on?'

'That's mine. You have no right to it.' I continued to cling on to one end of the envelope.

'No, it's my mother's.'

'She sent it here for me, didn't she? Didn't she?'

He closed his eyes and lowered his head. Not looking at me, he said, 'Don't.'

'What?'

But he only shook his head, and still held on to the envelope.

'Don't think I won't break your fingers to get it, Ed.' My

voice had a degree of calm which only came when I was sliding into hysteria.

He looked up then. 'Don't think I won't pick you up and throw you out of the nearest window if you try that.' His voice was equally calm, though I had no way of knowing what that denoted. For a moment neither of us said anything more, and then his mouth shaped itself into a sneer and he dropped the envelope on the floor and left the room.

I crouched down, knees touching the ground, and picked it up. The postmark said Quetta. I turned the envelope round to open the flap and saw a scribbled note: *This arrived during lunch. From Quetta? Tell me if it makes any sense. Shehnaz.*

I opened the envelope and pulled out a sheaf of encrypted, calligraphed pages.

I put the pages in my handbag, and exited the office, stopping only to mumble some explanation to the CEO about feeling unwell – he was on his way to the golf course and I'm sure it was impatience rather than concern that made him wave me out towards the door, towards my car, towards home as fast as the potholed streets would allow.

But once home, I climbed slowly, almost hesitatingly, up the steps to my third-floor flat. My life may be about to change, I thought. I became starkly aware of everything around me – the speckled pattern on the stairs; the mangy cat slouching through the driveway beneath; the multitude of potted plants in front of the doorway of one of the two first-floor flats accessible via this stairway; the tink-tink-tink sound from a nearby plot of land where someone repeatedly drove a hammer against nails, eliciting a rhythmic, near-musical sound; the rush of heat from a kitchen window; the glimpse, over at the horizon, of white-blue waves which might appear a mirage to an untutored eye seeing them, as I now did, through a wave of smoke from a fire in an empty plot; the fire itself, an even orange colour which made it possible to wonder if it, too, were a trick of the eye, really just a ragged piece of bright chiffon flapping back and forth in the breeze.

And most of all, most of all I was aware of the papers clutched tight in my hand.

I unlocked my front door, walked through the balcony and then through the second set of doors, locked the connecting door to Rabia's flat and, with a muttered prayer ('Silently,' I heard Beema tell me. 'Silently. Prayer is as quiet and as resonant as a single raindrop falling on a desert'), I sat down with the sheaf of papers in my hand.

The first line told me the Poet had written it.

. . .

I wonder if I'm still allergic to peaches.

It would be too absurd to bear if age and solitude worked their way through my body and mind erasing all defining characteristics, until nothing remained recognizable of the man I once was except my need to break out into gasps and hives each time I encounter that fruit.

I have a rash, therefore I am.

Sounds about right.

The Minions brought a bagful of peaches for me yesterday. My last experience with peaches was three decades ago, when you bit into a peach and then kissed me. Those were early days, before you learned I never did anything by half-measures; not love, not poetry, not allergies. I think of that experience now as a cautionary tale that stays my hand from the inviting plumpness of the fruit before me – remember how my tongue swelled up and nearly cut off all breath? I also have some memory of the momentarily overwhelming pleasure of your peachjuicemouth, but that is just background. And I remember what you said in the hospital room when we had ascertained I would live: even your allergies have to be poetic. Do you dare, Alfred Prufrock, do you dare?

That pleased me more than I ever told you.

If someone is reading this, it must be you, so you must still be alive despite claims to the contrary. I'm sorry I can't appear

111

to care more about this. I'll never see you again, so how can it matter? Still, now that they have allowed me to write at last, I'm writing to you. That must mean something.

I'm not really writing to you. How will this ever reach you, even if you are alive?

But why am I writing in our code, if not to write to you?

There is nothing like solitary confinement to make you lose any interest you ever had in self-analysis. Self-analysis! It's self-narrative, that's what it is. Create a story about yourself, and shape everything to fit that story. In my story I was always the one driven mad by love for you, even before I met you. I don't know how to interpret my actions now that I'm falling into an entirely different sort of insanity – the insanity of a twilight life, in which there is no distinction to be made between real and fictional worlds. Sometimes Rustum and Sohrab visit me in here, reliving over and over the battle in which father struck down son, until the room is so filled with recrimination and guilt that I have to banish them. The next day it's Virginia Woolf who wafts through. Hers is a curiously insistent presence; take your eyes off her for a moment and the next thing you know she's rearranging your syntax as though it were cutlery improperly laid out for a seven-course meal with some foreign dignitary who disdains your nation's table manners.

If I am no longer the man mad with love for you, does it mean I'm not me any more?

How tedious I've grown.

What should I tell you now, you who will never receive this?

Should I tell you I can't write poetry any more. Poetry? I can't write Urdu. My hand moves left to right across the page. There is a tide in the handwriting of men and I must flow with it. The first year they brought me here . . .

Why go back to that?

The first year they brought me here was the worst for many reasons but among those reasons was this: I had to break my addiction to writing. There was no paper anywhere. They kept me confined to the house – it was a room then; the Minions have added on over the years. Oh, the joy when they finally completed the kitchen! What a gourmet cook I've become, able to use anything they bring me. Sometimes they bring the strangest vegetables, things for which I have no vocabulary. I almost wonder if it's become a contest among them to try to produce something I cannot use.

Being confined to my one room meant I couldn't even walk out and pluck leaves from trees to serve as paper. And no watchband to write on either, as Hikmet did in his prison days. You know how fastidious I've always been, but enough days of remembering 'Make dust our parchment and with rainy eyes pour sorrow on the bosom of the earth' and I put aside the cleaning rags they had given me and let all surfaces around me become dulled. Then, a fingertip touched in saliva, and I was off! Words appeared, bright against their dust-covered surroundings. I who had always scribbled endlessly, covering page after page with doodles and letters and words that I merely liked to look at (you've noticed already the elaborate hand with which I've written this. I cannot bear the absence of physical beauty in the lines of the English alphabet. English has lines; Urdu has curves. Perhaps my use of English is mere sign of a dead libido. It's the sort of statement my critics would make. But no, look, haven't I restored splendour to this language with my near calligraphic flourishes?), I learned to hone phrases in my mind, and only write what I was sure of. The physical act of writing required me to suck dust off my fingers after every few characters. That made me think of you.

The Minions came in and found my words, remarkable words, the best I ever wrote, on every surface of the room. They filled buckets and drowned each image. Then they broke all my fingers, and left. This sort of thing went on for a while, though the first stands out in my memory most clearly.

Those were the early Minions. They've become more civilized since. Or perhaps I'm just too neutered to pose a threat.

You must have aged. In all the time I knew you, you only grew more beautiful.

Here is a memory of you that always makes me laugh:

It is 1971. I wrap around my shoulders that grey shawl you love. I haven't seen you in nearly four months, not since just before your wedding, haven't spoken to you since the day of the nikah when I phoned you to say I wasn't going to be dramatic and whisk you away on my white charger just seconds before you inked your contract and joined yourself in legitimate union to that weedy man, so you'd have to get out of the wedding on your own if you had the intelligence and courage to do it. I knew that would make you go through with the wedding which otherwise (I'm sure, though you always denied it) you were going to back out of at the last minute. I thought that was the surest way to win you back. I thought you'd last three days and then appear on my doorstep, humbled.

I underestimated your stubbornness.

In the end I had to make all the moves. I wrote *Laila* for you. Not the most conventional wooing poem ever written, but you knew it meant I was going insane with missing you. I alluded to you in an interview for a magazine to which I knew you subscribed. I flaunted my affairs in public, all with women you knew were not in any way to my taste. None of this was enough for you. You were silent, then more silent, and then, as though it were nothing, you announced to your friends who were also my friends that you were pregnant.

I still haven't entirely forgiven you for that.

So I wrap the grey shawl around my shoulders, let myself in through your gate and ring your door-bell. The Weed answers, and I think he or I would have put a knife through the other's heart if you hadn't been standing behind him asking who it was. He steps aside, and then I see you: your pregnancy still invisible to everyone including him, but to someone who knows your body as well as I do it is instantly obvious. You are holding a cookbook in one hand, a courgette in the other. I laugh so hard I have to lean against the door frame for support. 'Is that domesticity or a dildo?' I ask. 'Which of the two has this man driven you to?'

And bless you, you laugh with me.

'Both,' you say, and I know you are mine for ever.

This is why it's best not to write. Not even English. It jolts the memory. I had to put aside this page for days after writing that previous paragraph. I'll talk now only of my time in here, the years without you.

One day I just decided to stop. Stop trying to find ways to write in secret, stop writing in my head, stop remembering how it felt in those sweet moments when language obliterated me. You were so entwined in every word I wrote that I had to banish you too, though you did nothing to make that easy for me.

Then one day the Minions arrived with a book. A book! Not just any book, my love, but Shakespeare. The Complete Works of. That memory I wrote of earlier, the one from 1971, even that turns pale compared to this one. I kept thinking it meant they were going to kill me. Shakespeare as last meal. I didn't care. I held that book to my heart – black binding, faded gold lettering – and I wept. Huge great sobs from a place so far inside I didn't know it existed.

What I remembered then was Orwell. In *1984*, two years before they brought me here. Winston sometimes dreams of a world beyond the world of grey order, a world of green fields in which a woman takes her clothes off in a careless gesture that defies all authority. Without understanding why, Winston wakes up with the word 'Shakespeare' on his lips.

I told you once I would rather have written in English, despite its absence of curves. It was my politics that made me choose Urdu, more accessible to the public, less colonized. You rolled your eyes at me, but I was speaking the truth. I would rather have written English, purely because of Shakespeare. My first – and, it appears, most enduring – love. Another lie. The first love was Rashida, the schoolmaster's daughter, who was the only reason I went to his house for extra classes after school. Her hips, even at thirteen! And while I'm confessing lies, let me admit the choice of Urdu had nothing to do with public accessibility and everything to do with the fact that the grandeur of Shakespeare's language has gone out of English – it's a language that learned to use a knife and fork, though once it ripped chickens apart with its bare hands. Urdu still allows for lushness.

My favourite word in the English language: intrinsicate.

Shakespeare uses it to describe the bond between Antony and Cleopatra. The knot intrinsicate. He had the advantage, had Will, of living before dictionaries. He could do what he wanted with words and no one would use the awful phrase 'experimental', with all its connotations of impending failure. Intrinsicate. Both intricate and intrinsic.

My favourite definition in the English language: frass. It means 'excrement of boring larvae'. I choose to read 'boring' as a comment on personality. Is there any greater insult that you can think of? You frass! Not just excrement, not just excrement of larvae, but excrement of boring larvae. I yell it at the Minions sometimes. Frass! Frass! They continue to look impassive.

Did I always ramble this much?

They didn't kill me. (The Minions, I mean – keep up! – when they gave me Shakespeare.) They might even have looked amused. Since then, from time to time, they've added on to my library. I have to commend them on their tastes. Or on their knowledge of my tastes, perhaps. Or no, they are merely the delivery boys. For whom? There is the question to which I have no answer, though I've given it more than a little thought these last sixteen years.

Oh, and there you were, just as I wrote that last line, your eyebrows rising to impossible heights and your voice that extraordinary mix of sarcasm and tenderness: 'You always have an answer, sweetheart. It's just not always the right one.'

I'm beginning to miss you now, and I can't allow that to happen.

# IX

It had to be a hoax. It could only be a hoax.

Yes, a hoax. That's what it was. The Poet was dead.

But even if it was a hoax – no 'even if', Aasmaani, it is a hoax – who could have written it?

*I thought I was the only person left in the world who knew it, but it seems there are two of us now.*

My mother had said that the day I told her I still knew the code. If she was right, the only person who could have forged that communication and pretended it came from the Poet was her. Could my mother have tried to become the Poet just as Laila became Qais? I could feel myself falling into the strangeness of that thought, began picturing my mother running into barbed wire, and then I pulled my mind sharply out. It was an absurd idea, both too far-fetched and too neatly symmetrical – life never imitated art in quite that way – to be anything but false.

But if only three people ever knew the code and I could rule out my mother and myself as writers of that piece, what conclusion was left?

Someone else had to have known the code.

And yet it sounded so much like him.

Too much like him. It sounded too much like him. No, that wasn't true. There was a resignation to that tone which was never part of his voice.

So then it's proof he didn't write it.

But in sixteen years of course he would have changed.

He's dead, Aasmaani.

Yes, of course he's dead, but all I'm saying is . . .

Is what?

That it sounds so much like the way it would sound if it were true.

All right. List them. List the ways in which it sounds like him, and the ways it doesn't, and in those lists you'll find the flaw, the lie which will blow down that elaborate edifice.

And if I don't find the flaw?

You'll find it.

But if I don't?

Make the lists!

All right. All right.

The ways it doesn't sound like him: Resignation. Giving up poetry and my mother. (But he explains that. And the explanation makes sense. And he doesn't really give her up, does he, because he's writing to her.) Becoming an enthusiastic cook. The story of the courgette. There – that's the lie. That isn't how it happened.

See, I told you.

But . . .

What?

If it had happened that way, Mama would never have told me. We're talking about the moment she left my father. How could she tell me such a line as 'Domesticity or a dildo'? No, she would not tell me that. But I could imagine him – the Poet – I could imagine him saying it. There was that bawdy streak in him, and she loved it, though she pretended not to.

Keep going, then. Keep going with the list of all the ways it doesn't sound like the Poet.

That's it. That's the list. He's learnt resignation, he's given up poetry and he's become an enthusiastic cook.

So then, it isn't him.

But I've done all those things in the last sixteen years, though it seemed inconceivable when I was fourteen and he was alive.

The other list, then. All the ways in which it sounds like him.

Everything. The voice. *What should I tell you now, you who will never receive this?* That was a sentence structure he liked to use. *What will you become, you with the eclectic mind?* He wrote that on a card for me, on my thirteenth birthday. *You were silent, then more silent.* That's an echo of something he said when he described to me the first time he saw my mother. *She was beautiful, then more beautiful.*

But he's a poet. Of course he has a distinctive voice. It only means it's more easily imitated.

In Urdu. It's easily imitated in Urdu, not in English. Urdu was his public language. And then, there are all those details. The peach allergy. The schoolmaster's daughter and her hips. The grey shawl. Shakespeare. Yes, that particularly. I was there when he told my mother he would rather have written in English. That entire conversation. It was him and me and her. I was studying *Julius Caesar* for an exam. That's what started it. Just weeks before he died. There was no one there but the three of us.

He doesn't mention you. Doesn't that prove something?

No. Nothing.

But one of them could have told someone else about the conversation.

Gue.

Yes. I thought of that. Gue.

He loved finding oddball definitions in dictionaries. One day he called me up from Colombia, sat by the phone for hours waiting for the trunk call to be put through, so he could say, 'Look up "gue" in the dictionary, Aasmaani.' He and I had the same dictionary; he gave it to me as a present precisely so we could play this game. Gue is 'a kind of rude violin'. He loved that. He would love Frass. It is exactly the sort of thing he would love.

But it's impossible.

It's extremely improbable.

120

You can't allow yourself to start believing this.

But no matter how hard I looked for a sign that would prove, incontrovertibly, that is wasn't him, I couldn't find it. Hours went by, in which I first read and reread the pages, then wrote them out in plain English, just to have some different way of approaching them. When that proved fruitless I tried to impose order: start with paragraph one, I told myself, reread it and consider what it means. Why would someone put down that information rather than any other? Find the mind behind the words. But the only mind I encountered was the Poet's.

I heard Rabia come home. I wanted to call out to her, but then I imagined her look of panic if I told her what had happened, imagined her tearing up the pages, saying, someone's just playing a sick game with you, I'm calling Beema and Dad. And if I showed anything but utter willingness to agree with her and accept it as a hoax then it would all return to the days just after Mama left when I used to ask operators to trace calls, and searched everywhere for clues and conspiracies. In those days, Dad, Beema and Rabia were constantly accumulating and weighing evidence about whether I was getting better or not, watching me at all times, suggesting we 'talk' about 'feelings', forcing me to lie more and more convincingly just so that they would stop watching, stop gathering evidence, think I was improving. Sometimes I managed to fool Dad and Rabia, but never Beema. But now Beema had a dying mother, and the least I could do for her was allow that to be the centre of her world.

I heard Rabia and Shakeel go out. They knocked on the connecting door first but I stayed utterly still and didn't answer. It was only when they were gone that I wanted to take the letters to Rabia and tell her what they said.

Peaches. Broken fingers. My mother's kisses. Hikmet. The Poet alive. Someone trying to convince me – no, Shehnaz Saeed – that the Poet was alive. Why Shehnaz? The words were not my mother's. This wasn't the sign from her I'd been waiting for. I was no closer. And yet, the Poet alive. Not true. Domesticity or a dildo. Larvae. Her unforgivable pregnancy. I couldn't piece any of it together, couldn't hold on to one thought long enough to produce a reaction before another thought barrelled around the corner and derailed the first one.

At length, I stopped trying. I lay on my sofa, looking at the sun setting fiercely into the sea, individual words and phrases littered round my head like crumbs that can never be reconstituted into a slice of sense.

There was a cobweb in a corner of the room, so delicate my breath could send each thread spiralling into the darkness. Prufrock. Intrinsicate. Left to right. Right to left. Frass, Shakespeare, the grey shawl, no mention of me.

A shadow of an explanation swerved into my mind, and then swerved away again. I almost had it. A way out of here. That missing piece which would reveal the face of the mystery. But I would never have that missing piece – that was the torture of this near-delirium of overwrought thinking. I would only repeat the leaps from one thought to the other, each leap pushing the words further away from meaning. But I couldn't stop, I couldn't do anything but leap.

Someone was ringing the door-bell. Door-bells don't ring for ever. You just need the patience to wait them out. But this one kept on, an insistently merry 'ding' that soon grew frenzied, its cheer transmuting into increasing hysteria the longer I ignored it. Then the phone started ringing. At the same moment, my mobile beeped to announce a text message. The mobile was next to me. I raised a hand, pressed down on the keypad. Whose number was that? I pressed again and a message appeared: PLEASE OPEN THE DOOR. ED

Ed. Go away.

But then I sat up. He would prove it to me. I would read him the decrypted message, and he would tell me that it was impossible. He would tell me why it was impossible. My mind was too desperate for hope. I must be missing something,

something obvious. But Ed would see it. Ed was smart. Ed would release me from this.

I was on my feet, running to the door. I opened it, and there he stood, holding up a brown bag moulded in the shape of a bottle, in a pose reminiscent of the Statue of Liberty.

'I've brought a bottle of wine and an amusing anecdote as peace offerings.'

'Wine here tastes like vinegar.' I turned to walk back into the flat. There was a slight pause, and then I heard him following me in.

I headed towards the lounge, towards the encrypted pages, but Ed saw the kitchen, sauntered into it and came out with a corkscrew and two tumblers. I surprised myself by thinking that there was something in the way he entered my kitchen that I liked; not proprietary, not like so many men in Karachi who assumed they could walk into your home and act as though they owned it, but more familiar, as though we were past the need to be formal with each other. Then he held out a glass to me, and in that instant when it passed from his hand to mine I remembered the distaste with which he had thrown the envelope at my feet.

'Look, I'm sorry,' he said. 'My mother sent the letter for you. None of it was my business. It's just . . .'

'Yes?' When he was speaking, my mind could latch on to his words. Words which made sense, each letter slotting neatly into its place, all the letters together forming words and sentences with spaces between them, the spaces acting as transmitters of meaning and not as gulfs which kept each word, each sentence, separate and unbridgeable.

'You were treating me like some no-account delivery boy. My ego objected.'

'It wasn't about you, Ed.' I sat down on the sofa and glanced over to the papers on the low table.

'That's what my ego objected to.' He looked into his wine glass and then up at me again. 'You want to hear the amusing anecdote?' The sunset had been swallowed up in darkness and now a single beam of light from an unknown source came through the balcony window and lit up the wine in his glass to ruby, everything else in the flat existing in muted shades at the midpoint of colour and shadow.

'No. Do you want to know what was in the envelope your mother sent me?'

He had brought the rim of the glass up to his face again but the question made him forget to tilt the wine into his mouth, so he just stood there, his lower lip adhered to the glass, looking like a man who has seen a gorgon at a cocktail party.

Then he blinked, sipped, and put the glass down on the coffee table. 'I know it was more . . . what did you call it . . . calligraphy, if that's what you're going to tell me. I opened the envelope and looked inside before I brought it to you.'

'Your mother didn't show it to you?'

For a moment he was silent as though trying to decide what exactly to tell me. 'Let's just say I wasn't exactly pleased with my mother for giving you the first piece of calligraphy. So when that second one arrived during lunch she sneaked off without showing it to me and asked her driver to deliver it to you at STD. Fortunately the driver is a lazy bastard and decided just to wait until I was returning to the office and hand it over to me instead.'

'Does she know . . . ?'

'That I'm aware of her deception? No.'

'So it wouldn't be wholly inaccurate to say you have a somewhat strained relationship with your mother, Mir Adnan Akbar Khan.'

He smiled and looked just a little embarrassed. 'I love her, I really do. And I'm close to her, more than most men and their mothers. But that's why it just drives me crazy when she acts like we're in some soap opera in which every tiny moment has to have secrecy and suspense added to it. Really.' He was laughing now as though it had just occurred to him that he'd been living in a joke. 'The cook comes in with something that's been delivered in the letterbox. My mother sees the familiar handwriting on the envelope. She leaps up from her chair and darts to get it. The unsuspecting son asks her what it is. She says, nothing important. She is clearly lying. Then she says she just remembered she needs the driver to run an errand for her. She rushes out. When she comes back, she is clearly flustered. Exclamation exclamation.' He smiled again and rolled his eyes. 'It gets a bit exhausting.'

She had seemed so utterly different to me – too ironic about her profession to become the stereotype of the actress who cannot separate reality from drama. But I only said, 'Mothers can be that way.'

He came to sit next to me on the sofa and touched the back of my hand, very lightly. 'She told me about that code your mother and the Poet used. She told me she thought those garbled lines might be written in code. That's why I was angry with her for sending it to you. I thought she wasn't taking into account how you might feel about getting something you couldn't read and then wondering if it was your mother and the Poet's code. That's why, even with the second set of pages, I didn't know whether to give them to you or not. I was, I'll be honest, I was on my way to shred them when I heard a sound from your office and I went in to see if you were OK. I didn't intend for you to get those pages. I don't . . .' He ran his hand over his face. 'Look, my mother told me you still think your mother is alive and,' he held up his hands before I could react, as though anticipating a blow, 'I'm not saying she isn't. I don't know, I . . . that's your thing, your situation . . . I'm just . . . I don't think getting pages of weird writing you can't read but which you imagine is written by her will help anything. I saw that covering letter. It's obviously some crazy fan of my mother's. They send her all kinds of oddball stuff, just to get her attention.'

'Ed, I can read it.'

'Oh.' He leaned back against the sofa cushions. 'Oh. Oh, God. I really was going to shred it.'

I hadn't known until then if I was going to read the pages to him. I had no reason to trust him, to believe anything he might say about them. But right then it was clear – I needed to read them simply to give him a reason not to shred the next set of pages that might arrive at his house. With that clarity came such relief, as though all I had really wanted all along was a reason to have someone else share the burden of so inexplicable a secret. From the papers I had been holding, I pulled out the decrypted version of the coded pages and started reading out loud. He didn't say anything all the way through, just sat there sipping wine, first from his glass and then from mine.

When I finished reading, Ed said, 'Lordalmighty.'

'That seems as good a response as any I can think of. Did you follow all of it?'

'All?' He put a hand to his head. 'I don't follow any of it. It's not . . .' He frowned. 'Did you read that it's been sixteen years the writer of that has been trying to figure out who his captor is?' I nodded. 'And how long has it been . . . ?'

'Since the Poet died? Sixteen years.'

'But you can't really . . . I mean, it can't . . .' Those were the words, the ones I had wanted him to say and suddenly, passionately – I had to turn away so he wouldn't know – hated him for saying. Then he said, 'Can it?'

There was a single drop of wine on the bottom of my tumbler. I tilted the glass, reached in and held my finger lightly against its surface. When I moved my finger away, the drop came with it.

Ed stood up. 'There were all those rumours, weren't there? That he hadn't really died.'

'Yes.' I didn't know any more what I wanted of him.

'But your mother must have seen the body. Right? And she'd know if it was his body.' He turned red. 'I don't mean that in any vulgar way.'

It was the oddest moment of propriety. 'She never saw the body.'

'But . . .'

'But, it's still absurd. I know. And impossible.' There, I had said it, and as soon as I said it I saw it must be true. The flaw was not in his style, his voice, his anecdotes. The flaw was simply in the situation, so utterly ridiculous that no one could actually intend the whole fabrication to be taken seriously. 'I mean, for heaven's sake. How can someone be kept prisoner for sixteen years, with shifting sets of lackeys looking in on him, without anyone else finding out about it? You're right, it's absurd.' I stood up, feeling nothing but embarrassed for having revealed too much of my own weaknesses to him. 'I'm sorry for having taken up so much of your time.' I didn't mean for my voice to sound so distant, so formal. 'I see that it's absurd.'

He nodded, and stood up. I held out my hand to him, unable to move out of formality or to find some way to ask him to stay and talk to me of other things. He took my hand. Outside there was gunfire, rapid bursts of it into the sky. His fingers pressed down on mine in surprise and I remembered that he'd been away for years.

'It's just celebration,' I said. 'The Ruhat-e-Hilal committee must have seen the new moon. Ramzan starts tomorrow.'

'Of course,' he said, still holding my hand.

'I suppose that means you'll be heading off to film that Ramzan special. Guess I'll see you in another month. Hope it goes well.'

I tried to pull my hand out of his but he held on, rotated his wrist so that his hand was covering mine, clasping it. 'What would it mean to you?' he said. 'If I said, no, it's not absurd. Believing those pages might be genuine. It's not necessarily absurd.'

'How can it not be absurd?' My voice a whisper.

He smiled. 'Oh, you urban girl in your modern world. Have you no idea of the kinds of things that go on in secret, for generation after generation, in parts of the country that exist outside the reach of the law? When people have power, land, opportunity and no one to say no to them, the only limits on what they can do is the limit of their own imaginations. Years of secret imprisonment may be absurd, but it's possible.'

'Sixteen years, Ed!' I pulled my hand out of his.

'Sixteen days, sixteen years. What difference does it make? Ask this question—' All at once he was fired up. 'Why would someone imprison a man, and make his family believe he was dead?'

I stepped back and crossed my arms. It was as though we were in the office, talking about storylines for a proposed drama. 'You make them believe he's dead so no one comes looking for him. That's easy. You imprison him, I don't know. For hatred, fear, vengeance. Any unpleasant motive will do.'

'And how many people had cause to hate him, to fear him!' Ed said. 'Think about that. God, he spat on the powerful with impunity. He was fearless, utterly.'

No. If he was fearless, he wouldn't have left all those times, taking my mother with him.

She left. She chose to go. He didn't force her, he never once forced her.

'Once you imprison him and make the world believe he's dead, then what? You can't just let him go when you've had fun with the game. If you let him go, there'll be an invest-igation, there could be complications. He's too famous for there not to be complications. And really, why should you want to let him go? Once you've set everything up – set up the place you keep him, set up the loyal or terrified under-lings who attend to him – you can just leave him there to rot. Leave him there, hidden away somewhere in your vast land holdings, until he dies.'

'So you think it's a landowner who's behind all this?' I couldn't stop myself.

Ed held up his palms to the ceiling in a gesture that encom-passed all the strangeness of the universe. 'It's possible. I'm not saying it's true, but it's possible. Stranger things go on around here every day. There are vast parts of this country,

Aasmaani, which are still mediaeval in both their mindsets and their rules. And if these pages aren't some kind of forgery or game, well then, his jailer could be anyone, really, with enough money to pull it off. Can you pinpoint a location it's coming from? Postmarks?'

'The first from Multan or Mardan. The second from Quetta. And, anyway, the cover letter, I don't know, it . . .'

'Seems false. Yes. And why would someone send all that to my mother in the first place?' He looked suddenly unconvinced.

'I don't know. But there are things in there which sound so much like him, Ed, that it would be uncanny for someone to have made it up.'

There was a moment of silence in which we simply looked at each other.

'Aasmaani, do you really think it's him?'

I shook my head. 'I don't know. I don't know. It's too often, Ed, I've slipped into believing things only to find they weren't true. I can't keep doing it. And yet. If it is true . . .' I closed my eyes and leaned back against the wall.

I felt his hand brush my cheek. 'What can I do?'

I shook my head, my eyes still closed. 'Will you be offended if I ask you to leave?'

'Don't be silly. How could I be offended at anything you might choose to say right now?' My eyes were still closed, and I felt his breath on my mouth before his lips followed. I put my arm around his neck, and for a few seconds we stayed like that, our lips just resting on each other, the only movement my fingers stroking the nape of his neck.

When we moved apart, he said, 'I don't have to leave until tomorrow afternoon. So I'll see you in the morning, OK? Come and find me when you get to work.' He kissed my cheek. 'I'll let myself out.'

As soon as I heard the door close behind him, my body slid down to the ground. I pulled my legs up to my chest and wrapped my arms around them.

The Poet – my almost-stepfather – was being imprisoned

somewhere by an unknown captor. He had been there sixteen, nearly seventeen, years. Sixteen years during which he'd had no human contact except for his captor's lackeys who broke his fingers and erased his poems. He'd been told my mother was dead. He'd lost the ability to write Urdu. But he was alive. Omi was alive.

For a moment I felt something surge up inside and I had to clasp my hands against my chest as though that could push it down. I would not do this again. I would not move back into that seductive place which promised answers, that place which could only lead to despair each time an expected resolution revealed itself to only be a mirage. The Poet was dead. Omi was dead. Somewhere in the world there was proof. Where? Who knew the details of his death, who could give me the proof I had never before felt the need to search out?

Mirza the Snake. He went to the morgue and then to the funeral. He would have seen the body. Yes, he had the proof. Mirza had the proof. Whoever was playing this sick game with Shehnaz Saeed, and for whatever purpose, it had nothing to do with me.

I carried the pages to the bookshelf, paying no attention to the Fata Morgana shaking its head behind me as I placed them between the covers of *War and Peace*, two-thirds of the way through the book, and knelt on the ground to push the tome into an empty space on the bottom shelf.

# X

When the phone rang at five the following morning and woke me out of a dream about dreaming I thought it could only mean someone must have died.

'Are you coming over for sehri, or what?' Rabia said when I answered, panicked.

'Oh, bugger.'

Rabia laughed. 'It's the Holy Month. Be good. No abuse.'

I rolled out of bed and when my feet hit the bare ground in the space between my bed and the rug there was a thrilling sensation of cold. That promised winter had arrived, though it would probably be gone by dawn. I pulled on my dressing-gown, opened the window and leaned out. Over the loud-speaker of the nearby mosque came the impassioned chanting of Arabic. I felt a moment of irritation on behalf of the non-fasters who would have to put up with a sustained guilt trip for the next four weeks. Ramzan was a month when the holier-than-thous were in their element. We used to have one of them as a neighbour, and every year she'd make a list of people who weren't fasting, and every day of the month before daybreak she'd call someone on the list and recite Qur'ānic verses down the phone, hoping to affect a change of heart. She made the mistake of calling the Poet once and, with his limited knowledge of Arabic, he realized she was reading, at random, a verse about inheritance laws: being well aware of both the woman's identity and her family scandals, he responded by pointing out that under the God-ordained laws she had just read out she and her husband had cheated her sister-in-law of her rightful share of the family fortune.

Omi, if I could only believe you were still alive.

I made my way into Rabia's flat and found her arm-wrestling her husband on the living-room floor. I stopped a moment, unnoticed, to watch them. They made an incongruous couple – Rabia, petite and full of energy, and Shakeel, tall and languid. They had met at his first solo exhibition – Rabia didn't know who he was, just saw a skinny man with long eyelashes who seemed to be the only person not oohing and aahing over the paintings, and went over to him. Her opening remark to Shakeel was, 'So this guy claims he's not interested in being an artist for high-society ladies to collect and then he goes and paints such massive canvases that only really rich people with huge rooms will be able to hang up any of his paintings.' They were married within a year.

Rabia, yelling in frustration, had Shakeel's hand caught between both her hands. Shakeel was looking at her in adoration and making no attempt to win the struggle. Hearing me laugh, Shakeel looked up, and Rabia took that moment of distraction to slam his hand on to the floor and let out a cry of victory.

'Well, so much for being the brawn,' Shakeel said, standing up. He walked up to me and whispered, 'Who was the gentleman caller I saw leaving your flat as we were returning last night, young lady?'

I slapped him lightly on the shoulder. Shakeel liked to make much of the three-week age gap between us. He and I had a relationship in which frivolous conversation combined with deep affection in a way that meant I would never tell him any of my secrets or worries but was always perfectly content for him to be in the room on those rare occasions when I talked to Rabia about the things that were on my mind.

'If he turns out to be significant, I'll let you know.'

Shakeel laughed as he walked towards his studio – for him

Ramzan was an opportunity to start work early. 'He walked down the stairs like a man who thinks he is significant.'

It hadn't taken long after Ed left for me to regret reading the pages out to him, and to wonder what he really believed they meant. It was so sudden, his shift from disbelief to conviction, that I couldn't help wonder if it was a change of heart or manipulation. But it was no more sudden, I had to admit, than my shifts in thinking about him. Just as I felt relieved that he was going to be leaving for a month I'd remember the promise and lack of insistence of his lips on mine and then I wanted nothing more than for Ed to stay.

Rabia called out my name and I followed her voice into the kitchen, where she had tea and French toast ready for us – a sisterly ritual for the first day of Ramzan that went back as long as I could remember.

'I'm considering a boycott of Ramzan,' I said. 'To protest the rising power of the Machiavellian Mullah Alliance.'

'If you boycott religion because of them you only strengthen their claim to being guardians and interpreters of that religion.'

'Oh, shut up. I was being facetious.' I opened the window to the sounds of people clanking around kitchens in surrounding flats. This was one of the chief joys of Ramzan – this evidence of everyone engaged in eating before daybreak, the transformation of that solitary hour into something communal.

Rabia pulled up two high stools to the kitchen counter and sat down to eat. 'Day before yesterday, at seven a.m., I found biryani ingredients, chopped and ground, in your kitchen. They weren't there at one a.m. the night before when I went to get a glass of water while you were on the balcony. Therefore,' she pointed her finger at me, and I couldn't tell if what was to follow was a punch-line or a verdict, 'you were preparing a meal between one a.m. and seven a.m.'

'I'm sorry,' I said, sitting down beside her. 'Was there a spice curfew on during the night of which I'm unaware? Have I transgressed the unwritten laws of when a chicken can be chopped?'

Rabia crossed her arms. 'I know what it means when you cook at strange hours. What was on your mind?'

'Food, I imagine.'

'That's not even amusing.'

'Do I detect an edge there, Rabia? Are you trying to get angry with me?'

'Trying? You think I can't get angry at you?'

'You don't get angry, Little, you get compassionate.' I cut off a piece of French toast and held it in front of my eyes. There was nothing even remotely appealing about it.

'I was angry when you joined the oil company,' Rabia said. 'I was bloody furious then.' She attacked her French toast with knife and fork, cutting it into pieces with a concentration which suggested that the eating of the toast was an incidental afterthought. 'I still am. What point were you trying to make?'

She had been asking me this question at regular intervals over the last three years and the demise of my corporate persona had done nothing to put it out of her head.

'Some people, Rabia, have the luxury of doing things they love. Of knowing, this is what I want to spend my life in pursuit of, and then being in pursuit of it. Whether it's Shakeel with his art, or you with your women's upliftment projects – though, honestly, Rabia, that sounds like you're a plastic surgeon.' She didn't laugh, which was a bad sign. 'You're the lucky ones. You don't have to spend the greater proportion of your life in an office somewhere, unable to remember quite why it is that you're doing this particular thing rather than any of those other things out there, rather than any of those things you wanted to do when you were eleven years old. But we don't all have that luck. Some of us just go to work and get through the day. Now will you cut my toast?'

'No. Because impressive as that little speech is, it doesn't answer "Why you, why the oil company?"' She swapped plates with me, and began cutting my French toast.

Why the oil company, she wanted to know. Because why

134

not, Rabia? Because it makes no difference. That was what I could throw at her if she made me just a little angrier.

But she sat across from me, cutting the toast according to an elaborate system of diagonals, and she was still my baby sister. 'Why the oil company? For the same reason I'm not going to give you a straight answer: to irritate the life out of you.' I reached across and made an incision in the toast which ruined the pattern she'd been carving.

She didn't look at me. 'You have no idea how hard it is to be your sister sometimes.'

There was silence for a few seconds as we both chewed on our toast. 'Do I embarrass you?' I said at length, more bothered by her comment than I was willing to admit. 'Around all your NGO friends, when you have to admit that your sister used to work for the oil company, and now she's moved on to a quiz show. Does that embarrass you? Is that why it's hard being my sister?'

She looked at me in such surprise it made me want to weep. 'All the sadness in my life has to do with you. That's what's hard. And please don't tell me that you're fine.'

I held my mug up to the side of my face, the porcelain burning against my cheek. 'I get through the day, Rabia.'

'Oh, Smaani.' She pushed down on my wrist so the mug of tea came to rest on the kitchen counter. 'When did that start being nearly enough?'

I lifted my shoulders and let them drop again. 'So long ago I'm surprised you remember when it was different.'

She put her hand on mine. 'Don't you know how much I hero-worshipped you when I was a kid? You were Marie Curie crossed with Emily Brontë crossed with Joan of Arc to me when I was ten. And when I told you that, you said my cultural references were the sign of a colonized mind.'

'I didn't! You mean I was that irritating, even at fourteen?'

'You were that smart. That's how I saw it. Particularly when you were around the Poet. You and he were always talking about things I couldn't even begin to understand.'

There was nothing he ever believed I was too young to understand or discuss. Religion, politics, the tension that can be generated by the need for a rhyme. 'What do you remember about him?'

'The Poet? Not that much. I was so young when he died. And even before that, I always felt I would be disloyal to Dad if I went too often with you to your mother's house when they were in Karachi.' She shook her head. 'He really is the only person I can think of who could get Dad so riled up. And I don't even remember them having a single conversation, ever. But just the mention of his name and poof! Dad's face would turn red like he'd heard some incantation to overturn mild-manneredness. Do you think we'll ever hear the full details of the day your mother left him for the Poet?'

*Domesticity or a dildo? To which of those horrors has this man driven you?*

And Mama had laughed and said, 'Both.' What must it have taken for Dad to have agreed to allow her to move back into his house after the Poet died, with the memory of that 'Both' in his mind? And before that, what must it have taken for him to stand by and watch Beema and my mother become as close as they were without ever, to my knowledge, objecting? All because of me, I knew. Yet when I was growing up I only saw that he never allowed the Poet into his house, not even at my birthday parties, and that he barely spoke to Mama himself and always kept utterly quiet when Beema told me how much cause I had to be proud of my mother.

'But I also used to resent him a lot,' Rabia said. 'The Poet, I mean. Him and your mother.'

'Why?'

'Because they'd go into exile and take you away from me. Why is that funny?'

'It's not. It's ironic. I used to resent how much I got left behind.'

'Every summer and winter holiday, Aasmaani, you'd be

gone. Colombia, Egypt, wherever. I was the only girl in school who hated the holidays.'

Eleven weeks a year. That's all the time I had with my mother from the age of nine to twelve. She wasn't there when I got my first period, had my first crush, bought my first music album. She wasn't there for any of that. But I realized now that the time I spent with Mama, brief as it was, must have seemed immense to Rabia during those years. How old was she – only eight? – when they came back from the three-year exile? In those early years of her life I idolized my mother so completely and always yearned to be where she was – Rabia must have learned to fear that one day Mama would really take me with her, and then I would become a house-guest who occasionally flitted through my sister's life while on holiday from schools in distant parts of the world.

'I'm sorry.'

She shook her head, suddenly brisk with that air she had when she decided it was time to get to the bottom of a mystery – whether that mystery was a choked drainpipe or some knotty part of my psyche. 'What I want to know is when did it stop?' She gathered up the plates and walked over to the sink. 'Do you even know? When did you stop believing in all those things you were so passionate about? All those political ideals, notions of inspiration and activism and all that good stuff which you used to lecture me about in response to a question as seemingly apolitical as "Can I borrow your Walkman?" Was it when the Poet died or when your mother disappeared? I can't remember.'

The precise moment when everything inside you breaks. 'Neither. It was over a month after Mama left. It was 17 August, 1988.'

'Why does that date ring a bell? Oh. Oh yes.'

In June that year, General Mohammad Zia-ul-Haq dismissed the civilian government he had handpicked which, against expectations, was showing signs of independence. Amidst his grievances against the government, Zia included a lack of progress in the Islamization of the country and announced that henceforth sharia would be the supreme law of the land. This move towards theocracy sent violent tremors down the spine of the women's movement, which knew that Zia's Islam concerned itself primarily with striking down the rights of women and befriending fundamentalists. But when I heard the news, I felt that same impulse of joy that I relived just a few weeks before when the religious alliance won all those seats in the elections. Now Mama will return, I thought to myself, even though she hadn't yet removed her physical presence from our midst. She'll return to being herself. I wasn't the only one to think so; more than one of her activist friends called up to say they were planning a massive protest rally in Lahore, and would she come? She refused to take any of their calls. When I found that out, I ran into her room.

'You're going, you're going!' I yelled at her. 'And if you don't, I'll hate you for ever.'

'You're liable to do that in any case,' she replied, and before I could respond she had drifted away though she remained standing just feet away from me.

Later that night she came into my room so late she must have thought I would be asleep. She sat on the edge of my bed and stroked my hair. 'Mama, who will save the world if you don't?' I said, but though she wept a little my entreaties had no more effect on her than my anger. I kept trying, though – for the next couple of weeks I applied myself single-mindedly to convincing my mother to go to the rally. No manipulation, no cruelty was out of bounds. She put up with it for a couple of weeks and then, just days before the rally, she left.

But even when she was gone, I held on. To what, I don't know. I had no name for it, but I had a clear picture of what it was. The picture was of a group of young soldiers, looking up at a sky bursting with stars, their expressions purely of longing. My mother had that picture framed by her bedside when she lived next door to the Poet. She said it expressed so clearly that our greatest desire was for contentment, that was the strongest pull of all. To sit under a starry sky with your friends and dream. That is what the human soul wants, that is humanity in repose. Whether we're fighting unjust laws, or dictatorial governments, or the destruction of the mangrove swamps, Aasmaani, we're ultimately fighting for the luxury of that repose.

Even after the Poet died and the picture disappeared from her bedside, even after she left, I continued to believe the essential truth of what that picture had told me. Humanity in repose – that was a phrase I loved. She would find her way back to that truth, back to the necessity of fighting for it, I knew, and all the strangeness of the previous two years would be replaced by a return to the woman she was when she believed it. And that woman would come home.

But, instead, on 17 August 1988, General Mohammad Zia-ul-Haq boarded a plane in Bahawalpur, which exploded minutes after take-off.

When news reached me of his death, that was the moment I saw all my mother's stories of contentment and repose as nothing more than fairy stories. Even if true, they counted for nothing. That was the moment I broke. All those years she had fought against Zia's government – she and the Poet – with rallies and speeches and poems. And it had got them nowhere. It had got him tortured and killed; it had got her – well, there were no words for that, either. Those little victories they'd achieved, they were nothing but little. And that rally in Lahore, what had come of that? Nothing. Nothing. All those noble means of resisting came to nothing. But then someone – no one even knew who – put a bomb in a plane, and the General exploded, and already, within hours of his death, they were saying, there really might be elections now, real elections. There might be – oh God, I had been raised to whisper the word like a prayer – democracy. Because someone put a bomb on a plane. That is how things happen in the world. That is how you resist tyranny. By becoming it, by becoming it absolutely. It was the only effective way.

Everything you ever did, Mama, was nothing. All those years you fought, all those bruises, all the agonies I went through when you were imprisoned – for nothing. And you saw that, didn't you, well before I did? When the Poet died – no words of his powerful enough to turn away a hammer or a fist – you saw the futility of that life you had lived so passionately. That's why you made the choice you did, the one I started to understand that 17 August, though it would be a long time before I fully acknowledged it.

'Should we be happy?' thirteen-year-old Rabia had asked, coming into my room and hearing me say Zia was dead. When I heard that – my baby sister, all wide eyes and good intentions, wanting to know whether to feel happy about a bomb blast that killed a planeload of people – I banged my head against the wall and howled with tears that left my throat raw.

'God, you scared the life out of me that day,' Rabia said, her hands covered in soapy water. 'All that bawling and flailing. It didn't help that I'd just seen *The Exorcist*.'

I laughed, and ran my hand through my hair. 'Rabia, I've had a wretched week.'

'Hallelujah!' she said. 'An admission of misery. You going to tell me why?'

I shrugged and went to dry the dish she was holding out to me. 'Some days just seem to have so many hours in them.'

'I see. It's Aasmaani the Obscure again. Let me make a wild guess here – when you had lunch with Shehnaz Saeed, she spoke to you about your mother, didn't she?'

'She tried. She gave me the oh-how-the-nation-needs-her speech.'

Rabia dunked the frying pan in soap suds and flicked her wet hands in the direction of a hanging plant – a trick she'd learned from our snapdragon neighbour. 'Well, the nation does.'

'Oh, please.'

'You do, too – no one's denying that . . .'

'I'm not accusing anyone of denying that.' The words came out angrier than I expected. I was so tired of the way Rabia always approached me with such care around the subject of my mother, as though I might shatter into a million pieces if she didn't say exactly the right thing. 'Sorry. I'm still sleepy, that's all.' I kissed her forehead and started to walk away.

'We're just starting a conversation here,' Rabia said, but I shook my head and kept going. 'Why is it so necessary for you to believe that version of her life, Aasmaani?' she called out. I turned slightly. 'Why is it so necessary for you to believe her activism amounted to nothing?'

What was that line in the encrypted pages? *Create a story about yourself, and shape everything to fit that story.*

I entered my flat and locked the door behind me. Here, in my mind, were so many different images of my mother. My mother at twenty-three in a white kurta, lapis lazuli at her wrist. My mother at twenty-six, unable to resist an ex-lover in a grey shawl. My mother at twenty-seven, carrying me into a prison. My mother at thirty-four, rallying women together. My mother at thirty-five, running after the Poet to Colombia, leaving the women and me behind. My mother at thirty-eight, her body covered in bruises from a policeman's lathi, preparing to go out and lead another demonstration. My mother at forty, still dancing to old Donna Summers records. My mother at forty-one, allowing her grief over the Poet to consume her. My mother at forty-two, worse than she had been the year before. My mother at forty-three, gone.

What connected all the women in those images – the activist, the mother, the lover, the mourner, the dancer, the deserter? What allowed a single 'version' to arise from such variedness? There was a word for it: character. That imaginary tyrant. We pretend we all have one, and that it is something to be relied upon, something knowable and true, even when it oppresses and constrains us. When someone behaves 'out of character' we frown a little, a voice inside us whispering something that makes us uneasy, but then our brows clear. We've found a way to reinterpret the action as being in character. Or we say we were wrong about the person's character to begin with, and now, magically, our memory is able to furnish us with clues which would have revealed as much had we but picked up on them earlier. Otherwise, the person is deceptive; showing one face to the world while knowing all along that face was just a mask, ready to be ripped off with dramatic force. We don't dare consider that the internal voice which makes us uneasy is a voice that whispers: there is no such thing as fixed character, there is only our need to join the dots into a single picture.

Anything that doesn't fit the picture, we just forget about, or re-imagine.

I moved away from the door I had been leaning against and started to pace the length of the room. The joke of it, of course, is that we ourselves become slaves to the stories of our own characters. Our invented narratives of self determine our actions and reactions – I am brave; I am fickle; in such and such a situation I will behave in such and such a fashion. Character is just an invention, but it's an invention that serves as both reason and justification for our behaviour. It is the self-fulfilling prophecy that guides our lives, worming its way so deep beneath the levels of conscious thought that we forget there might have been a time when our 'defining traits' seemed less than inevitable. We are able to look back on our lives and chart our 'development of character', never seeing that it's the development of a storyline, and the longer we live with it the more boxed in we are by the rapidly diminishing variedness of our imagined selves. What we can't ever accept is that we might never know who we are.

I pushed open the door that led out to the balcony and breathed deep the carbon dioxide expelled by the plants around me. No – it's more terrifying than even that. What we can't begin to consider is that there is no consistent 'I', only a somewhat consistent outward form that houses such a vast set of possibilities that there would be anarchy if not for the tyranny of character. What frightens us most about this is knowing how easily we might have picked up another script, been governed by another tyrant, and so lived another life. I sank my hand into the loam in a flowerpot, and held it up to my nose. It smelt of hope, awful and richly glorious at the same time.

And all around us, people are reinforcing our notions by telling us, directly and in their treatment of us, who we are, what we believe in. At what point does character-playing become habit, something for which we are grateful because it allows us to go through the world with the ease that comes from being predictable to ourselves, even if that predictability takes the form of neurosis, hysteria, depression? And at what point does that habit turn darkly into addiction? I wiped my hands clean. We are so desperate to be explicable to ourselves, to rely on ourselves, that we need to believe a certain version of who we are even when evidence starts to mount that the version is a lie, even when the part of us which is not tamed by habit strains to break free and overwhelm the tired, repetitive creature that our character has become, mouldering at the edges.

When did my mother realize all of this and seek to break out of the character she and the world had invented for her? When did she see she couldn't successfully achieve that break-out so long as she was in the company of anyone who would try to re-impose that old narrative of character on to her life? Was it in the summer of '88 when all those activists and I demonstrated we still believed – well over two years after she had ceased to give us reason to believe it – that given the right opportunity, the right cause, she would become the Samina of *grazia* once more? And was it before or after that – the moment when she looked at me and thought, while I am discarding everything of myself I will also discard this child of mine?

I looked up at the starless sky. The dark began to diminish. Night was turning over in its sleep, turning to day. Surely there was some part of us that could be relied upon to remain consistent regardless of what life threw at us, some tiny kernel of being? Surely if Omi really had been locked up for sixteen years he would sound as he did in those hoax pages – still so like himself, despite everything? Surely some seed of the girl I had been when he was alive – the laughing girl who believed in belief and change – still remained within me, ready for reclamation? Or had that girl never existed – was she just part of the story I made up about myself? Self-analysis as the construction of self-narrative: I was once her, but she couldn't survive what was happening in her life, so I became me, but one day I'll be strong enough to go back to her. Was that the story I clung to? But if I still needed to believe that story, if I still had the will to want to be her rather than me, wasn't that hope?

In the cool dawn air, I was sweating. What I felt was anything but hope.

And it was time for the morning prayer. Every prayer of mine for the last fourteen years had been one single word: Mama.

Every prayer and every curse.

Without her here, I didn't know how to create for myself any story but that of the daughter she deserted, time and again; the one who never gave her a reason to stay. The one who now gave her no reason to return.

# XI

But surely, I thought a few hours later, my neck weaving in search of an opening in the short kurta tented over my head, surely our understanding of hope is entirely informed by a misreading of the Pandora myth. When she opens the box everything evil escapes into the world and only Hope remains for humanity, to comfort and lead us through misfortune. So the story goes. But what, I wondered as my head emerged out of the bright yellow fabric, was Hope doing mingled with all that evil? Why wasn't she off somewhere else with love and charity and friendship? Because her rightful place is amidst plague and sorrow, that's why. Hope stays in the box because she knows she can work her destruction best from within, in the form of a friend and a guide. Hope's crimes can only be successful if they are inside jobs.

I bunched up my hair at the nape of my neck, and twisted a band on to it. Hope was Zeus's ultimate revenge on humanity for Prometheus's theft of fire. And in what strange forms Hope comes to us – missives from the dead, lost languages brought to life, men bearing wine in paper bags.

I wasn't due at the office for another hour, but I picked up my car-keys and went straight there all the same.

Already, just a few hours into Ramzan, there was that feeling of something different in the air at STD. The kitchen was empty except for a pregnant woman who had the slightly guilty air of one who is so used to fasting in Ramzan that she feels she's betraying herself by brewing a cup of tea. In every other part of the studio, there was a sense of simultaneous deprivation and purpose. You could see it particularly with the chain-smokers who were constantly twirling pens in their fingers or fidgeting with paper clips. On the television mounted in the hallway, tea and biscuit commercials were replaced by washing powder and water cooler ads.

I went up the stairs – bypassing a group arguing heatedly about where the best jalaibees in the city could be found – and when I reached my office I found a piece of paper stuck on the door. There was no message, only a cartoon, expertly drawn, of a man handing a bottle to a woman, a smarmy smile on his face. The label on the bottle said VINEGAR in bright red letters, but the last three letters had been crossed out and the V turned into a W with a green marker. The woman's face was impassive.

I carefully peeled the cartoon off the door and walked down the hall to Ed's office. His door was ajar and I could hear his voice coming through, cold with fury.

'Well then, I'll be happy to treat your pay cheque as "just a little thing". Now get out.'

A man whom I recognized as a well-respected photographer, best known for his fashion shoots, walked out of the office and, seeing me, pointed back towards Ed's office and made a strangling motion with his hands before walking on.

I considered going back to my office, but Ed's voice called out, 'Is someone there?' so I pushed through the door and walked in.

His office was much larger than mine, and brighter. Sunlight angled in from the windows in two adjacent walls and converged on his desk, which was covered with black-and-white pictures. He was looking fixedly at the pictures when I walked in, but when I said his name he raised his head and smiled such a smile it made me feel I was a teenager again.

'Are those the reason you were chewing that poor man's

head off?' I asked, pointing to the photographs. They were all pictures of Shehnaz Saeed, standing at a window, looking out, one hand resting on the curtain. It was the hallmark Shehnaz Saeed photograph, taken during the filming of *Aik Ajnabi aur Mehbooba*, her first collaboration with Kiran Hilal, over two decades ago. The actor I'd dubbed Once-Leading-Now-Trailing man had played the man she loved, and in the scene during which this photograph was taken she is watching him leave her house after she's told him she can never marry him. How the entire nation had wept during that scene!

At second glance, I realized I wasn't looking at the old photograph but more recent pictures re-creating that scene.

'Bloody fool,' Ed grumbled. 'We need these for print ads that are supposed to start running next week for *Boond*, but just look at them.' He gestured angrily, and now I saw that the photographs weren't reproductions of a single image, but a series of shots nearly indistinguishable from one another.

'They look fine to me.'

'They're not fine at all. Look here, at this shadow, and here, there's too much curtain, and here, her hands just look old—' He stopped and looked up at me. 'I'm sorry. I seem obsessive, I know. It's all those years of working in advertising in New York. I've developed an eye for detail that is going to drive me crazy here.' He leaned back in his chair, closed his eyes for an instant longer than a blink. 'God, I miss it. New York. That damn city.'

At a student art exhibition I had once seen an installation called 'Shehnaz Saeed's Voice'. It was a replica larynx, with a pinhole at one end. When you placed your eye against the pinhole, some process of magnification allowed you to read a series of words inside the larynx, arranged in the space between two vocal cords – each word apparently written using the materials that the words themselves signified. Honey. Feather. Gravel. Velvet. Tears. Broken glass. As Ed spoke of New York, I almost believed that if I could direct a ray of sunlight towards his larynx it would shine through a pinhole and show me the proof that he was wholly his mother's son.

It was to continue hearing that timbre of voice that I asked, 'What do you miss about it?' as I sat down across from him.

He leaned forward and gathered up the photographs into a pile. 'What do I miss? Sushi.' He smiled and shrugged, as though to say the question could only be answered entirely unsatisfactorily. But I gave him a look to say, keep going. 'Pizza,' he offered. Then he exhaled and lifted his shoulders. 'The brunch scene. The cabs you can find everywhere, except when it rains. I miss talking politics in Urdu with cab drivers who are always left wing, and I miss being able to have anything delivered, free of charge – from dry-cleaning and saline solution to food from any part of the world. The Korean deli round the corner from me, particularly, which delivers ice-cream at four in the morning. What else? So much. Knicks games, and that New York attitude, and the way neighbour-hoods keep changing. The Trinidadian steel drummer at the 42nd Street subway station, and the Bangladeshi corner cigar-ettewalla who calls to me in the early morning as I pass by him on my way home from a night on the town. And the way the city clears out on long weekends. I miss snow in the West Village, and summers, New York summers, I miss those maybe most of all.'

As he was speaking, I thought at first that his look of pain resembled that of a man considering the end of a passionate love affair and then I realized, no, this is how the survivors of lost lands must look when they recall their former homes – Pompeii in ashes, Atlantis under the sea. 'Why leave, Ed? Really. Were the inconveniences so great that you couldn't live around them? I mean, there are inconveniences aplenty round here, though of a different variety. And surely your yuppie persona protected you somewhat?'

'I was made to feel powerless,' he said flatly.

'Is that really so terrible? I've always thought that the moment when Prospero renounces power at the end of *The Tempest* is when he's most powerful. The power to renounce power. What are those great Rilke lines about your friends, the scary angels?'

'"They serenely disdain to annihilate us. Every angel is terrifying."'

'Yes.'

'Don't look so surprised, Aasmaani. Even yuppies read poetry sometimes. Besides, the point is, I never renounced power. I just woke and realized I didn't have it, that's all.'

'So what? Until then you believed you could live the American dream – become a billionaire, donate generously to a political party and find yourself dictating government policy?'

'No, Miss Cynical. I believed I had the power to live freely, with no one bothering me if I only stayed within the law. The FBI knock on your door at two a.m. to ask about the flying lesson you took five years ago, and that illusion shatters in an instant. Listen, you want to know why I came back to the world of television after trying to live outside my mother's shadow? Because my mother's shadow is powerful. Because I walked into the CEO's office and said, "My mother might act if I ask her to," and now I'm all but running the place.'

'Karachi may not be New York but there are things to love around here as well.'

'People to love, certainly,' he said, looking up at me and then down at the photographs and then off to one side. Before I could think of something to say to that he was looking up again, smiling. 'I never did tell you the funny anecdote I promised yesterday. I was driving home from STD a couple of days ago – and you know I have to go past the police checkpoint near the US Consul General's house, right? So, as per usual, the police pull me over, write down my licence number and ask for my name—'

'You're right. That's a funny story.'

'I haven't got to the punchline.'

'Of course you have. You left your great life in New York because you disliked all the suspicion and prejudice, and you return to Karachi only to find that on a daily basis you get pulled over by the police who want to make sure you aren't endangering the safety of the US Consul General. How is that anything but the punchline?'

'I see your point. Thanks, you just killed my joke.'

'Oh, go on. What's your version of the punchline?'

'The police pulled me over, asked my name, and I thought, why do I always give them my real name? Let me lie. Let that be my attempt at resisting this nonsense. So I said, "Agamemnon." And the first policeman looked at me as though he was about to take me in for questioning but the second one said to him, "Write it down. Hurry up. Agha Memon."'

I laughed. He leaned further forward and rested his hand on mine.

And it was back again. The fizz. 'Hey,' I said, 'it's Ramzan. We're supposed to keep our thoughts pure until sunset. And while we're on the subject, don't stick bottles of wine on my office door.'

He lifted my hand and touched his lips to my knuckles.

I had almost forgotten how this felt; this anticipation, this drowning.

At length, he let go of my hand, stood up and walked towards the window. He jiggled the strings that controlled the workings of the blinds and held his palm against the windowpane as though to absorb its heat though it was far from cold in his office. Looking out at the garden with its pink-blossomed trees he said, 'Aasmaani, I don't believe the Poet wrote those pages. I think it's all some kind of hoax.'

'I think so, too.'

He turned to face me. 'Oh, thank God. I was afraid you'd actually started to believe . . .'

'No, no.' I could feel embarrassment spread across my cheeks.

'It's just, you know, it's so obviously, well, ridiculous, to start with. But also, everything you read to me. It's exactly what someone would write if it were a hoax, isn't it? I mean, if someone was trying to convince you that it was all real that's just how they'd do it. Drop in references to the peach allergy, dredge up a few old memories, throw in some clues about his present situation, do a quick summary of some aspect of all the intervening years. It's all too neat.'

'You knew he had a peach allergy?'

'Sorry?'

'The way you said "the peach allergy" as though it was something you know about.'

'Well, yeah.' He came closer to me. 'Once when your mother was over at my mother's place for dinner, there were peaches in the fruit-bowl. And Samina said that when the Poet was alive she never bought peaches. She said, "Now I can buy all the peaches I want, but as silver linings go that's pewter."'

I could hear her voice saying it. Her voice as it became when the Poet died – all hesitancy and brittleness.

Ed sat down on the edge of the desk, his shadow falling on me. 'Do you mind if I talk about her?'

I shook my head.

'Samina,' he said again, as though he hadn't said her name aloud in a long time and was surprised by the sound of it. 'She always insisted I call her that instead of "Aunty". I used to see her and the Poet, now and then, when I was growing up. Not often. Maybe a handful of times. But after the Poet died, she and my mother . . .' He stopped, unbuttoned and rebuttoned the cuff of his sleeve. 'She moves in and out of your features, you know? It's uncanny.'

'She and your mother.'

'What?'

'You were saying: after the Poet died . . .'

'Right. She and my mother became close, so she'd come by quite often. I used to drop in sometimes to see my mother and find her there. I wasn't living at home then – was at IBA, sharing a flat with a couple of guys near the campus.'

'Your delinquent university years. I remember hearing about them.'

151

'From your mother?'

'No. Just generally. When your mother quit acting.'

He stood up, rocking the desk. 'You mean when they all said she gave up the great passion of her life because of me. Because I was such a disaster she wanted to make sure she didn't make the same mistakes with the children from her second marriage.'

'Ed.' I touched his sleeve. 'I know how people in this town talk.'

'Yes. Of course you do.' He sat down again, closer this time. 'It was so unfair the way people treated your mother. All those years, she was only ever with the Poet. But because they didn't get married, and because they never really tried to hide the nature of their relationship, people thought they could say terrible things about her, and turn their backs on her when the Poet died.' He shook his head. 'All those people, married people, having their affairs, and no one says anything or treats them any differently as long as they keep it secret. As though there's some virtue in that. As though discretion and lies are the same thing. Your mother and the Poet, they were discreet. If you saw them in public and you wanted to believe they were just close friends and neighbours, hell, you could believe that.'

'Close friends and neighbours don't follow one another into exile.'

He waved his hand. 'There was just something so honest about their relationship. That's all I'm saying. They didn't flaunt it, but they didn't lie and sneak around either. They didn't deceive anyone. And you're the proof of that. You, growing up here, where everything goes on behind closed doors and yet everyone acts outraged about the tiniest suggestion of impropriety. You're not embarrassed or angry that your mother was involved with a man she never married. You don't hold it against her.'

'I loved him before I knew the meaning of the term "social convention", Ed. It's just that simple.'

'You never had to find out she was lying to you. It's that simple.'

Shehnaz Saeed had always confounded the purveyors of gossip by keeping her private life utterly private. Through all the years she was in the public eye there was never even a whiff of scandal attached to her. So, when she married her second husband, everyone was startled. He had been part of her wide social circle, but no one imagined he was anything more than that. Not even Ed?

'I remember the first time I saw your mother after the Poet died,' he said. 'At a supermarket – Paradise, maybe. Somewhere near Bath Island, at any rate.'

She never got used to thinking of the neighbourhood around my father's house as her neighbourhood. On those rare occasions when she did go out to shop it would always be back to her old haunts, the places where she looked on in exasperation as Omi took more time than seemed possible choosing the perfect watermelon, the ideal selection of green chillies. Even when it came to toothpaste and shampoo and soap, Omi would regard all the possible options as though being asked to locate a talisman, never choosing the same brand twice in a row.

'She looked so lost. And there were these two women staring at her and obviously talking about her. Samina was ignoring them. But then one of the women said, out loud, "Well, you can't expect people to treat you like a widow if you haven't been a wife."'

I folded my arms, pressed them against my chest. 'What did you do?'

'I went up to her, held her like this,' he placed his hands on my arms halfway between shoulder and elbow, 'kissed her on both cheeks and said how sorry I was. She seemed so grateful and surprised. There's nothing more unfair than your mother being placed in a position where she should have been grateful that some nineteen-year-old idiot didn't cut her dead when he saw her.'

I could love you, I thought.

He moved his hands slowly up to my shoulders. 'So, tell me something. What do you believe happened to your mother fourteen years ago?'

I leaned back, tipping my chair on to two legs, so that he had to let go of me to avoid toppling forward. If he had said 'think' instead of 'believe' I might even have answered him. But 'believe'? As though the fact of Mama's continued life was so implausible it could only belong in that realm in which atheists placed God, that realm in which faith and fantasy were synonymous. I could understand his scepticism, it wasn't something I would hold against him. But why did he have to look at me as though he were trying so hard – too hard – to convince me he was ready to double the numbers of this religion to which I alone subscribed, not because he believed the message but because he could not see me walk through the wilderness alone?

Come down to it, Ed was just another one of those men who wanted to fix me and believed that he could.

Take me broken, I wanted to say. But I knew already that in his eyes each one of my breaks would shift from challenge to reproach. Why can't you be fixed by me, he'd want to know. Why aren't I enough? Why do you resist my attempts?

I stood up and walked over to the wall without either window or door which was almost completely covered by an oil-paint poster advertising SHEHNAZ SAEED IN 'MACBETH'.

'If we're going to swap theories here, Ed, let's make it about a present-day mystery. Who's writing those hoax pages and sending them to your mother, and why?'

'Leave it alone, Aasmaani. It isn't the Poet.'

'I know that. But I'm still entitled to be curious, aren't I?'

'Of course.' He picked up the pile of photographs from his desk, pulled one out, and threw the rest into the waste-paper basket. 'But I can't help you. I've got no theories.'

His manner was so affectedly casual I knew he was hiding

something. Irritation, or even hurt, at the way I had brushed him off? Or was it something else? I looked up again at the poster. Shehnaz Saeed's face was painted on it with strokes so meticulous they avoided every flaw except that of excessive precision. There was no animation in the face; everything human had been replaced by perfection – except for the eyes, which seemed to look down at me in both invitation and warning. What was it I had thought the other day when I recalled her Lady Macbeth? Anyone in that audience would have plunged a dagger into a heart for her.

After the Poet died there was no reason for my mother to keep the code secret any more. She told me no one else knew it, but that was a year before she disappeared. What all did she say in that intervening year to the woman with whom she spent so much time? What did she say of codes and peaches and Shakespeare and shawls?

Ed said my name, his voice rising in a question.

I turned towards him. There he sat – Mama's boy and his own man knotted into one. It made perfect sense. Why else would he have brought the letter to my office, then refused to give it to me? Why else tell me the Poet couldn't be alive, then tell me that he could, then wake up the next morning and tell me no again? Poor Ed, caught between filial love and conscience.

He held out his hand to me. Not just conscience. There was something more going on here, something which Shehnaz Saeed couldn't possibly have anticipated.

Between Ed and me there was a sheet of sunlight, speckled with dust. I could walk to him through the sunlight and take his hand. I could play him. I could play his mother through him, pretending to be the fool while all along gathering information about what exactly was going on, and once I had figured that out I would find a way to turn it on its head.

'You're angry with me for something,' he said.

As he said it I realized how strange that, no, I wasn't. Not at all. I was – I felt this all along the muscles of my back – incredibly disappointed. And without the heart to keep this going any longer. Whatever Shehnaz Saeed's game, I wanted nothing more to do with it.

'Angry? No. Just a little guilty. Look, I'm going to have to be blunt here. You've outlived your usefulness for me.'

'What?' He looked so startled – so wounded – that it was all I could do to keep going.

'The pages are hoaxes, Ed. I looked them over again last night, and it was obvious they're fakes. Whoever wrote them did very well with the broad strokes, but there are certain fine details which are just completely wrong. So, sorry, but I don't need you or your mother in my life to act as the courier service any more.'

I moved towards the door, and he came through the sunlight and caught my arm. 'To hell with my mother and the letters. What about us?'

He was so beautiful right then.

'Listen, sweets, I'm sorry. I don't know what to tell you.' I pulled my arm away. *I don't know how to tell you what a monster your mother is.* 'Call me a bitch if it makes you feel better.'

'You're not,' he said. 'I don't understand what you're doing.'

'I'm saying goodbye.' I kissed him on the angle of his cheekbone. 'Safe travels, Ed.'

I walked out and returned to my office. By the time I was sitting at my chair, I could feel white-hot anger taking over my mind. I picked up the phone and called Shehnaz Saeed. I would tell her a thing or two. I would tell her she didn't have the intelligence to sound like the Poet. I would tell her all she'd done was make her son unhappy. I would tell her my mother used to laugh at her behind her back. I would tell her she was wrinkled and that everyone knew her husband couldn't bear to touch her any more. I would say 'casting couch' and 'neglectful mother' and 'has-been' and 'mediocre talent'.

156

I would have told her all this, I swear, but as I held the phone pressed against my ear until it stung all I heard was a ringing tone, repeating and repeating until the sound lost meaning and became the staccato victory laugh of Hope.

# XII

I called Beema at the hospital later that afternoon. Her voice was wrung out with exhaustion, and when I asked how her mother was she replied, 'Still dying.'

'Talk to me about other things,' Beema said. So I told her about life at STD, and my daily phone conversations with the architect responsible for renovating our house, and all the mini-dramas that were unfolding in the block of flats. When her voice finally seemed restored to itself, I said, 'Beema, what do you think of Shehnaz Saeed?'

'Gem of a human being,' Beema said without hesitation. 'One of the most generous, warm-hearted people I have ever known. The way she was with your mother – my God – it was extraordinary.'

'How was she with my mother?'

'Patient.'

I nodded, my chin bumping against the receiver. 'Unlike me.'

'Unlike everyone else in the world.'

'Please, Beema. You were patient.'

'Not always. I loved her, she was one of the dearest people to me in the world. No one braver or more charismatic than your mother. But I had other, stronger loyalties. Shehnaz didn't. Shehnaz didn't look at your mother and think about what her depression was doing to you, or to our household. She only saw Samina.'

Her depression. That was Beema's explanation for my

158

mother's behaviour before she left. Something unwilled, in which my mother played no part, had no agency. Everything could be explained away under the neat label 'depression'. Everything except the fact that my mother made a choice and slowly, painstakingly executed it.

'Would you trust her? Shehnaz Saeed?'

When Beema replied it was almost in a tone of revelation. 'You know, it's a strange thing. I've hardly seen Shehnaz in fourteen years. And we were never friends as such, just two people with a dearly loved friend in common. But now that you ask that question, I know the answer is yes, absolutely. Some people you can trust because of your relationship with them. Because they've earned your trust. And other people you trust simply because you know that they regard trust as a sacred thing, and if you hand it to them they'll hold on to it with their dying breath. And that's Shehnaz for you. Trust her? I wouldn't just trust her with my life, Aasmaani, I'd trust her with yours.'

The thing about Beema was this: for a remarkably generous woman she was also remarkably right about people.

When I ended the call and hung up the phone, I didn't know what to think any more. But it came down to this: if the pages were hoaxes, I could ignore them. I could call Shehnaz Saeed and say, if any more of those letters arrive, I don't want them. In her response perhaps I would learn whether to trust her or not. Whether to trust Ed or not.

But I couldn't call Shehnaz Saeed and say that because what if, what if.

I was back to where I had been the night before. Back to that need for a single piece of evidence that would assure me Omi was dead.

So I went down to the office of a news anchor, who was also a freelance journalist and a part-time sociology teacher, and, while chatting to her about the ideal consistency of a jalaibee (I came down on the side of gooey in the gooey/crunchy jalaibee divide), I flipped through the phone book on her desk, under the guise of being impressed by how many minor celebrities were filed in there and located and memorized the number I needed. I knew she'd have it – I had read the article on Ghalib she'd written in which she'd quoted Mirza the Snake.

And then, I did nothing. Nothing for the rest of that day, and nothing the following day and nothing the day after and so on until somehow we were into the third week of Ramzan and I had done nothing except have one brief conversation with Shehnaz Saeed.

It was very soon after my chat about her with Beema. I was in the office, rewriting bulletins from AP and Reuters for the evening news programme, when she called and invited me over for iftar the following day.

'No, sorry, I'm . . . I'm expected somewhere else. Relatives.'

'What a pity. But listen, drop in sometime, will you? It really was so lovely to see you the other day.'

She said it as though it were the most true thing in the world, and I found that I wanted Beema to be right about her, I wanted it almost painfully. 'I will, of course.'

'Good.'

'Oh, and thanks for sending me that second set of . . .'

'Any luck making sense of them?' she asked very quickly, as though the question had been lodged in her throat, straining to burst out.

'Not really, no. But I'm enjoying the challenge.'

She laughed. 'Imagine if you put hours into it and it turns out to be nothing more than recipes for cold soups. Should I continue sending you any more that I receive?'

'Sure,' I said casually. 'Why not? I'd hate to miss out on the gazpacho.'

The conversation wound down after that and I hung up thinking, I really have to call Mirza.

I had that thought each day, several times a day. No, more than several times a day. It was the thought with which I fell asleep and the thought with which I woke up. And in between, it was the thought of my dreams. But I was like a woman in the grips of a powerful addiction who keeps delaying that inevitable moment of last cigarette, last drink, last touch. It isn't as though I believed the Poet was alive. Not for a second did I believe that. But going to Mirza in search of that tiny scrap of evidence which would kill the possibility of *ever* believing that he was alive, that I couldn't do. Just as I couldn't call Ed, who made no attempt to get in touch himself. Just as I couldn't drop in on Shehnaz Saeed. Just as I couldn't speak to anyone about the coded pages, or keep from opening *War and Peace* and rereading the pages until they were burnt into my memory.

And also, I had to admit, I didn't want to call Mirza because he was Mirza – the most beautiful, arrogant man I had ever known. An angel undomesticated and with no need for earthly morality.

In any case, with Ramzan's strict structure it was all too easy to pretend there was no time for phone calls or visits. Wake at five for sehri, read the newspaper, return to sleep for a couple of hours, get to work by nine, leave by three, sleep until iftar, watch television with Rabia and Shakeel, have the lightest of light dinners, and then play night-cricket with the neighbours in the communal garden until it was midnight and time to sleep.

But finally one day, as I stood in the STD garden assisting in the painting of a sky-blue backdrop for the set of a religious discussion programme ('The sky suggests heaven,' someone explained as our brushes slapped against the canvas), a spray of paint arced through the air, came to rest on my arm, and when I turned to see who was wielding the guilty paintbrush I saw the journalist/newsreader/sociology teacher. 'Sorry, A,' she said. 'All this fasting has a really bad effect on my co-ordination. I can't believe we're only just past the mid-point of suffering. Doesn't it seem like for ever ago you stopped in and discussed jalaibees with me?'

'Yes,' I said, starting to walk away even as I said it, my brush dripping a trail of blue on to the grass as though I were a literal embodiment of my name, shedding a part of myself. When I was out of my colleagues' earshot I dialled the number which I'd stored in my mobile phone more than two weeks earlier.

On the first ring, an answering machine picked up and a familiar, slightly hypnotic voice came through. 'Ramzan is here. I am not. I swore into the phone just as the answering machine beeped. I should have known. He always used to say that there was no place for an alcoholic atheist in Pakistan during Ramzan, so as soon as the month started he'd leave the country.

'What's the matter?' the quiz show host asked, walking out into the garden as I was on my way back to my office. 'You look like a woman whose soufflé has sunk.'

I briefly considered advising him against using kitchen metaphors with twenty-first-century women who were already in a bad mood, but that wasn't a conversation for which I had sufficient energy. 'It's no big deal. I'm supposed to be researching something, but my source is out of town.'

'If you mean the Archivist, he got back from Lahore yesterday.'

The Archivist. Maybe, just maybe.

'Do you have his number?'

The quiz show host delicately scratched away at a dot of blue paint on my forearm. 'You don't need to call. During the day he's quite happy for people to just drop in.'

I patted his arm in thanks as though he were an old uncle and he shook his head, laughing again, and said, 'If I were even ten years younger than I am . . .'

'Instead of being at least ten years older than you claim to be?'

'Aasmaani, Aasmaani. So much like your mother. You whet words and use them to skewer our weaknesses, and we only adore you for it. Those of us who have any sense do, at least.' He took my hand and scribbled an address on it. 'That's where you'll find the Archivist.'

The Archivist was something of a Karachi institution. For

over three decades now he'd been clipping out articles of interest from all Karachi's English and Urdu newspapers and filing them away according to an elaborately ordered system. The All-Pakistan Newspaper Association had, some twenty years ago, passed a motion requiring that a copy each of all daily Karachi papers be delivered to the Archivist free of charge. The Archivist responded by saying that since he took his scissors to the newspapers he'd appreciate it if the motion was amended to require that either two copies of each paper be delivered to him or that the papers started printing articles on one side of the page only. There was some grumbling about ingratitude, but he got his two copies.

In all the years since I'd first heard about the Archivist, I had imagined him in a huge house with multiple floors, paper strewn everywhere. But it transpired he lived in a block of flats, near Clifton Bridge, and when he opened the front door to let me in my first impression of his flat was of extreme orderliness.

'What particular news item are you looking for?' he said, without waiting for an introduction. He was an entirely ordinary-looking man, old but not remarkably so, in nondescript beige shalwar-kameez, with thinning hair and a slight stoop.

'The Poet's death.'

He looked disappointed. 'Well, that's not very original. Are you sure you wouldn't prefer the kidnapping of a top bureaucrat's son in 1982? I've been transferring my files on to a computer and I just came across that old story.'

'Thank you, but no. It's the Poet I'm here for.'

The Archivist sighed, but beckoned me into the flat and led me down the brightly lit corridor past rooms without doors, each filled with floor-to-ceiling-high filing cabinets. In one of the rooms I saw a man standing on the top of a ladder, reaching into a cabinet near the ceiling. 'Some young scribe searching out information on the Builders' Mafia,' the Archivist explained. 'You need a good head for heights to be an effective researcher around here.'

163

We walked towards a room with a door and I stopped in front of it, wondering what top-secret files must lie on the other side.

'It's where I work,' he said, pushing the door open to reveal the voice of a perky American aerobics instructor ('One and two and work those abs!') coming through the television speakers. Across from the television was a large table; the chair at the end of it was pushed back to suggest the person who had been sitting in it had only got up to answer the door and intended to return to that spot with a minimum of delay. A scissor lay on top of the front page of one of the morning papers, which had a block of flower-printed plastic in place of a lead article. It took a moment for my brain to understand I was looking at a section of the tablecloth. Multiple stacks of papers, which had clearly already been through surgery, were on the floor near the chair, and a smaller stack, still unattended to, was on the table.

'You do this every day?'

He pointed at the aerobics instructor, who was now exhorting her viewers to 'Feel it! Feel it!'

'We all have our obsessions. At least I'm leaving something behind with mine.' He stepped over to the table, finished cutting out an article which was attached to the front page by only one corner, and placed it in one of the several piles of clippings in front of him.

'Do you enjoy it? Doing what you do?'

He looked up at me and smiled. 'This isn't what I do. It's who I am.' He looked at me a little more closely and nodded. 'And I know who you are.'

'I'm a researcher for STD television.'

'No, no. That's what you *do*. What I'm saying is, I know who you *are*. Those eyes. I've only ever seen one other set of those eyes. You're the daughter who can't let go. I've heard about you. What's it been? Near fifteen years now? Young lady, you put even me to shame.'

For a moment I considered turning on the ceiling fan, but

instead I straightened my shoulders and waited for him to show me what I had come to see.

All he said was 'Hmm.' Then he walked out of the room, gesturing for me to follow, and led me into a room larger than any of the others we'd passed so far. 'This is the murder room.'

I looked at the cabinets, wedged together in the white, uncarpeted, sun-drenched room, and felt dizzied. Extraordinary, how anyone in this city could walk around with the pretence of normality when there was so much horror pressing around us at all times. But the Archivist seemed immune to such thinking as, humming the song that had been playing in the background of the aerobics programme, he pointed to a cabinet level with his chest and said, 'That's the one. 1986.' He opened the cabinet, ran his fingers along the hanging folders and pulled out one which was disappointingly slim. He handed it to me and I read the tab, '31–7–6. Nazim: aka the Poet. Unsolved.'

'Please, no eating or drinking in here. And if you're using a pencil or pen keep it well away from the clippings. There's a reading room next door if you require it. When you're done, put the folder back in its place, and if you aren't sure where it goes, come and find me. Don't feel the need to say goodbye when you leave and don't take any item with you when you go, not even if you intend to return it within minutes.' He said all this with a slight air of boredom as though he'd said it so often the words no longer had any meaning. But then he leaned forward to me. 'What is it you hope to find here?'

I didn't entirely know. Something. Anything. Words to tell me he was dead. 'A reminder.'

'About the Poet's death?' He laughed. 'All you'll find in there is journalists parroting the official line, with one or two subtle suggestions that there's more to the story than they can say.'

'Such as?'

He expelled air noisily from his mouth. 'Who knows? Even the journalists didn't.'

He left the room, shaking his head. I opened the folder. The inside cover had two lines of handwritten text on it:

Master File: 1–10–1.
See also: Akram, Samina. Master File: 1–24–76.

See also. Was that the equivalent of reducing her to a footnote in his life?

'Bastard,' I muttered under my breath in the direction of the Archivist's room. I sat on the window sill, which looked down on Clifton Bridge with its steady stream of traffic, and turned my attention to the first clipping, pasted on to stiff white paper. The first thing I saw was a banner headline: WEEP, PAKISTAN!

The memory of his death stepped into my mind.

It was just a sound at first, a low sobbing. And then a taste – guava. I had been in the back garden of my father's house, eating fruit that wasn't yet ripe enough to be eaten without consequences, and my stomach hurt. So when I walked indoors and heard the sobbing I was in no mood to be sympathetic towards Rabia, weeping over her favourite pair of jeans which the dhobi had lost.

'Stop the melodrama!' I yelled towards the room from which I could hear the weeping. 'You'll find a replacement soon enough.'

The door, which was slightly ajar, opened, and I saw my mother through it, her face grotesque with mascara tears, looking at me with such shock that I knew I had given rise to an emotion within her which she never before knew she could feel towards me. Then Beema walked through the door, shut it behind her and put both her hands on my shoulders.

'Your Omi's dead,' she said. 'Jaan, I'm so sorry.'

My Omi.

It was the first time I learned about the body's ability to react to news which our minds haven't yet registered. I started crying right away, leaning against a wall, weeping, with my head in my hands. We never know the structure of grief until it comes to us, each time differently. Those of us who imagine a loss are always wrong in our predictions of how it will feel to find ourselves struggling to imagine emptiness in the shape of a loved body. I wasn't prepared for how unmoored grief could be; for days after, I was all tears, but not – as I had imagined – because of memory triggers, mention of his name, phrases of his poetry. It was just tears because there were tears and, within, not so much a desolation or sense of loss as a heaviness.

At some point in the hours just after I heard the news I locked myself in my bedroom to hide from my mother's blank gaze and the peculiar shuddering of her hands, and for want of something else to do, I scanned, without concentration, a newspaper. My eyes were arrested by an article with the heading: EVE TEASERS GO ON RAMPAGE: Modest Women Afraid to Leave Home.

And that's the first time I knew what it meant to be without him, because at that moment I wanted only to call him up and say, 'Have you seen the paper, Omi?'

I gripped the folder with both hands, and forced myself to start reading. The first clipping concerned itself mainly with extolling the Poet's genius, and lamenting the nation's loss. The only details about his death were that the body had been found 'with marks of violence' in the late morning the previous day, in an empty plot of land in Nazimabad. (Was the location mere coincidence? Omi used to love the fact that Karachi had a part of town called Nazimabad – Dwelling of Poets, he'd say, would you find such a locality in any of the so-called civilized parts of the world?) The Poet's wallet was found in the corpse's pocket, and Dr Basheer Riaz, who had been the Poet's doctor for years, was called in by the police to confirm that the body was the Poet's. A full investigation was underway. Nothing there that I didn't know.

But the next clipping was from one of the sensationalist Urdu tabloids. Here were details, graphic details, of the broken bones, the features smashed beyond recognition, the purple bruise that his face had become.

No teeth remained inside his mouth.

His tongue was a stump of muscle.

I dropped the folder. Pushed the window open and leaned out. Omi. Oh God, Omi.

They had protected me from this knowledge, all of them, everyone. I knew there had been torture, I knew there were marks of violence, but my father, my matter-of-fact father who never exaggerated or cloaked a detail in metaphor, was the one to tell me, 'He had the face of a man who was indestructible. So when he died, his face changed. It lost that indestructible quality and became unrecognizable. That's why they needed a doctor to confirm who it was. That's why a simple identification wasn't possible.' I knew they were keeping something from me, but I chose not to look any further for the details.

How could anyone do that to Omi? Why would anyone do that to Omi?

Smashed beyond recognition.

Beyond recognition.

I stood up.

Sometimes we find ourselves in a moment which feels like a pause; a suspension between the present and the possible. A moment in which our lives prepare to turn.

I bent down and sheafed together all the pages of the folder which had fanned out as they fell. My hands were utterly steady. I flipped through the cuttings – the tributes, the eulogies, the mention of the fire on the day after his death which destroyed all his papers, including the new collection he'd been working on – until I came to clippings from several weeks later, reporting the death of the Poet's doctor, Basheer Riaz. The one man who'd had the absolute proof, certain as dental records, undeniable as blood. The newspaper reports shed little light on the traffic accident which killed him – though almost all the reports, tellingly, mentioned that he had been the only person who was called in to identify the Poet's body. But there was also something that the Poet never had – a funeral notice. At the bottom left-hand side of the notice: MOURNER: Nasreen Riaz (sister). At the bottom right-hand side, a phone number.

It was a six-digit number, which started in 5–3.

I took my mobile phone out of my bag, and now my hands weren't quite so steady any more. Changing the 3 to an 8–5, I dialled the number. An automated voice told me the number didn't exist. I tried changing the 3 to an 8–3 and this time a woman's voice, elderly, answered.

'Nasreen Riaz?'

'Yes. Who is this?'

I reached out of the window and gripped the thin trunk of a bougainvillea vine that climbed along the wall. Purple, papery flowers twirled and drifted on to the concrete below.

'I'm a television researcher,' I said, and then, 'No, no. I mean, I am. But that's not why I'm calling. My name is Aasmaani. My mother . . . my mother's name might be familiar to you. Samina Akram.'

'Oh. Oh, I see.' Her voice was both curious and hesitant.

'I'm sorry to intrude like this, but I'm calling about your brother.'

'You're not another one of those conspiracy nuts, are you?'

I gripped the vine tighter. 'If you don't mind, I just wanted to know. I'm sorry if this sounds strange or callous. But were you close to your brother?'

There was the sound of something crashing to the floor. And then her voice came at me, furious. 'To hell with you. That's all anyone wanted to know. How close I was to my brother. Not because he was my brother and he was dead, but just because they wanted to know what he might have told me. His death was part of some grand plot, the tying up of loose ends. That's what everyone thought. He was not a loose end. He was my brother. Do you understand that?'

'I'm sorry. I didn't mean . . .'

'No one ever does. But that doesn't make it any easier. Listen to me. He died in a car accident. He had bad night vision, he shouldn't have been behind the wheel. But there was an emergency at the hospital and his driver was off sick that day. That's the story. That's all there is to it.'

'You're sure?'

'How is anyone ever sure of anything?' she said, her voice weary. 'You want to know if he was involved in a cover-up around the Poet's death, don't you? Well, I never asked him. It would have been a stupid question. But I know it was the Poet. I know it because my brother was an honourable man.'

'That's your proof?'

'That's my proof. I knew my brother. That's my proof.' She slammed down the phone.

The purples and reds of the bougainvillea flowers were sparks of a fire, burning his last poems.

I drew in a long breath. What sort of proof would be enough for me? His body was smashed beyond recognition. Even Mirza couldn't give me the proof I needed. No, the proof I needed could only come in the form of an exhumation of a grave in a distant village. I turned away from the thought. What would be in a grave seventeen years later? Nothing I wanted to see. And nothing that would be of any help, either, since he had no close surviving relatives that I knew of, except some branch of his father's family who never acknowledged him, and whom he never acknowledged, and who would only throw me out of their grand houses if I burst in babbling about DNA and opening graves and wild conspiracy stories. And in any case, I would never get permission for an exhumation, and I would never bring myself to ask for it either.

So there could be no proof.

Except his voice. His voice coming through to me in those pages, so utterly him, so utterly unlike any other voice I'd ever known. *I knew my brother. That's my proof*, she had said, and there was no way of arguing with that. But I knew my Poet.

Let's say, for the sake of argument, just for the sake of argument, I had to make a case for the pages being genuine. How would I construct the case?

First, stranger things go on. That was an important point. There was that story in the papers not so long ago – two feuding families, the infant daughter of one disappears and is never found. Fifteen years later, the families agree to end the blood feud that has gone on for generations between them. The patriarch of one family gives his absurdly young daughter in marriage to the elderly patriarch of the other family. The morning after the wedding night the bride's father tells her new stepson, *your stepmother is also your sister*. The young man takes an axe, bursts into the newly-wed's bedchamber, and kills the couple. The tribal jirga acquits him of murder, saying he did what was necessary for family honour.

Yes, stranger things go on.

Second, the only person to identify the body died mysteriously shortly afterwards. And though his sister refused to sully his memory by believing him involved in a cover-up, the fact remained that honourable men could be convinced into most dishonourable actions by anyone who knew just how and where to place the right degree of pressure.

Third. Third was a problem. Third was the matter of the burnt poems.

When Omi and my mother first moved into their adjoining houses, both houses belonged to my mother. Of the two of them, she was the one who was financially solvent, courtesy of her inheritance from her father. But when Omi received the first major cheque of his life, as prize money for the Rumi Award, he transferred the money to my mother's account and she responded by signing over the house he lived in to him, much to his irritation. How much she must have regretted that gesture the day she heard of his death! That was the day she learned exactly the price she would have to pay for never marrying him, the day she learned that their unwillingness to sign a piece of paper meant she had no rights, no claims to his life except the ones he accorded her while there was breath in him.

No one in the world of officialdom even bothered to inform her of Omi's death. It was Beema who heard the news from an uncle in the army, just before Mama came by Dad's house – she was supposed to take me to her tailor to have my first sari blouse fitted. And so it was Beema who broke the news to Mama. Mama wept for a while – wild, crazy tears – but then, while Beema held me tightly as I sobbed, Mama left the house and drove straight to the morgue. She arrived there to find that distant relatives of Omi's, who hadn't seen him in years, had already taken the body back to his village for burial. Was it a thought-out decision, or just instinct that made her drive home instead of coming back to Dad's house for me? Either way, she reached home to find the doorway in the boundary wall between his house and hers bricked up, and policemen barring her from entering through his front gate, saying they needed to search the premises for clues to his murder. There was nothing she could do but watch from her balcony as men who weren't wearing any uniform made a fire in his garden and burnt all his papers.

They say it made my mother scream like a madwoman – the smell of all those poems burning. I knew it was more than that; it was the memory of the fight I had witnessed between them just days earlier when he complained that she didn't take adequate care of the copies of his poems which he left in her house to safeguard against fire or theft. They rarely fought, but when they did their fights were monumental. She yelled, he blustered, and finally she said, fine, gathered her set of his poems into a pile and held a burning match above it. She wouldn't really have set it alight, I'm sure, but he lunged for her hand and, surprised, she dropped the match. They watched in silence as the papers burnt, flames spreading too fast to attempt any rescue, and when it was all ash, he rubbed his thumb in the greyness and wrote her name with it on a piece of paper.

'You see,' he told her. 'Everything I write can be reduced to a single word.'

Omi, how much you loved being the mad, passionate lover!

*If I am no longer the man mad with love for you does it mean I'm not me any more?*

Yes, it defined you so totally, your love for her. If that love ever dimmed or became an abstraction, you'd wonder if you were still yourself. I know you would.

A red bougainvillea flower glided into the room.

Return, then, to the case at hand. Return to the third problem. The problem of reconciling the burnt poems with the story of a faked death. Conventional wisdom has it that a government agency killed the Poet because they feared the effect his new poetry collection would have on a nation which had so recently received just a tiny reminder of the taste of democracy and was clamouring for more. No one had forgotten the impact his Hikmet translations, along with Habib Jalib's original verse, had on the popular – and successful – uprising against Ayub Khan in 1969. So the government had him killed – and tortured, to teach other revolutionary poets a lesson – and government agents entered his house and burnt his poems.

That was the story we'd all believed. It seemed to be the only story that made sense. After all, if the men who burnt the poems hadn't worked for the government, why would the police have stood guard outside while they gathered up the papers and stoked the flames?

There it was. That's what everything hinged on. The government burnt his poems after he died, so the government must have been responsible for his death.

I closed the file and walked back to the cabinet with it.

I opened the drawer for 1986 and there, in black marker, scrawled on steel in tiny letters was the word: WHY?

Why was it necessary to conclude that the people who burnt the poems were the very people responsible for his death?

I put the file back in its place and rested my hands on

either side of the drawer, as though it were a podium and I had just stepped up to expound my case.

Let's say – just for the sake of argument, let's say – that someone kidnapped the Poet, convinced the doctor to misidentify a corpse as his, and thereby spread the conviction through the nation – all the way to the very seat of power – that the Poet had died. Wouldn't it make sense, then, for government agencies to move in immediately to destroy his poems, knowing that his death would only augment their power? Yes, of course. His death would make his poems so much more powerful than his life ever could. How could a government be stupid enough to kill him while everyone knew he was working on a collection of political poems? How could a government be stupid enough to do that when, for all they knew, there were copies of his poems in someone's house, in someone's memory, making their way to someone's mailbox? It made no sense.

It made far more sense for the government to react to news of his death by burning his poems and hoping there were no copies. Simple as that.

Ladies and gentlemen, there is no disproving this thesis. I have explained away all your objections.

Explained away everything, except the most important thing. Motive. Why kidnap the Poet and imprison him for all these years?

Could it simply be 'any unpleasant motive'? Simply that someone despised him and wanted him to suffer?

That wasn't good enough.

Perhaps there was a reason that had not yet been revealed to us, or to him, just as the reason for the kidnapping of that young girl was not revealed until all those years later when the man she had come to think of as her father gave her in marriage to her real father and turned her brother to patricide and fratricide.

I moved away from the cold steel of the cabinets. What dark purpose, Omi, lies behind your capture, biding its time like Hera waiting for Hercules to become a father before she infects him with madness and drives him to kill his wife and children – a sweeter revenge than any she could have had before he knew what it was to love as only a parent can love?

As I stood in that room surrounded by murder stories, with the life of the city rumbling away beneath me on the bridge, it was obvious that in the absence of ultimate proof any story was possible, any belief was possible. The questions it came down to were these: did I believe that voice in the pages? Did I trust my ability to know Omi's voice? Did I trust the core of that man – that bawdy, tender, humorous, no-nonsense man with the razor-sharp mind – to remain unchanged even through all these years, all those trials?

Yes.

Simply, yes.

'Omi,' I said, and the word hung in the air, white-gold and sturdy.

He was still alive. Oh dear God, he was still alive.

I found I was kneeling on the ground, though I didn't know how I got there. Light streamed in through the window, almost liquid, almost tactile. The fist of muscle within my chest unfurled. With a great surge something molten shot through my veins – the sensation so unfamiliar, so overwhelming, that it took me a moment to recognize it as joy.

# XIII

In the hours, and days, that followed, life progressed on an ordinary path. Sehri, work, siesta, iftar, television, dinner, night-cricket. That was the outline of my days. But within that outline I was at once weightless and held fast, as though embraced by an Omi-shaped dream somewhere far above the gravitational pull of the earth.

While waiting to bat, and between innings, during the games of night-cricket I'd lean back on my elbows in the grass and look up at the sky. Only in its distant mystery could I find the language for my emotions. A knot of gas, made increasingly dense – perhaps by the force of a wave passing through it – will start to contract in on itself, heating up its core until it sets off nuclear fusion and a star is born.

Does that knot of gas recognize in itself an incipient star? Does it yearn for the wave to pass through it? Of course not. But even if it could, even if it had that faculty of imagination, perhaps it would choose not to use it. Perhaps it would only be at that moment (if millions of years can be a moment) when the knot of gas coalesced into luminescence that it would realize how diffused it had been, and for how long.

I couldn't speak of what was happening to me as I moved through the day with the outward semblance of a woman following routine. But whatever I did, this knowledge, this wave, was constantly making its way through me: he is alive, Omi is alive.

One evening, in my flat, I realized I had been looking out at the sea for hours without a single thought. That unthinking was the opposite of the deliberate, dark blankness I was driven to when the debris of facts could no longer fill my thoughts. It was the unthinking that came from being full with a certain knowledge, heavy with it. He was alive. That was not a thought, not something that came from the mind. It was knowledge in the form of sensation.

They noticed it, everyone around me – at work, during the cricket games, in the flat next door. They noticed it but couldn't pinpoint where it came from, or what it was, and didn't believe that I was being anything other than deliberately evasive when I just shook my head and smiled when questioned. How could I say, I cannot speak of it? This demands music, not language.

And it was music with which I filled my days. At the office, in the car, at home, I engulfed myself with the opera he had tried to teach me to love – here, here, he'd say, listen, and he'd make me sit through as much as I could bear of *Carmen*, *The Ring Cycle*, *Otello*, *Madama Butterfly*, or whatever else it was that he was listening to at the end of a session of writing. But what do the words mean, I would demand, and he'd shake his head. Never learn Italian, he warned me. Why do you think I prefer opera to qawaali? They both have the same degree of passion, but with qawaali I understand the words and that ruins it. As long as you don't understand the words of opera you can believe they match the sublime quality of the music, you can believe words are as capable as music of echoing and creating feeling, and you need only search hard enough, long enough, for the right combinations to create that perfection. Before the babble of Babel, Aasmaani, people spoke music.

For four days or five, I remained in the state of quiet joy, unbothered equally by the deprivations of fasting, the phone which kept ringing at odd hours with no originating number showing up on caller ID, the questions and strange looks that came my way. But then one night, as I lay on my stomach in the grass, watching the spinning of a cricket ball illuminated by the headlights of the cars parked side by side in the driveway alongside the makeshift pitch, Rabia lay down beside me and said, 'Does this have anything to do with your mother?'

The ball spun away from the bat's trajectory and dislodged a bail from the stumps. The innings ended.

I opened my mouth to say, 'No,' but the word didn't quite come out. Sensation distilled into thought, and the thought was: if there is such a thing as a core of being which remains unchanged, her core is her love for Omi. If she knows he's alive, if she knows his words are making their way to Karachi, then she'll return.

I put my head down, feeling blades of grass prickling my face. Rabia put her hand on my shoulder. 'You're so different these days, Aasmaani. I don't know if it's good or bad. You're more locked up in yourself than ever. But in a peaceful way, it seems.'

An understanding that I had been too blind to see in all these years forced me to look up at her. 'And you think, it can only be my mother who can bring me peace. My mother who left fourteen years ago, who used to leave so often before that, only my mother has that power in my life. You're the one who's always been my rock, you and Beema together the anchors who keep me moored to sanity. And you think you're so much less in my life than her, don't you?'

Rabia looked away, her fingers scratching at my shoulder in tiny circles. 'It's not a question of competition.'

'No, it isn't.' I turned over on to my back, and she pirouetted her body round to rest her head against my stomach.

My Scrabble girls, our father used to call us when we were young and there was no pillow in the world which Rabia would rather rest against than some part of me – shoulder, stomach, thigh – her body always perpendicular to mine so there was only that single point of contact between us.

Shakeel walked up to us, laughed, and lay down, his head on Rabia's leg. 'Double word score,' he announced.

'No abbreviations allowed, skinny man!' I said.

Someone had switched off the car headlights while everyone took a break between innings, and the stars were bright above us. I lay in silence for a while, looking up, listening to Rabia enumerate for Shakeel the different stars which made up the Orion constellation – Betelguese and Bellatrix at the Hunter's shoulders, Rigel and Saiph twinkling at his knees – and remembered when I had taught her to look up to the sky and greet the distant points of light by name.

Rabia the Patient, daughter of Beema the Sane.

I had never really thought to question why she maintained that scrapbook about my mother, long after I had discarded it; never stopped to consider that in those two years when my mother lived with me in the upstairs portion of my father's house, Rabia always kept a distance, not knowing how to react to that unfamiliar creature lurking beneath the shell of the woman she had once known; never wondered how much resentment Rabia felt towards Mama for being the strongest pull in my life. But now it was so clear.

I sat up, causing a reverse domino effect to take hold of my sister and brother-in-law.

'You have that look of purpose in your eyes,' Rabia said. 'What's that all about?'

'It just occurred to me to wonder something. When did you become such a fan of my mother, Rabia, and why? I know your feelings for her weren't uncomplicated when we were growing up.'

Rabia drew her legs up to her chest and put her arms around her knees. She didn't seem particularly surprised by the question. 'I admire what she did as an activist. I admire it particularly because I read all those condolence letters addressed to you in the months after she disappeared, which you used to throw into the bin after reading the first three words. So I know what a difference she made to people's lives, and how important she was to the women's movement in the eighties. But beyond that,' she glanced over at Shakeel, who nodded encouragingly, 'beyond that, Aasmaani, everything I think or feel about your mother is really just about you. I cut out those articles and put them in the scrapbook because your memory is so incredibly one-sided, so totally blinkered, that you need the black-and-white reminders of what you used to admire and idolize her for, just in case the day comes along when you're able to let go long enough to remember her as she really was, with all her flaws and in all her glory.'

There it was again. *Let go.*

I tapped my bare toes against her ankle. 'I don't think that's what it's about at all, Rabia. Reminding me of her activism won't make any difference to the way I think about her – it's not her activism I've ever resented. Admittedly, it turned out to be a waste of energy, but I don't resent her for not knowing that at the time.'

'It wasn't a waste,' Rabia said quietly. 'Read those articles. It wasn't a waste at all. What do you gain by believing it was a waste? Why are you so insistent about that point?'

'Don't turn this back on me, Rabo. We're talking about why you keep the scrapbook. And here's what I think. I think you cut those articles out to remind yourself that she was this creature of ideals and courage and everything else you admire so much. Because you need that reminder, don't you, to keep all your resentment at bay? All those years of resentment which only grows with every second she continues to be the siren pulling me away from you and the world of normality and good sense you live in. You can't let that resentment out, can't admit to it. You can't, because you're the rock, you're the anchor. Those are the roles I pushed you into when you were so young you should have been trying on different personalities every week just to find the one which suited you best. And even now, you believe that role so completely that you can't admit to your resentment, and you have to cloak it in concern for me. Rabia, you don't have to do that any more.'

When I was done, Shakeel said, 'Oh, boy,' stood up and

walked away, stopping long enough only to look back at Rabia and say, 'She's stronger than you think, you know.'

'What does that mean?' I demanded from my sister.

'It means,' she clutched her knees closer, 'it means, I'm not you, Aasmaani. People's minds, their psyches, don't all work in the same ways.' She made an exclamation of irritation. 'Do you want me to spell this out? Who is there in your life whom you once resented, then felt you weren't allowed to resent because it would be so selfish and so wrong, and whose memory you now revere above everyone else who has ever lived on this planet?'

I pushed myself off the ground and she sprang up next to me and caught me by the shoulder. 'Dammit, will you stop running away every time I try to talk to you about this!'

There was a crackle of lightning inside my head. 'You're talking rubbish. Yes, there were moments of irritation. I've had them with everyone. But you think I resented him? Rabia, the one thing I wanted most of all was to be his daughter. Not Dad's daughter. Not your half-sister. Not Beema's step-daughter. I would have given all that up to be his child, I would have given all that up in a heartbeat.'

For an instant I thought she was going to hit me, and then her face took on a concentration of utter pity. 'Of course that's what you wanted. Because if you had been his child, he wouldn't have made your mother choose between the two of you every time he went away and asked her to follow.'

'That's not how I saw it.'

'That's exactly how you saw it.'

There we stood, my sister and I, looking at each other from opposite shores of perspective. I was no longer in my skin, but hovering above, watching both of us with a curious detachment. We could spend all night out there, I knew, plunging our hands into the ice-cold river and pulling out squirming facts, entirely distinct from one another, which would wriggle out of our grasp almost as soon as we hoisted them above the fast-moving surface.

Then a chill hooked through me, and I almost cried out. It had gone. That peace, that joy, it had gone. With a great surge, questions finned in, jostling against each other, filling up all the crevices of my mind. How will you find the Poet? How will your mother know you've found him? What if no more letters come? Suppose Ed is angry enough to keep the letters from coming to you? How do you know you can trust Shehnaz Saeed? What if he comes back and she comes back, too, and they leave again and don't tell you where?

I squeezed my eyes shut. Please, not again.

'Aasmaani?' Rabia stepped closer to me.

I shook my head and held up a hand for her to stay away. Slow, heart, slow. Calm yourself. You'll find him. Look how far you've come already. He's alive. Say it. He is alive.

Omi.

It had the feel of a mantra.

Om Omi Om Omi.

How many of your Lord's blessings would you deny?

I opened my eyes and exhaled slowly.

'I'm sorry.' I took her hand in mine. 'I didn't mean what I said. I wouldn't give up being your sister for anything. And I know it seems like I take you all for granted. You and Beema and Dad. But it's just . . . it's just that sometimes it feels like I've spent my whole life missing Mama.'

Rabia wrapped her arms around me and pulled me to her. 'I know. Sometimes it feels like I've spent my whole life watching you miss her. You're wrong about me resenting her for being the stronger pull in your life. I've never resented her for that. But I've hated her for causing you so much pain. I've hated her for making you cry. Just as she hated herself for it.'

I pulled away. 'You think she did?'

'I know she did. I saw it.'

'Saw what?'

The cricket game was starting up again and we were perfectly positioned to be hit by a well-timed cover drive, so we stepped into the driveway and pulled ourselves on to the bonnet of a car, leaning back against the windshield.

'It was during those last two years. When she was living upstairs. She'd promised you she'd go to Sports Day to watch you in the long jump, but then she couldn't get out of bed that day. And you cried. You thought I didn't know. You always thought I didn't know.' For a moment a look flitted over her face that was nothing but the triumphant look of a twelve-year-old who has just discovered her big sister's secret. 'Anyway, the next day, you'd gone out with some school-friends and Dad was at work and Beema was giving maths tuition. So I marched up to your mother's room and I said, "We need to talk."'

'Aged twelve, you marched up to my mother's room and said, "We need to talk?"'

'Yes. I said, "Listen, lady." I think I'd just been watching some gangster movie. I said, "Listen, lady. It's OK with me that you're living in my room now, and I've had to move downstairs. But don't forget this is my room you're in, and if you're going to go on living here you owe me something. Let's call it rent."'

'You prepared this speech beforehand, didn't you?'

'Wrote it down, memorized it, practised it in front of the mirror. Your mother, bless her – she was having a better day that afternoon – just nodded really seriously and said, 'That seems fair.' So I said, "I don't want money. It's not like that. I want you to stop making my sister sad, that's the rent you owe me."'

'Oh, Rabia.'

'She started crying, Aasmaani. Really crying. I've never heard such crying, not even when Beema told her the Poet was dead. She just cried and cried like it was the only thing in the world she knew how to do any more, and I got so frightened I ran out of there. I've asked myself since, what was I so scared of? Because honestly, nothing has been more terrifying to me since. And I think it was this. That I saw, this is what can happen to a life, this can happen to anyone. That was the last day I ever hated your mother.' She wiped my eyes with the heel of her palm.

'You and Beema,' I said, blowing my nose. 'Saints-in-waiting, occasionally disguised as gangsters.' And in their saintliness so ready to choose pity over censure.

'She should at least have moved out of our house,' I said, balling up the tissue paper in my hand. 'If nothing else she could have done that. Why should you and Dad and Beema have had to suffer through all her suffering?'

'She tried to leave. Beema wouldn't hear of it. And she was in no state to look after herself, Aasmaani, you know that.'

I could have gone with her. I could have looked after her. I never offered. I never wanted, at that point, to have to be alone in a house with her, watching her strip away herself.

'How did Dad put up with it? I really don't know.'

'With gritted teeth.' Rabia shrugged. 'I don't think he was ever too happy about how close Beema and your mother were. It would have suited him better, I'm sure, if they got on civilly enough not to make life uncomfortable for you, and no more.' One of the cricketers yelled out that her feet were blocking the headlights, so she pulled herself into a cross-legged position. 'Remember Beema saying to your mother – this was before the Poet died, when they were back from exile and you were so happy you could hardly walk without dancing – Beema said, "Put us together, Samina, and the two of us form the one Superwoman that every individual woman needs to be if she's to go through this absurd world with even the barest sense of responsibility. We take on governments, buy the groceries, wrest religion out of the hands of patriarchs, raise our daughters into women, and accompany our men to places they'll never survive alone because they're still little boys in the bodies of competent adults." That was it, I think. The heart of their friendship. They saw themselves as complementary, and not only in your life. Your mother would never have left you all

184

those times, Aasmaani, if it wasn't Beema she was leaving you with.'

'She would never have left me unless she could bear to leave me.' I slid off the bonnet. 'She did me a favour, I know. I'm much better off having been raised by Beema, and in your company. But that was the result of, not the reason for, her decisions.'

From the fielders there came a roar of delight as the batsman struck a slower delivery back into the hands of the bowler.

'My turn,' I called out, making my way to the pitch.

I could tell, by the way my sister hovered near me when the game was over, that she wanted to continue our conversation. But I was sick of my own self-obsessed whining, and partly resentful for the dissipation of that utter peace I had known for the last few days, so after the game I loitered in the garden, talking politics with the neighbours.

During Ramzan, the country had finally got a government. Not a very convincing one, but the main reaction among the people I encountered at STD and in the communal garden was relief that the religious alliance had refused to join a coalition government. 'Bugger, but they talk democracy better than anyone else,' Rabia had groaned a few days earlier, watching the fiery leader of the beards lay into military intervention in matters of government as the inaugural session of the National Assembly was broadcast live on one channel after another.

I had looked at the scenes from Parliament, and I couldn't help wondering what it would feel like to be sitting there, part of the action.

Earlier in the year, soon after the President announced the new constitutional amendments prior to holding elections to end the three-year suspension of Parliament, I ran into a one-time friend of my mother, a man who'd been a brave and admired participant in the pro-democracy activities of the 1980s, only to turn into a corrupt, vindictive politician when democracy actually returned to the country and he found himself in a position of power. I hadn't seen him in years, but when we found ourselves at adjoining tables on the rooftop of my favourite restaurant his eyes registered delight.

'Aasmaani! How marvellous!' He pulled up a chair next to me, ignoring my three colleagues from the oil company who were sitting at the table with me. 'Heard about the new amendments? The reserved seats?'

I dipped a piece of na'an into raita and shrugged. 'My sister's been babbling on about it. Sixty reserved seats for women in the new parliament.'

'Right.' He drew his chair closer. 'So how about it? You want to be one of my party's nominees?'

My colleagues exploded into laughter. We had been discussing the amendments earlier and I had said the great benefit of having a quota of women in parliament was that it would add colour and a sense of fashion to the proceed-ings.

I spooned chicken ginger on to my plate. He picked up a seekh kabab and waved it in my face. 'Come on. You had a razor-sharp political mind when you were fourteen. Remember that time your mother and I got arrested . . .'

'You mean back in the days when you had integrity?' He bit into the seekh kabab and looked amused. 'We've all got to work with the system. Now, look. Say yes. Come on. This is your chance to do some good for the nation.'

I took the seekh kabab out of his hand and threw it to the cat which had been prowling nearby. 'The nation can sod off as far as I'm concerned.'

He clapped his hands. 'Even better. You're perfectly suited.'

I tried not to get irritated by the sight of my colleagues falling about with laughter at the thought of my entrance on to the political landscape. 'Right. So the way this works is your party gets to decide which women are suitable candidates. And then, with the fourteenth amendment firmly in place, once we join your party we're not allowed to vote against party lines, so if you decide to pass a law saying "Women are morons" we're legally obligated to vote with you? No thanks.'

'Well, that's a rather limited view of things.' He picked up another seekh kabab. 'A minimum of sixty women in the house is bound to affect business in some way or the other, don't you think? This is the chance for you to prove right your mother's theories about how women are the real dynamic and revolutionary force in this nation.'

'My mother's theories, like the nation, can sod off. And so can you.'

And that was that.

But now, standing in the garden at midnight, listening to everyone around me arguing different gloomy scenarios for the future of the nation, I couldn't help wondering what my mother would think if she turned on a TV one day and saw me sitting in the National Assembly.

What if he comes back and she comes back too, and they leave again and don't tell you where?

*Who, or what, would I need to be to make her stay this time?*
*a) member of parliament*
*b) apolitical quiz show researcher*
*c) capitalist corporate girl*
*d) translator of obscure Urdu diaries by day, party animal by night*
*Answer: this is a trick question. All depends on who she is now.*

I walked up to my flat, with an old, too-familiar heaviness tugging at my limbs. It was there the following morning, too, as I reached the studio and made my way to my office, to another day in which Shehnaz Saeed didn't send me more encrypted pages, another day in which Ed didn't call, another day in which I was no closer to knowing anything about where the Poet was and how to get to him.

Someone called my name as I climbed the stairs. I looked down to see an elderly journalist who had recently been hired to fill the spot offered to me as host of the political chat show. He was climbing up the stairs from the basement, wiping pancake make-up off his face.

'Word's got out about what you've been doing,' he said, as we met on the ground floor.

'The quiz show?' I said.

He took my elbow and steered me away from Kiran Hilal's team who had just walked out of the ground-floor conference room. The first three episodes of *Boond* had been filmed over the last week, and the STD office was still full of talk about the brilliance of Shehnaz Saeed and the idiocy of the Mistress's Daughter who had declared she couldn't film any romantic sequences before sunset because you're supposed to suppress 'those feelings' while fasting.

The journalist pulled me into the empty kitchen and turned to face me. 'There was a reporter at the Archivist's flat when you went there. The Archivist is a big gossip. He told the reporter who you were and which file you were looking at. Then Nasreen Riaz told her cousin, who works on our sports page, that you called her, too, asking about her brother's death. Now everyone at the newspaper office is speculating what you might be after.' He dropped his voice. 'Listen, you're still young and you might be fooled by the illusion of democracy. But believe me, power is still in the hands of the same old people. Nothing's changed.'

And with that, I was back to the habits of my childhood, looking around to see who was there, and then beckoning the journalist through the door into the back garden, out of range of any listening devices.

'What do you know that I shouldn't know?' I asked him. Even though we'd barely ever spoken before, I trusted him. Omi used to call him 'the press corps' voice of conscience'.

He smiled a little at my cloak-and-dagger antics. 'My guess is the only bugs in the kitchen are of the Osama Bin Roach family.' He grew serious again. 'But if you're asking me if I know who killed the Poet, I know only as much as everyone does. It's an open secret who those men were, the ones who ransacked his house and burnt his poems. Or, if not who they were, then certainly who they worked for. It was a government agency, Aasmaani, and the people who were involved are quite likely still in positions to know when people start snooping around where they shouldn't be.'

'So you're not one of those people who believed there was more to the story of his death than simply that the government had him killed?'

He looked at me with interest for the first time. 'If it wasn't the government, then who?'

I had to admit I had no idea, and then he looked offended, as though I were casting aspersions on his skills as an investigative reporter.

'There was no reason to point a finger in any direction other than the one in which we couldn't ever publicly point it.'

'But why? Why should they kill him, after all those years when they didn't? Why not just arrest him again?'

'Are you really such a child? Don't you know enough by now to know they don't need a reason for killing? You think of it as a big decision, whether or not to take a life. They don't. It's like picking teeth to them. Why shouldn't they do it? Who's going to stop them?' He pointed a finger sternly at me. 'If you're planning to find out who exactly gave the order and who exactly carried it out, if what you're looking for is a name, don't. I know how these people operate, and believe me, you don't want to find yourself in their radar.'

'You're the last person I'd expect to hear advising someone to lie low. Can I ask, would you be saying that if I wasn't a woman?'

'But you are a woman.'

'So's my mother,' I shot back.

'I rest my case.'

I opened my mouth to argue, but he straightened his

pointing finger into a vertical position to demand an end to the conversation. 'Keep out of trouble. The Poet and your mother were friends of mine. I owe it to them to tell you what a mistake you'd be making to continue with this madness.'

I remembered all the phone calls from unidentified numbers over the last weeks, the caller hanging up as soon as I answered. When had they started? The day I visited the Archivist, wasn't it? That very evening, in fact.

What surprised me then was not the feeling of panic that made me want to step on to a plane and leave the country as soon as possible, but the exhilaration that accompanied the panic. It was genetic, that exhilaration, and suicidal, too. But for a moment I let it wash over me. By God, I would give them reason to train their radars on me!

And then the exhilaration was gone. Who was 'them'? Who was behind Omi's captivity? Was it an individual or a group, and what were his or their allegiances and contacts and motives? Whom could I trust?

I looked at the journalist. Was he acting on behalf of my mother and Omi, or someone else entirely in telling me to stop my search for answers?

'You're right,' I said. 'It was just a moment of silliness. There won't be any more.'

No, no more pathetic attempts at playing detective. It would get me nowhere. The only person who could give me the answers I needed was Omi. If only he would write again. When would he write again?

It was much later that night, as I was drifting to sleep, that I thought, what if he has written again already? My eyes opened to the faint green glow of an octopus reaching its tentacles towards me. What if Ed told his mother I could read the pages? If she knew I'd been lying to her, why should she continue to send the pages to me? She owed me nothing, after all. She was, Beema had said, a woman who regarded trust as a sacred thing, and I had done nothing from the beginning but deceive her.

I thought, I'll call her first thing in the morning. And then I thought, Ed. I thought of his hand reaching out to mine on the other side of sunlight and how I turned away from him, choosing to see everything between us as evidence of his manipulation. When the truth of it was, all he'd done was show he was just as confused as I was by the coded pages. Over three weeks gone now since that last meeting between us, and I hadn't called to apologize, or to say what was simply true – that I missed him.

So, the following morning, as soon as I got to work, I called him. He must have seen the STD switchboard number on his mobile, because he picked up with the words, 'For the last time, no. We are not shooting her in soft focus.'

'Does the camera not love the Mistress as much as the CEO does?' I said. I had to speak loudly to cut through the static. 'Is that the nightmare in which you are living?'

'Aasmaani?' He said it hesitantly first and then with a great exuberance, 'Aasmaani!'

'Ed? Ed!' I replied, echoing his tone. 'You know you're going to have to get a new nickname. That one doesn't lend itself to passionate declamation.'

'Baby,' he said, his voice deepening into a Hollywood drawl. 'You can call me anything, just so long as you call me.'

'How's this, then? I'll call you Bogie and you can Bacall me.'

'Are we having a conversation or writing a song?'

'Actually, this is me apologizing.'

'Then this is me accepting your apology with a song in my heart. Should I sing it for you?'

'Sing it when you come home. When are you coming home?'

'Not soon enough. God, Aasmaani, I've missed you more than seems possible.'

'I'm going to linger on the compliment and ignore the backhand there.'

'This is going to sound odd, and maybe it has something to do with the phone reception, which is fairly suspect in these hills – most days I have to climb the tallest tree and lean at a precise angle to get a signal – but you sound lighter. Like someone's just pulled the sadness right out of you. Is it just the reception?'

I shook my head, though I knew he couldn't see it. 'It's him, Ed, it's really him.'

'Who?'

'Omi. He's alive.' It was the first time I had said it to anyone else and that joy welled up inside me again and made my voice crack.

'Omi?'

'The Poet, Ed. Don't be thick. The Poet is alive. I know it.'

'How . . . ?'

'Ed, don't ask. Just take my word. He's alive. It's not a hoax. Now listen, we have to make sure your mother keeps sending me those pages. Have you told her I can read them? Should we tell her? Ed?'

There was silence.

I moved the phone away from my ear and looked at the screen, expecting to see we'd been disconnected.

'Ed?' I pressed the phone against my ear again.

'So that's why you called.' His voice was utterly without expression. 'Because of the letters.'

'It's part of the reason,' I admitted. 'But – you're the other part.'

'Really? Can you break that down into numbers?' Fissures were appearing in his even tone, anger leaking out. 'What percentage of your reason for calling is about the letters, what percentage about me?'

'Ed. This is absurd.'

There was another pause. 'She doesn't know,' he said at last. 'My mother. She doesn't know. And though there's no reason for me to dispense good advice to you right now, I'd advise you not to tell her. It'll all become "They're my letters, this is about me."'

'She doesn't seem . . .' I stopped. 'Sorry. I appreciate the advice. Really, Ed.'

192

'If more letters appear I'll make sure you get them,' he said, his tone relenting. 'Now I really have to go.'

'Ed. Wait. Fifty.'

'What?'

'Fifty per cent because of you.'

'That's a lie, Aasmaani.'

'I want it to be the truth.' But this time he really had hung up.

What was there about this man that touched me so unexpectedly?

A girl I knew at university once spoke of 'secret societies of pain'. Her fiancé had died at the age of twenty-two, and she said sometimes a look in a stranger's eyes, a particular quality of desolation, would tell her the stranger had suffered a similar grief.

I tried calling Ed back to tell him about that girl but he didn't answer, so I sent him a text message saying, 'Ed. Call me.'

He wrote back, 'Signal buggered. No tall trees.'

It was impossible to discern the tone of that message – curt or humorous? – but I took it as a good sign when, three days later, Shehnaz Saeed's driver rang my door-bell. He handed me a note from Shehnaz inviting me over on Eid night to watch *Boond* with her and Ed. I read the note, standing in the doorway, while the driver waited for a response, and when I looked up to him to say, 'Tell her yes,' he was holding out an envelope, addressed to Shehnaz in childish handwriting.

. . .

We confuse conflict and suffering with tragedy. Hamlet is not the most tragic of Shakespeare's figures, nor is Lear. Hamlet is the most conflicted, Lear is the one whose suffering is most brilliantly rendered. But the most tragic figure is Macbeth, who has no illusions. Unlike Brutus, he does not attempt to justify murdering his friend and benefactor; unlike Othello, he is not drawn into murder by the perfidiousness of an Iago. Macbeth's tragedy is absolute self-knowledge allied to an unflinching awareness of the dire consequences of his action and a profound understanding of the immorality of his deeds.

I know whose voice that is: Darius Mehta, Impassioned Professor of English, Adjectivus Emeritus.

Myself, I have always gravitated to the tragedy of lovers. Laila Mujnu, of course. But also Antony and Cleopatra, Macbeth and his Lady (their passion for each other the real story of the play), Sassi Punoo, Samson and Delilah (of whom I owe my knowledge to Cecil B. de Mille rather than the Bible), Saleem and Anarkali, Oedipus and Jocasta (why pretend his tragedy is greater than hers; she who discovers she has married her patricidal son? She hangs herself – not because of incest committed in ignorance, but because of her continued desire for her son against all laws of morality and custom). But the saddest of love stories is Arthurian – not the story of Lancelot

194

and Guinevere, or even of Tristan and Iseult. Merlin and Nimue, that is the saddest of sad stories.

Not in all versions, of course. In some she is the cruel enchantress who seduces him, learns everything he knows and then imprisons him, leaving him to die a lingering death. But the story of Nimue and Merlin which I choose to believe is this: for love of the goddess whom she serves she must learn Merlin's lore, and so she seeks him out to seduce him. But Merlin will not fall for just any pretty face, particularly not when he knows he is destined to be betrayed in love. He is a man on his guard for falsehood in a beautiful guise. The only way for Nimue to convince Merlin is to fall truly in love with him. And so she falls, and he falls after her, and even at the moment of their falling she knows she doesn't love him quite enough to turn away from her goddess, and he knows that he truly loves, for the first time in his life, and if it is his destiny to be betrayed by the woman he loves then Nimue will be the one to betray him.

Why is this so great a tragedy? Because, like Macbeth, they always know the truth. Not for a heartbeat does she believe the goddess will release her from her obligation; not for an indrawn breath does he believe he can cheat destiny. I think this makes them gentle with each other; I think it makes them nostalgic for each moment before it's even past. I think it strengthens love to be thus caught in the fierce embrace of inevitability.

How did I get to that sentimental moment?

Oh, yes. Darius Mehta. He who, in the twilight of his life, was fired from his teaching job for discussing *Richard II* as a political rather than a literary text. You admired him for his courage in taking that stand. And I thought, what could he tell his students about politics that they didn't already know? What a waste – all those young minds that will now be deprived of the chance to hear Darius Mehta speak of Shakespeare and what it means to be human. What made him think he should be anything other than that of which he was so gloriously capable? Who made him believe that what he was wasn't good enough?

If someone came in here and started to talk to me of politics when I was reading *Richard II* I would shoo them away.

Stop it. Stop disapproving.

Woman who abandons her child for her lover and flaunts the affair in public while the child is growing up should know better than to disapprove of others.

Woman whose life achieved so little should know better than to demand political commitment in others.

How did this become about you? I promised myself I wouldn't let that happen again.

I'm beginning to resent pen and paper.

It was far better when I had only my books and my daily routine. My life was strictly regimented. But since I've started writing, you've come along, barging in at all moments, disrupting the tides that govern my day. Everything is infected by you, and I can't distinguish now between fiction, memory and my own imagination. Even now, as I write, I have to ask myself: is this gift or punishment? What game is being played with my life? All I know is, I want the Minions to remove from here all temptations to fill these blank pages. Only then can I begin again to forget all that I've lost. Only then can I attempt to forget all that someone else must have gained. Then, I don't need to ask myself questions such as: whose bed do you slip into at night? On whose body do you make your voracious demands?

Sometimes I am happier believing you dead.

Remember the beach that night. How we left the party and found our way to that musty cave and I wanted to leave because of the smell of stale urine, but you pulled me close and soon the cave was filled with another, muskier scent. Then that noise, someone was outside, someone watching, and you didn't care, you only grew more aroused. I could have accused you so many times of perversion, but I always loved you too much to throw that word at you. You had no such inhibitions when it came to my feelings.

How often thoughts of you can lead to anger. And then that goes, as fast as it came, and all I want, my love, is to hold you in my arms, away from all the world.

Come, find me, and let us fly away somewhere, away from all the world.

# XIV

If the door opened and the Poet walked through, I would kill him.

*Let us fly away somewhere, away from all the world.*

I scrunched the papers tightly into a ball, and hurled them across the room. 'You're not taking her away again!' I shouted. The ball of paper hit the window and ricocheted back to land at my feet.

*Woman who abandons her child for her lover and flaunts the affair in public.*

Bastard.

*I could have accused you so many times of perversion.*

Bastard. Bastard. You fat, old, ugly, scar-faced bastard.

For this man, Mama, you left Dad. For this man, you left me, again and again.

I knew those caves at the beach. The scent of them on days when it had been too long since the last time the tide came through and washed them clean of memory. I wanted to be washed clean of memory. I wanted to be embalmed. All fluids, all juices removed. If I angled my face down towards my armpit I'd catch the mingling of my body's odour and deodorant. Angle it further down. Concupiscence.

Things I didn't want to imagine, I was imagining. The beach at night, a cave, her eyes watching someone watching her as she pulled the Poet closer, deeper. I bit down on my knuckle, hard.

*Away from all the world.*

Rabia had been right. There was nothing unfamiliar in this explosion of anger, this desire to have him here so I could bang his head against a wall. I had grown up with this anger, it was almost like a long-lost friend.

'Bastard. You goddamn bastard.'

*Woman who abandons her child.*

How dare you? After all she gave up for you. After all you demanded she give up.

*Woman whose life achieved so little.*

Because of you, bastard, because of you.

In 1980, when the Poet went to Colombia she stayed in Karachi because of all those political commitments in her life. And what did he do? He sent her a postcard.

*S – I've been trying to work on a ghazal but all I can think is this: you are qafia and radif to me – the fixed rhyme and refrain of all the couplets that make up my life. That line would be adolescent drivel if it wasn't entirely true. Love, Yours. P. S. Call me! Write! Come here (I promised I wouldn't make that demand, but this isn't a demand, it's an entreaty. The Sufis were right – Hell is nothing more or less than the absence of the Beloved.)*

When that postcard arrived, I had hidden it away from her. For two days I kept it hidden until I couldn't bear the expectation in her eyes every time the phone rang or she saw the postman toss something over her gate. And so I handed her the postcard. She read it, and then she reached out and gathered me in her arms.

'What do I do?' she had wept into my hair.

I said, 'Go to him.'

What had I hoped? That by saying it I would make her stay? Didn't I know any better by then? But even though I wanted her to stay, I also wanted her to be with him. Theirs was the great love story I worshipped, even as it relegated me to a walk-on role. I was so proud – what a strange word, but that's what it was – of the way she was loved by him, and the way she loved him in return.

*Hell is nothing more or less than the absence of the Beloved.*

How did I see that as love, when it was so obviously just posturing? The Poet calling to his Muse, throwing himself into the drama of separation.

*If someone came in here and started to talk to me of politics when I was reading* Richard II *I would shoo them away.*

And they call you the great revolutionary poet. They put your name in a Master File ranked far above hers. What did you ever do in all those years she was out on the streets, risking her life, crying herself hoarse in rallies? Where were you, great poet? Hiding away in your study, writing and listening to opera, telling us all that you wouldn't publish anything until the collection was complete, tantalizing us all with little glimpses as you read out your politically impassioned verse. What were you going to do? Leave the country again and have it published from afar, while you were safely tucked away somewhere with my mother, having made sure your words were so inflammatory that there was no hope for a reprieve, no chance you and she would ever return from that exile?

Or were you never going to publish them at all? Three years you worked on that collection. How much longer would it have continued? We couldn't call you a coward as long as you were writing, couldn't say you had lost your nerve.

Did you stage your own death, Omi? Did you stage your death and arrange for your poems to be burnt so that my mother's reaction could give you a whole new world of inspiration to draw on for your next collection? Did you stage your death so that those poems would pass into legend as only lost works can? Never learn Italian, never publish your writing. That way it's possible to believe the words have transformed into music. Yes, those poems became myth, and you became legend. And what about my mother? What did she become? What did you make her, first by your refusal to marry her and then with your alleged and too convincing death? You always were, always have been, the Poet. Through everything. Through the scandal of your affair with my mother, through all the affront people took to the vulgarity of your early poems, through everything else, you always were, always will be, the Poet. But my mother who gave so much of her life to fighting forces she knew she had little hope of defeating, she is first and foremost the Jezebel, the fallen woman who abandoned her husband and child. And if anyone tries to say, but what about her activism?, there are all too many people ready to point out that her commitments to the cause must have been pretty feeble if she could run off for three years just because you snapped your fingers in Colombia.

*Let us fly away somewhere, away from all the world.*

You bastard, you bastard, I wish you were dead, I wish they had tortured you until you burst their ear-drums with your screaming.

I leaned forward and then jerked back, banging my head against the wall with all the violence I could muster. Before the pain could fully make itself known, a painting above me jiggled off its hook and fell towards me. I had a momentary vision of red and black swirls coming at me, and I put up my arms with a shout and batted it away.

The painting fell to one side, face down, and then I was just a woman with an aching head, looking down at a cracked frame.

I stood up, holding my head, and went to the kitchen. I grabbed a fistful of ice out of the freezer, wrapped the ice in a dupatta, and held it to my head.

A burst of gunfire punctured the silence which surrounded me. The dupatta fell from my hand. But then I realized what the gunfire must be about and I leaned out of the window to look for the shaving of moon which the Ruhat-e-Hilal committee must have seen in order to declare tomorrow Eid. I couldn't see it – but rounds of ammunition were now being pumped into the sky from all directions and there was no mistaking the celebration in the air.

When I heard you were dead, Omi, there was a moment in which I thought, at least now he'll never take her away from me again.

The thought made me stop as I was bending down to retrieve the fallen dupatta. My fingers dangled just inches from the cloth which was already seeping liquid on to the tiled floor. Leucippus, in the fourth century BC, wondered how water, having transformed into ice, could then melt into water again. He concluded that there was an essence which remained immutable through the transformation which allowed the water to move from one state to another and then back again. Leucippus coined the term 'atoms'. What would Leucippus say about the atoms of our character, the atoms of love?

I lay down on the floor, my head resting against the dupatta-wrapped ice, and held my hand in front of my eyes. There was the scar, cutting across my lifeline – a reminder of the penance I had exacted on myself with a kitchen knife for allowing any part of Omi's death to cause me even that briefest moment of relief. I had made sure to cut deep enough to scar, so that I would never forget my own small-heartedness.

I had been too hard on myself. Omi was capable of being far more small-hearted, it was clear.

There was a dusting of flour on the ground. I reached out and traced 'MAMA'. A name appearing in a cloud, a word emanating a ghostly-white mist.

*Your voracious demands. I could have accused you so many times of perversion.*

Somehow, that was the hardest thing to accept. That he would throw such an accusation at her. That he would join the ranks of those unable to accept her frank sexuality.

When I was an adolescent, Mama had sat me down to tell me about the facts of life.

'Oh, please. I've known for years,' I said, aghast at the

prospect of having to hear my mother even say the word 'sex'.

'I'm sure you know the technical side of things. The "Insert flap A into slot B" side of things,' she said, and I almost ran out of the room. 'But don't tell me you don't have questions.'

'Well.' I fiddled with something or the other, didn't meet her eyes. 'Does it hurt?'

When I looked up I could see her mind reaching back into memory. 'Mama!' I said. 'Please!'

'What?'

'You can't stand in front of me and start thinking about . . . that.'

She laughed her wonderful, unabashed laugh. 'Sweetheart, I can't stop being a woman just because I'm your mother. Stop looking so outraged. It's not as though I'm showing you pictures of myself in the act.'

'There are pictures?'

'Of course there aren't pictures.' She bit off the end of the sentence and frowned. 'Unless your father still has them.'

'Mama!'

'I'm joking, silly.' She placed her palm on the top of my head.

'You're really not a normal mother.'

'I know.' She sat down on her bed and pulled me down next to her. 'Do you mind?'

'Some days.'

'Aasmaani, I'm sorry.'

'Don't. Mama, don't.'

She leaned back, resting her weight on the heels of her hands, and smiled brightly at me. 'Let me tell you a secret. To answer your earlier question. The first time it happened, it didn't hurt. But it was definitely strange. And I thought, "You must be doing this wrong. Surely all that fuss can't be about *this*."' Then she rocked back with laughter again, and despite the blood rushing to my face I couldn't help but see the joke.

When we stopped laughing and I looked up, there was Omi

203

standing in the doorway, smiling. That look in his eyes as he walked over to her and kissed her hand – I had taken that look for nothing but love. And now, what was I to believe now?

The phone had been ringing for a long while now. My anonymous caller again. No one else had such persistence. I knew if I picked it up there would be no answer, and no originating number on my caller ID screen. I stood up to answer it anyway. I would say down the line, 'Bring him back to me.' I would say, 'Keep him locked away for ever.'

But when I picked it up it went dead almost immediately.

I lay down on the sofa. Omi and Mama – what was their great love? Did it end up a catalogue of accusations? Is that what all that early passion shifted into without my even noticing it? It didn't seem possible. But then, it didn't seem possible that he would accuse her of perversions. What all had I failed to see about them? How much can a fifteen-year-old really know of the relationship between a man and a woman?

Yeh aag bhee bujh jaye gee.

*This fire, too, will burn out.*

I pulled myself upright. I wouldn't start thinking of his poetry.

The phone rang again, my mobile this time, and my gratitude at being interrupted gave way to a feeling of disquiet when I saw the name on the display was MIRZA.

I let it ring two, three, four times. After the fifth ring it would go to voicemail. The fifth ring. I answered.

'Who is this?' said Mirza.

'You're the one calling me.'

'I just got home from holiday to a great many tedious messages.' His voice, as ever, was so languid it was camp. 'Only one of any interest. Someone swearing, with feeling, into my answering machine and hanging up. I put together the time of the call with the information on caller ID and it appears that obscenity came from this number. So, I just wanted to know. Should I take it personally?

'Mirza, you take everything personally. Even eclipses.'

There was a pause. 'Samina?' he said, the word barely above a whisper.

In my stomach, something somersaulted. 'Right DNA, wrong generation.'

Another pause, and then a soft laugh. 'Well, well, well, little Aasmaani.'

There was a crackle down the line. Was it tapped? Mirza had gone for the funeral. What did he know, what did he suspect? What could he tell me about how it really was with my mother and Omi all those years I was too busy weaving a fairytale of love to bother with anything so mundane as reality? 'Can we meet, Mirza? I'd like to catch up.'

'Catch up? Aasmaani, even at fourteen, you were way ahead of me.' He laughed again. 'But of course we can meet. No time like the present.'

We agreed on a café, which I knew would be free of the scores of Chaand Raat celebrants, and less than ten minutes later – having successfully avoided the traffic jams around areas where families had driven out to see Karachi lit up in lights like a bejewelled bride trying to draw attention away from the ungainliness of her natural façade – I reversed into an empty spot in a plot of land next to the café. As I pulled up the hand-brake I saw a man getting out of his car – a red, gleaming vehicle with aspirations to sportiness. Mirza the Snake.

I turned off my lights and ignition and watched him. The last time I had seen him he had been a man who wore creased kurta-shalwars and an air of glamorous dissipation. Long before heroin chic, Mirza had a startling beauty that was all about emaciation. Whether he picked up a book of poems or reached out to touch the Poet's shoulder, he treated his body as something that might just fall apart, and yet it was abundantly clear – even to me when I should have been too young to understand these things – that he subjected his flesh to all manner of torments, and that it wasn't glass but wire of which his bones were fashioned.

I never really had a personal relationship with him, the way I did with many of Omi and my mother's friends who teased me and spoilt me and asked me for my opinions on adult matters like politics and religion and books. But he was around so often that I knew quite intimately his face, his particular gestures, the cadences of his voice. And I knew he looked at me in a way that made me ashamed to like it. Many people thought he was just another one of the Acolytes – that group of men who I always believed were the main reason my mother and Omi lived in separate homes. She had no time for them – the vaunting egos, the self-absorption, the lachrymose intoxication. 'I loved him least after two a.m.,' she once said of Omi, who was always early to bed except when the Acolytes came over and kept him up until dawn with whisky, poetry and hashish. But though Mirza the Snake was always part of those late-night gatherings he wasn't really an Acolyte. He didn't ultimately defer to Omi the way the others did, nor preface every criticism with lavish praise. In many ways, Omi regarded him as an equal because he knew more about mystic poetry from a myriad traditions around the world than anyone else. An atheist obsessed with God, that's how my mother described him. Burdened with that love which was always just beyond reach because he didn't believe in the Beloved.

After we all thought Omi was dead, Mirza the Snake became the most persistent of his circle who tried to share my mother's grief with her. I remember him best from this period. One night, he walked up the driveway while my mother and I were sitting in Dad's garden. She had been avoiding him – and everyone – for weeks.

He ambled up to her and said, 'Push everyone else away, Samina – they're fools for thinking they understand what you've lost – but this is me, Mirza. You're the only person whose company I can bear right now and I suspect that's not a one-way street.' He held out his hand. 'Let's be each other's companions in grief.'

I was terrified when he said that. Terrified she'd agree. This must have been soon enough after the news of the Poet's death for me to believe I would have her to myself when the edge of grieving wore off. Before I knew that his death was the one thing with which I would never be able to compete.

But she narrowed her eyes at him. 'Let's not pretend to be friends, Mirza. He loved me, and that's one thing you can't forgive me.'

He reached out his long fingers, took the cigarette from her hand and held it to his lips. 'You burnt the only copies of his last poems,' he said, and turned and walked out, listing slightly with the breeze.

Sixteen years later, the walk had changed. It was the walk now of a portly man able to bear all manner of buffeting. The kurta-shalwar was made of richer fabric now, the kind that didn't wrinkle. And his features appeared to have had blotting paper held over them for a decade or more.

The Fata Morgana in the backseat of my car was gesturing for me to drive away. Mirza's real talent, my mother used to say, was for finding a wound and driving a nail through it.

I gestured impatiently at the backseat, got out of the car and walked up to the café. Pushing open the wooden doors, I looked around the cosy space with its five tables of varying sizes, of which only the long table had customers seated at it. There was no sign of Mirza, but one of the waiters, seeing my eyes scan the room, pointed up the stairs. I climbed the steps set alongside a long window which had a tree outside festooned in twinkling fairy lights and it was with a mixture of satisfaction and panic that I saw Mirza was the only person in the small upstairs section, his girth almost spilling off the cushion of the wrought-iron chair.

# XV

Mirza stood up when he saw me.

'Aasmaani Inqalab, all grown up,' he said. He moved forward, caught me by both shoulders and pressed his lips against my cheek. 'Chand Raat Mubarak,' he whispered, his mouth close to my ear, somehow managing to transform the greeting into something verging between intimacy and obscenity.

I pulled away and he smiled. 'I see I still make you nervous.' He sat down and gestured to the chair opposite him at the table which seemed incredibly small. Leaning forward, he almost entirely swallowed up the space between himself and the empty chair. 'Have a seat. And don't look so suspicious. You're the one who proposed this rendezvous.'

I pulled the chair away from the table and sat down, legs crossed, one arm crooked on the back. 'Sorry about the answering-machine message. I was researching something for STD – I work there now – and I had a pressing question I thought you could answer. I'm usually quite adept at hanging up before I start swearing.'

He reached into a bowl on the table and popped a pickled green chilli into his mouth. 'What was the question?'

I waved my hand dismissively. 'Something about the history of the ghazal. A minor matter really, for a five-minute segment of a show that never got made in the end – but the producer likes turning a feather into a flock of crows, so there are no minor matters, only minor pay-offs.' I was moving unthinkingly between English and Urdu, as was he, and though that was common enough, it had been a while since my Urdu vocabulary and syntax heightened into that old, now-vanishing courtly Urdu in which Mirza and the Poet always spoke to each other. I have Omi's voice in my mouth, I thought.

'But here we are after all these years. Hardly a minor payoff, I'd say.'

He was smiling pleasantly but even so I found myself looking down at my menu and pretending to read it intently just so that he wouldn't see my unease. Somewhere beneath that mountain of flesh was the first man who had made me wish I wasn't just a child. I used to fantasize about kissing him when I was too young to fantasize about anything beyond a kiss.

I felt slightly sick at the memory.

'So,' Mirza said, after the waiter had taken our orders – coffee for me, grilled chops for him – 'You're a dogsbody at STD. Is that your Raisin of Death?'

It was an expression the Poet used to use. His version of *raison d'être*.

'Is sycophancy your Raisin of Death, Mirza?' His sporty car and expensive kurta-shalwar confirmed the truth of the rumours I'd been hearing for the last decade: soon after democracy returned to Pakistan in 1988, five months after my mother's disappearance, Mirza became the unofficial Poet Laureate of Pakistan's politicos. On birthdays, anniversaries, in the run-up to elections, on the passage of new constitutional amendments, Mirza produced verses to fit the occasion for anyone willing to pay the price, regardless of their political affiliation. When the military had returned to power in 1999 the demand for his sycophantic poetry had only increased among his former patrons; politicians, it seemed, had a greater need for adulation when power was far from their grasp than when they were occupying high office. And with the recent return to pseudo-democracy, he was probably up to his eyeballs in rhymes about both the victors and those who were cheated of their rightful victories.

Mirza the Snake tried not to look irritated, and failed. 'Not all poets are fortunate enough to have rich mistresses,' he said. 'Being a kept man was the price your dear Omi had to pay for the integrity of his art. Face it, he was as much of a whore as I am.' He bit down on the tip of his thumb and looked at me as though studying my reaction, learning from it whether he'd found the wound through which he could drive a nail.

I smiled at him, with all the superiority I could bring to bear on an upturned pair of lips. Not even close, Mirza. Strange how, in testing for wounds, we look first to find our own wounds on the bodies opposite us. Mirza with his unbridled jealousy of anyone with a claim on Omi's affection – of course this would be the story he'd choose. And right then I saw how absurd it was – the notion that anything other than love had been at the very core of their relationship. Whatever else might have got mixed in, nothing could touch or diminish that core. That damned core which had always made it possible for them to fly away together, away from me and the world.

My smile was sagging, and Mirza's eyes took on an air of triumph. I laughed. 'That's a convenient revision of history, Mirza. It discounts the fact that he loved her most, and serves as role model for your poetic prostitution. Two birds, one stone. You were always economical with language.'

He shook his head. 'You were the most charming child, you know. And now – how hard you've grown. Or is it just brittle?'

The waiter appeared with my cup of coffee. I took a packet of sugar, tore the top off with my teeth, and measured out half a spoon. I was about to place the half-empty packet next to my cup after stirring in the sugar when I saw Mirza's eyes on it. An old habit of his which always amused Omi came to mind. I skimmed a teaspoon just beneath the surface of the coffee, lifted it out and then sprinkled sugar into the spoon, watching the white grains settle, thinned, at the bottom of the liquid. Carefully, I handed the spoon to him. He took it in his fingers at the point where bowl meets stem and lifted it to his mouth. We seemed to be caught in a painting, an artist we couldn't see drafting the lines of our bodies into positions of ritual that we didn't quite understand but which automatically transferred us into another time.

As he put the spoon down, with a nod of gratitude that acknowledged the tableau we had so unexpectedly found ourselves in, he seemed suddenly avuncular. He was a man who had known me when my hair was in pigtails. Uncle Mirza, I used to call him. More than that, he was a man linked to those golden years when my mother and Omi lived in Karachi, the three-year exile over; a man who knew me before the brittleness set in. All I wanted was to freeze the tableau, and I saw that he wanted it, too. That old tableau in which our presence in the same space always meant the two of them were somewhere nearby.

I felt tears prickling at my eyelids. I wanted both of them somewhere nearby, I wanted it desperately. I rubbed my thumb across the scar on my palm. If I put down the worst I had ever thought of her in a letter, all my anger, all my accusations, it would be so much more vindictive and poisonous than all that Omi had written. Sixteen years locked away from her, how could I expect him never to lash out?

*The Sufis were right – Hell is nothing more or less than the absence of the Beloved.*

Mirza first came to Omi's attention with a poem he had written which drew its inspiration from the Sufi version of Lucifer and Adam's expulsion from Eden. *Iblis aur Aadam*, it was called. A poem in rhyming couplets, creating a conversation between Iblis and Aadam, meeting thousands of years after Allah has banished both of them from heaven. It starts with recriminations and petty sniping, and moves on to Iblis challenging Aadam's love for Allah.

I loved him more than you, Iblis says. That's why being banished from his presence placed me in Hell, and you only in this middle ground of mud.

No, Aadam replies. My crime was merely disobedience; yours was pride. That is the reason for our differing punishments.

Our punishment is the same, says Iblis. Exile from his presence. We merely view that exile differently. But since you bring it up, your crime was far worse than mine. Yours arose from wilfulness, mine from love. I hated you because you supplanted me in my Beloved's affection. And if that wasn't pain enough, he asked me then to accept the falling-off of his love by bowing to you. He was unfair, Aadam, to both of us. He gave you curiosity, he gave me this faculty of eternal and undiminishing love – and then he turned those faculties against us. Admit it, we have been wronged.

Aadam replies, I cannot admit it. If I offend him further he may send me to where you are – to that place which is Hell precisely because it offers no hope of reprieve, no hope that I may return to Him in Heaven.

Soon, Aadam and Iblis are weeping in each other's arms. Allah sees this and knows the time has come. He turns the sky to the red of stained leather. Aadam turns joyfully towards Heaven as Iblis begins to make his weary way back to Hell.

Iblis, the Lord speaks. Where are you going?

To the prison of eternal separation to which you have condemned me, Iblis answers.

And the Lord says, Beloved, have you forgotten? Of all my attributes the foremost are these: I am the Merciful, the Compassionate.

Omi had loved that. It is the first and the final love story, he would remind my mother. It is the story in which we all live. Moses and Changez Khan and Marilyn Monroe and you and me, my love, we are all just players in that great story. Iblis and Allah. Love makes us devils, love sends us to hell, love saves us.

I brushed a tear away from my eyes. All these years of watching bad television instead of reading his poetry – it had almost got me believing that love was not a thing that could draw in anger and pettiness. I should have been reading him all these years, I should have been reading early Mirza.

I looked up at Mirza who was rotating the spoon in his hands, catching his face turning convex and concave by turn. How young he must have been when he wrote *Iblis aur Aadam*. He first joined the Poet's circle when he was still a student. The Poet used to refer to him as 'the next generation'. He was all fire and passion, then, constantly telling the Poet what he should be writing about, where his responsibility lay.

'They're out there,' he had railed once, walking up and down my mother's dining room, waving his finger in the air. 'They're out there, those men of war and politics, shouting about their God, insisting everyone own up to their relationship with Him, declare your devotion down on your knees, in Arabic, for all to see. It's an obscenity to make love so public.'

*It's an obscenity to make love so public.* He had said that with my mother in the room. Was that before or after the caves at the beach? I felt almost embarrassed now to think of those lines – for the first time it seemed simply rude to read words Omi meant for my mother alone. I felt I'd been caught peeping through a keyhole, and I had only myself to blame if what I saw didn't meet my expectations of what my mother and her lover should be saying and doing to each other behind closed doors.

'Can I hear some poetry, Mirza? Please. For old times' sake.' He looked startled and I realized he was as lost in his thoughts about those days as I had been. 'Go on. Recite a poem for me.'

'All right.' He leaned back in his chair. 'I'll do better than recite. I put this one to music myself.' He plucked at the air as though searching out notes on a sitar, and then, softly, he began to sing.

I closed my eyes. How I had missed this. The Poet never sang his own verse – though he was unrestrained about belting out arias with much confidence and little talent – but sometimes my mother sang his words for him. She had an arresting voice, unashamed to use its own smokiness to haunting effect.

Mirza's voice wasn't arresting, but it was beautiful. Words leaped clear from his throat. 'Subah kee shahadat . . .' The martyrdom of morning? Absurdly self-indulgent poetic moment. I opened my eyes. He was weaving his hand through invisible air traffic, gaze fixed far ahead of him.

I leaned my head sideways against the wall, and settled in to listen to the words. It was a poem about childhood, about picking falsas off bushes with friends now dead. Nothing remarkable in most of it. Nostalgia, lyricism, imagery of red, round berries bursting with juices into young mouths, which added a sexual undercurrent that ran through the whole poem and – how obvious and how irritating – got picked up again, more strongly this time, in the inviting fruit with maggots at its core. But amidst the clichés were startling images – the acned boy imagining falsas swelling to ripeness under his skin; the youngest of the boys biting into the fruit to discover a tooth already embedded in a falsa; the boys stuffing falsas down their clothes and then clasping each other close, red stains spreading across the fronts of their white kameezes as they pulled away from the violent embrace.

Mirza stopped singing. 'So what's your verdict?' he said.

'You should have been a much better poet by now.' I didn't mean it unkindly and somehow he seemed to see that.

'Yes,' he said, looking at his manicured fingernails. 'I should have found a subject to replace all this content. There are some wonderful voices in Urdu poetry these days, despite everything. I'm not even in the second tier. You keep up with it at all? The world of Urdu versification?'

I shook my head. 'All that went out of my life when he did. I don't even read his poetry any more, let alone anyone else's.'

214

'He.' Mirza shook his head. 'His fault. My failures, all his fault.'

'That's not fair.'

Mirza didn't look at me. 'I don't deny he was the best teacher anyone could have hoped for. But his death, Aasmaani. His death taught me the price poets have to pay for their integrity. I saw that price up close, every shattered bone of it.'

'You saw . . . you saw his body?' This is what I had wanted to know from Mirza when I dialled his number, and now it was as though I were hearing the news of Omi's death for the first time. In that instant it seemed possible – no, inescapable – that all those pages had been a hoax, and that 'shattered beyond recognition' had just been a turn of phrase to mean 'badly injured'.

But then Mirza said one word, the only word I could have hoped for: 'Unrecognizable.'

I released a breath I hadn't known I was holding. 'So it might not have been him,' I said before I could stop myself.

Mirza shook his head. 'His wallet was in his pocket, stuffed with all those little scraps of paper he used to jot lines of poetry on. And you could still . . . the size, the shape of him. And his doctor had medical records. They did tests. It was him. Why wouldn't it be him? Why would anyone fake a poet's death?'

'The doctor died just weeks later.'

Mirza finally looked at me. 'Aasmaani, don't you think your mother and I would have clung to any conspiracy theory that allowed us to believe he was alive if there seemed even the slightest chance?' He looked at his hands, turning them back to front. 'I saw him. I saw what they did to him. When the family went to get his body from the morgue – distant family, third cousins at best, to whom he meant nothing – I was there. I was there outside, and I told one of them that I was the Poet's illegitimate son. He believed me. They'd heard all sorts of stories about him – they would have believed anything.

So they let me go with them into the morgue.' He was still looking at his hands. 'The first part of him I saw was his hand.'

I put my own hand on top of his and squeezed. If only I trusted him just a little bit, I'd have told him the truth.

'I never told your mother what he looked like. I didn't want her to imagine what I had to remember. What I still remember. I looked at that hand, swollen, discoloured . . .'

Omi. Oh God, Omi.

It wasn't him. Breathe, Aasmaani. It wasn't him.

'. . . that hand which had written the sweetest words of the age, and I knew, right then, that I would never dare try to be the poet he believed I could be. And so here I am now, a middle-aged hack. And you, the closest thing he had to a child, who remembered more of his poetry in your head when you were fourteen than even he or I or your mother could, you're a media underling without enough information about ghazals to fill a five-minute segment.' He shifted sideways in his chair, stretched his legs in front of him and gazed disconsolately at his toes. 'Don't tell me I'm the only one who learned the value of certain silences.'

If they come home, what will they see when they look at me? A failure, a coward, a small-hearted creature.

I pressed the palm of my hand against the cold edge of the table, and turned to Mirza. 'And what happened to your love affair with all those poets in love with God?'

He waved his hand dismissively. 'God has become the most dangerous subject of all. I don't even think of Him any more.'

'Leave him in the hands of the extremists, is that your plan?'

I hoped to irritate him out of despondency, but he only shook his head.

I ran my hands along the edge of the glass-topped table. 'The Poet never said you had to write about God or politics to be a good poet. He said, to be a good poet . . .'

'. . . you must write good poetry. That's all.'

'You must have the freedom, even in times of war and barbarity . . .'

'. . . to write of first love, or the taste of mangoes, or the sight of a turtle gliding over the sand after she's laid her eggs.' He lowered his head into his hands. 'But I don't want to write about any of those things. I want to write about his death, and how it killed me, and I'm too afraid to do that, so I just go on being dead.'

My brother, I thought. My twin, my alter ego, my brother. I touched him on the sleeve and he looked up.

'All this emotion.' He brought his hands together in front of his face and traced a globe, his hands separating at the North Pole, meeting again at the South. 'How am I supposed to know how to react when you're sitting here looking so much like the girl you once were and also so much like the woman your mother was when I first knew her and the world was ours to shape?' He dragged the palms of his hand slowly down his fleshy cheeks. 'And I was beautiful then.' He caught my hand, brought it to his face and pressed my fingers down, beneath the layers of muscle and tissue, to where his sharply angled cheekbones still resided. 'I felt so breakable after I saw the Poet's corpse.'

'Tell me about the funeral. Who was there?'

Mirza made a gesture of not knowing. 'It was all done so quickly and quietly. I only knew about it because I was there when the relatives came for his body. The government's instructions, I suppose. They didn't want his funeral to start a riot. I was the only one there who really knew him. Even the schoolmaster's brother's family in Karachi weren't informed. And the schoolmaster and the aunt, the only two people in the village who ever meant anything to him, were dead. So I was the only one mourning. It was awful.'

'And who burnt his poems?'

Mirza flinched. 'I don't know. Some government lackeys.' Then he looked at me and I was startled by the greed in his eyes. 'Do you remember them? Any of them? Fragments, even?'

I shook my head. 'No, I'm sorry, Mirza. I wish I did. Mama and I, we both tried so hard to remember. But he only ever read them once or twice after he'd written them, so all we could remember was how it felt to hear him reciting those words with the ink still fresh on the pages.'

'Yes. It's the same with me. Your mother told me it was the same with her. You know it's the one proof of God's existence I find myself hoping for – words resurrected from ash.'

'When did she tell you?'

'Hmm? Oh, I don't know. Sometime after the Poet's death. I did keep trying, Aasmaani. You have to acknowledge that. I kept trying to pull her out of that listlessness she fell into. Usually she'd just hang up when she heard my voice or refuse to see me, but sometimes I'd get a sentence or two out of her.' He shook his head. 'What a waste.'

'The burnt poems?'

'Your mother.' He touched his flabby cheeks again. 'I always knew I was a coward. But there were all those people who were turned to flame by his death, who wrote and marched and resisted, above all, resisted all those tyrannies he'd fought against. And I would have sworn your mother would have been foremost among their ranks. But no. She and I, we were the two who loved him most and we were the two who failed him most spectacularly when he died.'

'I loved him, too.' At that moment I knew it to be true, however complicated that truth might have been, however mixed in with jealousy.

'Yes. I suppose you must have. It was hard not to.'

'What did you love about him?'

Mirza looked at me as though I were a child again, asking a question that revealed nothing so much as my ignorance. 'I loved him. That's all there is to it. I loved him the way I've never loved anyone else.'

I wiped the ring of coffee on the saucer, wiped the bottom of the coffee cup. 'And who hated him, Mirza? Hated him enough to do what was done to him?' *Hated him enough to imprison him all these years?*

A great weariness took over Mirza's face. 'That's what we like to believe, isn't it? That he had to die in such a brutal fashion because of some great reason. Some great fear. Some great hate. That's the only way we can accept it, isn't it? How often do you replay it in your mind, Aasmaani? How do you see it happening?'

I shook my head. 'Replay what? See what?'

'His death.' He was whispering now. 'I see it every day, even now. I see it as avoidable.' He smoothed the tablecloth between us with his fingers which still retained something of their old elegance. 'I see some low-ranked government lackeys picking him up, taking him for a drive, just to scare him. The way they do with journalists all the time. His new book of poems was nearly done. That wasn't a secret. So some thugs pick him up just to have a talk. Just to scare him out of publishing. It had happened before. He'd got a few punches and a lot of threats and came home to write a poem about the whole thing. But this time, this time something happened differently.' He kept smoothing the tablecloth though there was nothing to smooth. 'He mocked them, that's what I think. His tongue could be a scythe when his compassion didn't get in the way. I think he mocked them. Mocked their clothes, their occupation, their car, their manhood. Mocked their looks. Mocked their attempts to frighten him. Mocked violence. And one of them picked up something heavy, something that could bludgeon, and hit him, just to shut him up. And then hit him again. And again. And kept on. And the thing about keeping on, Aasmaani – whether you keep on hitting or you keep on obsessing or keep on lying or keep on deceiving – at a point that's all you can do. Keep on. Keep on. Sever his tongue, break each unbroken bone—'

'Mirza. Stop it. Stop it. Stop it.' I took his hand in mine, and squeezed tight. He drew a deep breath, and for a moment we were equals, with nothing in common but our pain, with everything in common because of our pain.

'Why did he have to be so arrogant? Why couldn't he just have pretended to be scared? They would have let him go. We would all still be whole. The Poet, your mother, you, me. We would all still be whole.'

'It might not have happened that way, Mirza.'

'Then how? How do you see it happening?'

I shook my head. 'I don't know what happened.'

'But how do you imagine it?'

'I don't.'

There was a sound of footsteps. The waiter, coming up the stairs with Mirza's food. Mirza waved him away.

'You don't imagine it? In all these years you haven't imagined it?'

'No.'

'That scared of what it did to your mother?'

'Meaning what?'

'Meaning, if thinking about it could drive her mad, mightn't it do the same to you?'

'Drive her mad?'

'Yes. Drive her mad. Imagining his death and knowing that if she hadn't insisted on coming back to Karachi it wouldn't have happened. If she hadn't insisted on coming back because of you he wouldn't be dead. If it wasn't for her and you he wouldn't be dead.'

I took a long sip of coffee. 'Well. Things keep coming back to Lady Macbeth. Is that how you imagine her final two years here, Mirza? Years in which you almost never saw her. You think she floated around in a white nightgown, holding a candle above her head, sleepless with guilt, whispering, can all the seas of Arabia wash this blood from my hand?' I tried to put the coffee cup down, but it kept missing the middle of the saucer and hitting the edges. On the third attempt, I managed it.

Then I looked up at him. 'She didn't come back for me, Mirza. I was never reason to stay or to return for either of them. Neither were you. That's what kills us.'

'Their shadows kill us, Aasmaani. The shadows we cower in. They asked, how do we change the world? How do we take on dictators without sacrificing the metre of a line? How do we keep from surrendering this nation? And you and I, their heirs, what do we ask? Where did my mummy go? Did my father-figure love me? We look at the mess of our lives, we look at the mess in which we live, and we say they failed us. We say it because that is so much easier than saying we are the ones who have failed. God, Aasmaani, what is this world we're living in? How did we let it get like this? They would never have let it get like this.'

The roots of war are seeped in oil, so we join an oil company. A city we love becomes suspicious of the people of our religion so we leave that city. We don't resist the abuses of power, we just make it clear we're smart enough, aware enough, to understand our powerlessness. And at some level we believe that makes us admirable.

'Mirza, things keep on. Like you said. They keep on and they keep on. Macbeth again. Remember, Omi always used to say the key to understanding Macbeth is understanding that he doesn't keep killing to retain power. He keeps killing because he's just following the momentum of that initial thrust of a dagger through Duncan's heart. So the world keeps on. The momentum is more than you or I can fight against.'

'Enough with Macbeth. You know, I don't even think the Poet much liked the play. He was commissioned to translate Shakespeare, so he chose the shortest play.' He laughed shakily. 'We keep trying to construct meaning out of things. Why was he killed? Why did she become the way she became? Why did he choose Macbeth? We want grand reasons. We always want grand reasons. It was the shortest play. That's it. That is it. Yes. I stopped believing in grandness when the Poet died. Greatness and grandness, stopped believing in them. And you? What do you believe in, Samina's daughter, when you look around at this world in which the only grandness that exists is the grandness of opposing extremisms? What did they teach us, after all, that would be of any use in this stinking mess of a world?'

'Nothing.'

'Don't tell me "Nothing."' His voice was shaking with anger. 'It can't be nothing. Tell me what they taught us.'

'They taught us to fight only with words. The words of an individual poet, or the words of a gathering of thousands chanting their slogans of protests.'

Mirza made a noise that would have been a laugh if it wasn't so humourless. Here we both were, Mama and Omi's heirs, drowning in words. We each had thousands at our disposal. And I suspected that Mirza could still see, as I did, that they were right – words continued to be both the battleground and the weapon. Mirza and I could recognize, as well as they ever did, the outrage in the discrepancy between 'what is' and 'what is claimed'. But Mirza and I would do nothing about it. We would do nothing because we knew that in our refusal to fight for language with bombs or lies lay our defeat. No, it was nothing so grand as that. We knew how voices could be silenced. We knew that most shameful secret which Mama and Omi had tried so hard to keep from us: violence is more powerful than language.

'So we lose,' I said.

'So we are lost.' Mirza looked past me out of the window and I knew he wasn't seeing the fairy lights outside, or even the sky.

We sat there in silence until it became unbearable. And then I left. As I drove away I could see him silhouetted against the window, still looking outside, seeing my mother and the Poet, and seeing himself, too, that version of himself that had existed when he still thought he was unbreakable.

Omi, how will your heart survive everything that has happened here in your absence?

# XVI

The following morning was Eid. Despite everything that had happened the previous evening, I woke up smiling. Not true. I woke up, first, with a feeling of panic. A month of rising at dawn made waking in broad daylight feel like a transgression. But then I remembered, oh yes, Ramzan's over. It's Eid.

Eid had always been the day when I was simply Beema and Dad's daughter, Rabia's sister. The Poet was dismissive of organized religion ('The more I sin, the more God will want me in heaven where he can keep an eye on me,' he'd said in one of his more inflammatory interviews) and my mother said it seemed false to celebrate Eid when she hadn't fasted, so even when they were in Karachi I never saw them on that day. And so Eid became, for me, the one day of the year when I could take a break from being her daughter and look around the table at Beema's relatives, who descended on us en masse for lunch, and think, this sanity is, but for a technicality, my family.

Year after year, Eid in Dad and Beema's house followed a pattern as unvarying and comforting as the progression of the moon from sliver to sphere marked with dark seas and craters. We'd wake up early – though it seemed late compared to the dawn rising – and someone (usually Beema) would hold up the morning papers to let us know that once again ritual had been maintained and the papers had prophetically announced that Eid would be celebrated 'with fervour, festivity'. Before long, the house would fill with the smells of Eid lunch being cooked in the kitchen, and my father would give Rabia and me kulfis on sticks, bought the day before at Sony Sweets, and take us for a drive to get us out of Beema's way as she made her elaborate feast. This was how Dad liked to celebrate Eid. Driving with his daughters, Indian film songs from long ago blasting through the speakers, consuming food in public for the first time in a month. He was always too lost in the music to communicate, so before long whoever was in the passenger seat would get tired of twisting around to talk to her sister and would clamber into the back seat.

Then, Rabia and I would categorize everyone we passed on Karachi's streets. Men whose white shalwar-kameezes were creased in a way that showed they'd been kneeling and prostrating at morning prayers; women whose harried tailors had only finished stitching their clothes late the night before and still hadn't quite got it right, leaving the women to tug at the seams around their armpits or pull up the neckline which revealed just a little too much skin; couples, stiff-backed and silent in cars, who had just been arguing about which relatives they had to call on and how long they had to stay; Parsis; drivers sent out by frantic housewives to find that one missing ingredient needed for today's lunch, in a city where all the shops were closed for the holiday; children disgusted with their parents for running late, because it meant skipping visits to relatives known to be generous with Eidi. Every so often, when we saw someone who didn't fit into any category and who had an air of general dissatisfaction (as opposed to all those with Eid-specific dissatisfaction) we'd whisper to each other, 'Atheist.' I knew atheists aplenty, thanks to the Poet, but it always seemed possible to forget that on Eid mornings and regard the unbelievers as strange creatures whose afflictions could not be spoken of out loud.

We'd return home in time to greet the mid-morning callers, and every year, without fail, there was a moment of panic between Beema and my father when some distant relatives who hadn't been invited for lunch dropped in to say Eid Mubarak and looked as though they planned to stay beyond the consumption of savaiyan and the distribution of Eidi ('prize money for being young', my mother used to call it). When the suspense of their unknown intentions grew too much to bear Beema would say, 'Of course, you're staying for lunch,' and then they'd turn red, get up quickly, say no, no, and start to leave, whereupon Beema would get so embarrassed about appearing to force them out (though that was, of course, exactly her intention) that she'd plead with them to stay, plead so intently that they would grow quite confused, unable to discern what protocol demanded of them. But then – blessedly – they'd remember that, no, they really were expected somewhere else, and couldn't possibly stay for lunch without offending whoever had invited them. When they said that everyone's shoulders would slump in relief, and the relatives would leave, and for a few minutes we'd believe they were really lovely people, next year we should invite them. Then the lunch guests would arrive – about fifteen or twenty of them – and gossip and eat for hours. After they'd left, we'd lock the gate from outside so it appeared no one was home, and settle down to watch a video, some romantic comedy usually, since Beema always got to choose it as recompense for the effort she'd put into getting the lunch organized.

This year, with Beema in Islamabad, Rabia had taken over the responsibility of the family lunch, and as I was still lying in bed enjoying the light streaming in between the curtains, I heard her push through the connecting door and yell, 'Smaani! Help! There are six disasters already, and one of them involves the Tyrant!' The Tyrant was one of Beema's aunts, and I knew immediately that the disaster was related to the Tyrant's decision, three years earlier, that she would climb no more stairs. Concomitant with this decision came her discovery of her love for ice-cream, and the sprightly slip of a woman had now transformed into a great mass of lethargy who caused many a marital row in the family when husbands

225

declared that at the next family gathering someone else could help hoist the chair in which the Tyrant got carried up the stairs. And Rabia's flat was on the third floor.

I got out of bed, laughing. And then I continued laughing all through the morning and afternoon, as I helped Rabia and Shakeel prepare lunch, spoke to Beema and Dad who had tales of two mobile phones destroyed in one evening during Dad's attempt to demonstrate the principles of aerodynamics to one of his neighbours, and then received the relatives (the men and women resolving the crisis by taking it in shifts to carry the Tyrant up the stairs). I even managed to remain in good humour while being lectured about my unmarried state by old great-aunts who didn't allow the absence of blood ties between us to stand in the way of their familial right to lecture me. 'You could die a virgin!' the Tyrant said, clutching my hand. 'It happened to a cousin of mine. And she, poor woman, was married.' All the women of her age nodded, some of them whispering the name of the cousin to each other with hands covering the side of their mouths to protect the identity of the dead woman, while the younger generations looked for a place to hide their embarrassment, the uncles started talking very loudly about cricket and the new government, and Shakeel sprinted into his studio, from where we could hear him explode into laughter.

There is this narrative, too, in my life, I thought, late in the afternoon when everyone was filing out, and more than one of the female cousins near my age whispered, giggling, 'Don't die a virgin!' as they left. There has always been this narrative. Just for this one day I will not be hostage to that other past of mine.

Next door, the phone started ringing.

'Aren't you going to answer it?' Rabia said. 'It's been going every fifteen minutes for the last couple of hours.'

Here we go again.

I went into my flat, picked up the phone. No answer, no originating number. I disconnected the phone, trying not to notice the tiny fibrillations of my heart that occurred each time I heard that ring, and the rush of gratitude I felt when I answered to hear a voice on the other end, even if the voice belonged to no one I had any interest in speaking to.

I took a long siesta that afternoon, with dreams in which the sound of a ringing telephone followed me everywhere, even though I was transported back in time, trekking in the middle of desert and rock in a world in which I knew phones hadn't yet been invented.

I forgot about that dream when I woke up, but it returned to me later that evening as I was driving to Shehnaz Saeed's for dinner, replaying the day's amusing moments in my head and finding that I had almost entirely exhausted my determination to laugh at the world. I turned on to Chartered Accountants Avenue and, in the rearview mirror, I saw a motorcycle weaving its way through traffic towards me. I heard an echo of a phone ringing in my head, recalled the dream, and the nausea I felt then came from the realization that the motorcycle had been following me through the dense Eid traffic for over ten minutes now, ever since the Bar-B-Q-Tonite roundabout, just a short distance from my flat. The man driving had large dark glasses on, and the man seated behind him had a shawl loosely wrapped around him, though it wasn't really cool enough to warrant such attire.

The traffic stopped and the motorbike drew level with me. I was boxed in on all sides by cars. The man with the shawl looked in through my rolled-up window, and slowly – unbearably slowly – removed his hand from the driver's shoulder and reached beneath the shawl.

'Eid Mubarak,' he mouthed, the hand beneath the shawl scratching his stomach, and then the motorcycle continued to snake through the traffic and turned towards Gizri.

I bit my lip and willed myself just to continue driving, without any further looks in the rearview mirror unless they were necessary to prevent an accident. A few minutes later, it was with the relief that travellers in the desert greet

Bedouins bearing palm fronds and coconut water that I saluted the chowkidar at Shehnaz Saeed's house when he opened the gate for me.

The front door was ajar, and as I walked up to the doorway I saw Ed standing in the hallway, arms crossed, looking at the paintings of his mother.

I was absurdly glad to see him. 'Hey, stranger.' I walked up to him, not sure whether to hug him or kiss him on the cheek or put my arms around his neck and see what followed

He turned around, arms still crossed, making all three options physically awkward to manage. 'Hello, Aasmaani.' He didn't smile or show a sign of anything except indifference at my arrival.

'Well, this is a strained moment.' He half-shrugged. 'I see. And getting worse by the second. Should we try polite chitchat? When did you get back?'

'Yesterday.'

'Uh-huh. And how did filming go?'

'Fine.'

'Glad to hear it. And clearly the rugged wilds of Pakistan allowed you to get in touch with your inner Heathcliff. How is that experience going for you?'

'Oh, stop it, for God's sake.' He strode into the nearest room, slamming the door behind him.

I heard footsteps and turned in their direction. The woman who had let me in when I came for lunch with Shehnaz Saeed was walking down the tiled hall towards me, her clothes white this time, as though she had switched sides in a game of draughts. 'When he does that it means he wants you to follow him in,' she said.

'Maybe I should just leave him alone.'

She shook her head. 'Even as a little boy he used to think he needed to do all kinds of drama to get attention. Because his mother was so busy with her acting.' She held up a hand, cutting off a statement that I hadn't been about to make. 'I won't hear any criticism of her. That husband went off and left her without any money, what could she do but work? But my little Adnan,' she pointed towards the door, 'he was too young to understand that. So he'd jump out of trees and break his legs to make her stay at home. His heart,' she beat her hand against my chest, 'it's so large he doesn't know what to do with it.' And then she was grinning suggestively at me. 'Maybe you can teach him.'

In a surprisingly quick motion, she opened the door and pushed me inside.

I was in a study, dark save for an up-lighter on the floor, directed at a large mirror which reflected the dim light on to the bookshelves and sofas and Ed, sitting in an armchair, rocking a millefiori paperweight in his hands. The door closed behind me.

'Is this about me or are you just in a bad mood?' I asked, staying near the door.

'Too much these days is about you. I don't know how that happened. I can't seem to stop thinking about you.'

'And this is a terrible thing?' I walked up to him as I spoke, resting my hand on his shoulder when I came to the end of the question.

'Why did you call me?' He was looking down at the paperweight, which he was twisting as though to pull the clear glass off the enclosed blue, green and yellow flowers. 'I had just convinced myself that you wouldn't call, that you weren't thinking about me. That it was over before it had really begun. Then you called. And hearing your voice, Aasmaani, it was like . . . like that moment in *The Wizard of* Oz when Dorothy opens the door and the world is colour. Remember that haiku of yours? How did she recognize emerald, ruby and yellow when all she'd known was grey? She dreamed of colour, that's how she knew. And that's why she had to return home to grey Kansas. Because there's nothing more frightening than stepping into the dream closest to your heart. If it lets you down, you won't even have a dream of colour any more, you'll have nothing but grey.'

'Is it really so impossible to believe I won't let you down?'

He looked up at me, finally. 'You already did. When I realized you weren't calling because of me. You were calling to ensure you kept getting those damned messages from your beloved Poet. If it was the CEO giving you the letters, you'd have been calling him instead.'

I sat on the arm of his sofa. 'Do you know the story of Merlin and Nimue?'

'Yes. She imprisoned him in a tree.'

'That's one way of looking at it. She needs something from him. But she can't get it unless she falls in love with him.' Then I did what I'd been wanting to do since the first time I saw Ed. I ran my fingers through the thickness of his hair. 'I don't deny the Poet's messages are what brought us close, or that they continue to make it essential that you don't step out of my life. But, Ed, do you really think that if the CEO had been the one to give me the messages I would be sitting here playing with his hair?'

'No. He's bald.' He glared at me as he said it. And then – it was like alchemy – he smiled. He put an arm around my waist and pulled me on to his lap.

'Eid Mubarak,' he said. 'How's your day been?'

'It's had a couple of low moments, but on the whole, pretty wonderful.'

'Am I the low moments?'

'You were most of them. There's also a whole phone thing going on which is starting to get to me.'

'What phone thing?' He reached up to my hair and pulled off the band that tied it up.

'Oh, I don't know. Probably just a crank caller. I'm being paranoid. Result of getting a lecture from an esteemed journalist about staying under the radar.'

'You've lost me. If you ever cut your hair, Aasmaani, I'll run through the streets wailing like a madman. What journalist, what radar? What have you been doing?'

'Nothing very effective.' I held up a lock of my hair over

his upper lip to see what he'd look like with a flowing moustache. 'Unless alerting reporters and Archivists and doctor's sisters and God knows who else to my attempts at discovering what happened to the Poet can be termed effective.'

All the playfulness vanished from his face as he took hold of me by the shoulders. 'Aasmaani, you stupid woman. What have you been doing?'

I pulled myself away, and stood up. 'Don't talk to me in that tone.'

'What have you done?' He was standing up too, now.

'Nothing. Nothing that led anywhere. I went looking for answers about the Poet, that's all.'

'You did what?' He caught my shoulders again. 'Hasn't it occurred to you that maybe everyone was right all along? That really powerful agencies were involved with his death?'

'He's not dead.'

He slammed his hand on the desk. 'Whatever happened to him sixteen years ago, Aasmaani, someone – maybe several someones – planned it, and executed it, and has kept it a secret all these years. And you just decide to wake up one morning and let the world know that you've decided to be Nancy Drew.'

'Hey!'

'Don't "hey" me. These people are dangerous. And they're without compunction. Who do you think you're dealing with here, some incompetent cartoon goons? They can hurt you. They can kill you. They can do to you what they did to him. And that may not matter to you, and it certainly won't matter to them, but it goddamn well matters to me. Do you have any idea how much it matters to me?'

I didn't know what to say to that. I just stood, looking at him, wondering where this terrifying and terrified stranger had come from.

What an odd life I've had, I thought unexpectedly. Because it was my life I didn't stop very often to think how it must look from the outside, or how distinct it was from other lives.

But here was Ed, almost delirious with panic because I had been asking questions about the Poet's death – seeing his reaction I couldn't help but feel silly about those moments of concern I had about ringing telephones or men wrapped in shawls. This was nothing. Compared to what I'd grown up with, this was nothing. I was nothing. There wasn't a thing I had yet done to shake the complacency of those men who were so assured of their ability to know exactly what was going on that they wouldn't strike unless someone posed a threat. I posed no threat. I had, to all intents and purposes, come no closer to finding Omi than in all those years I believed he was dead. That was the terrifying part. And I had no idea how to start looking for him. That, that was what was unendurable.

'You don't really believe he's alive, do you?' I said at last.

'Oh God, Aasmaani.' He stepped back and covered one side of his face with his hand. 'I don't care if he's alive or not. I don't care about him. But you. You . . .' He came closer to me. 'What if he really is dead?'

I shook my head. 'No. It's him. I know it is. And it's like a miracle.' I was speaking slowly now as for the first time I tried to explain what it meant to me to read those pages. 'It's like . . . stepping into a dream of colour.'

'I see.' He shrugged. It took me a moment to understand why that mechanism of self-defence had come into play.

'I'm sorry, Ed.'

He shook his head. He was unshaven, and I could imagine how his stubble would feel against my lips, the rasp of it. 'How do you not resent him? The Poet. How? My mother . . . everyone she ever . . . I always . . .' He stopped, drew a long breath.

'You resent your stepfather?'

Ed made a dismissive gesture. 'That nonentity? Hardly! I resented all the others.'

'Oh.'

'And I resented her for having them.'

232

'We've all got our different wounds, Ed. At least she didn't ever leave you. See, that's what I obsess about. The leaving.' He stood there with his hands jammed into his pockets and I could see the young boy who jumped off a tree and broke his leg to distract his mother away from everything else in the world.

And I had hidden Omi's postcard from Mama.

It was the second time in twenty-four hours that I had felt this tug of recognition towards the man opposite me – but with Mirza that recognition had only led to self-pity. With Ed, it brought on something more complicated. Here stood a man of such intelligence and ability – a man of such potential – unable to regard the scars of adolescence as markers of injuries he'd survived rather than as evidence of the pain inflicted on him. And what reason did he have to be scarred? Because he was something less than her entire world?

'It's none of my business, but, you know, she didn't stop being a woman because she became a mother.' Wasn't that really, ultimately, what I had wanted of Mama? That she be my mother to the exclusion of all else? Is that why I remembered all the days and weeks and months she went with the Poet, and never the ones during which she stayed with me? She was twenty-six when I was born. Twenty-six years old: a mother and a woman desperately in love – could she have known right away that she would, at so many times in her life, be forced to choose between those two incarnations? If yes, then the wonder of it is that she didn't choose that moment to disappear, to step right out of the heart-cleaving complication that her life became the moment I was born.

'Think about it, Ed, she wasn't even twenty-five when your father left. What did you want her to do? Take a vow of celibacy for your sake? Would you, at twenty-five, have sworn off sex for ever, under any circumstances?'

'Please. You can't compare . . .'

'What? Can't compare the needs of men to the needs of women? Ed, try not to be an insufferable bastard.'

'Why are the things you can't get past any more accept-able than the things I can't get past?' he demanded.

'Oh, don't even try that. You didn't want your mother to have anyone in her life other than you. I never demanded anything quite so selfish.' No, I didn't want her to have no one else. I just wanted to always be first. And why shouldn't I? I was her child, I was the defenceless one. But I couldn't even pretend to believe that. In the sanctuary of Beema and Dad's house the only thing I needed defending against was my mother's absence.

He looked down at the carpet, the toe of his shoe tracing over the intricate paisley pattern, and when he spoke his voice was very soft. 'But I didn't have anyone in my life other than her. No father who cared to know me, no siblings, no cousins, no real friends.' He looked up. 'Don't you have any idea how lucky you are, how fortunate your life has been? I have every right to be obsessive. You have none. Why are you wasting your life being obsessed? Don't you have any idea how wonderful you could be if you just gave yourself the chance?'

I shook my head. 'I don't know who you see when you look at me.'

He leaned back against the desk, giving himself the extra distance to see me in my entirety. I couldn't help pushing my hair off my face. 'A woman no one could ever choose to leave.' He took a step closer to me. 'So don't run away to pre-empt a move I'm never going to make.'

'You're not the first man to be fascinated by the enigma that is Aasmaani, Ed. And you won't be the first to—'

'You aren't even remotely enigmatic. I've never met anyone less opaque. Are you fashioned of different material to everyone else in the world, Aasmaani, and is it possible that I'm the superhero whose only talent – whose unparalleled talent – it is to see you clearly, down to the atoms of the stuff of which you're made? I'll take that superpower over all others in the world, even if I'm promised nothing more than just the seeing.'

234

Memory prickled the back of my neck. Omi had spoken of my mother in those terms. Mirza had once asked him whether he thought that by marrying my mother the mystery would go out of their relationship, and Omi had said, 'There is no mystery – that's the beauty of it. We are entirely explicable to each other, and yet we stay. What a miracle that is.'

The paisleys were a bridge between us across the blue sea of the carpet, each one the footprint of a god as he searched for his Beloved.

'Are you going to start wearing a cape and spandex leggings, SuperEd?'

'Whatever works,' he smiled back. I started to move towards him and he held up a hand. 'First promise me something. Promise you won't go asking more questions about the Poet. Promise you'll keep yourself safe.'

'I don't even know where to go looking . . .'

'Promise me. Promise me you won't ask questions. Promise me that.'

'Ed, I have to find him. However I can.'

'Then rely on him. Rely on his letters. If you start asking questions—' He looked around as though something in the room might end his sentence for him. When nothing did, he settled for, 'I don't want to think about what they could do to you.'

'I have to be willing to risk something. You have to be willing to risk some things when the stakes are high enough. Don't you see that?' There was my mother's voice coming out of my mouth, her very words.

'But what if you alert them?' He came up to me and took me by the hands. 'What if your questions arouse their suspicions and they find out about the letters?'

'I don't know how not to fight for this.' *Mama, how long have you been hiding inside me?* 'Don't talk to me as though there's a choice involved. I must do whatever I can.'

His grip on my hands was almost painful. 'If you won't

protect yourself, protect him. Secrecy is your ally here. If anyone knows you've discovered he's still alive . . .'

I leaned my head on to his chest. His heart was like a piston. I was no threat, but Omi was. If anyone started to wonder why I was asking questions and traced the encrypted letters back to him . . .

'Yes.'

'What?' he said.

'You're right.'

He exhaled and kissed the top of my head.

'This doesn't mean I'm giving up, Ed. I'm just going to have to think through my next move carefully.'

'Can I think with you?'

'It's really not your mind I'm interested in, spandex boy.'

He put his arms around me and laughed. 'Ditto, darling.'

There was no gloom any more in the shadowed room; the dull light was a softness of colour against which I could close my eyes to transmigrate into that darkness in which all discovery occurs through touch and smell and taste. Sea-blown citrus, and the sliver of skin at the borderland of stubble and lip.

And sound. There was also sound. A hand jiggling the door-knob.

Ed and I pulled apart, each of us stepping backward along the paisleyed bridge as the door opened and Shehnaz Saeed entered.

# XVII

In her chiffon sari, with a diamond bracelet around her wrist, Shehnaz Saeed looked so utterly the part of the star that it was possible to believe the rectangle of illumination she stood in hadn't been thrown by the bright lights of the hallway but simply followed her everywhere she went.

'Oh, there you are. I thought I heard you drive up. Eid Mubarak, Aasmaani.' She walked over and kissed me on the cheek, then looked at Ed and raised her eyebrows. 'Am I interrupting something?' she said low into my ear.

'You don't have to whisper.' Ed's voice was cold, even more so than it had been when I first walked in. I glanced at him, wondering what I had missed. I was suddenly very conscious that this was the first time I was seeing the two of them together.

'And you don't have to be so edgy,' Shehnaz Saeed said in that not-in-front-of-the-guest tone which I had often given Beema reason to employ during my adolescence.

Ed picked up the paperweight again and tossed it from palm to palm with affected casualness. 'You should have walked in a few minutes ago. We were having a conversation I'm sure you could have added a lot to.'

'Oh?' She seemed not to see that he was baiting her. 'What about?'

'Mothers and sex.'

'Ed!' I couldn't believe he'd actually said it.

Shehnaz Saeed looked from him to me, her cheeks colouring. 'What has he been saying to you?'

I shook my head, mute with horror at the impropriety of it all.

'I haven't said anything, Mother.'

She continued to look at me, and I shook my head again, this time to indicate no, he hasn't said anything.

At last she turned back to him and said with simple dignity, 'Aasmaani and I will be in the lounge. Join us when you've had time to grow up.' She put her hand on my arm. 'Come on, darling.'

'Get your hand off her,' Ed said, his voice still icy. 'Otherwise I'll tell her all those things you don't want told, and she'll push you off herself.'

'Ed, enough with the Jekyll and Hyde bit,' I said.

At that, Shehnaz Saeed dropped her hand from my arm and turned to her son again. 'You'd be a fool to let me get between you and her. I can't undo what I've done, or who I am. Tell her. Go on. I don't mind. I'm not ashamed of it. And I won't have your shame over it – over me – wreck your own chance of happiness.'

All of a sudden, Ed looked as though he was going to weep. 'I'm sorry, Amma.' He came up to her and leaned his head on her shoulder. 'I'm sorry.'

'My boy,' she said, stroking his hair. 'My baby boy.'

I stood to one side, wishing they weren't between the door and me so that I could simply slip away. My God, Ed, have you any idea how lucky you are that she's still here to forgive you? Let her do that. Do yourself a favour, and let her forgive you for everything. For all the accusations, all the hurt, all the betrayals, all the ways in which you weren't enough.

'Aasmaani?' Shehnaz Saeed held a hand out to me. 'The horribly awkward moment is over. Come on, let's go into the lounge.'

We walked into the hallway together, all three of us, and

in that magical way in which families can be restored to good humour seconds after they've all but cut out one another's hearts, Ed and his mother had their arms around each other, their voices as they spoke consisting of nothing but lightness.

'Have you told Aasmaani about the dictionary man?' Shehnaz Saeed said. 'Aasmaani, did you hear about the dictionary man in Multan?'

I shook my head, and Ed and his mother laughed.

'You tell her, Amma. You tell it better than me.'

'I wasn't even there when it happened.'

'Never mind. You tell it.'

Shehnaz Saeed stopped walking and put a hand on my wrist. 'So Ed's in Multan last week, filming the Ramzan special. And at the end of a long day he's relaxing in the coffee shop of his hotel . . .'

'Drinking instant coffee.'

'Drinking instant coffee. And in walks this irate man with jowls so droopy they could carry him away in a strong wind. And he's got a book in his hand which he starts waving at Ed like a fanatic holding the Word of God, ready to produce the black-and-white evidence that drinking anything other than percolated coffee is an unpardonable sin.'

'And he comes up to me and slams the book down on the table in front of me, flipping it open to a page which his thumb had been marking. And I see it's an Urdu dictionary he's holding. And he says – Amma, tell her.'

'He says,' her voice turned squeaky, its rhythms truncated, '"I've found your dirty secret. You TV people with your loose morals. Why *Boond* of all names, I wondered. Why a drop of rain? What sort of title is this? And now I see you're having your vulgar jokes at the country's expense.' And he points to the definition of *Boond* and – even I didn't know this, Aasmaani. In addition to rain or blood, which is what Kiran had in mind when she came up with the title, it also means—'

'Semen,' I finished.

239

'You knew?' Ed laughed.

'Of course. One of the Poet's early ghazals has "boond" as the radif. It also means spotted silk, by the way.'

'We must talk about his poetry one day,' Shehnaz Saeed said. 'It would be such a pleasure to discuss it with you.'

As she said it, I imagined calling her up to say I was coming over to discuss poetry, and then leading Omi into this house with me. The look on Shehnaz Saeed's face.

She had walked ahead of us into the lounge, and Ed was about to follow when I caught hold of his hand and squeezed it. He looked away as though he couldn't bear my hopefulness. He didn't quite believe Omi could still be alive and I knew, as though he'd whispered it into my ear one night so that it made its way into my dreams, that he couldn't bear the thought of what it would do to me if I had to face Omi's death again. The sweetness of Shehnaz Saeed's character resided in Ed, too, but in a concentrate at his very core. I rubbed my thumb along the back of his palm and he looked at me, eyes grave.

For a moment I thought he was going to say something and then he shook his head and we walked through the doorway into the room of Bukhara rug, Gandhara Buddhas and muted elegance which I had seen through the partially open door my first time in this house. On the walls were prints of Indian landscapes and monuments etched by English artists from the colonial era.

Shehnaz Saeed switched on the television, and put it on mute. There were only a few minutes to go before the start of *Boond*. 'I'm so nervous I might throw up,' she said, sitting down on a plush cream sofa. 'I never used to be this nervous about watching myself.'

'You'll be fabulous.' Ed sat down next to her. 'You are Shehnaz Saeed. How could you not be fabulous?'

She looked up at him in surprised gratitude.

He can do and say anything he wants, I thought, and she won't stop loving him. He'll always be her baby boy. For all his faults, she'll blame herself, not him. That knowledge made me tired, and again I thought of leaving. But Ed reached out and caught hold of my hand, right there with his mother watching, as though to say, no backing out now. We're official.

Difficult, but worth it – that's how my mother had once described life with Omi. I could see myself saying that about Ed.

As I sat down, still holding Ed's hand, I caught Shehnaz Saeed looking over at us, and I thought I saw some wistfulness there, but not unhappiness. I wondered if she'd been in love with any of those other men Ed had talked about.

'So you want to hear about the travails of my month?' Ed asked. 'Dictionary man aside. My mother's already sat through part of the story.'

'Oh, I'm more than happy to hear it again. Go bring the camera so Aasmaani can see the pictures.'

Ed nodded and left the room.

'Now, I'm not one of those mothers who interferes in her son's relationships,' Shehnaz Saeed said, leaning over to me and lowering her voice. 'So I'll say only this. I'm glad it's you. I'm glad enough to give you this piece of advice: what you did back there – standing up for me when he started to attack me – don't do that again.'

'I wasn't standing up for you. I was objecting to his bad manners.'

'Whatever it was. I've been the stumbling block in every relationship he's had. Don't stumble over me, Aasmaani. Kick me out of the way if you must, but don't stumble over me. I'm so tired of being the reason for his loneliness.'

'You feel guilty about him, don't you?'

'I wasn't the mother I should have been.'

'You could have done what my mother did. Sent him away to be raised by someone more fitting.'

Shehnaz straightened up, almost offended, it seemed. 'Samina loved you.'

'Abstractly.'

241

'Relentlessly.'

'For her, loving the Poet was addictive. Loving me was merely habit-forming.'

'What is it with you children? Don't you understand that lovers can never be to us what you are? You don't occupy the same space.' She stopped and raised her eyebrows. 'That sounded really vulgar, didn't it?'

'I wasn't going to be the one to mention it.' I laughed and pointed to the clock. 'The show's about to begin.'

Ed came back into the room, carrying a digital camera. He had just started to cycle through the pictures, sitting next to me, his arm around my shoulder, when there was a cry of expectation from Shehnaz Saeed. Ed raised the volume. Shehnaz Saeed's come-back began.

Within the first few minutes it was obvious that *Boond* would not send critics scrambling for their thesauruses, as had happened with Kiran and Shehnaz's first collaboration, nearly two years ago, which the newspapers proclaimed 'a miracle, a revelation and possibly a hallucination'.

But, although *Boond* was clearly not going to inspire the same sort of outpouring, it was solid, eminently watchable, with the occasional marvellous moment. The Mistress's Daughter could actually act, and the only disappointment was the one I'd dubbed Once-Leading, Now-Trailing man, who looked strangely uncomfortable, as though too aware that this might be his last chance to restore his reputation as an actor of subtlety and depth.

And then. Shehnaz Saeed stepped on to the screen and into a flashback. I hated flashbacks in television shows – everyone seen through a soft-filter lens to make them appear younger – but even so I caught my breath at how the lighting turned her back into the woman I remembered from the days of Lady Macbeth. The flashback occurred in Shehnaz Saeed's mind as she lands in Karachi – from where, we don't know – and we see her returning in her memory to the early days of her marriage, Once-Leading walking with her along the beach, an anatomically unlikely bulge under her kameez denoting her pregnancy. It was the worst kind of flashback – sappy music drowned out all conversation as the young couple wandered barefoot in the sand, shadows falling across their path with the exhausted air of overused metaphors. Compared to the light touch evidenced in the rest of the episode, it should have been laughable. And yet. Something remarkable happened in that scene: Shehnaz Saeed. I couldn't believe that just minutes earlier Ed had snapped at her and, despite her dignity, she had seemed reduced, weak, when he did that.

On screen, she was remarkable. She turned away from Once-Leading and held her face up to the breeze, and in her expression she told us everything about her desire to feel the clichéd happiness that this scene demanded and her inability to stop yearning for something beyond this moment. And Once-Leading, who had been moving through his lines like a man weary of wasting his talents, suddenly started to act. He was madly in love, hopelessly daring to dream that she was in love with him too. An echo of their long-ago perform-ance as the Macbeths flickered through them, not enough to be distracting but enough to make us feel that anything could happen from here – regicide, insanity, love, hauntings.

The sub-plot of Once-Leading's fiancée worrying that he was still in love with his ex – a sub-plot which I'd taken to indicate terrible insecurity on the part of the fiancée – reshaped itself as I watched that scene. The fiancée is right, I thought, watching the man rest his hand on his wife's head to prevent her hair from blowing into her eyes as a gust of wind raced in from the sea.

How could he not be blindly and – in some way – eternally in love with her? Even her Lady Macbeth hadn't moved me so profoundly, and yet she had done little except walk across the sand, miming the actions of a smoker because although her pregnancy demanded she give up the habit her hand stayed addicted to the motion of lifting a cigarette to her lips and . . .

I pulled myself upright. 'What are you doing?' I said to the Shehnaz Saeed sitting just feet away from me.

She had been looking at her hands instead of the screen, and now she looked up at me. 'I don't like watching myself.'

'No.' I pulled myself off the sofa and pointed at the screen. 'There. What are you doing there?' In soft focus, she repeated the gesture. She brought her index and middle fingers to her lips, held them there for two long beats, her eyes closed, their lids tremoring lightly. Then she turned her head to one side and let her hand move away to the other side, slowly, as she exhaled from between barely parted lips. As she exhaled, her fingers curled back into a fist.

'That's my mother.' I was aware of the curious flatness of my voice. 'You've turned that character into my mother.'

'What? No.' She looked up at the screen, and the denial caught in her throat.

Beside me, Ed had covered his face with his hand, muffling whatever words were coming out of his mouth.

I knew what would come next. Shehnaz Saeed's character would return. Back to Karachi, back to her daughter, back from all those years of disappearance. She'd speak in a smoky voice with a lisp so buried you wouldn't notice it unless you'd grown up with it, heard it every time she spoke your name. Every time she said Aasmaani. Every time she said sweet-heart.

I stood up. I couldn't quite feel my limbs but I managed to stand up and move towards the door. Shehnaz Saeed was saying something, and Ed, too, but all I was aware of was the Fata Morgana's hand pressed against the small of my back, keeping my shoulders straight as I departed without looking back.

# XVIII

My father sat across from me at the dining table, warming his hands around a cup of tea. It wasn't particularly cold – not in this sunlit spot around my dining table, in mid-afternoon – and it occurred to me that this way of holding a cup was a habit he'd picked up in the colder climes of Islamabad. Was that all that had changed in his life since he'd been gone? His way of holding a tea-cup?

He was here because Rabia had told him I needed some talking to. I knew this even though no one had told me so. This morning, when I woke up at dawn, having slept only a very few hours, I heard Rabia's phone ringing. I thought she'd still be asleep. She had been up until late, holding me as I wept after returning from Shehnaz Saeed's. When she had asked me what was wrong, her question had set off such a bout of inexplicable, painful crying, the sort that seems to pull the flesh from your ribs, that she had fallen silent. She was still holding me when I finally fell asleep, exhausted and aching from the physical toll of weeping, and only after that did she leave my room to return to her flat. So when I woke up in the morning and heard the phone, I went through the connecting door to answer it and allow her and Shakeel a little more rest.

But just as I walked through the door I heard her pick up the extension in her bedroom. 'Why didn't you call back last night?' she said, and from her tone of voice with its echoes of adolescence, I knew she was talking to Beema. 'Oh . . . oh . . . when are you bringing her home? . . . Oh. Ma, I know you have enough going on but seriously it's bad here . . . Yes. Yes. I don't know . . . I don't know, I'm telling you, I don't know. She doesn't talk to me. It's worse than ever before. Can't you leave Nani for just a day and fly down? Just a few hours even . . . Send Dad?' Rabia's voice was incredulous. 'What can he do with her?'

But here he was, holding on to his cup of tea for dear life as though it was a lifebuoy that would save him from drowning in this attempt to converse with his first-born. No newspaper, television, fused light-bulb, broken door hinge, Beema, or Rabia between or beside us to obscure the fact that my father and I had nothing significant to say to each other, never had. When I had become a cricket fan at the age of thirteen, Dad – who had always disdained sport – decided it was time to give himself over to the national passion too, just so that he and I could have something in common. It sometimes seemed to me that the only reason I kept up with cricket as avidly as I did, despite my growing disgust at the state of the national team, was to fill the silence between us. I suspected he felt the same.

He cleared his throat. 'Your mother sends her love,' he said. Then he gripped the cup more tightly. 'I mean, Beema.'

'I didn't think you meant anyone else.'

'No, of course you didn't.' He peered down into his tea. 'I saw that television show which you helped out with. There was some interesting . . .' If the sentence had an ending, it got lost in the tea-cup as he brought it to his lips.

Had he, too, recognized Mama on the screen? And if so, did he think the actor opposite her was him? Once-Leading Man. Did he think that character was based on him? After my one meeting with the *Boond* team I had told Beema I had helped with the Shehnaz Saeed storyline, and she would doubtless have passed that information on to him. Did he believe I had helped turn his marriage with my mother into material for a television series that would have all of Karachi whispering and bringing up the past once more?

'I only saw the first few minutes of it,' I said. 'At Shehnaz Saeed's. Then I left.'

He nodded his head slowly. 'It was the damndest thing, wasn't it? I had forgotten she used to do that.'

'Was there more? After that first scene?'

'More?'

'Did she go on playing that character like it was Mama?'

'Oh God, no. No. Just that one mannerism. So that is what made you cry so much. I thought it might have been.'

I didn't know where to take the conversation from there. We never talked about my mother, except obliquely. In the two years after Omi's death when they lived under the same roof I never saw them being anything but utterly polite to each other. He never ventured upstairs, to the best of my memory, in all that time, and she largely stayed confined to her room and to Rabia and my communal play area. When she did come downstairs – to have a meal in the dining room instead of eating from a tray upstairs – it was always for lunch, and always when he was at work. The rare exceptions to that rule, in the early days, were such strained occasions – with neither of my parents able to simulate ease in each other's presence – that I think everyone in the household was relieved when they ceased altogether.

'So you want to talk about it?' my father said.

'Talk about what? The fact that I miss Mama? There – I miss her. We've talked about it.'

'Hmm.' He tilted a spoonful of sugar so that it fell a few granules at a time into his cup.

'You mind, don't you? That I miss her. That I love her as much as I do. You think she never deserved that.'

'Don't you think I understand anything about loving your mother? She broke my heart when she left me. And if she'd been even slightly less brutal about the way she did it, I expect

I would have gone on loving her and missing her through all eternity.'

'Domesticity or a dildo.'

His hand jerked, spilling tea on to the tablecloth. 'She told you about that?'

'No. I . . . overheard it. Once when the Poet was speaking to her.'

He nodded, took off his glasses and wiped them absent-mindedly on a tissue he'd taken out of its box to sop up the tea.

'Dad, I'm sorry. That was cruel of them. You've never done anything to deserve such unkindness.'

He put his glasses back on and pressed the tissue against the tea stain. 'It was for the best. Someone leaves you like that, you don't waste time harbouring thoughts of reconciliation. Anyway. It was a long time ago. All I'm saying is, I didn't love her without reason. There was always all the reason in the world to love Samina. So how can I mind that you loved her? How can I mind that you loved your own mother?'

'Tell me about you and her. How it really was.'

'It was great. It was perfect.' He smiled at my look of surprise. 'When we were seventeen. It was the best thing in the world during those few months we were together before university split us apart. You know, first love and all that. We'd talk on the phone for hours every night. About every-thing, everything. And we used to play an idiotic form of "chicken" in which I'd drive through Karachi with her hands covering my eyes, trusting her to tell me when to brake and go. We drove all the way from KDA to Clifton like that once. She told me afterwards she made me run three red lights along the way. We never played that game again.' He shook his head, as if he couldn't really believe he was talking about himself.

'So what happened? How did first love go bad?'

'She went to Cambridge. I stayed in Karachi. She wrote to me to say it was great, now it's over. That was the gist of it, though she phrased it more kindly. By the time she finished university and came back to Karachi, she was someone else, and then I met your stepmother, and she and I were at that point of silent acknowledgement that something was about to happen between us. And that should have been it. But then one day Samina just bursts into my office, eyes sparkling, and I haven't seen her in months, haven't had any conversation with her in years, and she says, "Well, are you going to ask me to marry you or not?"' He laughed, chin resting on his hand, and I saw the young, infatuated boy he had been. 'I knew about her and the Poet. Who didn't? But she looked . . . luminescent. And I was chafing at the person I was turning into – this responsible, practical banker who would never play "chicken" for even five seconds, let alone from KDA to Clifton – and she was my way out of that. So.'

'So you just dumped Beema?'

He looked away guiltily. 'I hadn't exactly, you know, picked her up at that point.'

'I'm amazed she ever spoke to you or Mama after that.'

'Well, that's your Beema for you. After Samina left me, she was so incredibly kind. I found I was only going out to social gatherings if I thought I'd run into her. And then Samina called me one day – she was about eight months pregnant by then – and said, "Get a move on. She's not going to wait around for ever for you." I said, "What business is it of yours?" and she said, "You're still technically my husband. I'm allowed to interfere in your life. Besides, she'd make a wonderful mother to our child." It was all weird and so utterly right.' He put his hand on mine. 'Sometimes there's so much of her in you. Your voice, your eyes, your quickness with language. And it reminds me of the Samina I loved, that girl who stole my heart. So for the last time – I have never minded or been even slightly surprised by your love for her.' He moved his hand away, wrapped it around his cup again. 'But if there's something I mind about you . . . well, not even mind. It's just something I think about from time to time. Not that there's anything to be done about it, or . . . it's just that, of your four parents, I'm the one you've always loved least effusively, and sometimes I've wished that wasn't so.'

I touched the back of his hand with the tips of my fingers. 'Sorry.' And I was. Sorry and profoundly ashamed.

He shook his head to indicate there was nothing to apologize for.

'I don't know about the four parents bit, though. I don't think the Poet was ever a second father to me.' What I meant by that was that I could see no correlation between Dad's and Omi's positions in my life. Fathers were efficient in matters of finance, and rewiring. They didn't lack emotion, they simply didn't express it except in tiny bursts. And they were always there. That was their most abiding quality – their thereness. That was Dad, that was fathers. Omi was nothing like that.

But my father didn't understand the meaning behind my words. He looped his finger into the handle of the tea-cup and spun it in slowly oscillating half-circles. 'It's childish and immature and my wife would be horrified to hear me say this, but: good.'

I looked at his neck, the one part of him which belonged on a much older man, and for the first time his mortality became real to me. 'You hated him, huh?'

My father nodded, still watching the tea-cup.

'Because you lost her to him?'

'I suppose that would have to be the core of it. But, even apart from that, I just disapproved of everything he stood for.'

'Poetry? Resistance?'

'Debauchery. Selfishness.'

'Debauchery?'

'All those nights he stayed up with his artsy friends, imbibing whisky and God-knows-what-else until dawn, laughing at those of us who had to go to work for a living. Vertical readers, he used to call us. Because we'd spend our days poring over numbers in columns instead of words written

250

across a page.' My father waved his hand through the air to indicate lines of print and the tea-cup went crashing on to the floor. His face was red as he bent to pick up the pieces.

'How do you know?' *How have you managed to keep from making me feel I'm betraying you every time I spoke his name with affection?*

'Because one night you were spending the night at your mother's house and I came to pick you up for school on my way to work. As I drew up, the gate next door opened and those friends of his stumbled out, eyes red and puffy, slurring goodbyes to each other. He was there, seeing them out, and when he saw me he said, "It's a vertical reader." You know, it's just as well your mother didn't marry him. I don't think I would have allowed you to stay overnight in a house with all that going on.'

'Just as well she didn't marry him?' I couldn't believe he'd said that. 'After everything she went through after he died because she wasn't his wife, you can say it was just as well she didn't marry him?'

'You know I didn't mean it that way. You know that. Dammit, Aasmaani, why must you always make me feel as though I'm failing you?'

I sat back down on the chair opposite him. 'They didn't sit around talking about your day in the office. The Acolytes. That's not what they were about. They talked about poetry, and politics – don't do that' – he had dropped his head into his hands – 'and what language could and couldn't do in a censored and censorious world. Some evenings I'd wander in there and I'd sit and I'd listen to them, just listen. Then I'd go back to Mama's house and she'd be sitting with her friends, her fellow activists, and they'd be talking about forcing changes in laws, about setting up schools and defining curricula, about appealing to international bodies. I went from one house to the other, listening to all that, and it was exhilarating. It made me feel like I was on fire, breathing fire, walking on fire.'

'And what have you got to show for it?' As soon as he said that he was reaching for my hand. 'No, I'm sorry. That really did come out wrong.'

'Did it?' I pulled away from him.

'See, you still glamorize both of them. I'm sure it was exciting, Aasmaani. I used to see it in your face some days when you'd come back home after spending a day or a weekend or longer at her house. You'd come back and you'd look around at us, your other family, as we talked about renting videos and going to the Chinese for dinner, and there would be this look on your face saying: is this it? Is this all you're capable of? Well, I'll tell you something. Something they were capable of and we weren't: leaving.'

'Stop it.'

'You want to know why I hated him? That's why. Because he kept forcing her to choose between him and you. He kept getting himself into situations and then he'd have to leave the country, or he'd get carted off to prison, and then she'd be gone, poof! just like that, and I'd have to hear my daughter crying herself to sleep at night. That time they stayed away for three years. Three years, Aasmaani. Why? Because it was dangerous for him to come back, and when she wanted to return, she even called me to let me know which flight she was on, he scared her into thinking they'd arrest her to get to him. He even made her think she might put you in danger.'

'No.' As soon as I said it, there it was. A memory making its way to the surface in that inexplicable way of latent memories which need just the right spark to wake them up. I stood up, sat down again, tried to bring my father's face into focus. It wasn't Omi who told her to stay away. It was me. When my father came to my room to say he'd spoken to her and she was coming back, I was the one to call her back and say, 'Don't.' I wanted her with me. It's not that I didn't. But when she was abroad, I felt safe. Omi wouldn't be imprisoned, she wouldn't be beaten and bruised in demonstrations, or spirited away in the night, never to be seen again, as happened to so many people she and Omi knew. I said, stay away, I'll come to you in the summers and winters. I said, what if I'm at your house when they come knocking at your door in the middle of the night, looking for you? What will happen to me then? I said that knowing, with all the assurance in the world, that she might be willing to risk herself, but she wouldn't risk me – not my physical self, not my state of mind. I said, Mama, when you're here I get scared.

Only now, when I had a mere fraction of the reason she ever had to jump when the phone rang, to hold my breath when a motorcycle seemed to be following me, to know what it meant to feel you were being watched – only now, in those moments when the ringing phone made me look next door and think, suppose it isn't just paranoia, suppose someone is after me and they come here and find Rabia instead of me – only now did I understand something of what I must have put her through when I said, supposing I'm in the house when they come to take you away?

I opened my mouth to say, 'Dad, she stayed away for my sake,' but then I saw the expression of anger still on his face and I knew he'd think I was just trying to defend Omi. So I said, 'What did you want him to do? Stop writing? Write pretty little verses about the sparrows and the rainbows? You expected him to stop writing because of me? For God's sake, Dad, I wasn't even his daughter.' Everything my father had said, I'd thought a million times over for more than half my life now. But I had blamed her, not him. I wasn't his daughter, but I was hers. And she chose him over me every time – that's what I had believed for so long.

My hands were rubbing the length of my thighs. I couldn't quite stop them, couldn't render myself into stillness.

But even if you thought of coming back, Mama, and I talked you out of it, why did you allow me to do that? I was a child. How could you let me make those decisions for you unless they were the decisions you wanted all along? Even if you wanted to come back, that does nothing to change the fact that you left to begin with. It's not natural. Mothers aren't supposed to choose anyone else over their children. You unnatural woman. Oh, stop, stop, stop.

I got out of the chair again and walked away from the table, aware of my father's expression beginning to cross from concern into worry. Unnatural? I wasn't going to fall for that one; she'd taught me too well to allow me to buy into such stories.

When I was twelve and Mama was at the forefront of political activism with the Women's Action Forum, the mother of one of my friends said I mustn't be angry at my mother for getting thrown in jail when she should have stayed at home and looked after me; after all, the woman said, she was doubtless just doing it because she thought she could make the world a better place for me. I looked at the woman in contempt and told her I didn't have to invent excuses or justifications for my mother's courage, and how dare she suggest that a woman's actions were only of value if they could be linked to maternal instincts. At twelve, I knew exactly how the world worked and I thought that by knowing it I could free myself of the world's ability to grind people down with the relentlessness of its notions of what was acceptable behaviour in women.

'I had you and Beema and Rabia,' I told my father, things that I once believed coming back to me. 'Mama knew that. The Poet had no one really, except her. I mean, there were admirers aplenty, but people who would follow him into exile, relocate their lives to see him in jail, no. No one except her. Don't ask me to hold it against her that she stood with him. Didn't stand *by* him, didn't follow him, didn't give up her life to the dictates of his plans. She stood with him. Would you have preferred it if she took me with her every time she left?'

'Oh, come off it, Aasmaani. Don't pretend that everything you had to give up was OK by you. All in service of the greater goods of freedom and poetry, which – I might add – have got this nation nowhere.'

It was nothing that I hadn't thought myself. The futility, the utter futility, of everything Mama and Omi did in the name of politics. But they didn't know it was futile, a voice in my head insisted, and I recognized it from a time in my life when I knew how it felt to walk on fire, unharmed. A voice which didn't blame or whine but simply remembered the facts as they had been before hindsight changed the shape of everything Mama-related. I pushed back my chair, and strode into the lounge to retrieve Rabia's file about my mother. My father sat watching me as I flipped through the articles. When I came to the one I wanted I meant to turn it towards him, but instead I found my own eyes unable to pull away from it; I had never before been able to do more than just glance at it.

It was a newspaper article from an Egyptian paper, two decades old, covering a protest rally against the Hudood Ordinance. One of my mother's friends in Cairo had sent it to me shortly after my mother disappeared, along with a message about the importance of my mother's role in linking Muslim feminists from around the world; the message sounded too much like a letter of condolence to be bearable, so I tossed it, and the article, into the garbage from where Rabia retrieved them. What Arabic I had learnt in '82, the year my mother and the Poet moved from Colombia to Egypt and I visited them over my summer holidays, I had now forgotten, but the text wasn't what was important about the article.

In grainy black and white, my mother is the centre of both photographs that accompany the text. In the first, she is surrounded by policewomen brandishing lathis. She is holding on, with both hands, to a pole that must have helped support a banner, but she's been separated from whoever held the second pole, and the banner has ripped in two. They must have held on tight to each pole, she and the other woman, to make that banner tear down the middle as they were pushed apart. The half-banner is furled in on itself, making it impossible to read the words on it. Even so, one of the police-women is reaching for the pole, which my mother holds upright, resisting the temptation to wield it like a weapon. A second policewoman holds a lathi horizontally. The photo-grapher has caught the moment when the policewoman's arm recoils after striking my mother across her midriff with the lathi, and my mother is just beginning to double over, mouth open, eyes closed, face strangely serene.

In the second picture she is down on the ground, several of her friends gathered nearby, not daring to help pick her up. A policeman is standing about five feet away from her. In his right hand is a lathi, and in his left a much longer stick, slightly pliant, which he uses to keep my mother pinned to the ground as though she were an animal. But she will not be defeated. Although she's on the ground, her head is raised, looking straight at the policemen, and one hand is gripping the long stick, making clear her intention to use it to lever herself to her feet. In the background, other men walk past, not even looking at her.

Mama, how did you find the strength? And why did it leave you so utterly when you thought the Poet had died?

My father turned the file towards himself, and winced when he looked down at the images. I thought that was a sign of sympathy for my mother, but he said, 'As long as you carry on looking at pictures like this you won't allow yourself to admit you have reason to be angry at her.'

I touched my hand to my mother's midriff. I remembered the bruises the lathi had left, remembered walking into her room as the Poet, crying, rubbed balm on to them. When she saw me she pushed his hand away and lowered her kameez to try to hide the vicious purpling of her skin. I ran and threw my arms around her, and though the Poet gasped as my body collided with hers, she only ran her fingers through my hair and kissed the top of my head.

'Hello, my sanctuary,' she said.

I looked up from the picture and saw my father – so unbruised, so safe.

'Of course I've allowed myself to be angry.' Saying that, I felt my heart quieten down. 'I've been nothing but angry and resentful, Dad, for so long. For the leaving. Not for this—' I gestured to the pictures. 'I will not be resentful for this. How dare you make me try? The one thing I've hated most about this place – ever since I was a child – is all the attitudes here which tell me I should be angry about this, I should be resentful. No one says, be resentful of the people who made it necessary for her to choose between staying home to help you with your homework and going out to fight laws which say rape victims can be found guilty of adultery and stoned to death. No one ever says, be resentful of your father and stepmother and everyone else who didn't go out and join that fight and make her burden lighter.'

My father's face took on an expression that told me what I had said was so absurd he didn't even believe that I really believed it. 'What, so now you're angry Beema and I didn't get beaten up and thrown into prison, leaving you and your sister to look after yourselves when you were eight and twelve?'

'Stop it. Stop doing that. She made one choice. You made another. And it's purely a matter of perspective which one of you let me down. At some abstract level, I really do believe neither of you did. But it's just hard sometimes to know that in my heart.'

'In your heart, she takes up so much place that there's almost no room left for the rest of us – let alone for anyone new.' His tone was slightly peevish, and that made it impossible for me to be angry.

I looked at his neck again and felt such tenderness that I almost cried out. Let us leave this room, Dad, and meet again somewhere far away from every shadow around which we've peeped at each other all our lives, and let us talk. Let's talk about who you are, who I am. Let's talk about the heroism of staying at home with your children, and the heroism of leaving them in order to fight. Let's talk of the archaeologist

257

you wanted to be, and why you wanted to hold history in your hands. Let's talk about losing Mama. Let's talk about the simple pleasures of finding order in the working of an electric fuse. I never saw until now that my ordering, if not ordered, mind is your mind.

'If it's any consolation, I know she's far from perfect, Dad. I know she has her faults.'

His eyes opened wide and there was such fear in them that I glanced over my shoulder, muscles tensing to face the threat that must have entered.

'*Has* her faults? Fourteen years later you're still saying, *has* her faults?' He reached across the table and caught me by the elbows. 'Aasmaani. Aasmaani, your mother's dead.'

I knew they'd been saying it, all of them, for years, but it was the first time I heard the words. I knew it would happen some day, and I thought I'd be prepared, but I wasn't. I wanted to hit him, simple as that. Wanted to strike the mouth which had uttered that obscenity.

I stood up. 'Get out of my flat!'

'No.'

'Get out!'

The connecting door swung open and Rabia came running in.

'What happened? Dad, what did you say to her?'

My father pushed his chair back and stood up slowly. 'Something I should have said many years ago. Aasmaani, she is dead. She is dead. There's no other explanation. She is dead.'

'Rabia, get him out of here.'

But Rabia only took our father's hand in hers. That was the betrayal for which nothing had prepared me, and I felt such desolation it took away all my will to argue.

'She was miserable with her life.' Dad reached for me, but I drew away from him. 'She couldn't see a way out of it. She left the house and never came back. She was last seen walking towards the sea. She never came back. Put it together. Allow your mind to do what it does best. Put the pieces together.'

'I have. But you'll excuse me if I don't choose the same pieces you do.'

Dad crossed his arms. 'Fine. Educate me, then. What happened to Samina? She's still alive – yes? Yes?'

'Dad, don't,' Rabia said.

Our father held up a hand to stop her. 'Enough, Rabia. You and your mother have tried it your way for years now. It hasn't worked.' He turned his attention back to me. 'Go on, Aasmaani.'

'Dad, she could . . .' Rabia started, and then broke off.

'I could what?'

'You could become the way your mother became when the Poet died,' Dad said. 'Except, you won't. And if you do, we'll find a way to help you. But I can't tiptoe around you any more and allow this to continue.' His face softened. 'Darling, why force yourself to believe she's alive and staying away from you? Don't you see that damages you more than the truth ever could?'

'What do you know of the truth? You're a small man with a small mind. You can't possibly understand.'

'Stop it. Both of you,' Rabia pleaded.

'Tell me what I can't understand,' Dad demanded. 'Go on. Explain it to me.'

I reached for my handbag, slung over the back of a chair. Omi's pages were inside. I touched the bag as though it were a talisman. If he could still be alive, anything was possible.

'Soon, Dad, you'll see what strangeness the world is capable of. Then you'll start to understand.' I brushed past him and walked into my bedroom, locking the door behind me.

. . .

There is nothing to do now but wait.

It sits across from me, the television, reflecting the room back in grey concaves. I feel like a creature of the wilderness newly acquainted with this magic box, wanting to peel away the greyness – which doesn't move unless I move in it – and find beneath it those layers of coloured images which, yesterday, moved by so fast they gave the impression of continuous motion.

The Minions brought in the television and VCR. Late, late at night. Early a.m. today, if I am to be precise. I woke to hear them moving about in the second room and when I went to see what they were doing they made me sit down, told me there was something I had to watch. They turned on the television and everything was grey-and-white specks and a noise of static. It had been so long since I saw a television that even the static seemed fascinating. Lice jumping round a middle-aged man's hair! I said to the Minions. They told me to sit, and they played the tape. A single word of Urdu appeared on the screen. The first word of Urdu in so long. And then my old friend, my old Macbeth, walked into a room. No, I suppose we were never friends, really. I translated a play, he acted in it, we met once or twice. But he belongs to that other life of mine, and so I recognized him with a joy that might be more suited, under normal circumstances, for encountering a long-lost twin.

260

And when I realized it was in Karachi. Oh, that moment. What was it? He said something. He said: this isn't Funland. Funland! I hadn't thought about it in years, but when he said that I remembered taking Aasmaani there and how she loved that ride, what was it called? Hurdy-Gurdy! Show me outdoors, I started to scream at the images. I've forgotten the passive art of television viewership. Show me the sea, please show me the sea. But it was all interiors. The ad breaks were edited out. I have never wanted so desperately to see ads. What's being sold, what's being used to sell it? Sixteen years of living outside the world and suddenly I was hungry for any kind of knowledge. So there I was, examining fashions. The women weren't all covered up, that was a huge relief. Very short sleeves and near-revealing necklines for the younger actresses, as well as streamlined shalwars that could almost pass for trousers. Kameezes shorter than I remembered, though not as short as in the seventies. And hairstyles, compact. Thank God for that. The volume of hair we had to contend with when I was last part of the world was just embarrassing.

Me, looking at clothes and hairstyles. Who would have believed it possible?

Still, I couldn't understand why I was watching it. And why the Minions were standing around, watching me as though preparing mental reports about my reactions. I couldn't understand it at all but I kept watching and at last we had an exterior. An airport. Big and new and marble and clean. The words 'Quaid-e-Azam International Airport' in large letters across the top of the building.

Karachi has a new airport? I said to the Minions.

They didn't say anything, but one of them – who I've caught before showing signs of sympathy – nodded briefly.

Then I forgot them. Forgot everything.

Because, disembarking from a plane, setting her foot down on the tarmac and looking up and around, as though seeing a sky she hadn't seen for a very long time: Shehnaz. Almost before I was able to believe it really was her, she looked up at the sunset and then the scene was changing to another sunset and there she was again, pregnant at the beach.

I don't know how I didn't have a heart attack. Shehnaz and the waves, Macbeth at her side, and I said to the Minions, 'Stop. Pause it. Pause!' They just looked at me, and I stood up, tripped, fell over and crawled to the VCR, my hands the hands of a trembling old man as I pressed the pause button to freeze the moment.

I put my hand to the screen. I touched the water. The waves nearest to shore were bowing, a gesture of self-effacement that was a split second away from annihilating them. I touched the sand, first where it was wet, then where it was not. I touched Shehnaz's face, her shoulders, the swell of her stomach. I put my forehead against the screen, wrapped my arms around the box, and tried to breathe in the scent of the ocean, the scent of her skin. I know what I looked like to the Minions: a whimpering old man trying to make love to a television. I didn't care. I am long past dignity.

At length, I sat back and pressed 'PLAY'.

And there you were.

Don't ask me to relive what I felt. I cannot separate the emotions into discrete words. Three of the Minions looked away; they couldn't watch my emotions spilling on to the floor.

Sweet, sweet torture, that's what it was. I never realized until then how much my captor hates me. Nearly seventeen years locked in here, you'd think I wouldn't be left in any doubt about that. But I'd begun to believe he just thought of me as some pet, not domesticated enough to be allowed out of my cage, nor interesting enough to be worth a personal visit. But to make me watch that, to have his Minions stand around as observers while I wept and flailed, and to have them tell me afterwards that this was a new television show, they would bring me one episode every week as long as it lasted but who knows how long that would be? To do all that, he has to hate me.

Was I growing too comfortable for him? Too resigned?

Or am I wrong about this? Do I merely amuse him? The revolutionary poet turned television addict.

Put that way, it is more than a little entertaining. Of course, you and I know that even when there was nothing so personal at stake I had a terrible weakness for television. And lowbrow television, at that. *Charlie's Angels*! Loved those girls. You could never decide whether to approve of them or not. I said, why can't feminism show some cleavage? We were standing in your bedroom. You raised a threatening eyebrow. I said, are you going to throw something at me now? Yes, you said. Your hand moved towards a pillow and then – with one of those sudden gestures of yours – you reached up, your index finger crooked into your shirt's neck, tugged the kameez over your head and flung it at me.

Quick! I said. The curtain's open. Anyone could be looking. Get down! I pulled you on to the bed. You were laughing and I held my hand to your bare stomach and felt the muscles move under my palm. You locked your arm around my neck as I bent to kiss your shoulder and your voice was fierce when you spoke. Never love anyone but me, you said.

Samina, are you even still alive?

They told me you were dead. The Minions did. One morning, many years ago. It was your birthday, and I have never been able to banish you so completely that you'd stay away on that day. I may go weeks without thinking of you but every 8 October morning when I wake up, there you are, pressed up against me, your leg thrown over my thigh. Sweet bliss of it!

But that year the Minions walked in without my noticing. I was singing Puccini, mixing omelette batter, and calling out to you: 'Samina! Get out of the shower or I'm coming in after you.' I heard footsteps behind me, and for a minute I allowed myself to believe I could smell your shampoo. But when I turned, it was them. One of them said, 'She's dead,' handed me the new pair of glasses I'd been long demanding, and then they all left.

They have said nothing on the subject since and will not be drawn into any discussion of you.

My love, I think I could have borne your death with some courage. I think I would have wept with grief and then with gratitude for every second I had with you. But this not knowing. This inability to discern if he had been speaking the truth or just playing tricks with me. They do that sometimes – play tricks. They told me once that India and Pakistan had tested nuclear devices; they told me once that the Berlin Wall had fallen; they told me once that Atlantis had been discovered; they told me once that a sheep had been cloned, and named Dolly (it was the absurdity of that name which revealed the lie immediately); they told me once that brain transplants are now possible, and would I like to sign a donor card so that my thoughts could live on after my death?; they told me once that Mandela had been freed and after twenty-nine years of becoming a legend behind bars he emerged into freedom and did not disappoint the world. Ha! Can you imagine trying that one on me?

They told me all these things, and more; and some they retracted, some re-retracted, some refused to discuss any more.

Let anything happen in the world outside, I don't care. But tell me if I should mourn for you or not. I said earlier that it didn't matter if you were alive or dead since I'll never see you again.

It matters, my love. It matters.

If you are dead, I'll take kidney beans by the handful and whisper a prayer over each one before dropping it on a white sheet. I'll knot up the beans in the sheet and tell the Minions to take it to a mosque. In this, I know they'll oblige me. They are men who respect rituals. Then I'll walk out into the garden which they now allow me to tend, and I'll dig up a handful of mud to fill my nostrils with the smell of earth. I'll close my eyes, lie upon the ground and imagine every detail of your funeral. Who was there, who helped me carry your body –. or no, though others might carry you to the gravesite I would insist at the very last on taking you in my arms and lowering you into the grave. Then I'll place the handful of mud back in the ground, pat it down, and drop a flower on it. Every day for forty days I'll step out to this spot, and lay a fresh flower. And when the mourning period is over, I'll know that there'll never again be an 8 October when I'll wake to feel you pressed against me, and in that knowledge I will find peace.

It's so lonely here without you. But it's lonelier when you flit in and then leave, and I don't know if it was my imagination or a ghost.

# XIX

The intersecting ropes of the charpai tickled my ankle as I pulled myself into a cross-legged position, feet tucked under thighs to escape the attention of the mosquitoes. Across the splintering table Ed was bent over his plate, his fingers hovering over the mounds of haandi chicken, chapli kabab, daal and raita as he contemplated which combination to pick up with his na'an. Above us, there were more stars than you could ever see in any of the hearts of Karachi. From the other side of the restaurant's low boundary wall came the sound of trucks traversing the highway. A group of men and women walked in through the gate and were directed towards the 'family section' where Ed and I were, thus far, the only patrons.

It was two days after Eid. It was a few minutes after I had decided I did believe in miracles.

I looked back down at the encrypted pages in my lap and then at the decrypted version I had just finished writing out on the back of five menu-cards. This set of pages had arrived earlier in the day, in an envelope with no stamp. Hand-delivered, Ed supposed, though no one on his street had seen it pushed through the letter slot in the gate. He had asked, yes, repeatedly. There was a tyre mark on the envelope, proof of nothing. He'd driven over it without noticing it when he came home from the gym. Then he'd got out of the car, seen tyre marks on a white rectangle, gone closer, recognized the handwriting on the envelope. He got back in the car and drove straight to my flat, the letter in his glove compartment. We made the long drive out to the restaurant without him telling me it was there.

We didn't speak of mothers or codes or *Boond* during that ride. Instead we talked of the ordinary things of our lives. We talked of music and movies, school days, university years, the different jobs we'd held, the people we discovered we knew in common. He told me why he'd rather watch basketball than cricket. I told him he was a fool. He described waking up in New York one Thanksgiving and opening his window to see the air full of feathers – an event that remained unexplained. I told him about finding a dying dolphin on Karachi's beach, its dark skin like rubber, its large eyes more gentle than any human eyes. Only when we pulled up outside the restaurant had he opened the glove compartment and handed me the envelope.

'I wanted to be with you while you read it. Do you mind?'

I found I didn't mind at all. 'You'll have to shut up while I decrypt it; can you do that?'

He'd done it with an astonishing degree of patience, not even asking questions when I said, 'It can't be. It can't be,' as the series of letters became words and the words became sense which I was so afraid of misinterpreting that I had to read it over and over, once I'd written out the decrypted version, until I was finally able to accept it.

I placed the menu cards on the table between us. 'He saw the first episode of *Boond*.'

'Wh—?' His mouth was full as he spoke, but the question mark at the end of that garbled sound was unmistakable.

I pointed to the menu cards. 'Read it. Read it, Ed.'

While he was reading it, I rocked back on the charpai, pulling my shawl close around me. Ed pushed the plate of kababs closer to me as he read, but I couldn't think of eating.

There was so much else to think of. That he had watched the episode and would be watching more, yes, that seemed important. That was more important than I fully realized, I guessed. But my mind kept moving on from that to other things. How reading my name had almost made my stomach flip over, much as it did when I rode the Hurdy-Gurdy with him. He always stepped off that ride slightly nauseous. And that part about *Charlie's Angels*. Love and laughter and desire sparkling in the air between Mama and Omi, restoring to me my memories of them which had been more shaken than I had admitted to myself by the previous set of pages with its accusations of perversion.

I closed my eyes and my mind skimmed over those moments. But where it settled was nearer the end of the pages, the moment which had made my breath catch.

*It's lonelier when you flit in and then leave, and I don't know if it's my imagination or a ghost.*

I knew that loneliness, the exact and exacting desolation of it. Made lonelier by my aloneness in it; everyone else had given up on her years ago. I had never realized how much I wanted a companion for my grief until, coming to the end of the Poet's missive, I had heard, for the first time, a voice which understood my dreams. The dream of a mermaid, particularly. The dream of a burial without a body, and the anticipated release of a ritual of farewell.

I opened my eyes. The sky was almost too beautiful to bear. And it was only then that I finally asked myself the question I had failed to ask all this while: whose corpse had been found in the empty plot of land, nearly seventeen years ago? Who was the man disfigured beyond recognition for the simple crime of having the same build as the Poet? Someone inconsequential, that's who his captor, or captors, would have chosen. Someone whose disappearance wouldn't make newspaper headlines, whose relatives couldn't afford to push for an extensive investigation. In all the years since, had some woman been waiting for her husband to come home, had some child grown up wondering if he'd been abandoned by his father? And if I could discover the identity of the corpse, would it be an act of benevolence or brutality to seek out his

268

relatives and say, he's not coming back, and this is how he died?

'This is unbelievable.' Ed put down the menus. 'And weird.'

'Weird?'

'Why would someone go to the trouble of bringing in a VCR and television to show him *Boond*?'

'To torment him with that glimpse of my mother. Ed, it was uncanny the way your mother did it. I mean, I don't know if you ever saw Mama do that, but Shehnaz got it so right . . .'

'So whoever's keeping the Poet captive knew your mother. Knew her well enough to recognize my mother's impersonation of her.'

'Yes.' It felt like a triumph. The first clue of any kind we had to the identity of the Poet's captor.

'It's all happening very fast,' he said. 'It's been hardly more than forty-eight hours since the show aired.'

'There's another question here. Whoever the captor is, why did he tape *Boond* in the first place? Was that just coincidence? He taped it, saw the impersonation and decided to give the Poet a viewing. Or . . . ?'

'Or?'

I shrugged my shoulders. 'I can't think of an "or". I guess that's how it happened.' I was lying. I could think of another way for it to happen. If Shehnaz Saeed was connected to the conspiracy, that's how it could have happened. If she played the scene that way precisely in order to send it to the Poet and make him weep with longing for my mother. I ladled daal on to my plate and started spooning it into my mouth, just to have something to do.

'What is it?'

I smiled at him. 'Nothing. I'm just overwhelmed.' If Shehnaz Saeed was involved, Ed knew nothing about it. I was sure of that now. Sure of him.

'I'm having an idea,' he said. 'It could be crazy. But I'm distinctly having an idea.'

He called out to the waiter, gestured for the bill. 'I have to get to STD. There's something I need to do there. You can take the rest of the food home.' I waved away the suggestion. 'I'm sorry. I know I'm acting strangely. But there's a reason. Promise. Tomorrow you'll see. Or not. Once I think it through it may just be nothing. But I think it's something. I think it may well be something.' He was standing up now, almost hopping in his excitement.

I was more than happy to leave the restaurant and forestall any conversations that might lead to me airing my suspicions. Ridiculous, I was being ridiculous. Beema said I could trust her, and Beema's instincts were always better than mine.

Although, really, my instincts were to trust her, too. When I was in her company I couldn't imagine her involved in any form of deception. It was only away from her, when I looked at the evidence, and remembered the moments in which Ed had spoken of his mother as a creature of overwhelming narcissism that I wondered, was all that sweetness just an act?

If so, it was such a good act that even now I was far more convinced by it than not. It was easier to believe Shehnaz Saeed was being manipulated than to see her spinning webs of deceit in which she and her son and I were bound.

Ed paid the waiter, batting away my attempts to reach for my purse, and we left the restaurant. Both of us were quiet as we drove away, a distracted but comfortable quiet. My hand rested on his shoulder, and when his left hand wasn't changing gears it reached up to caress my fingers. Soft music drifted out of the open windows – the artist was a singer I'd never heard before who threatened in every track to cross the line which separates mellow from soporific, but never actually did.

When he pulled up outside my flat, I said, 'Will you come up?'

'Of course. But not tonight.' He pulled me into a swift kiss – there were neighbours walking down the driveway towards us and even that brief liplock felt risqué – and drew away, grinning like a boy who's run through a stranger's kitchen and stolen a hash brownie. 'Ask me tomorrow. By then I may be your hero.'

'All I really want is a toyboy,' I said, stepping out of the car and blowing him a kiss.

He drove away with a screech that was entirely for the benefit of the neighbours.

I was smiling on my way up the stairs when I bumped into Rabia, Shakeel and Dad, headed down.

'Where've you been?' Rabia complained. 'Dad's plane leaves in an hour. We have to get to the airport.'

I looked guiltily at my father. Yesterday, after I'd locked myself in my bedroom, I hadn't come out for hours, and when I did I refused to talk to Dad about anything to do with my mother. And so our interaction in the last twenty-four hours had returned to centring around cricket and home repairs. He'd spent much of the day correcting the imbalance of my bookshelf, oiling rusty hinges and doing something elaborate with the pipes under my sink which hadn't yet given me cause to complain. In the evening he'd gone with Rabia and Shakeel to have a look at the renovations being done on the house, and I'd said I would cook dinner for the three of them when they returned. But then Ed arrived to whisk me away and I'd left a note saying, 'Sorry. Forgot prior commitment. Rain-check?'

'I didn't realize you were leaving tonight.'

'I can stay until tomorrow if you'd like,' he said.

'No. No. I'd just be keeping you from Beema. She needs you right now.'

'Well, you're coming to the airport, aren't you?' Rabia said to me, her tone belligerent.

I was still looking at my father. The boy who played 'chicken' on the streets of Karachi with Mama. One drunken evening, I had been talking to some friends at university and said, 'Not that I've ever imagined my conception, of course, but I'm sure it occurred entirely by accident. My mother must have bumped into my father in the dark as their paths crossed somewhere in the vicinity of the linen closet.'

They never stood a chance as a couple, that had always been clear. But since talking to Dad the evening before I had been able to believe that for a moment they – not just he – might not have known that. And, in that moment, perhaps, I happened.

'Airport goodbyes are horrible,' Dad said. He came down the stairs until he was standing just beneath me and we were the same height. He put his arms around me. 'We're not done talking. I'm just giving you a pause.' He kissed my cheek and released me. When he got to the bottom of the steps he turned around again. 'If she were alive, she'd let you know. She loved you.'

After they'd driven away, I went upstairs and sat on the low cement wall that surrounded my balcony, my back pressed against the building's edifice. The temperature had dipped sharply and there was nothing except a shawl between my short-sleeved cotton shalwar-kameez and the glass-and-tinsel air.

Yes, she loved me. All the years in which she went off with Omi, she loved me. But then he died and she broke that habit. I could never explain that to Dad or Beema or Rabia. I could never say – you want to know what I think happened to her? All right. All right. Here it is: she saw the falseness in everything she had believed. She saw the futility – in activism, in protest, in peaceful resistance, in all those things she had built her identity around. So she decided to un-become the woman she had been for so long. That's what happened to my mother. She cast off her own skin, and became someone else, someone opposite. It took time, but she was patient, and determined. My God, was she deter-mined. She would let go of everything that held her to her past self. Everything, including me. And when she saw that she couldn't do that here, because this place and all of us had too many memories of the woman she used to be, she left. She and Omi, they knew so many people who had to vanish from the country, leaving no trace of where they'd gone. She knew it could be done. She knew how to do it.

I could never explain that to my family because there was, within all of them, nothing that would allow them to believe such a monstrous act was possible.

She never deceived herself about the brutality of what she was doing. That's why she wept as she did when Rabia confronted her with her selfishness. She knew exactly what she was doing, and she kept on. That's why she had never come back. Because she knew what she had done was unforgivable. She realized it even before she left. Those days she was reduced to an almost coma-like state, lying in bed, her eyes fixed on nothing. Those were the days she was paralysed by the horror of her own decision. She knew exactly what she was doing, and the price she was exacting from all of us who loved her. And she knew, also, that the price she was exacting from herself was this: that she couldn't change her mind. She couldn't come back and say, sorry for what I put you through, but here I am and everything's OK.

But here's the thing, Mama: you can. I'll forgive you.

I pulled the shawl closer and for the first time in my life I wondered if I could really do that. Could I forgive her who I had become since her departure?

Would I forgive her if she came back for Omi after all those years in which she didn't come back for me?

This habit of blame, had it become an addiction, the defining feature of my character? If she came back, would I find it impossible to rein in the momentum of my incessant accusations? Would I find it necessary to interpret her every act as a sign of betrayal or desertion?

Questions without answers. My life seemed filled with them these days.

But Omi would give me all the answers. He'd come back and teach me how to be the girl I could have been. He'd teach me how to step forward instead of circling old wounds. He'd teach me that – and I'd teach Ed the same.

The door-bell rang, and I smiled. Dad was notorious for discovering, halfway to the airport, some crucial item he'd left behind.

But when I opened the door there was an unfamiliar man standing there. His hands were much too small for his body. I noticed this right away and I can't say why but it struck me as threatening.

'You live alone,' he said.

With a quickness I didn't know myself capable of I slammed the door shut and locked it.

There was no sound from the other side of the doorway, but when I stepped back I could see, in that slice of space beneath the door, his feet, unmoving. Then, there came a gentle rapping on my door, of knuckles that knew they didn't have to exert any strength to achieve their effect.

'Madam,' said the soft voice. 'I only want you to see this.'

A paper slid beneath the door and stopped at my feet.

I picked it up. Amidst columns of words, a colour picture of a man lying on the ground, his head cradled in blood.

I knew, right away, that they'd intercepted Omi's letters. Intercepted them, and killed him. And now they were here just to tell me what they had done. That was all they needed to do to me.

The caption beneath the picture said: DON'T LET THIS BE YOU.

The voice behind the door warned, 'Madam, it won't take long.'

'You bastards.' No fear, only rage.

'Madam?'

And then I looked down at the paper in my hand again. SECURE-CITY SECURITY said the words at the top of the page.

It was a newsletter from a private security company, one recently hired to manage the block of flats. A circular sent around the building had said representatives of the company would be stopping by to speak to all tenants, on an individual basis.

There was suddenly no strength in my legs and I had to lean all my weight against the wall.

'Madam?' And now the voice was concerned.

'I'm sorry,' I said. My lips felt numb. 'Please come back later.'

'Sorry to bother.' Footsteps moved away from the door. Then they stopped and the man's voice said, 'Be assured, we will be watching at all times.'

The footsteps started again – towards, and down, the stairs.

Just the security man, I told myself. But why hadn't he stopped next to knock on Rabia and Shakeel's door? I leaned over the balcony and looked down. Ten, eleven seconds went by. He was talking to the downstairs neighbours, no doubt. But then he stepped out of the stairway, into the driveway, his small hands lighting up a cigarette, and walked towards the gate, without stopping at any other flat along the way.

I ran inside and called one of the neighbours.

'The security man?' she said. 'Oh, there've been many of them through the day. I got my visit this afternoon while I was asleep, 9D was woken up at seven a.m. to get her briefing. What nonsense is this? Why not just have the whole block get together and tell us in one shot?'

This is not sinister, I told myself, putting down the phone. None of this is sinister.

I lay awake at night repeating that thought over and over, and when I finally slept I dreamed of pushing my way through tangled weeds in murky water, ahead of me a bend in the river which would lead to sun-dappled waters and herons in flight if I could only swim clear of the little hands which wrapped themselves around my limbs.

# XX

The following morning, when I walked into STD, there was a palpable air of victory about the place. Telephones, e-mails, websites, internet chat rooms, newspapers – praise for Shehnaz Saeed's comeback had choked all mediums of communication. So today, the first day most of us were back after the Eid holidays, the ground floor had the air of a school hallway in the intense flicker of time between lessons. All the previous night's fears seemed absurd.

'Did you see, yaar, that moment? Oh my God, that moment.'

'The one when Shehnaz . . . ?

'Yeah, yeah. Man, wow.'

'Who taped it? I need to see the whole thing again. That look when she sees the daughter.'

'Taped it? Taped it? Oh, ehmuk, we work for STD. We're in the building with the original tapes.'

And then the knot of people dissolved into near-hysterical laughter.

How had Shehnaz played the moment when she sees the daughter?

A door opened and Kiran Hilal held her fingers up in victory. 'Pulled it off, didn't we?' She danced, unexpectedly sinuously, across the floor. Then she stopped, mid-gyration, and turned to me. 'Any idea why Ed's taken a rough cut of the second episode? He's not going to start interfering, is he? They say he's a little strange when it comes to his mother.'

I shook my head, shrugged and then ran to find Ed. At some point in the middle of the night I had woken to realize, for the first time, the full impact of what it meant for Omi to be watching *Boond*. It had taken every atom of self-restraint within me not to call Ed and demand to know his plan but instead to do what he had asked and give him until the morning.

As I rounded into the hallway, I saw Ed standing outside his office watching *Boond*'s director stalking away from him. Halfway down the hall, the director turned around – as though she'd just thought up a punchline – and said, 'It's prostitution.'

'No, it's a box of tissues,' Ed replied with elaborate patience, and the director stormed her way past me.

Ed came down the hall towards me, caught me around the waist and waltzed me down to his office.

'What?' I said, laughing. 'What's going on?'

'Product placement, baby,' he said, closing the office door behind him and picking up a box of A-TISHOO tissues from his desk. He twirled the box on the tip of his fingers. 'The day after *Boond* aired I got a call from an old classmate of mine who works in marketing at the company that produces these luxurious, two-ply wisps of heaven.' He pulled one tissue after another out of the box and threw them in the air. 'And my friend said, "Ed, yaar, remember how you asked me if we wanted to buy spots to advertise our wares during *Boond* and I said no? Well, mea mucho culpa. Is it too late? Can we still get in there? We'll pay double the rates." And I said, "Ali, yaar, I don't think so."'

'Punchline, please.'

'Punchline is this. Last night, after reading the decrypted pages, I thought – product placement. Why not? Instead of giving A-TISHOO a spot during the ad breaks, why not have their product placed in every home and every office and every back seat of every car in the *Boond* universe? And make the folks at A-TISHOO pay through their running noses for it.'

'You read Omi's pages and it made you think of how to generate revenue for STD?'

He threw the last of the tissues at me. 'Don't be silly. Look, watch this. It's the last scene of episode two, to be aired in four days. Obviously, we can't reshoot the whole episode to include tissue boxes in every scene. But we can make a start.' As he was speaking he ushered me into his desk chair and pressed some combination of keys on his computer keyboard.

An interior shot appeared on the computer screen. Some generic living room, so tastefully decorated it was entirely without personality. The only sign that it wasn't just a show-room in a furniture store was a newspaper carelessly tossed on the coffee table. There was the sound of a door opening. Then someone – the camera didn't show us who – walked into the room and placed something on the coffee table. The figure turned and walked out. The camera panned back to the table. There, lying on top of the newspaper, was a faded picture of Shehnaz Saeed, her on-screen ex-husband and their infant daughter – Shehnaz's eyes had been poked out.

Ed pressed another key and the picture stilled.

'The black magic storyline?' I said.

'Forget the storyline. This is the last shot of the episode. This is the shot on which the episode "freezes" as the credits roll. Don't you see? It would take very little effort to reshoot the scene. They're still using those interiors for the new episodes. They can reshoot the scene, with a tissue box placed on the coffee table, and have it ready in time for the second episode to be aired.'

'Thrilling. A tissue box in episode two!'

'The thrill isn't in the tissue box. It's in the fact that we reshoot the scene. We reshoot the final shot which has a news-paper in it.'

I took a closer look at the newspaper. It was open on the

LOCAL NEWS page, which was largely dominated by a photograph of a burst sewer.

'Aasmaani, you're being uncharacteristically slow here. They won't still have that old newspaper lying around. And even if they do, I'm going to go over while they're reshooting – under the excuse that I want to make sure the tissue box is properly placed with its logo and brand name clearly showing – and pay whoever is in charge of set design or props or whatever the hell it is to place today's newspaper in the scene instead.' He picked up the morning paper from his desk and folded it to isolate the crossword. 'Like that.' I made a gesture of appeal, and he sighed and spoke very slowly. 'Episode two will end with a shot that has the crossword clearly showing. The crossword grid will not be empty. Some clues will be filled in with bright red pen that draws your eye to it. Do. You. Understand?'

I looked from him to the crossword to the red pen he was holding out to me. I understood.

I took the pen from him.

'Something simple,' he said.

I tapped the pen on the back of my hand, its nib emerging and retracting. Something simple. In two of the across clues I wrote: JAZZ and FUGUES. Then I used the first letter of FUGUES to write FRASS vertically.

'What are jazz fugues?' Ed asked, watching over my shoulder.

'He'll know. Omi will know,' I said, going over the letters one more time with the pen to ensure they'd stand out. I closed my eyes and leaned back. All I could hear was the twittering of a sparrow outside and my own heart. Omi would know, Omi would understand. And when he realized his words weren't merely echoing into silence, he would start to write differently. He'd write clues to where he was. Sixteen years of being in a place, you must pick up some clues. A man as smart, as observant, as Omi, he couldn't fail to pick up clues. He'd tell me how to find him, and then I'd bring him home.

I'd bring him home. He'd be home. Aged, yes. Frail, perhaps. Unaccustomed to the din of city life, no doubt. But his first day back, I would take him to the sea. Just Omi and me, walking through the sand towards the surf, taking turns to lead, taking turns to plant our feet into the other one's footprints as we had been doing since the days when he had to stand on the tips of his toes in order not to stamp out my prints. He'd wade into the water, trailing his fingers – now swollen and misshapen from all the times the Minions had broken them – just below the surface, and he'd beckon me to come alongside him. As the first wave loomed ahead of us, we'd shout out together, leap up into its maw, bodies colliding with water, and in that sting, that slap, that wheeling over and floundering, we'd know ourselves to be alive again.

I stood up and put my arms around Ed's neck. He lifted me off the ground and swung me around.

'I'm going to speak to him, Ed. I'm going to speak to Omi. My Omi.'

'Can we not talk about him all the time, please?'

I unlooped one arm from his neck and tweaked his ear. 'Why, Mr Ed, are you jealous of a seventy-year-old man?'

Ed let go of me and I slipped to the ground, yanking his ear as I did so. We both cried out and glared at each other.

'What?' I said.

He picked up the crossword. 'I'm going to go and find the director and get this taken care of.'

I caught hold of his sleeve as he started to walk away. 'What? What is it?'

He looked at me and shrugged. 'It's just a little thing. A tiny little thing, Aasmaani. You'll never love me as long as you're obsessed with the two of them.'

I loved him a little, right then.

'Sometimes I want to burn them,' he said. 'When I have the envelopes in my hand, before I give them to you, sometimes I want to burn them.'

'You can't, you know you can't. Ed, promise me.'

280

'You don't need a promise. You know I won't. I can't.' He said that as though pronouncing a sentence on himself. Then he looking accusingly at me. 'Even though you won't tell me what "jazz fugues" means, I won't burn them.'

I let go of his sleeve. 'It's the key to the code. It's two words from the key. You want me to explain the whole thing to you?'

In response, he kissed me, holding my face between his hands, and everything else in the world ceased. When he finally pulled away his smile had nothing boyish about it.

'No,' he said. 'I just needed you to make the offer.'

Then he left with the crossword to find the director again.

When he was gone, I drew a long breath. Everything was falling into place, everything was falling. I made my way to my office, placing one foot carefully in front of the other as I walked. Suddenly it all seemed so precarious, no room for any mistakes. Is this how they felt – explorers in search of lost treasures when they saw the spot indicated by 'X' on the map and knew, finally, there was no stepping back? Were they surprised to find the exhilaration they expected replaced by dread?

I reached my office, sat down, and ran my hands along the cracks in the leather of the desk chair. Today it was cool enough to dispense with the fan, for the first time since I had joined STD, and without that whirring of the blades this room, with its tiny dimensions, felt even more sealed up than usual. Six weeks. Six weeks only since I first stepped into this office with Ed.

Could it really just be chance, everything that had happened since then? The questions worrying at the back of my mind were no longer irritants to be pushed aside. The Poet's messages and I had moved into the world of reactions and consequences. Was it really possible that there was no ordering principle behind anything that had happened – the messages to Shehnaz, her guess that they were written in code, the intersection of her life with mine? Stranger things had happened by chance, it's true. And yet, there was that possibility that I was being played. What game is being played with my life, Omi had asked. Whatever it was, was I now part of it? Had I been placed on the board myself? To what end? What was the purpose behind his captivity, what was the plan?

But even if I were part of the game, how could I act differently, how could I pass this opportunity by? If the explorers knew the treasure map was written by a malevolent hand, would that stop them from digging deep into the earth in search of what was buried? If the box they pulled out said 'Property of Pandora' would they, even then, find it in themselves to place it back in the earth, tear up the map and turn away?

To understand the game, you must understand the mind that created it. For all my amateur detective work I was no closer to doing that than I had been the day all this started. All I had done in these last weeks was make myself visible, my investigation into Omi's death anything but a secret.

Now comes the gathering.

I switched on my computer and checked my e-mail. There were messages aplenty with the heading *Boond*. I read only a few before deleting them all. Did every person at STD feel the need to send an office-wide message about what their friends and relatives said about the show?

I leaned back in my chair. If my life were a top-rated television show, how would it go from here? I'd send a message to the Poet through a crossword puzzle. He'd realize his scribblings were getting through to me. He'd send messages back. Details of the flora, the fauna, the weather around him. He'd write about a brief but intense shower of rain. I'd find a weather-man. My next-door neighbour would happen to be a weather-man. I'd ask him, where did it rain yesterday, with a ferocity and brevity reminiscent of most passion. He'd say, there was one cloud only, right above this spot here on the map, that's where it rained yesterday. And I'd tell no one, I'd enlist no aid, but I'd make my way to that spot, I'd face down the Minions, I'd rescue the Poet. And somewhere, far away, my mother would open a paper, hear of his return from the dead, and that would dissipate the amnesia she'd been suffering from these past fourteen years and she'd catch the next plane home.

Wasn't that the only season finale that would leave me satisfied?

I turned my attention back to the computer and continued to scroll down my inbox. Near the bottom was a message from my father.

The subject heading: Remember her?

I clicked on the message. It was just a few sentences and a weblink.

*I just found this. My first time hearing this side of her. My God! Love, Dad.*

I clicked on the weblink and my computer's audio player popped up.

A voice trying too hard to sound purposeful and trust-worthy said: Samina Akram, 2 January 1986, Karachi. In conversation with Maulana Moin Haq.

The voice cut off and the audioplayer started rebuffering the sound file.

I had been there. I had been in that audience in an audit-orium in Karachi, 2 January 1986, watching my mother and the maulana square up to each other – an extraordinary match-up that only took place, Omi said, because both my mother and the maulana were convinced of their ability to decimate the other in discussion. I had been sitting between Omi and Beema in the first row of the audience, and while the moderator (the term caused Omi much amusement) was introducing my mother, Omi and I were making faces at her up on the stage, trying to make her laugh, while Beema shrugged apologetically in her direction. At one point, Omi had bunched his features into a exaggerated grimace and it was the maulana, not my mother, who caught his eye. The

283

look on the man's bearded face almost made me fall off my chair with suppressed laughter.

I rubbed my hands over my eyes and my mother's voice filled the office: 'Maulana Sahib, is it asking too much of you to look at me while I speak?'

A man's gentle voice came back: 'Mohtarma, if you don't respect yourself and the laws of the Qur'ān enough to keep your head covered in public, I at least respect you enough to keep my eyes averted.'

'The laws of the Qur'ān?' ('Now she's got him!' Beema had whispered.) 'Maulana Sahib, it embarrasses me profoundly to have to remind a scholar such as you of what is written in the Qur'ān – and I don't mean in your translation of it, which I have read with astonishment and wonder.' (Laughter from the audience.) 'Within the Qur'ān itself, as you well know, there are two verses which refer to the apparel of women. Verse thirty-one of Surah An-Nur and verse fifty-nine of Surah Al-Ahzab. In one, the word "khomoorehenna" is used and in the other the word "jalabib". Your translation, I'm afraid, seems utterly unaware that khomoorehenna comes from the word "khumar", which simply means "a covering" rather than "a veil". It doesn't specify what is covered or how. And "jalabib" means a shirt or cloak. If the Almighty had wished to use the word "hijab" to more precisely indicate a head-covering I'm sure He would have done so. I know you would not want to suggest any deficiencies in His vocabulary or precision.' (Muffled laughter from the audience, as well as some shouts of objection.) 'It seems fairly evident from a close examination of the text that women are being enjoined, Maulana Sahib, to cover our chests in public, which I am really more than happy to do when in your company.' (Loud laughter, in which Omi's raucous guffaw was unmistakable.)

'Mohtarma, I am impressed that a woman such as yourself should have taken the time to read our Holy Book. But as Shakespeare said,' and here he switched to English, '"the devil can cite the scriptures to his own purposes". I could mention verses from our own tradition which have similar warnings but I suspect Shakespeare of the West might carry more weight with you. The strictest definitions of "khumar" are irrelevant – what is relevant is its commonly accepted usage. I implore you not to spread your poison through the ranks of our young Pakistani women. It is precisely because of the divisiveness caused in religion by acts of re-interpretation that the gates of Ijtihad were closed in the thirteenth century—'

'Maulana Sahib, there's a difference between re-interpretation and reading.' (And now there were hoots of delight, in largely female tones.) 'The strictest definition of a word is never irrelevant to the intended meaning . . .'

'The unity of the ummah is of paramount importance. Anyone who works against it works against Islam.'

'And you know all about the unity of the ummah, don't you?' Her voice moved down a register and hearing it I knew – as I had known nearly seventeen years ago – that no jokes would follow. 'Last night I was talking to a friend, Maulana, who has seen those planes fly to our border with Afghanistan, with volunteers – young men, little more than boys – ready to join the Afghans and Pakistanis already in the training camps preparing to battle the Soviets. Planes with volunteers from all across the Muslim world. Jordan, Syria, Sudan, Algeria, Egypt—'

'Mohtarma, a second ago we were sitting here in Karachi talking about women's religious obligations and suddenly you're taking us all on a world tour.' (He got his laughs, too.) 'Please don't stray from the subject.'

'The subject is your obligations to the ummah. You take a territorial issue in Afghanistan and you make it into a matter of religious duty – you and your unlikely bedfellows in the West – and you spout phrases like "the unity of the ummah" as you hand those boys – those young, idealistic, confused, angry, devout, ready-to-be-brainwashed boys – the most sophisticated weapons and the best combat training in the world and tell them to get the infidel Soviets off Muslim soil. Soil has no religion, Maulana. If you had left those boys without that call to unity, they would be separate, untrained, spread all across the world. Some would have picked up guns, yes, and some would have lectured their sisters on how to dress. But some would have turned to local politics, or maybe even to writing bad, impassioned poetry. Or maybe, Maulana, maybe even very good, impassioned poetry.'

'You are, of course, the expert on impassioned poetry.' (There was no laughter now. Even through the computer's speakers I could hear tension crackle through the room.)

'What happens after Afghanistan, have you considered that? Where do they go next, those global guerrillas with their allegiance to a common cause and their belief in violence as the most effective way to take on the enemy? Do you and your American friends ever sit down to talk about that?'

The sound file ended.

Mama, could you have known that as your voice took on a power that left us all speechless, and brought tears to Omi's eyes – as it brings tears now to mine and not just for reasons of hindsight – you were singing your swansong?

It was only five days later that she was told Omi had died, and that version of her – that Activist and Icon and woman of *grazia* – we never saw again.

I left the office and drove down to the sea, my windows open to the cool winter breeze. I drove past the lingering Eid revellers, past the theylawallas selling juice and chaat and roasted corn, past the camels with mirror-worked cloth spread over their humps who bowed each time they sat or stood. Finally, in a spot of relative isolation in front of the sea-wall, I parked the car and breathed in the scent of brine.

Omi and I used to come walking here some evenings. He told me, on one of those walks, about the first time he came to Karachi. After his mother's death, when the rich landlord who was his father continued refusing to acknowledge Omi as his illegitimate son, the schoolmaster in the village took him under his wing and sent him to the city to live with his brother and enrol in the school at which the brother taught. Still mourning for his mother, Omi was desperately miserable the first days in the home of the schoolmaster's brother, despite all the kindness everyone in the household lavished on him. The schoolmaster's nephew, three years older than Omi, was the only one who didn't fuss over him and try a little too hard to make him feel welcome. Instead, he left him alone for two days and on the third day told Omi to climb on to the back of his father's Vespa, and drove recklessly through Karachi's dusty streets all the way to Clifton beach – clear blue waters and fine sand, before the waste of cargo ships slicked down its wild beauty.

That was as far as Omi took the story, but it was enough. He stopped walking, looked out towards the water, scanning the horizon from right to left, and I knew that in some way he pitied me for having grown up so near the sea that I couldn't help but take it for granted.

Is this really the most we can ask from them, the ones who have raised us? That they leave us with memories we can cherish?

My mother won that round with the maulana, no one could deny it. But to what end? She was the safety-valve who allowed us all to release some of our frustrations as we cheered her on and said that she, too, was a voice of the nation, a voice that would make itself heard. But what came of it except a lesson to all the daughters in the audience, learnt slowly over the years, that voices such as hers could be ignored or stifled or extinguished completely? My mother's life as an activist, brave as it had been, was a lesson in futility – and in the end, she knew it.

So I had been telling myself for a long time now. But now I had her voice echoing in my ear, the laughter of the women in the audience echoing with it. And then all the sound of the world fell away and I was left in that silence – that almost holy silence – which had grown up around her, sentence by sentence, as she so artfully moved the debate to the exact space in which she had all along intended it to exist – that accountable space. How could I call that nothing? And the thrum of my own blood as I heard her speak, how could I repudiate that?

Why is it so necessary for you to believe the version of her which you cling on to so desperately, Rabia had asked me.

Because. I looked out at the water. Sunlight cut a path through the sea.

Because. Just because.

# XXI

It had been forty-six hours and seventeen minutes since the second episode of *Boond* ended with a shot of the crossword grid, perfectly in focus. Forty-six hours and seventeen minutes, and no word from Omi. Forty-six hours and eighteen minutes now, and I was lost in a vision of dark blues and reds and jagged lines.

'What are you thinking?'

I turned my attention away from the ceiling of the Sadequain gallery and towards my brother-in-law, who was gesturing around the large room as though he were a game-show host and this was the grand prize. Less than fifteen minutes ago he had received a phone call offering him a solo exhibition at the gallery, and he'd run into my flat and insisted that I had to accompany him to the gallery so that I could watch him leap with joy around it and then describe it all to Rabia when she got back from her weekend trip to Islamabad.

'Don't you mind having that as competition?' I said, pointing my thumb at the gloriously worked ceiling.

'Silly girl. Sadequain's not competition. He's the giant whose shoulders are imprinted with my feet. He's the guy who made me stand open-mouthed in front of a painting at the age of twelve and think, my God, this is possible. You can be just human, and do this.'

'He died a poor, depressed alcoholic, didn't he?'

Shakeel rocked back on his heels and looked up at the ceiling. 'Yeah. But that doesn't erase a single line he drew.'

As we were walking down the stairs – after Shakeel had, quite literally, leapt with joy around the gallery – my phone rang.

'Where are you?' Ed said. 'I'm standing outside your flat ringing your door-bell. I'm paying you a surprise visit.'

'Well, we're a bad O'Hara story, then. I'm around the corner from your place contemplating dropping in on you.'

'I'm turning around. I'm walking towards the stairs. I'm almost tripping over a cat. I'll see you at mine in a few minutes.'

Shakeel was smirking at me when I hung up. 'We're a bad O'Hara story,' he said in a high-pitched voice, batting his eyelids. I slapped the back of his head and he put an arm around me. 'When do we meet this guy? I want to see the man whose name need only be mentioned to send my sister-in-law into a paroxysm of blushes. Let me demonstrate: Ed. There you go. Beetroot Inqalab!'

'Oh, shut up and drop me at his house. And no, you can't come in and wait for him.'

It took only a few seconds to get to Ed's, and it wasn't until the chowkidar opened the gate for me and Shakeel drove away that I realized Shehnaz Saeed might be home, and if so, there could be no avoiding her any longer.

She had called me the day after we'd watched that first episode of *Boond*, and I had seen her number flash up on my caller ID screen and let my answering machine pick it up. Her message had been brief. Just, 'Please call me.' I hadn't – and when I mentioned it to Ed he said, 'It's between you and her. If you don't want to talk to her, don't.' I didn't know if she'd tried calling in the last few days. I had pulled my phone out of its socket several nights ago when the crank calling had become intolerable.

If I was lucky, I thought, pushing open the front door, I would make it up the stairs to Ed's section of the house without bumping into her.

But the sort of luck I needed wasn't possible in a house with a yapping chihuahua. I was only a few feet down the entrance hall when the creature heard me and launched into what sounded like a demented version of 'O Sole Mio'.

'Who's there?' I heard Shehnaz Saeed call out, and then I had no option but to walk into that elegant room from which I had so dramatically departed nine days ago.

'Ed's not home,' were her first words.

'I know. He's on his way.' I was sufficiently ill at ease that I was grateful to have the canine falsetto twirling at my feet, giving me an excuse to bend down and fuss over her. I thought that would pass the conversational ball into Shehnaz Saeed's court but she didn't say anything, and when I couldn't bear having my hand licked any more I stood up and said, 'I'm sorry I didn't call you back. Things have been very busy. My father was in town, and work's a little crazy.'

'Aasmaani, you don't have to lie. I understand that you're angry. Ed's told me you have no desire to hear my excuses. And I'm sorry for that, I really am.'

'I never said that to Ed.' The chihuahua's front paws were scrabbling at my shins. 'Director, basket!' I ordered and the animal darted out of the door.

'Your mother never liked chihuahuas either,' Shehnaz said.

And once again, in her presence, it was impossible to feel anything but utterly at ease. I walked over to the sofa and sat down across from her. 'So why did you do it? Imitate my mother?'

'Why do you imitate your mother?'

'When?'

'All the time. You have all these gestures. Like now. The way you're sitting. The way your arm is crooked on the back of the sofa and your head is resting on your hand. That. Right there.'

I moved my arm down to my side. 'I'm not . . .'

'No, of course not. You're not imitating her. You're just sitting. That's how you sit. You may have learnt it from her.

You may have copied her at one point in time, but now that's just the way you sit.'

'I don't understand your point.'

'Look, my character in *Boond*, she smokes. It's a big plot point. She smokes a very particular imported brand of cigarette from Guatemala or Ecuador or some other place that exports bananas. She has always smoked that brand, ever since she was a college student. In episode three, someone she's trying to hide from will know that she's been in his office because he'll find a stub of her cigarette in his waste-paper basket. So, she's a smoker, always has been. When we were filming that flashback pregnancy scene, the director said, OK, no smoking in this scene because she's pregnant. She said, Shehnaz, do that air cigarette thing you did in *Nashaa* to show us she's trying to quit. Did you ever see *Nashaa*, Aasmaani?'

'Yes.' It was the last telefilm she acted in before she retired.

'Yes. Here.' She uncurled herself from the sofa and put a tape in the VCR. 'I was thinking of sending this to you with my driver but I didn't know if it would make things worse.' She pressed 'PLAY', and there, on-screen, was a young Shehnaz Saeed smoking air cigarettes as my mother used to.

'I got it from her, from Samina. When I did *Nashaa*, early on when I was still finding my way into the character's skin, I was having dinner with Samina and she'd run out of cigarettes so she started air smoking. And I said, can I borrow that mannerism? Take it, she said, and continued to demonstrate it for me so that I'd get it right. But once I got it right it became mine. That's how I smoke cigarettes that aren't really there. I don't think of it in terms of your mother any more than you think of her when you rest your arm on the back of a sofa. I learned gestures and expression from her, Aasmaani, turns of phrase and a way of squaring my shoulders when I don't want to show that I'm intimidated. All these things and more, I learned from your mother. But in time you internalize all that you learn, and it becomes yours. I wasn't imitating your mother in *Boond*.' She gestured to the screen once more. 'I was imitating myself imitating her all those years ago. I'm sorry that I didn't stop to think that it would upset you. Believe me, that possibility didn't even cross my mind.'

'I see.' I looked down at my hands. 'You said, I have all these gestures which are hers.'

'Gestures, cadences, entire sentences of speech.'

'Like what? Tell me.'

'It'll only make you self-conscious. You are your own woman, Aasmaani. But it does make my breath stop sometimes, the way Samina peeps out from behind your eyes.'

There was something in her voice as she said my mother's name for which I couldn't quite find a word.

'You should come for dinner next week,' she said, her tone changing into briskness. 'My husband will be back from Rome for a few days. I think you'd like him. Although, no, actually, let me retract that invitation until I check with Ed. The two of them alternate between being civil and pretending the other one doesn't exist.'

I'd almost forgotten there was a husband. 'Why does he spend so much time in Rome?'

'His boyfriend lives there.'

'Oh.'

She cracked a peanut shell open with her teeth and looked remarkably pleased with herself. 'That was almost exactly your mother's reaction all those years ago. Don't start giving me those pitying looks, darling. He's a lovely man and he's given me both unstinting friendship and stability.' She gestured around the opulent room. 'In exchange I've given him the freedom to be with the love of his life, his university sweetheart, who, being Jewish and male – a terrible combination, in these parts – was entirely unacceptable to his family, who threatened to disinherit him. Also, his mother kept having a stroke each time he said he would rather live without money than live a lie, and he's a real mother's boy. So, he married me. Made Mummy happy – and convinced

293

her that homosexuality is cured with just a little bit of parental firmness and a friendly doctor who's happy to mis-diagnose heartburn. And after that, he could spend as much time as he wanted in Rome on "business trips" with David. Close your mouth, Aasmaani, you look undignified.'

'But . . .' I looked at her curled on the couch, unsure if she was playing another game with me as she had that first time we met. 'But you're Shehnaz Saeed. You could have found plenty of men who would have given you financial stability and also . . .'

'Sex?'

'In a nutshell.'

'Yes, well, there's the rub.' She squared her shoulders.

And just like that, it was clear. The Others, Ed had called her various lovers, and it hadn't occurred to me to think about the absence of gender in that term.

'You and Mama. You were in love with her.'

She looked steadily at me. 'Yes.'

'Oh.' I leaned back in my sofa and tried to form a reac-tion to that. 'When did that happen?'

'Why?' she demanded, with sudden force. 'Does the timing of it alter the unnaturalness of the emotion?'

'Unnaturalness? Is that what you think I think? Shehnaz – Aunty – my mother didn't raise any bigoted children.'

At that she ducked her head and smiled, and I smiled back, my mother's disdain for the sheer stupidity of narrow-mind-edness filling the room around us.

When Shehnaz Saeed looked up again, there was almost palpable relief on her face. 'It probably started the first time we met. At least that seems inevitable now. But I became aware of it a few months after the Poet died.'

'And how did she . . . ? Did she reciprocate?'

Shehnaz Saeed laughed. 'It's sweet of you to pretend to believe that's a possibility.'

'Well . . .' I spread my hands. 'You're a total babe. And I can't pretend to know the range of my mother's . . . interests.'

'You really are so much like her. Her way of letting me down gently was to say, "My hormones are too inscribed with the habit of Him to consider anyone else. Of any gender."'

'And that didn't stop you loving her?'

'Oh no.'

For a little while we both sat where we were, looking straight ahead. Then I went over and sat down beside her. 'Thank you.'

'For what?'

I leaned back and breathed in deeply. 'For loving her unreservedly after Omi died. I've thought she didn't have that from anyone.'

'Oh, darling. She had it from you.'

'We both know that isn't true.'

Shehnaz Saeed sighed. 'She understood. She said adolescence is horrible enough without having to deal with a mother unable to cope with the world and a father-figure brutally killed.'

'She talked to you about me?'

'Of course she did.' She rested her palm on the top of my head. That was one of my mother's gestures of affection, but somehow I knew this time that Shehnaz wasn't imitating, merely replicating a gesture she'd learnt from my mother and made her own through using it unselfconsciously. 'She talked to everyone about you. You were the world to her.'

'The Poet was the world to her.' Despite everything, that particular scar still bit down into my bones.

Her hand slipped off my head. 'They were mythic,' she said. 'The Poet and the Activist. They walked into a room and crowds parted for them. The sea itself would have parted for them if they'd so demanded. That's how we felt, all of us who were their audience.' She looked down at her finger nails, and pushed a cuticle back to reveal a tiny sliver of a half-moon between her nail polish and skin.

'Tell me,' I said. 'Tell me about her. Tell me about you and her.'

'You sure this doesn't make you uncomfortable?'

'Why should it?' And then I knew: Ed. The Others, he had spat out. 'It's your son, isn't it? He's the one who called it unnaturalness?'

'Don't think badly of him for it. If there'd been other men in my life he wouldn't have been any happier. Oh, and I dealt so badly with it. It wasn't until several years after my divorce that I was able to face the truth about myself, and then I was ashamed, Aasmaani, of who I was. Ed was such a sensitive child. I think he picked up that feeling of shame from me. And of course I wasn't going to tell him outright. So I lied and sneaked around. Made him spend the night at the homes of cousins he didn't like. I don't even know when or how he found out – but one day in his adolescence he hurled it at me. You're not a real woman, he said.'

I could see him saying it. And I could see him hating himself for saying it afterwards.

'He was angriest about your mother. He thought we were having an affair and I never denied it.'

'Why let him think something that would make him so angry if it wasn't true?'

'Because it wasn't any of his business. That's what Samina taught me – that it wasn't anyone's business and no one had a right to question me about it and demand answers. She was, you know, the person who finally made me dispense with all feelings of shame. My husband was largely responsible, too, but it was Samina who took that final filament of shame off my skin and just blew it away.'

'How?'

'I delivered some tortured monologue to her one evening. About desire and identity and what we admit to ourselves and what we admit to others and how do we know when reining in desire is repression and when it's just good manners? I went on and on about this. And when I finally stopped to draw breath, Samina shrugged and said, "I've never liked mangoes. People say it means I'm not a true Pakistani, but

I've never liked mangoes. Nothing to be done about it, and frankly I don't see why I should bother to try. The way I see it I'm just expanding people's notions of what it means to be Pakistani." And that was the entire conversation for her, right there.'

Mama. Always a woman who could cut to the quick of things.

'I do wonder sometimes,' Shehnaz Saeed went on. 'Did I love her enough to love her unselfishly, really unselfishly? If she'd pulled out of her depression and found herself in a frame of mind to consider being with someone else, and that someone else wasn't me, would I have been able to accept it?'

'We're back to the depression storyline, are we? The one which meets with such high viewer approval it's going to keep running for ever.'

'You don't accept that she suffered depression?' She was looking at me as though I'd just told her the world was flat.

I shrugged. 'She stepped out of her character.'

'She did what?'

'Nothing. Nothing. Forget it.'

'Stepped out of her character?' I didn't know if she was ignoring me or if I hadn't actually spoken aloud. 'That's an interesting way of putting it, I suppose. Though it's more a question of your character stepping out of you, isn't it? Or of the different parts not holding together, or one part overwhelming the rest. There's still so little we understand about it, isn't there, for all the strides science has made in the last decade and a half?'

'Uh-huh.'

Shehnaz Saeed walked over to her bookshelf and pulled out an armload of books. 'Here. Take these home. Read them.' She opened her arms and the books fell on to the sofa with a thomp! which released a spray of dust from the sofa cushions. I looked at the titles. *Living With Depression. Brain Chemistry. What Can We Do? Virginia Woolf: Diaries and Letters.*

I looked up at her, my eyebrow arching. 'Virginia Woolf? Oh, come on.'

She sat down again. 'Sometimes, near the end, I didn't see her for days or weeks because she couldn't even come to the phone or get out of bed. I used to go to your house in the morning, while you were at school, and just sit by her bedside talking to her, or not talking, just sitting there. Some days she'd come over and all she'd do was weep. Your stepmother and I, we convinced Samina she should get professional help. But we were both so clueless. We just saw a sign outside a clinic saying "PSYCHOTHERAPIST" and we took her there. Without a single reference. The man was a complete nightmare. He told her that what she was experiencing was delayed guilt about having an extra-marital relationship for all those years. She said – it was one of her stronger days – she said, "Doctor, then I'm afraid things are going to get much worse for me. Because I think I might do it again, and this time it might even be with a woman."'

'There you go. She was making fun of him. And of the whole process. Because she knew it wasn't depression. She knew she didn't need to seek out professional help.'

'It was one of her periods of reprieve. That's what she called them. She always knew they wouldn't last very long.'

I hated those periods most of all. Those moments, those days, sometimes weeks, when she reverted to her old self and became the Samina of *grazia* again. I didn't understand then what she was doing, what was happening to her, what she was making happen. And so those days were just reminders of what I'd lose when she retreated into her self-imposed darkness again.

Incandescent. Aflame. Those were the words we all used about her. She was supposed to be the Olympic torch, the fire that never burnt out. I would have thrown myself into that fire to keep it alight, but that power was never mine. So all I could do in those last two years was watch with dread each time she emerged into brilliance.

298

'That was the cruellest thing she did. Remind us what she used to be like, what she could be like.'

Shehnaz Saeed closed her eyes for a long moment. 'It was like watching beautiful, fragile butterfly wings exploding out of a chrysalis. It could never be anything but short-lived.'

Stay believing that, I thought. Keep loving her without anger. I won't be the one to tell you the truth.

'Can I ask you something?'

'Of course,' she said. 'Anything.'

'Why did you stop acting? It wasn't because you were planning to have more children, was it?'

'I don't know how that story got started. I never publicly gave any reason. Well, I suppose that is how the story got started. People need reasons, don't they? If you don't give them one, they'll pick one for you. I just stopped. That's it.'

'So it's just coincidence that it happened just a few months after the Poet died? No correlation there?'

She stood up and walked towards the windows. It was dark now. She drew the heavy silk curtains. 'I was offered a part which would have required being away from Karachi for several weeks. I didn't want to leave her. And I was recently married – he'd put this house in my name – so my bank account didn't require me to work any more. Things snowballed in my mind after that.'

'You quit acting so that you could be around for my mother at all times?'

'Yes. But don't think of it as a sacrifice. It was entirely self-serving.'

'Tell me another. I know how difficult it was to be around her in those days.'

'What was difficult was the jealousy, in the beginning. Before I understood the way depression works. What was difficult was the period in which I'd think, why can't I make you stop going mad with grief over him? Why does he have such complete power over you, even in death?'

Hearing her say that was like flipping through an old family album and finding one of your own features – the one you most despise – on the face of someone who's turning deliberately towards the camera at an angle designed to pronounce that exact feature. And looking beautiful doing it.

'And then what? You just learned to live with it?'

'I learned to understand what she was going through.' She gestured to the books beside me. 'What an odd breed humans are. We climb mountains, delve beneath the sea, discover how to leave the planet entirely – but the ultimate zone of exploration, the unknown country more mysterious even than death, is right here.' She tapped my head. 'Right within us. We use only ten per cent of our brain, and that figure is high compared to how much of it we actually understand. We think it's a part of us, and it is, but it also controls us. It's smarter than us, so much smarter. Always several hundred steps ahead. Some of its decisions, it lets us in on – other decisions it simply executes and we never know about them even as they shape our entire lives.'

'The tyranny of character,' I whispered.

'Tyranny. Yes, that's a good word. All power dynamics – all instances of repression and authoritarianism and manipulation – are just failed metaphors for the ways our own brains interact with us. That was the grand irony of your mother's life – she could fight all those external tyrannies, but not the internal one.'

'Wait. What?'

'The Poet's death released it. Released something in her brain. Something that ate her up. And once it was released, it stopped having anything to do with the Poet. That's the thing I needed to understand. That's what you must understand, Aasmaani. Understand the tyrant within her.'

'How do you know you're not just making up a story that's bearable?'

'Darling, there was nothing bearable about watching your mother go through that. Near the end she even said, "I would give anything to believe this is about his death. I would give anything to have something to which I could attach this. If there's a cause I can grapple with it. If there's a reason, there's a way out." But in the end, that's what she couldn't believe – that there was a way out.' There were tears in her eyes now.

'You tell yourself one story, I'll tell myself another. Either way, Mama is lost to both of us. Does it really matter how we get to that bottom line?'

'It isn't the bottom line, Aasmaani – it's the starting point of how we learn to live without her. She didn't kill herself because you weren't reason enough for her to stay alive – that's not why she did it. And it isn't that she was leaving you for the Poet. Those aren't the reasons. You must accept those aren't the reasons. She hung on to an intolerable existence for two years because of you. Not me – I've always known that. She didn't hang on for me. She did it for you. She did it until she simply couldn't do it any more.'

I stood up. I couldn't even be angry with her for consigning my mother to the role of suicide victim. If that was the panacea she needed to cope with Mama's disappearance, let her have it. 'I really have to go.'

Someone blew a car-horn outside the gate. 'That's Ed. He's home. Please, don't let me make you leave. He won't forgive me for that.'

I nodded. 'Did he hate my mother? If he believed you were having an affair . . .' The enormity of what he had kept concealed from me was only just beginning to register.

'Oh no. Not at all. He adored her. He hated me for what he believed was my seduction of a grieving woman. Or used to. But it's the funniest thing. Sometimes there's almost a symmetry in the world, isn't there? The other day, just after he'd spent an evening with you, he came into my room and he said, "Amma, I'm beginning to understand love."' She stood up, put her arms around me and kissed my forehead. 'Thank you for that. Now, go on, go up and wait for him. Tell him as much or as little as you want about our conversation. I advise the former. And Aasmaani, borrow these books and read them.' She gestured back to the pile on the sofa. 'That's all I'm asking.'

I embraced her without answering and then ran up the stairs to the second floor. I stopped at the first door on the left. It was a linen closet. I laughed softly to myself and opened the second door, which led into a TV lounge. I was about to walk in when I changed my mind and stepped through the third door into his bedroom.

It was a long room, with a bed at one end, next to a window which looked out on to the garden. At the other end was a built-in wardrobe and a desk with a laptop computer on it. There were bookshelves along the length of one wall. I walked over to the bedside table. A lamp, a copy of Rafael Gonzales's *Umbrellas*, which I had been urging him to read, a framed picture of a very young Ed hugging his mother. I opened *Umbrellas*. A bookmark fell out. I picked it up and saw it was a picture of me, which he'd taken from my flat two days earlier when he'd come over to watch the second episode of *Boond*. We'd stayed up talking until late that night, and I'd fallen asleep on the sofa with his arms around me. I'd woken up the following morning to find myself in bed; on the pillow beside me were buds of raat-ki-rani which had filled my dreams with gardens and moonlight.

The door opened, and Ed walked in. He saw me, smiled, and held out an envelope.

．．．

Samina, if we turn away hope when it flies down on to our shoulders and offers its wings to those of our limbs which have long been accustomed to stooping, then how shall we be forgiven?

That's a metaphor I could once have turned with precision in Urdu. Stooping limbs makes no sense. Can arms stoop? You would not let me get away with such slippages of language. A bird must be a bird before it can be hope, you would remind me, and rightly so. And so, you'd continue, what kind of bird are we talking about here? The shambling vulture with its own stoop or a drillbeaked woodpecker, destroying your antique furniture? A nightingale! I'd say. Oh please, God, not that cliché again; you'd roll your eyes.

I sit here in the fading light, and remember the pleasure of writing while you slept, your breath my only metronome.

For today, for this moment, I can banish the thought that you weren't speaking to me through the crossword (how did my words about Frass get to you? Is it the sympathetic Minion who takes away everything I write? The first time he did that, it upset me, but then I began to see it as an act of charity. If everything I wrote remained on my desk, I'd know you'd never read it. By taking it away he created the illusion that perhaps, somehow, my words would reach you. It was never an illusion I really dared to believe.) For today, I can banish the thought that it wasn't you speaking (it can be no one else. No one else knew of the jazz fugues).

But for today, I must also think of all those words I've written to you these last weeks. All the words which might have reached you. There was some cruelty in there. If I had the chance I would take those pages back and swallow them, letter by letter. Since that is beyond me, let me say this instead –

Through me, Samina, you found love. If you were to be faithful to me in all my years of absence, you'd be unfaithful to love. I am embalmed memory to you now, and love is not a cucumber – it gains little from being pickled. (That's a joke – my metaphors haven't degenerated to that extent.) If the Minions were female, or if my desires were differently constructed, perhaps one of them would have found a place in my heart and my body and my mind.

So, love. Love deeply and passionately. Love foolishly.

If you can.

If you can't, remember what I now remember, what I have remembered so often all my time in here: Samina, we lived.

We were the Phoenix and the fire, the flight to the sun and the radiance at the end of it. Even when thorns pierced us, they were plucked from Yggdrasil.

Only the language of legend can suffice for our lives.

If I am to remain in here for the rest of my days, if they take all my books from me, take away pen and paper, they will not take away those years I had with you. You, and Aasmaani.

My God, Aasmaani.

She must be a woman now.

Has she eclipsed us already, that brilliant, brilliant child?

JAZZ FUGUES. FRASS. Such simple messages can change our lives. You may never find me, Samina. I have no way of knowing where I am. But don't let that cause you pain. Your

304

words have reached out to me, all these years later. The worst I feared was that you had ceased to love me. I know now that isn't true. That's enough. There's very little life left in me now, but you've given me enough to carry me in joy through all the days that remain.

So don't spend the life that remains to you in a search for me. I can see too easily how you would do that, destroying your own chance at happiness. Put this paper down, and step out to embrace someone near enough to embrace.

Let it be whoever it is, I will accept it. Let it be Shehnaz.

They were right all along, the poets who redefined the Raqeeb. Not just a rival in love but, as a consequence of being a rival in love, also a twin soul, an alter ego, the only one who understands what it means to be afflicted with love for the Beloved.

I used to see the way she looked at you, all those years, and I knew exactly what it meant because wasn't it how I looked at you, too?

That first time you met her, during the rehearsals of *Laila*, you said: I hear you do a remarkable imitation of him.

Yes, she said, and she took a strand of your hair between her finger and thumb just as I had done a few minutes earlier. Your two pairs of eyes locked and just before you laughed and turned away, there was an instant when I saw a possibility occur to you which had never occurred to you before.

How well she must know you, how intimately, to have captured you so perfectly on-screen in those heart-stopping moments. And now here she is helping you to send messages to me, though it must kill her to imagine my return.

Am I right about this?

I suspect I am. The surprise of it all is that I feel no jealousy, only a great tenderness for Shehnaz, a desire to sit and talk with her, to grow maudlin in the moonlight discussing your charms. You would not stay for such a conversation, you would not countenance such sentimentality. But Shehnaz would revel in it. Yes, if there must be a Raqeeb then let it be Shehnaz.

> Oh, love, I am awash with tenderness now.
> Your eyes, your mouth, the taste of you.
> Samina, how lucky we have been.

# XXII

Ed's bedroom window looked down on the garden. Bougainvillea grew along the boundary wall, though not to such a height that it could obscure the palm trees next door. A boy climbed one of the trees, barefoot, his shalwar rolled above his knee. I watched him until he disappeared into the leaves and darkness. Seconds elapsed, and a green coconut dropped down into – I knew though I couldn't see it – a pair of hands waiting below.

Coconut thieves. Some crimes have such charm attached to them.

I lifted the pages and read the last sentence as though it were a prayer.

> Hfanof, jkm gpesb mc jfzc tcco.
> Samina, how lucky we have been.

He had written her name in ash before my eyes. Everything I write can be reduced to one word. And what was that one word to him? It was language become music. Samina. In it, the timbres of love, jealousy, rage, friendship, admiration, passion, hurt and adoration came together in a single pitch. These qualities didn't exist side by side, didn't vie for supremacy, didn't form separate narratives which confounded his attempt to settle on a single definition of her. He knew better than to make such an attempt.

Omi. My Raqeeb, my rival, my father, my twin.

She loved you, always. You're right about that.

And me, what about me?

Then, this memory:

*I have my arms around my mother. It's just after I've been screaming at her for not going to the rally in Lahore. My screams have exhausted into tears. She strokes my hair.*

*'Don't think I don't know the horrors of adolescence, Aasmaani. One day we'll raise a glass, you and I, to having survived these concurrent, awful periods in our lives.'*

*A glass of what, Mama?*

*A glass of air, sweetheart. We'll drink buoyancy.*

Ed stood up from his desk chair and walked towards me. 'Have you finished?' he said.

Love deeply and passionately. Love foolishly.

I held out a hand to him, and when he took it I pulled him down into a deep kiss. Everything else could wait.

'Aasmaani.' His face, when I touched it, was hot. 'If what you're feeling right now is because of what you've just read, then I can't. I can't take advantage of that.'

'Of course you can't, Ed. You can't take advantage when you're the one being seduced.'

He laughed and lay down, his arms around me. 'You can't seduce someone who wants you so desperately.'

I sat up and pulled off my kameez. 'We could argue definitions all night, or we could think of some other way to pass the time.'

'OK. What's Ginkgo Biloba?'

I lay down on top of him and it was with a satisfaction that came from far within that I felt his fingers move up my spine. 'A character from *Lord of the Rings*?'

I didn't feel the earth move that night. I didn't feel the boundaries of the universe dissolve. I didn't feel a single cliché. What I felt was abandon. Not sexual abandon – we played it safe, too aware of the specificities of each body's desire and too aware also of how our bodies were all but strangers to each other; in those moments when we allowed our past lovers' proclivities to guide us what ensued was disaster saved only by humour. ('I'm sure your intentions are good, Ed, but avoid doing that again,' I had to say at one point.) But in the end, we got it right, and though the earth didn't move, no part of the universe dissolved, I was moved, I dissolved, and, immediately after, I found myself thinking, love is a fugue, the call and response of it, the improvisations; it was the first time that I understood it wasn't a misleading euphemism to refer to sex as the act of love.

And that was the abandon – I abandoned myself to imagining, as I lay in Ed's arms, a future. I abandoned myself to anticipating, with pleasure, how we'd grow to know each other – each muscle, each nerve ending, each scar, each kind of scar, even the kinds we couldn't see for ourselves and needed someone else to point out to us. It was not a process to be hurried, there was no need for hurry, let each new discovery be a source of pleasure. But one day, eventually, I'd find I had no secrets from him. In all my past relationships I had never once thought the man I was with would ever know everything there was to know.

Our sweat cooled, turned chilly, forced us to huddle closer under his duvet. His fingers were tangled in my hair and his breathing changed to the deep rhythms of sleep. I wanted to stay in his arms, to fall asleep there.

All those years, when I stayed with my mother, she made the Poet sleep next door. Even when they were in Colombia and Egypt he'd have his own room. Such strange nods to social convention. As if I would have cared. I thought it was a tiny thing, for them to sleep apart. But now, as Ed shifted and his mouth touched my shoulder, I thought, Omi, I'm sorry. Mama, you didn't need to.

I looked at my watch. Rabia would have flown back from Islamabad by now and it was well past the hour when I usually called to tell her not to worry if I was staying out late. The trappings of family. I eased myself out of Ed's arms, dressed, and picked his cordless phone off the receiver. I'd left my mobile in Shakeel's car. Another reason for Rabia to worry. I stepped outside into the hallway. It was eerily quiet. The window shutters threw shadows in front of me. If I stepped into the shadows I would be caught between slats.

I dialled Rabia's mobile, and she answered on the first ring.

'Aasmaani, where are you?'

'Sorry. Just lost track of time. I'm at Ed's.'

There was silence on the other end, and then Rabia pushed aside whatever questions came to mind and said, 'Are you going to be there much longer?'

For a moment I wanted to laugh. Shehnaz Saeed may have told me she'd been in love with my mother, but she would still consider it a terrible breach of etiquette if I came down for breakfast with Ed in the morning. I'd probably be too embarrassed to speak myself.

'I don't have a car here.'

'You wouldn't be driving alone at this hour in any case,' she said. 'Isn't that Ed of yours going to drop you home?'

'He's sleeping.'

There was another pause. Then she said, 'OK, we're on our way home from the airport.' Now I could make out the intermittent sound of late-night traffic in the background. 'We're coming to get you. Should I call this number when we get there?'

'You'll wake up the whole house. Tell me how long it'll take you to get here and I'll come down.'

She told me three minutes. I ended the call and went back into the bedroom.

'Ginkgo Biloba,' I whispered next to Ed's ear as I bent down to kiss his neck.

I looked around for a pen to write him a note and found, instead, his laptop on the desk at the far end of his room. I lifted the lid, pressed the space bar, and the computer hummed to life. He'd been using the word processor and hadn't exited the program, so as soon as the computer retreated out of its hibernation a blue screen appeared, awaiting white letters to fill it up.

I turned to look at Ed, my fingers moving across the keyboard as I watched him sleep.

*Ed, I love you, isn't that funny?*

Pithy, but to the point.

I looked back at the screen.

It said: Cr, N gkzc bkp, nho'i ijfi xpoob?

# XXIII

Ed, I love you, isn't that funny?

*Cr, N gkzc bkp, nho'i ijfi xpoob?*

Ed, I love you, isn't that funny?

I kept looking at the sentence, my brain too attuned to decrypting the code to doubt what I was reading, yet knowing that it was impossible, what I thought I was seeing was impossible.

Mama, I wrote.

*Afaf,* the word appeared.

The Minions came again today, I wrote.

*Ijc Anonkoh efac fyfno ikrfb,* the screen spat back at me.

My ex calls

*Ab cd efggh*

I jerked my hands off the keyboard. Now it was only my own breath I could hear, ragged.

The light from the street lamps outside made everything around me part visible. I looked at the bookshelf along the wall, and certain books seemed to draw my eyes to them. *Morte d'Arthur. Urdu Poetry: A Study. The Complete Works of William Shakespeare* – gold letters, black binding.

My hands were poised in the air, halfway between the keyboard and my eyes. I brought them down – this required great concentration – on to the desk, one on either side of the laptop. My index finger touched a pen, half-hidden under a piece of paper. I lifted it up, unscrewed the top. A calligraphy pen. I remembered the scrawl of Omi's handwriting in that postcard he'd sent my mother from Colombia. No curves, no loops. For him the aesthetic of language was in its sound, not its visual appearance.

'I don't understand,' I whispered.

In the quiet of the room, the words carried. Ed shifted. I turned to look at him. He reached out for me, found I wasn't next to him, and sat up in bed.

'Oh,' he said, smiling a beautiful half-asleep smile. 'There you are.'

'I was going to tell you something, Ed, but I think you already know.'

He smiled again, lay down and closed his eyes. 'I love you too, Aasmaani.'

'I was going to tell you, Ed, that my ex calls the ochre winter autumn as we queue to hear dock boys play jazz fugues in velvet dark.'

For a moment he didn't move and then he was throwing the covers off, running across the room, absurdly naked, his hand reaching out for the laptop and slamming the lid shut.

'A bit late for that, I think.' I stood up, my face inches away from his. 'I don't . . . I can't quite understand this, Ed, but I think you need to tell me the truth and I think I'll know if you're lying.'

'Oh God, Aasmaani.' He cupped my face in his hand, gently stroking my jaw-line with his thumb. 'Why did you have to do that?'

I didn't know how to answer except literally. 'I wanted to leave you a note. I saw the computer before I saw the pen.' I frowned, trying to make some sense of things, pulled away from him. 'Are you one of the Minions?'

But he only looked at me more sadly.

'No, of course not. That wouldn't make sense.'

If the people we've buried walked back into our lives would we recognize them or would our brain be so assured of their deaths, and of death's insistence on obliterating our corporeal

313

selves, that it would make us glance at their faces and then turn away, thinking, I cannot look at this person who reminds me of what I have lost? As I stood there with Ed – the computer screen, the pen, the books all at the edges of my vision – I did not allow myself to see what I was seeing, I did not allow that information to overturn the certainty that had built up in my mind these last weeks. I think I would have believed any lie Ed told me, if it seemed even partially plausible.

He said, 'All those encrypted pages you read, I wrote them.'

I waited for him to laugh. I waited for him to say, 'And if you believe that one I've got a cloud to sell you.' I waited, and while I waited I knew that I might not survive the inescapable truth that he wasn't lying.

'Please don't do this.' My voice was not something I recognized.

'I love you, Aasmaani. This is all because I love you.'

'What are you saying, Ed? I don't understand what you're saying.'

His hands dropped away from me. 'You weren't even supposed to see it, that's the ridiculous part. That first message. The Minions came again today. You weren't supposed to see it. I didn't even know you when I wrote it. I wrote it for my mother.'

'I don't understand.'

'I knew the code, Aasmaani. There was no need for your mother to keep it a secret in the end. One night she was here for dinner, and I was here, too. I was at university at the time, I didn't live here, but . . .'

'Ed. Please. I don't need domestic details.'

'She explained the code. She gave us the sentence. The jazz fugues sentence. I went away and wrote it down. Kept it all these years. I was sure my mother would do the same. There was no distinction in my ideas of love and obsession until you.' He lifted a hand to touch me and then dropped it again. I could still smell him on me.

'Put some clothes on, Ed.'

He walked past me to the wardrobe, and I watched in silence as he put on jeans and a T-shirt.

'So why did you write it?' I said at last.

'For years I'd been wanting my mother to act again. I knew she wanted to, only she was scared to take that first step. So I thought, OK, she needs a reason to say yes after all those years she's been saying no. So I got a job at STD, and I came home and said, Amma, enough of this retirement stuff, OK? And she said no.' He pulled some tiny clinging thing off his shirt. 'I was so angry. All these years everyone thought she stopped acting because of motherhood. She didn't. She stopped because of Samina.'

He was looking at me as if everything depended on my response to that.

'I know.' I shrugged. 'Conventional mothers are overrated.'

He nodded. 'Well, I wish I could share your attitude, I really do. When she said no, again, all those years later, with me back in Karachi, working for a TV studio, I thought, if she were here, if Samina were here and she told you to act again, you'd do it in a second. It became important for me to prove that to myself, to have that evidence against her, that proof of how little she loved me in comparison. So I mentioned the code in passing to her one day, just casually, "Oh, remember that night when Samina told us . . ." and then a couple of weeks later I sent her the message in code. You know, to make it more authentic. Just four lines, with an absurd covering note saying, "Act again and I'll send you more."'

'And so she agreed to do *Boond*?'

'No. She thought it was a deranged fan and ignored it. She couldn't read the code, she didn't believe your mother was still alive. And I felt stupid for having sent it to her.' He ran his fingers through his hair. 'It should all have ended there. A few weeks went by and that actress dropped out of *Boond* and Kiran Hilal came to me and said, I think your mother should do it. Let's all gang up on her. So a whole group of them came to dinner – Kiran, the director, her former co-stars, the costume designer, the sound guy. A whole bunch of people she'd worked with before, and they all said, come on, Shehnaz, take the plunge. And she said no and no and no and maybe and perhaps and then, at about four a.m., she said, OK, I'll do it. OK.'

'But she kept the encrypted letter.'

'Yes, she kept it. And when she heard you were at STD she must have had a moment of wondering, what if it is that code of Samina and the Poet's? So she sent it to you. And when you told me you needed to speak to her because she'd sent you some calligraphy I realized what she'd done, and suspected you were able to read it. And then everything became about you.'

He walked over to the desk I was leaning on and switched on a lamp. It had the effect of making it more difficult to see him, the dull yellow light shining at the periphery of my vision and Ed directly behind it, so that to look at him I had to see almost straight into the light. I swung my hand and the lamp fell to the floor, the bulb shattering. Ed barely moved, though there was glass around his feet.

'It was the most extraordinary thing. There you were, walking around the office, bantering, joking, being witty and poised, and yet it was there. That same vacancy I used to see in your mother's eyes. It was there, always. I started to ask people questions about you and they all said, Whatever you do, don't try talking about Samina to her. Do you know the reputation you have around town for becoming ice-cold when anyone mentions her?'

'It appears there's a lot I don't know.'

'Stop it, stop it. Be angry, but not this.'

'Don't tell me what to do. Keep talking.'

'I tried to get you to talk to me, just to talk, about anything. There was so much we had in common, so much we could discuss. But you just treated me like I was nothing. My God, you made me angry. I thought, watch it, girl, I'll get a reaction out of you.' He finally lifted his feet, shook the glass off almost daintily, and stepped away from the shards. 'And instead, I went and fell in love with you.'

I had got so used to touching him. Even before tonight. I hadn't realized the extent to which I would reach out for him, even if it was just to rest my fingers on his wrist or playfully slap his shoulder. I had to keep my arms hugging my chest because otherwise I didn't know what to do with them. I suspected I would hit him, just for some physical contact. His hands were balled into fists, perhaps for the same reason.

'When my mother said you'd asked her to send any more messages I felt sick. And then we bumped into each other on the stairs in STD and we were laughing together and something happened . . .'

That spark, that fizz.

'I was going to tell you the truth. That I wrote it for my mother, that I was sorry if it had upset you. I practised a little speech, trying to explain it, and I came to your office to ask you out for coffee, so I could tell you. But you just pushed me away, with that vacant look again. You made it so clear that what had happened on the stair, that connection I had felt, meant nothing to you. You were so lost, you looked so lost. And I just wanted to do something that you couldn't turn away from with that blank look, that look which told me I was nothing. So I thought, I'll write another message. But I couldn't write in your mother's voice. I couldn't put Samina's voice on paper, couldn't capture it at all. But the Poet was a different matter. I had been weirdly fascinated with him since I first found out about your mother and mine –'

I opened my mouth to correct his misconception, and then closed it without speaking.

'– so I had all these interviews of him, all his poems, all his letters to Rafael Gonzales which were published when Gonzales got the Nobel. And I had stories about him, stories

317

your mother would tell us over dinner. About riding the Hurdy-Gurdy with you and how he ended up in hospital with the peach allergy. I could write in his voice, I knew I could.'

'No. No, that's impossible. Why are you lying to me, Ed?'

'For the first time, Aasmaani, I'm not.'

'I know his voice. I know it. No one else has a voice like that. No one else writes such sentences.'

There was unbearable pity in his eyes. 'That's what made it easy.' He lifted a book off his desk. *The Letters of Rafael Gonzales*. 'Read this?' I shook my head. Beema had given me a copy, but I'd known it would bring me nothing but pain. There was a 150-page section of letters between Omi and Rafael – lovely, shaggy-haired Rafael who was the only one of Omi's friends whom Mama didn't turn away from in the last years of her life; Rafael who was on his way to Karachi to see Mama, months before she disappeared, when he had the stroke which left him incapacitated for the last ten years of his life.

'The Poet wrote to him about everything. Poetry, politics, food, childhood, your mother – always your mother. It was one of those friendships you almost never see between men.' Ed opened the book to a bookmarked page and held it out to me. 'Every sentence construction, every literary allusion, every shift in tone that you read in those encrypted letters is in here. I took the content of one sentence, forced it into the structure of another. Took a story your mother told me, transposed it onto the stories he told Rafael. Look, look at this.' My eyes couldn't help following his finger as it moved across the page. *Mirza appeared, a spark against the ashen-brained surroundings.*

'Words appeared, bright against their dust-covered surroundings,' I said, that line from the second set of encrypted pages falling instantly off my tongue.

'Yes. You see? All I did was imitate him. The distinctiveness of his voice was what made it easy. That, and your desire to believe.'

'I don't understand,' I said, again.

'I know.' We were both leaning against the desk with our hands clasped together, not making eye contact, not daring to touch. 'I just wanted you to wake up. No, no, that's not true. When you looked through me, Aasmaani, you made me feel powerless, and worthless. It set off, I think, a little madness in my brain. You will not ignore me, you will not treat me like scum, I thought. I will make myself important in your life.' He unclasped his hands and looked at his palms as though trying to find, in their intersecting and dividing lines, an explanation. 'I wasn't thinking very clearly.'

'Keep going.'

'And so I wrote another message. Oh, here—' He pulled open a desk drawer and I saw an inkpad and stamps from different postal districts in Pakistan rattling around. 'When I moved into my office, the CEO handed over boxes of supplies and it included all these postmark stamps. I don't know what he used them for. Something shady, I imagine. But anyway, I dropped the second envelope into the letter slot at home. When my mother saw it she told her driver to give it to you – and the idiot handed it to me instead. I took it to the office, unsure what to do. Finally I realized I was acting crazy. I took the envelope and I was heading towards the shredder downstairs. But I stopped in your office on the way, and you saw the envelope.'

'And made you give it to me.'

'Yes. I was sick with guilt, again. That's why I went over to your place that evening. To tell you. To explain. And then I got there, and I just couldn't. Because it would have meant saying goodbye to you.'

We were both silent, thinking back to that evening.

'I couldn't tell you the truth. I couldn't even tell you it was impossible that he was writing the pages. I just couldn't. It just kept going from there.'

'Things keep on and keep on.'

'Yes.'

'For how long were you planning to keep it going, Ed?'

'Today's was to be the last. I thought maybe – I hadn't thought it through properly – but maybe I'd send you a final letter from one of the Minions to say the Poet had died peacefully in his sleep.'

'You were going to make me lose him again?'

'I would have helped you get through it. I'm sorry, Aasmaani. It got beyond my control. I couldn't continue lying to you any more than I could tell you the truth.'

'One letter from the Minions and it would have been over? You really believed that?'

He lifted his hand in a gesture of futility. 'I knew I had to find a way to make it stop. I just didn't quite know how.'

'The crosswords. Why, Ed? Why intensify the fantasy by making me believe I could speak to him?'

'I had to. For your sake. How else could I keep you from continuing your public enquiries about what happened to him? God, you terrified me when you said you were doing that.' He took my hand, finally. 'I loved you almost from the first moment we met. I knew instantly that something was happening between us, something that I couldn't control or stop. You knew my heart, Aasmaani. You *had* my heart, it was beating in your chest, my damaged, obsessive heart.'

I gripped his hand more tightly. I wanted to kiss him quiet, kiss him wordless, but he was looking at me so intensely that I couldn't move.

'And those letters, they were the only way you'd let me into your life. As the delivery boy.'

'You didn't have to be the delivery boy. You were you, that's enough. You don't have to jump off a tree and break your leg to make someone stay with you, don't you know that?' But even as I said it, I knew it wasn't true. I had become so adept at walking away from people. Ed was here with me now because he'd found the one chink, the one part of me which was wound instead of armour.

'Let's be honest. The only way I could get into your life

was as Merlin, possessing the information you needed. I'm sorry about that letter – the one about your mother's perversions. I was so angry when I wrote that one. But all the others, all the others, Aasmaani, they weren't cruel, were they? When I saw all that unhappiness in your life, I knew I could use the letters to make it better. I only wanted to make you happy in the end. I couldn't do it on my own. But in the Poet's voice, I could. This one today, it was to be the final letter. The one you could go back to and know that he and your mother had something together which no one could take away from them. I didn't know that myself until I met you. Isn't that strange? Between you and the letters, you rewrote me. Turned me into someone who could understand love, and what a blessing it is. Two nights ago after we saw *Boond* together, when you fell asleep in my arms, I knew I couldn't continue the deception any longer. I had to put an end to it. I realized that as you slept. I started working out the contents of that letter in my head as you slept – your breath my only metronome.'

I smiled. 'It was the first detail you got wrong, as far as I know. I would have realized it if I'd had time to think it over. He didn't write when she slept. He wrote in the mornings after they'd had breakfast together.' I said that, and then I saw Omi, bent over his desk. I saw him, because I was in the room with him. I was the only person in the world he allowed into his study when he wrote. I'd sit there, and read one of the books from his library – Elizabeth Bishop and Mir were two of our joint favourites – learning to love their word combinations before I really understood what they meant.

I pulled my hand out of Ed's grasp.

All the while he'd been talking, I had followed along his story, Ed the conflicted hero at the heart of it. It was his story I was listening to and concentrating on, the camera was on him alone. How could it have taken so long to think what I should have thought instantly?

'Omi died sixteen years ago.' I stepped away from him.

'Aasmaani?'

A hammer smashed down, all the weight of a grown man's body behind it. A bone split in two. Omi called out, 'Samina!' The hammer lifted again, smashed down again. Another bone split. They pulled his teeth out, one by one. Took the hammer to his bones again. His body becoming pulp. 'Samina. Samina.' My mother every day after his death had to imagine this. Every single day she could not help but imagine this. They cut out his tongue. He continued to mouth her name. Samina. Their fists on his face, his nose, his cheekbones. Bruises spreading across his face like rivers melting through ice, crawling together into a mass of blue. The only thing recognizable in him any more the shape his mouth kept forming. Samina. My love. Samina.

I was down on my knees. Ed was crouching next to me, saying something, but I couldn't hear him through the screams. And then the door was flung open, and Beema ran to me, Rabia and Shakeel and Shehnaz Saeed behind her. Beema put her arms around me, pulling me close to her, never letting go until there was no voice left in me and then Shakeel lifted me in his arms, and they thought I had stopped screaming as he carried me down the stairs and into the car, but I hadn't. I didn't stop screaming for a very long time.

# XXIV

They have it easy, the ones who can mourn the dead.

I sat hunched over in bed, in the spare bedroom of Dad and Beema's Islamabad house, staring into the red bars of the electric heater. If I looked long enough that image would sear itself on to my retina and when I shut my eyes those bars would be all I'd see. Not Omi, not rivers melting through ice, not my mother drowning in the thought of those rivers.

I had never properly mourned Omi. I realized as much the day Beema packed my clothes and took me away from Karachi and Ed and Shehnaz Saeed, into the green, unreal calm of Islamabad. That he had left my life, yes, I mourned that, but never the manner of his dying. And now that I tried to complete the process of grief, the man I mourned was the Omi of the encrypted pages. The man who shouted, 'Frass! Frass!' to the Minions, who wanted to grow maudlin in the moonlight with Shehnaz Saeed discussing the woman they both loved, who spoke of my mother's 'peachjuicemouth', who wondered if I had overshadowed him yet. I mourned him and, while mourning, remembered that the man I was crying for had never even existed, and I had no language then to articulate my loss.

And Ed. I tried to tell myself that the Ed I loved had never really existed either, but I knew that wasn't true. I had loved Ed most for the pain he carried around, and the secrets which he revealed that night in his room did nothing to lessen the pain – quite the contrary. And also, that voice in the pages, the voice I thought was Omi's, the voice I had loved, that was Ed's voice, too.

A shadow fell across the red bars. I looked up and saw Beema standing in the doorway.

'Do you ever sleep?' she said.

'I suppose I must. There are lost hours of almost every day, these days. Do you?'

She partway lifted her shoulders, and then dropped them before the gesture could become a shrug. The doctors had said there was nothing more they could do for Beema's mother, so we'd brought her home to die. Beema spent hours at a stretch sitting by her mother's bedside, holding her hand, moving only when someone opened the door to let in a draught – then she'd smooth down the goosebumps that appeared on her mother's skin, though the old lady was well past being aware of such things. Watching her, I sometimes felt envy.

She moved towards the heater, and held her hands inches from the red bars, her back towards me. 'You know, you shouldn't give up on yourself. You shouldn't just decide you'll never be OK again.'

I didn't respond and a little while later she said, 'What he did to you was unspeakable, and if I ever see him again I'll probably draw blood. But there's a part of me that's almost grateful to him.'

'To Ed?'

'You'd been slipping, Aasmaani, away from us and from yourself for so long now. I can't remember a time when I wasn't worried about you. And you'd just say, I'm fine, I'm fine.'

'So now I know I'm not fine, and how does that help me?'

She straightened up and turned towards me. 'Fight for yourself. My God, child, what you've been through, from such a young age. It's a wonder you're still standing. My guess is, you're stronger than all of us.'

Strong? I could barely get out of bed any more.

It might have been two minutes or two hours later that Beema left the room. I heard her whispering something to someone outside, and then my father's voice, carrying clearly through the night's silence, said, 'You have to allow her this.'

'That's what we said about Samina.' Beema's voice was fierce with anger. 'For God's sake do something. I don't know if I can bear this any longer.' And then I heard something from her that I hadn't heard in all the hours I watched her sit by her mother – weeping. I tried to feel some sympathy, some shame, but there was nothing in me to give, however hard I tried to locate it.

I suppose I slept at some point that night. It was something my body did while my mind proceeded relentlessly with its continuous feed of images – hammers and rivers and a thread of blood on Omi's tongue as the razor cut through it. Or maybe I didn't sleep. Maybe I just closed my eyes for a moment, and when I opened them there was daylight and my father stood beside my bed with a book in his hands.

'This was your mother's,' he said, and placed the book beside me before leaving the room.

It was the Poet's collected works. The book that lay on her bedside in the years after his death, which I was unable to pick up without picking up her grief along with it. Or my own grief, perhaps.

I opened the front cover. Turned to the table of contents. Turned past that. Kept going.

And there he was, rising out of the pages.

So many of the poems carried memories of Omi reciting them, Omi listening to my mother sing them, Omi talking about them. Here he was bawdy, here funny, here tender, here impassioned. In some places he sounded exactly like the man who had written about frass and minions, and in other places he sounded like someone else entirely, a voice that could never be imitated. It was mostly in his poems about my mother that I heard that inimitable voice. What struck me most about his poems – what I had quite forgotten – was not his mastery of form, or the complexity and concision of his thinking, or even his extraordinary sensitivity to the sound of each syllable. What struck me most was, simply, the greatness of his heart. Here was a man who faced exile, imprisonment, betrayal and deprivation without losing his sense of wonder. In his prison poems, the bars on his windows are merely the grid through which he sees shooting stars, each lash of a whip is a reminder of the insecurity of tyrants, and a rumour that orders for his execution have been dispatched is reason to weep for the executioner.

As I read I found with surprise how many of the poems were still stored in my brain, allowing me to anticipate the line ahead when I paused to turn a page. I found the girl I had once promised to be within the pages of that collection. The girl who knew his poems, who listened to him argue God with Mirza, poetry with my mother, political responsibility with Rafael. The girl who believed without question – I owed this to both him and my mother – that some things in the world you fight for, regardless of the cost to yourself, because the cost of not fighting is much higher. The girl he would have fought for, the girl my mother would have fought for. The girl I had to fight for.

I didn't move from my bed all day as I made my way through those 312 poems, and as I read the last line of the final poem and turned to the end-page I saw, tucked into the inside flap of the back cover, a sheet of thin blue paper.

I think I knew what it was even before I unfolded it and saw the encrypted writing, with a date on top – 28 April 1979 – which told me this was composed just days after General Zia had Omi imprisoned.

I read the first three words of that letter, and for a moment it was Ed writing to me. And then I continued through the sentence, and it was no one but Omi speaking to Mama.

*Forgive me, beloved, but your last letter was a thing of such absurdity I had to tear a corner off it and place it beneath my tongue as I slept, knowing it would fill my dreams with barking cats, suns that revolve around the planets in zigzag courses, and Siamese twins on stilts trying to tie each other's shoelaces.*

*You can't help worry, you wrote, about my imprisonment.*

*O my beautiful jailer, why would you wish upon me the indifference of freedom? These bars, those walls, the guards who shoot at unauthorized shadows which slide towards me in the prison yard – do you think I haven't yet recognized them for what they are? Do you think I don't know you're responsible? You have always been so literal about the metaphorical, and I can't deny that there are moments these days – particularly around meal times – when I wish it were otherwise. I know all the things I've said to you – I'm held captive by your heart, imprisoned in your grey-green eyes, and if you hold out the key of freedom to me it will melt with desire the instant my fingers touch yours to take possession of it.*

*That, Samina, was figurative language.*

*So I really didn't expect to wake up within this cell, and at first, I'll admit, I was a little irritated. But now that I've learnt to look more closely at the metaphor – did it turn concrete or have I become an abstraction? – I can't help but applaud what you've done. In here, I am nothing but the man who loves you. All else is stripped away. Love and separation and longing – those are the stages of my day. The sun rises in one and sets in the other and darkness embraces me in the third.*

*I think of Qais in exile, so consumed with the rapture of his love for Laila that love becomes entirely self-obsessed, unwilling to drag its gaze away from itself long enough to recognize the object of that love walk across the surrounding wasteland. The object of my love, Qais thinks, would make the ground grow verdant at the touch of her feet, not like this sensibly shod woman who creates only shadows as she walks, her clothes sweat-stained from travel. And as I recall*

*Qais I begin to fear – for how can the woman in my head really exist, how can such a love bear reality? That is the only fear I have in here. The only thing they could do to hurt me, Samina, is to make you other than the woman I believe – no, I know – you really are.*

*I will not be in here for ever, I promise. All metaphors need to come up for air. When I can bear no more of separation, when I have learnt all that absence can teach me of desire, the walls will shimmer and I will step out of the mirage, into your arms, to lose myself and find myself inside you.*

*Give Aasmaani the largest possible embrace from me. Ask her to explain metaphors to you if you find yourself struggling with your tendency towards the literal – she understands these things better than either of us could imagine.*

*Forever and always yours, entirely.*
*Aashiq*

Aashiq.

The name he was given at birth, which no one but my mother used once his childhood had passed. 'It's not a name, it's what I am to Samina,' Omi used to say. 'No one else can use that word for me. I'm her Aashiq, her Beloved.'

I turned my head away from the page so that my tears wouldn't smudge the already smudged words. Only now did I have the answer to the question I'd been unable to stop turning around in my mind: how had Ed done it? Even given his obsessive mind, his intelligence, his copies of all those letters to Rafael, how had he been able to re-create Omi on the page, having never known the man at all? And now I knew: he hadn't.

If I had put the letters to any kind of serious scrutiny – if I had really looked at the conditions under which the Poet was allegedly writing and considered the things he chose to write, or rather the glaring omissions from the letters – I would have known instantly. How many times in all those weeks after getting the first letter had I thought of Laila and Qais, Iblis and Allah, the Sufis and their interpretation of Hell? And yet it had never crossed my mind. Even when I read those lines in which he declares Merlin and Nimue to be his favourite love story – those lines I read the very day I met Mirza and remembered how the Poet loved *Iblis aur Aadam*, recalled him saying, 'This is the first and final love story, the one in which we all live' – even then I didn't allow myself to see that I was reading lies.

In all his poems, that is the one trope he always returns to: The absence of the Beloved is Hell, is imprisonment. And that absence fuels love until the prisoner becomes a conflagration of yearning. Sometimes the absent beloved is a woman, sometimes it is democracy, sometimes it is the dreams of youth. But always, always, separation is just a catapult to a new level of love.

Each time he was imprisoned, each time he and my mother were forced apart, he would write to her – half-teasing, half-tender – of his immersion in that metaphor. In part because he believed it; in part because he would do everything he could to keep her from pain. That great heart of his – it would never have written of broken fingers or of love slipping away, not even if there seemed only the remotest possibility she would ever see the words.

How had I been so blind?

Ed had known. Ed had known that the greatest assistance to his deception didn't come from the poet's letters to Rafael or his memories of my mother's stories. It came from my desire to believe. Why had I so suddenly convinced myself that the letters were genuine? In what moment had that decision taken hold? I leaned forward, so that my forehead touched the back cover of the Poet's collection as though it were a prayer mat. It was in the Archivist's room, with news cuttings in front of me telling me how Omi had died. Face this, the news cuttings told me, or else convince yourself it wasn't him who died. And I had taken the latter option. I chose to believe an impossible life over an unbearable death.

Just as I had done with Mama.

I raised my head and closed the book.

My mother suffered from profound clinical depression. She lived with it for over two years until, unable to believe in the possibility of recovery, she killed herself.

I said the words to myself, silently and then aloud. They didn't seem to mean anything.

So I got out of bed and went into the lounge, where Dad was cutting an apple carefully into eighths and reading a book which I recognized from the package Shehnaz Saeed had couriered over to me last week.

'Mama killed herself because she was depressed and didn't think she could get better,' I said.

Dad took off his glasses, put the book to one side and looked up at me. 'Yes.'

I sat down beside him on the sofa. He picked an unbruised apple slice off his plate and handed it to me. He seemed to be waiting for me to say something more but I was over-taken by a curious sensation of flatness, as though all metaphors had fled and what remained was irreducible, irrefutable fact.

'Why weren't you able to accept it all this while?' he said finally and not without hesitation. 'Did you think if you had to face her death you'd react the way she reacted to the Poet's death?'

I shook my head slowly.

All those things my mother had done in the first fifteen years of my life which outsiders saw as signs she wasn't a good mother – every time she left, every occasion she followed the Poet to another city or another country, every school play she missed because she was in prison or at a rally – I had, at the time, forgiven, understood, even been proud of. All those things could be understood as signs of her strength – strength of love, strength of purpose, strength of belief in my ability to understand why she couldn't be ordinary. I forgave her all her strengths. But I couldn't see her collapse for what it was because that, to me, would have been a sign of weakness – and I would have regarded that as betrayal.

'I wasn't willing to accept that she was human, Dad. I wasn't willing to accept she could be broken.'

And that was it – so small a thing, and yet it had defined every aspect of my life. It was the conclusion with which I had started when I tried to understand her disappearance – and I had worked backward from it, interpreting and reinterpreting my notions of the world to make the conclusion seem plausible. I didn't stop and see the idiocy of what I was doing even when the only way to retain the myth I had created was to jettison the things she held so dear – her faith in activism and her love for me.

'Do you see her suicide as desertion?' He held my hand as he said it.

I shook my head again. I had played myself as victim of my mother's lack of love for too long, had wrung myself out thinking it. It would be easy enough to go on, step from one narrative of desertion into another – but when I closed my eyes to allow in that old familiar, almost comforting, story I saw Ed scribbling an encrypted note to his mother to make her believe the woman she loved was still alive; the intended cruelty there double-edged, shredding his own heart as he watched it shred hers.

'I think Shehnaz was right. In the end it wasn't about the Poet, or me or anyone. It was about a minute, five minutes, ten minutes in which she believed, with utter certainty, that she simply could not endure any more.' It seemed impossible, already, to have denied this truth for so long.

'You know what?' Dad said. 'She really was the bravest woman – the bravest human being – I ever knew.'

I smiled at him for that. 'Really?'

'Really.' He tapped the spine of the book he'd been reading.

'I've been rethinking her, too. And I'm sorrier than I can say that I didn't try to understand earlier.'

I gripped his hand tighter. 'I would have liked to have known her.' Then, feeling so self-conscious I had to rush the words out, I said: 'I'd like to know you.'

Dad put his arm around my shoulder, with only a slight trace of tentativeness. 'Let's start with this. Your mother and I had one conversation a little before she died. She was sitting in the garden one evening when I came home from work, and she said, "I have to confess something. When we played 'chicken' from KDA to Clifton and I said I made you run three red lights, I lied. I made you stop even when they were only just turning amber." And I replied, "Samina, I didn't love you because you were the girl who ran red lights. I loved you because when you covered my eyes with your hands, I knew I could trust you to get me home." She was afraid of running red lights, Aasmaani. She wasn't an unbreakable creature of myth. She was entirely human, entirely breakable, and entirely extraordinary.'

I rested my head against his chest. 'I miss her,' I said, and at last I cried for her death.

Maybe a bird didn't start to sing outside the window in notes of heartbreaking beauty. But when I recall that moment, that's how I remember it.

# XXV

That was January. Now it's April. I'm back in Karachi, and yesterday I saw Ed.

It was at the café at which I'd met Mirza, the café to which Ed had invited me for coffee that day in the office when he decided to tell me the truth, though I don't think even he knew if he really would have done that when the moment came.

I was driving near the café when I saw Ed's car parked outside, and knew I would have to stop.

'You look terrible,' I said, when I entered and saw him sitting alone, though that was a lie.

His frame seemed to shrink at the sound of my voice. He looked up from his coffee-cup. 'You don't.'

'I just want you to know, Ed, in case there's any confusion about this, that what you did to me was unforgivable.'

He blinked in weary agreement. 'But you've survived it, as you survive everything, Aasmaani. Whereas I, well, I've lost the only two people who have ever mattered to me. You and my mother. She doesn't want anything to do with me either, it appears. Let that give you some pleasure.'

I felt achingly sorry for him, despite everything. I remembered lying in his arms, and the abandon of believing we had a future together, and it would be a lie to say I didn't regret most bitterly that things hadn't worked out the way I had wanted them to in those few moments when Ed and I found each other and found completion.

'I owe you a great deal,' I said.

He looked up with a twisted smile, as though waiting for the punchline.

'I mean it. What you did really was unforgivable—'

'I think you've made that point.'

'But it made me look at all those other things I've thought of as unforgivable in my life. And it made me look at all the reasons I have to ask for people's forgiveness. You're among those people, you know.'

For a moment, the corners of his mouth started to lift up. And then he said, 'But you can't forgive me.'

'I can't trust you. However much I may continue to love you.'

He opened his mouth, but I shook my head and he smiled a little sadly and looked down into his coffee-cup. There was nothing more we had to say to each other, and we both knew it.


I walk along the beach. I walk slowly. The sand is shot through with silver and I have to dodge the clumps of dried seaweed. There's a tear in the sand. I lift it up, careful not to squash it. A tentacle emerges, translucent. It straightens and then curls, seeking something that will help it sustain life. I carry it to the water which abandoned it on shore and place it in the waves.

A boy on the rocks at one end of the beach is shouting something, his voice lost in the wind. He raises two pieces of wood, held together in a manner that suggests a gun, and pumps invisible bullets into the sea. He is a boy enraptured by the glamour of certainty: you can read it in his face.

I draw closer and now I can hear him. There are no words coming out of his throat, just a cry of triumph.

Did they cry out like that, the men who broke Omi?

There was no way to find who they were, not when the trail was seventeen years cold. They weren't men who left clues. And my pathetic attempts at investigation hadn't caused them the slightest twitch. All those phone calls, it had transpired, came from a lonely man at STD who spent his day calling different women and hanging up when they answered. Sometimes the world is so sad, and so senseless.

That's what they did, Omi and Mama: they gave meaning to the world when it seemed senseless.

It's true, of course, that I'm just creating another story for myself, another version of my mother's life, and Omi's, and mine. But if, in the end, the ways in which we apprehend the world are merely synonymous with the stories in which we feel most comfortable, then this is a story I am willing to claim for my world. And one I'm determined to spread.

I've been in touch with one of STD's rival companies to volunteer my services as researcher for a documentary about the women's movement in Pakistan, to be broadcast in time for the twentieth anniversary of the Hudood Ordinances. At first the executives at the company weren't too enthusiastic. It would be a direct assault, they said, on the religious parties in the Frontier. Well, yes, I said, and I have other plans in mind, too. When they continued to dither I called Shehnaz Saeed and she said she'd narrate the show and consider talking to the TV channel about future projects, too. There was no dithering after that.

And Shehnaz did something else for me, something remarkable. Yesterday she sent me a home movie she'd shot at a party, in 1983, and within it, for just a few seconds, Mama and Omi come into focus. They're standing a few feet apart, and he's watching her as though he's never seen anything so beautiful. She's talking to someone – that journalist who had warned me against prying that day in STD – and the camera finds her halfway through the conversation.

'Look,' Mama says. 'It's not about the ultimate victory. It's just that a nation needs to be reminded of all the components of its character. That's what we do when we resist, just as it's what the poets do, what the artists and dancers and musicians and,' she shot a glance over towards the camera and smiled, 'don't pretend you're not hoping I'll say this, Shehnaz – what the actresses do: we remind people, this, too, is part of your heritage and, more importantly, it can be part of your future. Be this rather than those creatures of tyranny.'

'Why should they listen if the creatures of tyranny are the ones with power?' the journalist said.

Mama exchanged smiles with Omi, as though somehow the conversation had stumbled into some private area of discourse that they'd long ago traversed. 'It's true, that in concrete battles the tyrants may have the upper hand in terms of tactics, weapons, ruthlessness. What our means of protest attempt to do is to move the battles towards abstract space. Force tyranny to defend itself in language. Weaken it with public opinion, with supreme court judgements, with debates and subversive curriculum. Take hold of the media, take hold of the printing presses and the newspapers, broadcast your views from pirate radio channels, spread the word. Don't do anything less than all you are capable of, and remember that history outlives you. It may not be until your grandchildren's days that they'll point back and say, there were sown the seeds of what we've now achieved.' She looked at Omi again.

'What will Aasmaani say about us when we've gone?' he said, smiling at her, ignoring everyone else. 'That's the real test.'

I called Shehnaz to thank her for that reminder of their lives, trying to find the words to express how moved I was by just those few moments in which they were both alive again and so utterly delighted to simply be in each other's company. But before I could explain why I had called she started weeping for her son.

'Find a way to forgive him,' I said to her. 'For your own sake.'

'Can you do that?' she asked.

'No. But you're his mother. That changes everything.'

Rabia is watching me from a distance. She's been watching me closely since I got back from Islamabad last week after

Beema's mother's funeral. She doesn't know whether to trust that I'm well.

I'm not well, but I'm getting there. I still wake up some nights screaming from dreams of Omi. I still miss Ed. I find myself weeping uncontrollably in moments when I least expect it, and I know it's for Mama. But already I can feel this begin to pass into a quieter grief, one that will become part of my character without destroying me.

I make that sound so easy. Nothing about this has been easy. But somehow I find I really am strong enough to bear it. And I recognize how remarkable, and how unearned, a gift that is.

Rabia calls out my name. I hold up a hand to say I'll be there in a minute. There is one thing that remains to be done, one ritual to fulfil.

I walk away from the water, but not too far away. The sand here is wet and packed solid. I write my mother's name in the sand. Did she and Omi really make love in a cave with someone watching? Was that someone Ed? In all those sentences Ed wrote about her what was truth, what false-hood, what his own interpretations? They had dissolved into my memory of her – all those words had – and I didn't know if I'd ever be able to separate them out.

With the little plastic spade I've been carrying I cut out the patch of sand which has my mother's name inscribed on it.

Some days she'd leave the house and walk down to the beach nearest us. It was no more than a twenty-minute walk but we'd always tell her she shouldn't be out on the streets alone. She replied that no one ever bothered her. The last time anyone saw her she was walking down the street towards the sea. It was the monsoons, not a time to go to the beach, not a time to put even a toe into the water. The undertow could carry you out so far you'd never return.

She never returned.

Her absence was proof of her death. She loved me too

much to allow me to believe she was dead when she wasn't. Despite all the lies, somehow that memory, that certainty, had come to me, urgent and unshakable. And for that, I'd always be indebted to Ed.

Did she throw herself into the sea, or simply let it carry her away? Or did she struggle in the end, trying to find her way back to shore? I'll never know. I don't even know for which of those options to hope.

I take the block of sand in my palms and walk forward until I am knee-deep in the cold, clear water. The bright winter sun throws a net of silver between the horizon and me. I bend my back and lower my cupped hands just below the surface of the sea. Her name and the sand stream out between my fingers, dissolve into the waves, and are carried away.

## A NOTE ON THE AUTHOR

Kamila Shamsie was born in 1973 in Pakistan. She has twice been shortlisted for the John Llewelyn Rhys/*Mail on Sunday* Prize and has received The Prime Minister's Award for Literature in Pakistan. Kamila lives in London and Karachi.

## A NOTE ON THE TYPE

The text of this book is set in Berling roman,
a modern face designed by K. E. Forsberg between
1951–58. In spite of its youth, it does carry the
characteristics of an old face. The serifs are inclined
and blunt, and the g has a straight ear.